CLIMBING IN HEELS

CLIMBING IN HEELS

Elaine Goldsmith-Thomas

ST. MARTIN'S PRESS
NEW YORK

This is a work of fiction. All of the characters, organizations, and events portrayed in this novel are either products of the author's imagination or are used fictitiously.

First published in the United States by St. Martin's Press, an imprint of St. Martin's Publishing Group

www.stmartins.com

Designed by Jen Edwards

Staircase © nikit_a/Shutterstock

The Library of Congress Cataloging-in-Publication Data is available upon request.

ISBN 978-1-250-27478-6 (hardcover)
ISBN 978-1-250-27479-3 (ebook)

Our books may be purchased in bulk for promotional, educational, or business use. Please contact your local bookseller or the Macmillan Corporate and Premium Sales Department at 1-800-221-7945, extension 5442, or by email at MacmillanSpecialMarkets@macmillan.com.

First Edition: 2025

10 9 8 7 6 5 4 3 2 1

I dedicate this book to the two women who not only left their imprimaturs upon my heart but opened the door to Wonderland.

The first is my mother, Frances Goldsmith, who would cringe if people remotely compared her to Beanie's mother, Miriam Rosenswag. "Make sure you clarify that I'm nothing like that woman," she would have insisted, demanding that I set the record straight lest anyone conclude that it was somehow a send-up of her. It was not. Okay? They are nothing alike. Except maybe for the fact that they were both singularly focused on their daughters' waistlines and would take not only pride but ownership in their achievements. Also, on occasion, they would Zamboni zip codes to trade up on reality. But for Beanie, her mother was her kryptonite, the voice in her head that made her doubt her worth. While for me, my mother was my hero, making me believe that anything was possible. Oh Lord, I miss her laugh and her loyalty and the way she would insist that everyone buy this book, and then quiz them to make sure they'd read it. And when they didn't, or if they didn't, she'd take names . . . and never forget.

So, Mom, while it's not about you, it's for you, and it's because of you.

The second woman was Gayle Nachlis, an inspirational, insanely witty and brilliant powerhouse agent who was kind enough to hire me as her secretary once upon a time at the William Morris Agency, and generous enough to let me climb.

Beware that when fighting monsters, you yourself do not become a monster. For when you gaze long into the abyss, the abyss gazes also into you.

—Nietzsche

PROLOGUE

In the second half of the twentieth century, there were two industries dominating Southern California: aerospace and entertainment.

This is not a story about aerospace.

By 1980, approximately 230 million people got in their cars each week to pay $3.50 to sit in a crowded, dark theater and experience the thrills of a movie with a group of strangers. The films—romances, mysteries, musicals, and thrillers—were driven by stories and peopled with stars.

In order to hire the stars, one needed to get to their agents.

And in order to become an agent, one needed to break into the club.

This is a story about breaking in.

SHE'S DEAD

1995

"She's dead," said the woman's voice on the other end of the line. "Beanie's dead."

Beanie Rosen, when she died at thirty-five, was the most powerful agent in Hollywood. She had summited, passing countless men and the few women who had come before her, outlasting, outwitting—at least for a moment. But by harnessing that moment, freezing it in time, she would always, at the very least, keep the title. And titles were important to Beanie. They cemented truth, even when truth was in doubt, and sustained the legend long after the legend was gone. So, while others would disappear into the ether, her impeccable timing for endings ensured that she would not.

Everything with Beanie was about timing.

"That's how you sign the stars," she liked to say. "You keep it short, hit the point, make them laugh—but not too much, never too much—then you end it by saying something that makes them think that you're the missing piece to whatever the fuck they need." Beanie Rosen signed a lot of stars. And for her services she took 10 percent of their salary and 50 percent of their heat. The more stars she signed, the hotter she was. And Beanie, for a while, was the hottest. But stars, even suns, burn out. So, the trick was to leave them before they could leave you.

"At least she died on top," said the unknown voice on the other end of a phone that Moze Goff had answered at five in the morning after getting off a red-eye. Goff, thirty-seven, a top New York agent who was considered by many to be equally as powerful and infinitely smarter than Beanie Rosen, sat up in bed, stunned and disoriented. Holding the slim black receiver to his ear, he heard a voice telling him that *Beanie Rosen had died.* Was it a prank? A sick joke? Usually, his houseman would have answered, or his service, but the incessant ringing during off hours informed an urgency that circumnavigated station.

"Who the hell is this?" he asked, searching for a Gitane, his cigarette of choice, only to find that they had been replaced by a carton of Merits in some asinine attempt by his on-again, off-again lover to get him to quit. "Hellooooo?" he said, growing more annoyed.

"Yeah, sorry," said the voice, between sobs. "It's Ella. Gaddy. I didn't mean to wake you, but I figured that I should call you instead of Mercedes Khan. I mean, that might be awkward."

"Who?" he asked, trying to shake the sleep from his brain.

"Mercedes Khan. She called me. That's how I heard. Beanie's mother called her and asked that she notify people." The irony somehow eluding Ella was not lost on Moze. Mercedes Khan was married to the president of the Sylvan Light Agency, and Moze hadn't spoken to her since he worked there, and even then only rarely due to the fact that Beanie detested everything about her.

They had been roommates once—Beanie, Mercedes, and Ella—starting out, climbing the ladder three-girls-three, that kind of thing. But Mercedes had used Beanie and then tried to destroy her, at least by Moze's recollection. So she being the messenger of Beanie's demise seemed like some kind of cosmic joke.

But obviously not to Ella. "Mercedes is having a little gathering at the Stone Canyon house day after tomorrow, and she wanted me to ask if you'd fly out. We could all be there together. Beanie would have liked that."

No, she wouldn't, Moze thought, walking through his Greenwich Village apartment to his outdoor terrace, high above the city. *Beanie hated Mercedes. And you hated Beanie. At least that's what you told me yesterday.*

Of course, he didn't say that aloud. Not to Ella. He wanted to stay on her good side. She was an important manager who had important clients she was going to bring to him.

Or so she'd said twenty-four hours earlier when she'd sworn to Moze that her friendship with Beanie was irrevocably broken. "I'll never work with her again," she had vowed, and now here she was, sobbing over the fact that she couldn't.

He wondered momentarily if Ella had killed Beanie. She had been mad after all, and not particularly forthcoming about the details. Could she have done it out of rage or spite or perhaps envy? Of course the thought was crazy, but when everything is crazy, nothing is. That's what Beanie used to say.

The city below was still asleep.

Jesus Christ, this makes no sense, he thought, running his hands through his short curly hair. Beanie was still so young, and while not exactly the picture of health, she was robust, he presumed, though he hadn't seen her in almost a year. But he'd heard about her, certainly felt her presence, her imprimatur on the industry as her legend and fluctuating waistline had grown and shrunk and grown again. There were always jokes about her, inside barbs, cruel remarks. But that's what happens when you push and pull and leverage your way into a club that never wanted you in the first place.

And now she was dead.

It was hard for him to get his head around it. Moze had loved her. Once. Or maybe he hadn't. He wasn't sure anymore. Perhaps he didn't have the right to judge any of them. By force or by leverage or quite by accident Beanie Rosen had changed the rules for women, then bent them enough so Ella Gaddy and Mercedes Baxter Khan could follow. Driven by mothers who wanted more in a time when less was given, these women knew no other way. Their backgrounds were as unique as their talents, and their passion to be heard was as fierce as their rage at being silenced. Unwilling to settle for less in a world where less was expected, they stood on each other's shoulders, craning their necks to get a better view of the well-established patriarchy that for years had barred them from entry.

Neither feminists nor activists, they just wanted in.

Theirs was a story of survival, of friendship, of betrayal; of saying *fuck you* instead of thank you, of standing up when they pass you by, of saying "I won't quit" when they want you gone. And it's also a story about how some of those women became the very monsters they had fought against.

But it had all started with Beanie.

If not for her, where would any of them be?

WE LIVE IN ARLETA

BEANIE ROSEN

Zamboni-ing their way one zip code at a time.

1961

Beanie Rosen was born in New York City in 1961. Her given name was Bertha Rosenswag, but like everything else about her, it was Zambonied. That was her word. She'd invented it when she was ten years old while watching a Zamboni machine polishing ice until it was smooth and perfect.

That's my life, she thought upon reflection many years later, *ice smoothed over, like a smokescreen. Or Botox.*

Perfectly suited for Hollywood.

They were, after all, image makers, but first they remade their own.

Or their mothers did.

The Zamboni was a technique that Beanie had acquired from her mother, Miriam, who Zambonied the truth until it fit her reality.

That was how she survived disappointment.

Miriam Cantor married Harry Rosenswag, Beanie's father, in 1957. He came from a well-to-do family, and Miriam had assumed that Harry, in due time, would get his share. But when Harry's father passed in 1959 and left the bulk of his estate to Harry's two older brothers, Miriam was enraged.

"They owe you," she roared.

"We're fine," he responded.

"You're weak," she screamed.

"You're cruel," he said.

They were both right.

They fought. A lot. Mostly about money.

Miriam wanted Harry to take a stand, but instead he took a job, an insurance salesman out west in California, where they covered their tracks with revisionist history and Zambonied their names. Now the Rosenswags were the Rosens, and their daughter Bertha became Bernice, and Bernice became Beanie, and Miriam never looked back.

Or so she claimed. In truth, Miriam always looked back. And worse, she kept score.

They had moved to Pacoima, a suburb forty-five minutes outside of Los Angeles, where affordable housing was available for ex-GIs and their families. Beanie's father thought they had arrived. Her mother thought they had stalled. But Beanie thought it was paradise. There were orange groves and lemon groves and big fields called empty lots. Baby palm trees were planted alongside baby boomers, both trying to take root in unfamiliar ground, claiming it as their own.

It was nice, but it wasn't Arleta.

Arleta was an upscale neighborhood a few miles closer to Ventura Boulevard, Ventura being the great divide: the line between what Miriam had and what Miriam wanted. And if you lived south of the Boulevard in the Hills, well, Jesus, you were someone. Beanie would often hear her mother whisper, "They live in Sherman Oaks." There was something reverential about Sherman Oaks or Encino. Houses had pools and central air and cool tile floors with housekeepers on their knees polishing them.

The housekeepers lived in Pacoima.

"If anyone asks," her mother said as she was taking Beanie to her Brownie meeting, "we live in Arleta."

"No, we don't," Beanie protested.

"Yes, we do, Beanie." End of discussion.

And so, by decree, she learned not only that wherever she was wasn't good enough, but that image was more important than truth.

"She knows we don't live there, right? I mean, she knows it's a lie?" Beanie asked her father.

"*She* lives there," he said softly.

For Miriam Rosenswag, it was less a lie and more a vision, making Arleta one step closer to her truth.

SOUTH OF THE BOULEVARD

Everything is better in Encino.

1969

"They have a built-in," Miriam Rosen said, showing both her husband and daughter a brochure for the fancy pool at the fancy synagogue she'd been pestering Harry to join. They were sitting at the dining table, fronted by a curio cabinet where the little Lladro salt and pepper shakers sat shiny, pristine, and protected; safely displayed but never used. Harry glanced at the booklet where young upwardly mobile couples swam with their children, either pre- or post-worship, enjoying the view south of the Boulevard.

"Why would a temple have a pool?" Beanie asked, thumbing through other photographs showing a young rabbi welcoming smiling congregants in party dresses and business suits.

"Because it's more than a temple, it's a community," Miriam said, showing pictures of the young families listening to lectures, running charity drives, having picnics, and swimming. "Wouldn't you like to swim there, too?" Miriam asked, pointing out the diving board and the chaise lounges and the oversized umbrellas protecting congregants from too much of the Lord's light.

Beanie nodded. It was impressive. A built-in, she knew, was something that was landscaped and architectural, with tiles around the periphery and a diving board that gave air and acrobatics to the swim and the swimmer, while a Doughboy, common in Pacoima, was a plastic aboveground drum that you could get for peanuts at any Sears.

"I'm tired of Beanie swimming in watering holes and praying in a church," Miriam told Harry, referring to the local Temple Ahavat Shalom—which was otherwise, six days a week, Our Lady of Peace. Miriam, who was neither devout nor religious, had no qualms about leaning on God to win an argument. "How long can we disrespect Hashem by reading scripture out of a rented Torah?" she asked. It was hard to argue with Hashem.

Harder still to argue with Miriam.

In May of 1969, Harry conceded. They would live in Pacoima, call it Arleta, and worship in Encino. South of the Boulevard.

If Miriam's happiness was a balloon, then Temple Beth Torah, with its built-in pool and community of young affluent people, would keep it afloat. Cost be damned.

Miriam dressed carefully for their first High Holiday service at Beth Torah. It was Rosh Hashanah, and for $15, which Harry had shelled out, there would be dinner and dancing afterward. She spun around in her purple and yellow floral party dress, cinched at the waist, showing off the swishing crinoline underneath along with her phenomenal figure.

"How do I look?" she asked Beanie while putting combs in her red wavy hair.

"Perfect," said Beanie, lying on her mother's twin bed. The Rosens had two beds, separated by one night table and a good amount of dissatisfaction. Beanie studied her mother, who was, inarguably, at thirty-one, a knockout. Her skin, which she carefully kept out of the sun, was unblemished and lily white, and her eyes, a blue green, contrasted with her red hair, giving her a sort of Maureen O'Hara look. Or at least that's what Harry said.

Only more beautiful, Beanie thought.

Harry looked equally handsome in his double-breasted suit and tie. His black hair, combed back with Brylcreem, looked like polished patent leather.

"You look like William Holden," Beanie told him, having heard her mother reference the movie star once. And since Miriam had said it, it had become an absolute.

Like Arleta.

After the services, people milled around outside the synagogue, waiting for the outdoor dinner dance to start. There were twinkly lights strung under a gazebo and buffet tables with carving stations under an adjacent canopy.

Harry spotted Alan Steinway, who had a chain of shoe stores, standing by the hi-fi. "I'll be right back," he told Miriam.

She grabbed his arm. "Don't embarrass me, Harry," she said, knowing that he was going to try to sell a policy, and reminding him that Steinway didn't believe in insurance. "He already turned you down on Mitzvah day," she said, but Harry was out of earshot.

"Damn him," she hissed, spitting mad. "It's bad enough he sells insurance, but not here. Not to someone as important as Mr. Steinway."

Beanie, unsure if Miriam was talking to herself or to Beanie, was confused as to what made Steinway so special. After all, they both were salesmen, only one sold shoes and the other insurance.

Miriam looked at her eight-year-old daughter, sighing. "Mr. Steinway," she said, taking a drag off the Viceroy cigarette she'd just lit to calm her nerves, "is the boss."

She didn't need to explain to Beanie that her father wasn't. Beanie had heard it enough in their fights. Still, from afar at least, it looked friendly, like Mr. Steinway was enjoying his conversation with her father. They talked for at least twenty minutes before Beanie's mother, anxious and fearful, sent her in.

"Mom says it's time to eat," Beanie said.

Her father put his arm around Beanie and continued with his story as Miriam anxiously watched from afar. Finally, after an excruciating fifteen minutes more, Harry walked with Steinway and Beanie back to the tables.

"I hope he hasn't talked your ear off," Miriam said to Steinway to ease what she presumed had been an uncomfortable situation.

"Not at all," Steinway said, shaking Harry's hand. "Your husband is quite the salesman."

As Steinway walked away, Miriam, perplexed, turned to her husband, who put his arm around her and whispered, "Platinum, baby."

"What?" Miriam said, barely able to absorb the enormity of the whisper. Had Harry, her Harry, just sold a platinum policy?

Even Beanie knew how big this was. No one bought Platinum. Ever. Her father would be hailed, written about in the MetLife newsletter, and maybe even get a raise. Beanie looked from her mother to her father. They were both afloat in a sort of platinum-bliss bubble as Frankie Valli sang "*You're just too good to be true*" on the outdoor speakers.

"Dance with me, handsome," her mother said as they floated under the twinkly lights. For that moment, her father was enough. She was enough. And the world was good.

"How did you get Mr. Steinway to buy the platinum package?" Beanie asked a few nights later. She and her father were walking hand in hand to the empty lot around the corner. A neighborhood landmark, the empty lot had been purchased months earlier by a grocery store, and a steel skeleton now rose from its weeds. They liked to walk there for different reasons: her father to chart the progress, Beanie to pay homage. This had been *her* lot. And now it was gone. Or soon would be.

She was having trouble wrapping her mind around the futility of it all; to have existed, and then—*poof!*—without ceremony or sentiment, be wiped away, transformed into something sterile and lifeless.

"Future home of Safeway," she said, reading the freshly painted sign which, to her, was a confirmation that everything she had loved would soon disappear. And that made her profoundly sad. It wasn't the empty lot, per se, or even the trees, transplanted to a more forgiving lot, she hoped, one that wouldn't displace them without thought or memento. It was the *idea* of the empty lot. The *idea* of it somehow had provided comfort. And soon that idea would be gone.

Beanie clung to ideas. They protected her when reality didn't. Like pretending to have parents who didn't fight.

Beanie pulled at her thick dirty-blond hair until the plaits her mother had carefully braided that morning began to unwind. She needed to take her mind off the impending future of the empty lot.

"How did you sell a man who didn't want any insurance a platinum policy?" she asked again.

"By not trying to sell," her father told her, going on to explain that Mr. Steinway didn't buy insurance, he bought Harry Rosen.

"You see?" he asked, trying to land the message. "They buy you," he told her, adding that "People need to see and appreciate the person behind the sale. Understand?" he asked.

She turned it over in her mind, nodding slowly. It made sense to her. In a way. If people think you're on the make, they might get suspicious. "What's the angle?" they might ask themselves. But if they can get to know you, and like you, then they might be able to hear you better, and trust that what you're saying is helpful. After all, Beanie's father was doing Mr. Steinway the favor. Only Mr. Steinway couldn't see it, until he got to know who Harry Rosen was. She looked up at her father with a mix of curiosity and pride and slipped her hand in his.

Beanie loved her father's hands. They were strong and smooth and made her feel safe when the rest of the world didn't. They sat together under the one remaining orange tree in the corner of the lot that Beanie hoped would somehow remain.

He picked an orange and began to peel it. "There's a secret to getting the yes. You want to know what it is?" he asked conspiratorially.

She nodded her head yes and waited anxiously, elated that she was being let in to some secret club.

He leaned in. "You have to know your audience," he said, explaining that each time he met someone, he tried to learn a little bit about who *they* were, what *they* wanted, and how and if he could help. "You have to genuinely *want* to help," he told her, pausing before popping a section of orange into his mouth. That, apparently, was a key component: authenticity.

"A good salesman," he said, "is a fixer, trying to fill whatever need they might have with what he's selling. So when you hear a no . . ." he said.

"You keep going back until you get the yes?" she asked.

He nodded, and Beanie smiled, enjoying the sweetness of the fruit and the lesson. "A no is like a wave in the ocean," he continued, as she visualized the two of them standing in front of the waves at Zuma Beach every summer. He would hold her hand, and together they would figure out how to make it through. "Sometimes you wipe out, right?" he asked. She nodded. "So you try again," he told her. "Even if you don't sail through the wave, the mere act of doing it makes you a better swimmer for the next one. But Bean," he said, looking intently at his young daughter who stared at him, wide-eyed, "you need to tell the difference between a hard no and a maybe. If there's an opening, even a little one, you take it. If that door's closed, you respect it, and move on. There might be some waves you should avoid."

It was, Beanie later said, her lightbulb moment: Helen Keller understanding that the word Annie Sullivan was spelling in her hands was the "water" running over them.

"No matter what you do in life," her father said, "you need to learn how to stand up to the no without fear and, if there's an opening you keep going back until you get the yes."

And that evening, in front of a once empty lot that would soon be transformed into something inorganic and air conditioned, Beanie understood that some no's meant "Try again." And when you do, you never give up until you "get the yes." And just like that, the empty lot with the one remaining citrus tree became a place for Beanie to park her dreams.

EGAD!

ELLA JOY GADDY

What a beautiful little . . . bonnet.

—A GADDY FRIEND UPON SEEING BABY ELLA

1959–1967

Ella Joy Gaddy grew up the second daughter of Boo and Eve Lynn Knox Gaddy, a wealthy conservative Southern family with strong beliefs about right and wrong, good and evil, black and white.

Her father, Boo Gaddy, a raucous good ole boy, ran the third largest distillery south of the Mason-Dixon, which kept the family well-oiled, enabling him to dabble in his true love: betting the horses. Their farm, two hundred acres in the rolling hills just outside Lexington, Kentucky, had been, like the business, passed down for generations. Boo ran the farm and the distillery but happily ceded all household duties, including the rearing of their three children, to his wife, who had a definite opinion on both. As a celebrated ex-debutante from Savannah, Eve Lynn Knox Gaddy was firmly dedicated to upholding the gloved standards of the Old South, where manners and decorum came first.

And where separate *was* equal.

She met her husband at a debutante ball thrown by her father, Clayton Knox. "We need a party," Clayton had said, "where the women look like women again." Believing that society had turned upside down during the Second World War, Knox belonged to a circle of like-minded individuals who wanted their women in the kitchens, looking pretty. He didn't understand a world where girls grew muscles, attitude, and a sense of entitlement that they could do a man's job, and he raised Eve Lynn, being his only daughter, to understand her role and her place, so that when she married and had children, they would understand theirs.

But Eve Lynn's second daughter Ella never understood. An anomaly in both appearance and disposition, Ella was the youngest of three children. The eldest, Alice Lee, five years Ella's senior, was a miniature blond replica of her mother. A dainty debutante in training, she shadowed her mother to charity luncheons and dance recitals wearing her ruffles and her gloves like declarations of her pedigree. Knox Gaddy, the male heir, two and a half years older than Ella, was also blond, quiet, and obedient, never challenging or questioning the rules in place.

Ella, different in both looks and manner, was a freckled redhead with long legs and a short temper. Bawdy and bodacious, she lived out loud with a wildness and a stubborn streak that, much like her unruly and curly hair, could not be tamed.

"She is far more comfortable with the farmhands than the delicate ones," Eve Lynn observed at a Fourth of July picnic when Ella, not yet seven, showed an affinity for off-color jokes and Gaddy bourbon.

"She'll grow out of it," Boo had told her. But what happened was actually quite the opposite.

"Mother, I swear she's going to be a little slut," said Alice Lee, fourteen, to an alarmed Eve Lynn, who had tasked Ella's older sibling with supervising her younger sister while she and Boo were out of town.

Specifically, Alice Lee had been charged with bringing Ella to two engagements. The first, a picnic at the lake with her fifth-grade class, turned into a naked free-for-all led by Ella, who stripped off her clothes and insisted that everyone go skinny-dipping.

"There were boys there," Alice Lee later said to her mother, as if she needed more of a mental picture.

"I hope you didn't tell the teachers it was Ella's idea," Eve Lynn worried.

"I didn't need to," said Alice Lee, explaining that they had all tried to stop her.

Eve Lynn nodded in a sort of daze.

The other engagement, a birthday party for Sue Anne Peabody, the daughter of one of the South's oldest and most conservative families, had also been a bust.

"Was there nudity?" Eve Lynn asked Alice Lee, her voice barely above a whisper.

Her daughter shook her head. "She left ten minutes after I dropped her off," Alice Lee said, explaining that Ella had feigned sickness, gone home, and spent the entire day with Harlan and his cousin Darnell on the lake. Harlan was the son of Essie and James, the cook and groundskeeper, and Darnell was their eighteen-year-old nephew who had lost both his parents and would often spend summers and holidays on the Gaddy farm.

Still, there was no reason for alarm until Alice Lee created one: "There's gossip that Ella likes to play doctor, or should I say *patient*, with all the boys," she said, adding in a whisper, "And that Darnell is pre-med at Howard University, so you do the math, Mother."

THE HELP IS THE HELP

Drinks and people should not be mixed . . .

—EVE LYNN KNOX GADDY UPON TAKING HER VODKA STRAIGHT UP

1967–1973

After that disturbing conversation with her eldest, Eve Lynn began watching her youngest more carefully, noting how Ella would run to Harlan after breakfast or after school, and the two of them would talk quietly for hours. She also clocked when his older cousin Darnell visited, and watched as Ella hung on his arm, and on his every word. While nothing seemed untoward on the surface, Eve Lynn had no idea what was bubbling underneath, and she didn't want to wait to find out.

Such friendships had to be stopped, or at least discouraged, and she approached the subject with her husband cautiously, since he, like his youngest daughter, saw nothing wrong with fraternizing with the help. And he was especially sensitive when it came to Essie and James, who were, at least in Boo Gaddy's eyes, beyond reproach. Essie and James had met as children on the estate and married there with Boo's uncle, the local reverend, officiating. This was a needle Eve Lynn had to thread carefully.

"I'm concerned about Ella," she said one evening when they were dressing for a formal dinner honoring the old mayor and his new wife. "She needs to make friends of her own, and venture out from the employees."

"No harm in having friends here," Boo said, more interested in his tie than the conversation.

"Well, I'm sorry, Mr. Gaddy, but I don't agree," she said, walking over to straighten out the knot he had made both in his bow tie and in his lack of boundaries. "Where I come from the help is the help." With a few deft moves, Eve Lynn perfected the bow, standing back to admire her masterpiece. "Now, don't you look handsome," she said, smiling at her husband's reflection in the mirror. He smiled back, which she took as a sign to press on.

"I think I'll have a talk with Essie, and suggest she speak to her boy," she said, patting her husband's lapel in punctuation of a decision he had neither made nor agreed to.

"A conversation with Essie about what?" he asked, instantly suspicious.

"About their boy," she said, as if his name didn't merit mention.

"Harlan?"

"Yes, Harlan," she said, somewhat exasperated, "and that nephew of theirs who seems to be constantly visiting."

"Darnell," he said, reminding her that the young man had no other family, and that Essie and James were his de facto parents.

"I don't care if they're his parents, Mr. Gaddy," she playfully scolded, "that boy's in college."

Boo looked at her a beat. "What exactly are you implying?" he asked, the tenor of the conversation suddenly shifting. He knew when Eve Lynn wanted something he might otherwise find objectionable she would often pour on the sugar to hide the bitter. He was well trained in her tactics.

"I'm not implying anything," she said, "other than Ella Joy is spending far too much time with the both of them." Boo, aware that his wife had strong beliefs when it came to class and race and white and wrong, didn't want to insult Essie or James with untoward accusations.

"Well, I like the gaggle close to home," he said, trying to lighten the mood. "And I'm particularly fond of Harlan and Darnell. Let's not make problems where they don't exist."

Picking up her pink beaded clutch, she headed toward the door, signaling an end to a conversation that had somehow gone belly-up. Boo's meaning was clear, she was to refrain from mentioning anything to Essie or James.

The truth, which she didn't share with her husband, or another soul, was not that Harlan or Darnell might take advantage of her daughter, but quite the inverse. "It'll all come out in the wash," Boo liked to say. For Eve Lynn, the question was, would the stain be permanent?

"I'm going to go to Howard University," Ella announced at the dinner table six months later. It was the day before Christmas, and Ella, not yet twelve, had decided it was time to let her parents in on her future plans.

"*If* you go to college, which remains to be seen," Alice Lee replied, "you will not be going to Howard University!"

"Yes, I will," Ella said with a stubborn finality that enraged her sister. "That's where Darnell goes, that's where Harlan will go, and that's where I'm going."

"You are an embarrassment," Alice Lee declared.

"You are!" said Ella, defiantly holding her ground.

"Mother!" Alice Lee appealed to Eve Lynn, as she often did when conversations with her younger sister grew contentious. Both Boo and Knox knew well to steer clear when the sisters did battle.

Eve Lynn wiped the corners of her mouth, put down her serviette, and calmly addressed her youngest daughter. "No, dear, you will not be attending Howard University." Ella looked over to Alice Lee who smiled, smugly.

"Why not?" she shouted, less outraged by the collusion between mother and sister than the verdict which gave no room for appeal.

"Ella Joy, you lower your voice right now," Eve Lynn told her. Then, pointedly looking at Essie, who was clearing the plates, added, "We will discuss it *another* time."

But Ella was mad, spitting mad, and got up from the table without asking to be excused. She ran to Essie and James's cottage, where Darnell, who had just gotten into town, was wrapping Christmas gifts with Harlan for his aunt and uncle.

"It's a school for colored people," Darnell explained.

"*Only* for colored people?" she asked.

He nodded.

"That makes zero sense," she said. "It's like having a school for people with blue eyes."

Darnell didn't say anything. How could he? From Ella's point of view, *she* was being kept out, which she hated. And, beyond that, Alice Lee was right, which she despised.

Three months later, when Martin Luther King Jr., was assassinated, Ella mourned with Essie, James, Harlan, and Darnell. She even grew her curly hair into an Afro so she could stand in solidarity.

"I just don't know what to do with her anymore," Eve Lynn said, distancing herself from the young rebel and her new 'fro. Again, Boo didn't seem distressed by his daughter's activism or social awareness, but Eve Lynn urged him to look again with new eyes. After all, he was being groomed for political office by the Republican Party who, at least according to Eve Lynn, would look at the Gaddys, particularly the girls, through a microscope. "And what will they see?" she worried.

While Alice Lee was interested in the carefully curated world around her, with friends who cared as deeply about the coming debutante season as they did about literature, Ella was interested in the world-around-the-world-around-her, with a deep and growing passion for fighting for social injustice and civil rights.

But it wasn't until 1970, when twelve-year-old Ella Joy Gaddy spoke on the record to the *Courier Journal* about desegregation and equal rights for women, that Boo Gaddy took notice. He had just been elected to state assembly and a local journalist had interviewed Ella and a few of her classmates about the world they would inherit.

"She's not changing, is she, Boo?" Eve Lynn asked rhetorically, after reading and re-reading her daughter's comments.

For once, Boo didn't have an answer.

At the dawn of adolescence, Ella Joy Gaddy—first to laugh, first to smoke, first to take the dare—had turned into not only a firecracker and an activist, but a liability.

"All we are saying," she told her confused parents when she was thirteen years old and had been suspended from school for ditching classes to do a sit-in, "is to give peace a chance."

Six weeks later they enrolled Ella in a boarding school in Hanover, New Hampshire, where her opinions and appearances would be limited to visiting days.

MOTHER'S DAY

MILLICENT BAXTER

As is the mother, so is her daughter.

—EZEKIEL 16:44

1966

Millicent Baxter's character and trajectory was formed and informed by her older sister Lucille, who Millicent believed was the only person on earth who truly loved her. While Millicent could easily settle for less, Lucille could not, which worried her.

In early June 1966, at the age of twelve, Millicent arrived home from school and stood just outside the small flat in the East End of London, where she lived with her aunt Fifi, uncle Jack, and sister, Lucille. On that afternoon, Aunt Fifi and Lucille were having a terrible row, screaming obscenities through open windows while passersby made comments or wagers or just made fun.

Millicent, noting the crowd outside, counted the seconds until the screaming stopped or until the crowd dispersed. It wasn't that she was ashamed or embarrassed by the unseemly display, it was that Lucille might be.

Lucille, a raven-haired beauty who, at twenty-six, was fourteen years Millicent's senior, cared deeply what people thought and harshly judged the circumstances surrounding her life. She hated the East End and its smells of poverty and grime. It wasn't meant for her, Lucille was convinced, and late at night when she and Millicent would lie in their shared twin bed, she'd plot their escape.

The sisters shared not only a bed, but a bond, and a mother who had died shortly after Millicent's birth. Their aunt and uncle had taken them both in out of obligation, and also out of a desire to have a family. Ten years later, the obligation and the family had worn thin. And not just for Aunt Fifi and Uncle Jack.

"We need to be the architects of our own future," Lucille would say, explaining that unless you have a blueprint for how to get from Point A to Point Wherever the Hell You Bloody Well Want to Be, you'll end up stuck in a dead-end life like Aunt Fifi: bitter, jealous, and petty. It was an ominous forecast designed, Millicent thought, to ensure that she'd stand beside Lucille. And in truth, while Millicent saw nothing wrong with her aunt, nor their lives, all she really wanted was Lucille's approval. They were a team, and Lucille promised they always would be.

And so, with dreams that were more strategic than whimsical, Lucille would outline their exit plan. "We need zeros, Squeak," she said, using the nickname she'd given Millicent after her favorite comfort food: bubble and squeak. "Zeros," she told her, pulling Millicent close, "are people with money who never had to worry about living in stinking flats above dank butcher shops and next to smelly fishmongers."

"And how do we find zeros?" Millicent would ask, thinking that maybe she'd help Lucille look for a few.

"By securing a patron to be our saint and our savior," Lucille explained. And then she set out to do just that. Landing a job as a part-time salesgirl displaying new cars on giant spinning discs in convention centers for rich men in the market for the newest model, auto or otherwise, Lucille made eye contact, made small talk, made unspoken promises that would set her apart, she hoped, from the other beauties twirling nearby.

"Take me for a ride," she'd say. And they would. It was all fair game, and she played the game strategically until she landed the grand prize.

Sir Rodney Goldstone, an Australian millionaire who was sophisticated, charming, and thirty-three years her senior, fell hard and quickly for Lucille Baxter. He was, she liked to say, her Henry Higgins, and she his Eliza.

But when Aunt Fifi heard about the relationship, she was disgusted. "As I recall," Fifi chided, "Henry Higgins wasn't married."

Goldstone was. The more time Lucille spent with him, the more the fighting between her and Aunt Fifi increased until the fateful day in June of '66 when Millicent came home from school and heard her aunt call her sister a whore. Millicent, alarmed less by the words and more by the actions, watched as Lucille, suitcase in hand, turned to Fifi before heading toward the door.

"Please forward my mail to the Dorchester," she said, adding, "*Mrs.* Rodney Goldstone, that's how they know me."

Millicent watched Fifi's eyes bulge, and face redden, as she processed this new information. "It was the final straw," Aunt Fifi would later say.

There was simply no holding back her words. "Take it all!" she screamed, "and take your bastard daughter with you."

And that was how Millicent Baxter found out that her sister was her mother.

THE SQUEAKY WHEEL

. . . gets silenced . . .

—LUCILLE BAXTER

1966

"Can we talk about Aunt Fifi?" Millicent asked a few days later while waiting in the tearoom at Claridge's to meet sweet Uncle Rodney. The tables, set with fine bone china cups and saucers, and sterling silver spoons, had at their centers three-tiered serving plates piled high with finger sandwiches and scones. Crystal jars of jams and marmalades sat nearby.

Millicent, who had never seen anything so grand, had wanted to sample it all, but was told to wait until Sir Rodney arrived. Rodney Goldstone, who was neither sweet nor uncle, had rescued the girls, believing that Lucille had extricated them both from a volatile and potentially violent homelife.

"I made a promise to Mum on her dying bed I'd take care of my sis," she had sobbed to him. "I had to get her out of there."

Sir Rodney's heart broke as his wallet opened, offering to put them both up in a suite at Claridge's until he could set them up in an apartment.

Lucille thanked him with tears of gratitude but was disappointed, secretly hoping that he'd offer his Knightsbridge flat, which she'd never been in but had heard was magnificent, with three stories and five bedrooms all en suite, and maids' rooms and butlers' pantries, and a dining room that seated fifty. But his wife, who just weeks before had filed for divorce, had only recently vacated, and since he didn't offer, she didn't ask.

"Millicent Baxter," Lucille said, jerking Millicent's arm and pulling her closer, "we are not discussing Fifi. Do you understand?"

Millicent nodded, frightened.

"Never mention her name."

Millicent looked at her, wide-eyed. Lucille had never before spoken to her that way. And her arm, she was hurting it.

Lucille loosened her grip and apologized, saying she was nervous about introducing Millicent to Rodney, that was all. This was too important a meeting, and she couldn't have a careless outburst unravel her plans. Not when she was so close. Lucille explained that until and unless Sir Rodney proposed, she was in a much more precarious position than she had been before his wife had filed the divorce papers.

"After all," she told her, "Sir Rodney Goldstone is now on the market, and the presumption that I will fill the vacancy is just that, a presumption." While she didn't share this with Millicent, Lucille knew that she had to subtly and consistently let the older man find his way to giving her exactly what she wanted. And what she wanted was legitimacy. It was a dance that she performed flawlessly, never making demands, never arguing, just slowly applying the gas, reminding him with love, encouragement, and a nightly blowjob that he had found his way to the next Mrs. Goldstone.

"We're going to stay at the hotel for a while," Lucille told her. "And there may be a few nights where you're on your own."

"On my own?" Millicent asked, astonished.

"Don't be a ninny," Lucille said. "You're nearly thirteen years old, and this is Claridge's. I'll be round to check on you."

Millicent considered this, then told her in that case she'd like to go back to Aunt Fifi's.

"They don't want us anymore," Lucille snapped. "And we don't want them."

But Millicent did. Very much. She wanted things to be as they were. Surely they could all sit down, have tea and a cuddle, then call it a day. This was just a terrible quarrel, much of which she didn't understand, or hadn't taken the time to process.

It had all happened so quickly. Lucille had grabbed Millicent and left her aunt, her uncle, and all her worldly goods, until she sent for them later—the goods, that is. It was a pattern Millicent would later emulate; take everything of value, then wipe away the tracks.

Pulling Millicent close, Lucille tried to reassure her. "Put the past behind you," she said. But somewhere in the past was a truth, Millicent's truth, and that had been deviling her. Could Lucille be her mother? If so, who was her father? Was he still alive? And how did Aunt Fifi fit into all this? Could she be her grandmother? It was simultaneously too much information and too little. Millicent needed a home and answers. If she couldn't have one, she was determined to get the other.

"Am I your bastard daughter?" Millicent asked as Lucille passed Sir Rodney, who had arrived only moments earlier, a cucumber sandwich.

Rodney looked at Lucille, baffled, but Lucille, not one to lose her composure, simply smiled and said, "Of course not, Squeak." Then she offered her a scone.

"But what is a bastard daughter?" Millicent asked, this time addressing her question to Sir Rodney.

"Well, it's an illegitimate child," Sir Rodney told her. "Why do you ask?"

Lucille shot a look at her sister, who realized instantly that she had done something wrong.

Millicent was surprised. Genuinely. All Lucille had said was not to bring up Aunt Fifi. The bastard-daughter question was an entirely different subject. She looked at her sister. Was Lucille upset? Had Millicent somehow ruined her chances of marriage?

But Lucille's veneer was calm and serene as she simply asked, "Where did you hear such language, Millicent?"

Millicent looked to her sister and then to sweet Uncle Rodney. "On the telly," she lied, and then, avoiding further eye contact, focused on her scone.

A week later, Millicent took her first airplane ride with a nanny charged with her safe deposit to her new school, the Lycée le Rosey, in Switzerland.

THE WEIGHT

BEANIE

I cannot have a fat daughter.

—MIRIAM ROSEN TO THE FAMILY PHYSICIAN

1971–1975

Beanie's happiest memories revolved around food, and gatherings on warm summer evenings when her parents seemed happy, and everything was delicious. Sometimes they'd go to potlucks at friends' houses, where there would be barbecues with sloppy joes and hot dogs and chips and s'mores and all the foods her mother didn't keep in the house because she was always watching her father's weight.

Her father's brothers were morbidly obese—emphasis, at least for Miriam, on *morbidly*—and Miriam was determined not to let that happen to her Harry. But Beanie's father, less concerned and certainly less cautious, would wait until Miriam left the house every Sunday for her Sisterhood meeting, and rush to make fudge with Beanie, hiding it in the back of the deep freeze in the garage where both would stealthily sneak pieces out during the week while watching *All in the Family* or *M*A*S*H.* Food equaled love.

So, when her parents would turn on each other, she would turn to love.

Beanie had a "just in case" drawer under her bed. It was a Steinway shoebox filled with Sugar Babies, Chic-O-Sticks, M&M's, licorice, and Butterfingers. Late at night when harsh words escalated to shouting matches, she would reach for the box and quiet the noise.

Miriam found it once and confronted her in shock. "What is *this*?" she said accusatorially, as if each piece of candy were illegal contraband that Beanie had hidden from authorities.

Beanie hung her head in shame and listened as her mother compared her to her father. "You're two of a kind," she said, as if that wasn't something to be proud of. But Beanie well knew what her mother meant. Her father also squirreled away candy and chips and other foods he wasn't supposed to eat. Miriam confiscated all hidden boxes with haste. "If it's something to be hidden, it's something to be stopped," she told them both, ending the discussion and the habit, she hoped for good.

But Beanie soon found another container and began rebuilding reserves, hiding it better this time, a box within a box within a suitcase that she could retrieve, just in case . . . She was more careful from then on, opening wrappers ever so quietly, hiding the contraband inside pockets, under blankets, or balled up in her fist. But she didn't need to be so vigilant.

No one was paying attention to Beanie, or the candy hidden in a box within a box within a suitcase. Her parents were too busy fighting. Sometimes she could hear them all the way down the street. She'd be walking home from school with friends who would make comments or make fun, and she would join in, praying no one would discover that it was coming from her home.

And when fights broke out spontaneously at dinner or on weekends she'd run outside, embarrassed, leaning against the garage door, willing them to stop. Her parents would scream hurtful things, their words vile and nasty while Beanie would gird her soul and guard her house, making sure no one nearby commented, and if they did, when they did, she'd challenge them with a look that said, *Go away.*

The truth was most of the families on her block fought. They were all young couples, barely out of their twenties, who had borrowed their down payments, raced to have kids, and then found themselves saddled with dreams that didn't match reality, and bills that didn't match bank accounts. They were scared, unprepared, and ill equipped to raise children. And the children, equally frightened, never spoke of it, not to each other at least. But they would steel themselves when their houses flared up, and everyone around would cut them a wide berth, hoping the words and the anger weren't contagious.

But the fighting at the Rosens' became more frequent, which frightened Beanie. She'd heard of families that had gotten divorced, and she wouldn't let that happen. Not to hers. Divorce was a no you couldn't turn into a yes. Divorce was unthinkable.

Beanie would close her eyes, waiting for them to finish, and eat to recapture some sense of calm. *They love each other,* she told herself soothingly, hoping that her father would do something truly spectacular to make her mother happy. But in truth, he couldn't. Not really. He'd promised her the world but they lived in the valley, the undesirable part. And Miriam never let him forget it.

"What do you want?" Harry asked one night as the three of them sat at a restaurant, about to order.

"More," Miriam said, not referring to the menu.

So her father borrowed money from her rich uncles and moved them all to a large ranch house with a small built-in pool in Sepulveda.

Her mother called it Northridge.

In "Northridge," the yelling stopped. Beanie wasn't sure if it was because her parents were finally happy or just tired of fighting.

She chose to believe they were happy.

She chose wrong.

In April 1975, Miriam got a job working for Dr. Leonard Spitz, a dermatologist in the Encino Hills, who was toying with the idea of getting into plastic surgery because that was where the money was.

He was singing Miriam's tune. And they began harmonizing. Often.

Dr. Spitz, a thirty-six-year-old divorcé whom Miriam had met at Temple Beth Torah, was a good-looking man who found her engaging and fun. At first she was flattered, then intrigued, as nine-to-five became nine-to-seven, becoming nine-to-weekends.

It was inevitable, Beanie thought, looking back. Miriam Rosen felt that life had cheated her from the go, and she would not be silenced by her husband's acceptance of mediocrity. Beanie's mother was a fighter and her father a dreamer, and together they produced a daughter fueled by a sense of injustice and the belief that she could do anything in the world except keep her parents together.

When Harry confronted Miriam about her relationship with the dermatologist, she didn't deny it. He moved out, she moved on, and they were done. Just like that. They sold the Sepulveda house and split the proceeds, with Miriam taking the good china and the Admiral Color TV with remote control.

"The rest is crap," she said, with an all-encompassing gesture that made Beanie wonder if she was included.

Beanie was numb. And it wasn't just because her mother had moved on. It was because her father had. "You didn't fight to keep me," she said to him, disbelieving.

And though he tried to explain about mothers getting custody and that he would see her on weekends, it was all just noise and emptiness that she later ate to quiet. The man who had taught her to keep trying until you get the yes had held at no. And that rearranged her.

After that, the just-in-case box got bigger, and the eating escalated.

In November of 1975, Miriam and Beanie moved into Dr. Spitz's two-bedroom condo in the Encino Flats. He had previously given his wife the fancy home in the Hills, and his daughters—twins Esther and Sarah, who he'd see every other weekend and two days a week—shared the second bedroom. Beanie moved into his office with the convertible sofa and no door.

A scorekeeper by nature, Miriam wouldn't allow *her* daughter to have less than *his*. "We just need to get a new place," she told him, leveraging the inequity into a new home and a firm wedding date. Miriam booked the Terrace Room at the Sportsmen's Lodge in Sherman Oaks for July 4, 1976.

"The two hundredth anniversary of the United States and the beginning of the rest of your life," Dr. Spitz said wistfully.

"The beginning of the *best* of my life," Miriam corrected, never considering her daughter who sat between them at the kitchen table.

She began looking for houses. Not his. Not hers. Theirs. Though her budget was not a penny over $75,000, Miriam took Beanie to look at several $110,000 homes on Mulholland Drive with acres of land, koi ponds, and guest houses with security gates.

Beanie cringed at the thought of what Dr. Spitz would say, but he just laughed at Miriam's ambition, redirecting her to a sprawling four-bedroom, three-bath Spanish hacienda in the hills of Sherman Oaks that was $81,000, proving to Beanie that her mother always won, if only by degree.

In January 1976 they moved into the 4,614-square-foot home Dr. Spitz had purchased as a wedding gift for his wife. Finally Miriam Rosen, soon to be Spitz, had *her* own maid scrubbing *her* own floors, and she didn't need to pretend to live anywhere else anymore.

"But I do like Bel Air," she told the Realtor, with an eye to her next push.

In Sherman Oaks, Beanie had her own room with Peter Max bedsheets, posters of Andy Gibb and David Cassidy, and sliding glass doors that overlooked the lanai and the built-in pool with a distant view of her old life north of the Boulevard. She would have to change schools, Miriam told her, and since it was the middle of the year, they would skip her a grade. But the good news for her, at least according to Miriam, was that she'd be in the same grade as the Spitz twins.

"They'll introduce you to all of their friends," she told Beanie. And though the twins never did, Beanie didn't want to burst Miriam's south-of-the-Boulevard bubble. She had worked too hard to get it. And so, that January, Beanie Rosen left her friends behind and started school at Sinai a year younger than her classmates, and feeling, at least initially, quite alone.

Food became the elixir, the panacea that comforted, calmed, and narcotized her until all she felt was full and, afterward, guilty. It was a vicious cycle that she promised each night to end, then would start again the next day, wondering what she could eat to stop the noise. She'd plan out her meals and make sure her just-in-case stash was well stocked and well hidden.

Since the twins were at the house infrequently, and Dr. Spitz and the soon-to-be Mrs. Spitz were out every night, Beanie would break open the box within a box hiding the contraband, usually peanut M&M's,

underneath Jiffy Pop popcorn in case anyone came home unexpectedly. Then she'd curl up on the couch in front of the television, wearing her Lanz of Salzburg nightgown, which was flannel and flowery and tented just enough to hide the growing evidence of her binge, and lull herself into a kind of hypnotic state, eating robotically as she escaped into *Little House on the Prairie, The Brady Bunch*, or *The Waltons*: a triptych of family, harmony, and love.

And when they weren't on, she'd find old movies or watch reruns of *To Tell the Truth* or *What's My Line?* where famous people, dressed in minks and pearls, exchanged witty repartee and inside jokes about theater, literature, and all things terribly important. Beanie would slip into their world, laughing along with them, because she too, as long as the food lasted, would be in on the joke.

In early February 1976, five months before the wedding, Miriam took Beanie, just fifteen, along with Esther and Sarah, who were sixteen and a half and twenty-five pounds thinner, to Miss Jane's on Ventura Boulevard.

Miss Jane's was a boutique in Encino where wealthy mothers shopped for their wealthy daughters, buying Bat Mitzvah gowns or other special-occasion dresses. Miss Jane, rail thin and bird-like, was impeccably dressed in vintage Chanel with big white pearls hugging her neck and heels high enough to make her eye level with fifteen-year-old Beanie.

She looks like a sandpiper, Beanie thought, referring to the tiny birds that run up and down the shore at Zuma Beach.

Miniscule and meticulous, Miss Jane gave hushed instructions to the salesgirls who brought out sample dresses with matching hats and shoes.

"The twins," Miriam said, indicating Esther and Sarah, who wore co-ordinating halter tops, high-waisted jeans, and platform sandals to show off their tiny waists and elongated frames, "will be my junior bridesmaids, and my Beanie"—she put her arm around her daughter, adjusting Beanie's poncho which hung low over her faded jeans and Wallabees—"my maid of honor."

Miss Jane smiled as the salesgirl pulled sample dresses. "Let's just try these on for size," she said, leading the girls toward the dressing rooms.

But when Beanie took off her poncho and Miss Jane noted the girth around the middle, she pulled Miriam aside. "We only go up to size twelve," she whispered.

Miriam looked at Miss Jane quizzically, then snapped her head to her daughter, moving her eyes up and down Beanie's body, now uncloaked by the heavy poncho. Beanie, her Beanie, was *FAT*, like her father and her uncles and their wives. How had she not noticed?

"This all stops now," Miriam told her once they got home and the skinny twins, in bikinis, were lying by the pool, sunbathing though it was February and overcast.

Freaks, Beanie thought, watching them from her bedroom view until her mother and her vitriol snapped her out of it.

"You get this from your father's side," Miriam said, spitting out the words as if the fat gene might be contagious. Beanie, like her father, was reminded that she was never enough, or in this case was too much. "We have five months, for God's sakes," she said, pointing to the calendar with the big red heart around the fourth of July. "You simply must take off *the weight.*"

Miriam, who vacillated between a size four and size six, enrolled her daughter in "Chubby Checkers, Sherman Oaks," a diet program designed for overweight youth, south of the Boulevard. At their suggestion, she had the bathroom scale moved into the kitchen so Beanie could visualize her weight *before* opening the fridge.

"It'll make you think twice," Miriam said, and reminded Beanie that they were all in this together.

"Leggs goes to queen size," Esther whispered to Beanie that night, reminding her that they weren't.

By the middle of May, with Beanie still hovering at 151 pounds, Miriam decided to have a dress custom made.

"Perfect," said Miss Jane after taking Beanie's measurements and noting that the material for her dress would be slightly different. "Now your maid of honor will stand out!"

"Yes, she will," said Miriam, unable to hide the double meaning. Beanie's weight was a reminder of all the promises broken, the years of disappointment, and the fat uncles with their fat wives.

"She's going to be just like them," Miriam told Dr. Spitz a few nights later when she thought her daughter was asleep, sending Beanie into her just-in-case stash to self-fulfill the prophecy.

Finally, to quell or perhaps silence Miriam's dissatisfaction, Dr. Spitz prescribed diet pills once a day, which quickly helped Beanie lose some water weight.

"Take two," Miriam told her, hoping they would miraculously trim her down.

They didn't.

At the wedding, Beanie wore a *custom-made* A-line lavender granny dress, dyed-to-match lavender satin pumps with enough of a lift to elongate her frame, and, at Miriam's insistence, her first girdle.

"All women wear them," Miriam said, ignoring the fact that neither she nor the twins needed to. Beanie's dirty-blond hair had been straightened and flattened, and a wreath of flowers encircled the crown of her head, with lavender ribbons flowing down her back. "You *are* beautiful," Miriam said, reassuring Beanie and perhaps herself. "You just needed a little help."

THE SCHNITZ

It was a night of many firsts.
—BEANIE ROSEN'S JOURNAL

July 4, 1976

Crowds cheered coast to coast as fireworks exploded in night skies and tall ships sailed down the Hudson River to celebrate not just the two hundredth birthday of the United States, but an even more perfect union: the joining of Dr. and Mrs. Spitz.

Miriam Rosen walked down the aisle in an ivory gown with a fascinator veil, her wavy red hair cascading to her shoulders, while Beanie—stretched, flattened, girdled, and much less puffy—stood proudly by her side. Though the ceremony was brief, the reception was opulent as the upwardly mobile crowd celebrated the Dr. and new Mrs. Spitz while eating hors d'oeuvres of mini blintzes, latkes, and caviar, and waited for the seated dinner to begin.

Beanie, standing near a carving station, looked pretty not only in her mother's eyes, but also in the eyes of one pockmarked seventeen-year-old boy standing across the room near the Tiki Bar.

"Joel Schnitzer's checking you out," said Beanie's new stepsister Esther, gesturing toward the boy. "He's Rabbi Schnitzer's nephew. He always helps at big events."

"Oh," said Beanie, looking over, then quickly looking away. *Holy shit,* she thought. Joel Schnitzer was in fact checking her out. And that made her nervous.

"He goes to Sinai," Esther reminded. "He's a senior."

Beanie glanced over at him again.

He's creepy, she decided. That was her catchphrase for anyone or anything a little off. And instinct told her that Joel Schnitzer, while perfectly presentable in his three-piece, wide-lapelled, powder-blue leisure suit, was definitely off.

He was also headed her way.

"Have fun," Esther said with a conspiratorial smile, making Beanie wonder if she had arranged this whole thing.

"Hiya," Joel said, looking her up and down. "Joel Schnitzer, but you can call me 'The Schnitz.' Everyone does."

She nodded.

"You go to Sinai."

Again, she nodded.

"Junior?"

"Next year," she said.

Somewhere in the background, the expensive eight-piece wedding band that Miriam had hired instead of a DJ—no one south of the Boulevard hires a DJ—began playing Chicago's "25 or 6 to 4."

"Wanna dance?" he asked.

Her heart was pumping double-time. Beanie wasn't sure if it was from the diet pills or his question. No boy had ever asked her to dance.

She hid her nerves best she could and shrugged nonchalantly. "Okay."

They walked into the dining room adorned with twinkly lights and pink and white peony centerpieces. The Schnitz navigated Beanie through the fifteen round tables of ten surrounding an almost empty dance floor.

"I lead the youth group choir at Temple Beth Torah," he shouted proudly to her as he moved to the song.

"You should hear our 'Dayenu'" he joked, raising his eyebrows and tapping an imaginary cigar à la Groucho Marx. While half of her was nauseated by this senior who somehow thought his temple choir duties were cool or funny, the other half couldn't help but notice him studying her body, lusting fiercely, obviously. Her A-line dress, coupled with her girdle and push-up bra, put her ample breasts on display. She watched Joel watch them.

And that made her feel powerful.

And pretty.

And wanted.

It was a sort of game, albeit a dangerous one, and she decided she'd play for a while. Never before had anyone lusted after her.

Other couples joined them on the dance floor as the band began playing their rendition of "My Love" by Wings. The Schnitz pulled her toward him. It was her first slow dance.

It would be the first of many events that night at the Sportsmen's Lodge.

She could feel his ardor on her leg, pressing against her. Ardor—that's what they called it in *Once Is Not Enough* and the other racy books Beanie had found hidden behind other books on Miriam's bookshelves. But beyond those books, Beanie had no reference nor experience. She knew about sex, of course, in a biological way, and had talked about it generically with friends, but she had never seen nor felt an actual penis pressed against her, which simultaneously excited and repulsed her.

"Let's get outta here," said The Schnitz, his voice thick with lust and urgency.

Ewww, she thought to herself. But she followed him.

The Schnitz brought her outside to the garden with the peacocks that Dr. Spitz had paid for—$20 per cock—and led her to a bench hidden in the corner. He played with her hair, then nibbled her ear. It tickled, and she reacted, indicating, he must have thought, that she wanted more.

But what she really wanted was to run back to the beautiful room where "Tie A Yellow Ribbon" wafted through the air, where people were laughing and dancing and probably being seated for dinner. Miriam had wanted two choices, filet *or* salmon. "All the best weddings give options," she had said to Dr. Spitz, cuddling up to him. And though it was costly, the good doctor, as usual, yielded to his bride. "We should get back for dinner," Beanie told The Schnitz. "I really want to try the meat."

The Schnitz smiled. "That can be arranged," he said, as he popped a Certs into his mouth and found his way to hers.

Beanie's first kiss was more like a tonsillectomy.

A lot of tongue, she thought empirically, as she tried her best to navigate the invasion of face, minty breath, and hands. It was too much. She tried to disengage, but The Schnitz was all over her in a kind of frenetic, desperate exploration that left her feeling overpowered, out of control. Neither romantic nor seductive, it was an assault.

Game over, she decided, pulling away.

"Hey!" The Schnitz gasped, surprised.

"Sorry," Beanie said, "but they're going to introduce Mom and Dr. Spitz."

"You already know them," he said jokingly, taking her hand and placing it directly onto his crotch. "Besides, I'm so fucking hard."

She had never felt anything like that. Repulsed and frightened, she tried to pull away. "Let me go," she said. But he held her. Tight.

"Come on," he pleaded. "Just touch it."

"No," she said, louder this time, freeing her hand and shooting him daggers. This had gone too far. Much too far. She turned around, heading back inside.

"Can you just wait a minute? I was just messing with you. I don't want you to be mad," he pleaded.

"I'm not mad," she lied.

"You're a really good kisser," he told her. "You really turn me on."

Run, she thought. *Just turn and leave.* But she didn't.

"Let me show you how much," he whispered. She stood transfixed as he unzipped his pants. Even in the shadows she couldn't miss his erect penis unleashed, like a jack-in-the-box, springing free with a buoyancy that suggested a life of its own.

She was astonished. Shocked.

He watched her watch him. "Touch it," he whispered.

She shook her head, willing her feet to move, but they stayed right where they were.

"Okay, okay, I won't ask again. I promise," he said, reading her mind, trying to keep her close. "Just stay here," he told her, "and watch me." Slowly, he began stroking himself. "Like this, see?" he whispered. "Just like this."

She couldn't take her eyes off The Schnitz's erect penis.

Or his hand. Up and down. Up and down.

"You start at the bottom and go over the head . . . like this," he said, offering a tutorial, then a shiver, which had an effect on her she wasn't ready to acknowledge.

"You're so fucking hot," he whispered as he continued jerking himself off.

"And your mouth," he said, jerking harder, getting closer to climax. "Red, and moist . . . wrapped around my cock."

Her face flushed, and he could see his words were having an effect.

"Do you like me to talk dirty?" he asked softly, studying her.

She stood transfixed, refusing to reveal how much she liked it.

He stroked faster now. Even the peacocks kept their distance.

"Do you ever touch yourself?" he asked.

And her face revealed the truth.

"I knew it," he said, panting. "You rub your clit every night, don't you?"

She was taken aback. Not because of the word, obscene in the way he had shortened it, but because somehow . . . somehow . . . he knew.

"Do it," he commanded, reaching out for her. "Show me! Touch yourself!"

And, instantly, that snapped Beanie out of her momentary paralysis. She'd had enough. She'd seen enough. She was done. "You're gross," she said, leaving The Schnitz, haloed by the expensive purple lighting that Dr. Spitz had paid extra for, spread-eagled on the bench, to resolve his issue.

But that night in bed, ungirdled, she replayed the events over and over while slowly, methodically, resolving her own.

Joel Schnitzer's penis would leave an indelible mark on the Fourth of July, the Sportsmen's Lodge, and the blessed joining of Dr. and Mrs. Spitz. As both reference point and benchmark, it had opened the door to a world that Beanie was anxious to explore.

THE BOOM BOOM

ELLA

Shut up! I think I said for you to shut up!
—CHRISSY, *IN THE BOOM BOOM ROOM*

1974

Ella, sixteen, who had been quieted if not tamed in boarding school, had become interested in theater in general, and the Williamstown Summer Festival in particular. Ella's parents, while loving this blossoming side of their creative and outspoken daughter, were also loving the space that the theater and specifically the summer internship could offer. Her father was in the middle of a senatorial run, and the distance between his conservative campaign and his liberal daughter created a cushion that allowed him to celebrate her accomplishments—from afar.

But first, in order to get into the famed Williamstown Summer Theatre Festival, one had to audition. Ella chose a monologue from David Rabe's *In the Boom Boom Room.* This was a new play they were going to do in repertory that summer, and she desperately wanted to play Chrissy, the lead. It was an audacious reach, one that her limited résumé did not support, but that only fueled her belief that it was her manifest destiny to land it.

Her theater teacher, Edith Rood, had suggested that, at her audition, she do something to get noticed, and so, halfway through the monologue, Ella stripped and did the remainder of the piece in the nude. The admittance committee, comprised of three actors, one director, and two playwrights, thought the gesture bawdy, lewd, and brave, and though the odds were against her, she was waitlisted for the first company, but accepted into the second.

With a permission slip signed by Eve Lynn and a donation signed by Boo, Ella Joy Gaddy was accepted into the prestigious summer program at Williamstown and offered small roles in that season's *The Seagull, The Threepenny Opera,* and the pièce de résistance, understudying the role she most dearly wanted, Chrissy in *In the Boom Boom Room.* She would be understudying Tamasin Sullivan, a senior star on the rise who was in the drama program at Yale.

Tamasin's reputation for excellence, and the fact that she had had a small but significant role in John Schlesinger's *Marathon Man,* created a mystique around her. It was rumored that agents from William Morris and Sylvan Light were flying in to try to sign her away from her small East Coast representatives who had discovered and nurtured her from the age of fourteen. She was, in Ella's estimation, a legend, or at least one in the making, and Ella was awed to be in her presence.

For the first two weeks they didn't talk at all; Ella just understudied, over studied, and generally observed everything about Tamasin. She mirrored her mannerisms, her gait, the way she'd hold on to a phrase or punctuate a word with a breath, a stare, or an elongated pause that made the audience and the actors onstage lean in. *Pay attention,* it said, without saying it. And people did. There was little about Tamasin Sullivan that Ella didn't love, admire, and perhaps for the first time in her life, envy.

Rarely intimidated, Ella couldn't find words when it came to Tamasin.

"She probably thinks I'm a moron," Ella told Harlan, who was visiting with Essie. They had come to help Ella get situated as Eve Lynn was busy campaigning with Boo. By that time, Darnell was in his last year of medical school in nearby Boston, and he'd come as well.

Ella and Darnell hadn't seen each other for a few years but had been writing regularly, and despite their nine-year age difference, they'd developed a deep friendship.

"No one would ever think you were a moron, E," Darnell said. They always used initials when referring to the other, something Ella had started as a child. "Just be yourself," he told her, winking. "Can't do better than that."

But for the first time in her life, Ella Gaddy was shy, and insecure. Being underage, she felt a bit outside the circle of actors and stagehands who would all get together after rehearsals, listening to the Stones or Zeppelin and getting wasted, then getting laid. She kept her distance.

It was Tamasin who approached her. "Got a fag?" she asked.

Rehearsals had just ended, and a group of kids were going to Digby's to dance and drink and stretch their legs with the locals.

Ella pulled out a box of Virginia Slims from her embroidered shoulder bag. "You've come a long way, baby," Ella said, smiling at the reference as she lit Tamasin's cigarette. Tamasin looked at her, confused.

"What's that supposed to mean?" she asked.

"It's, you know, the slogan in the cigarette commercial," Ella said, feeling her face redden. "You've come a long way?" Tamasin's emotionless stare made Ella self-conscious.

"Never mind," Ella said, wanting to disappear.

Tamasin took a long drag. "I heard you stripped halfway through your audition, and that's how you got to be my understudy."

It was more of a statement than a question; an acknowledgment that Tamasin had done some research. And somehow that gave Ella back her footing.

"Yeah," she said. "Maybe if I would've stripped from the beginning, I could have landed the role."

Tamasin looked at her for a moment, then let out a deep laugh, which made Ella relax a bit. "I bet you could have," she said, impressed, and then, referring to the busload of kids, "You going with 'em?"

Ella shook her head.

"Good," Tamasin said, taking another drag. "Neither am I." And then she looked at Ella again, with her signature pregnant pause, as if she were weighing a decision. "Wanna walk?"

Ella nodded, shivering, though it was a billion degrees. They headed round the lake back to the cabins that housed the repertory company. They were both wearing shorts and sandals, Tamasin in cutoffs, a Lynyrd Skynyrd T-shirt, and Birkenstocks, Ella in cuffed shorts and a flowered sleeveless blouse.

"Very twin set," Tamasin commented, regarding the shirt that matched the shorts. "When I first saw you, I thought you'd be a Southern priss."

Ella didn't know how to respond.

"So, are you a Southern priss?" Tamasin asked, squinting as she took another drag. Ella considered the question.

"Truth be told I do come from a long line of prisses, and I can't really abide any of 'em, so I sure as hell hope I'm not," she told her with a candor and authenticity that was not only refreshing but absofuckinglutley charming.

Tamasin smiled.

And in that moment Ella knew she had passed some test.

The walk back was three-quarters of a mile, but for Ella it felt like two steps. She hung on every word Tamasin said. It wasn't just that she was talented, that went without saying, but she was brilliant. And honest. And curious. And fucking magnificent.

At five feet nine inches, Tamasin Sullivan was as tall as Ella, but less lanky, with a natural beauty that Ella found refreshing for its lack of pretense.

"Thirsty?" Tamasin asked just before they got to the cabin. Ella nodded.

Tamasin's cabin, which housed four to a room, was conveniently empty, and smelled of incense.

"You like?" Tamasin asked, holding a cone of Nag Champa.

Again, Ella nodded.

"Light it," Tamasin told her, bringing over a bottle of Coke and sitting on her bed. She patted the spot next to her and Ella obediently walked over and sat down, taking a swig from the Coke Tamasin offered. The Nag Champa gave the air a heavy, spicy aroma that Ella found intoxicating.

Tamasin studied Ella as she drank. "Is that natural?" Tamasin asked, referring to Ella's vibrant hair color.

And for the third time, Ella, tongue-tied, just nodded.

"You're beautiful," Tamasin said, reaching for a strand of Ella's hair.

"You are," Ella whispered back. Her throat was dry, and her heart was pounding. She wasn't sure what she was feeling except the need to be closer, and not wanting it to end. She had never had sexual feelings for a woman, never even considered it, but now it seemed as natural as breathing as Tamasin gently leaned in and kissed her.

Ella kissed her back, passionately, hungrily, as she had an out-of-body experience, wondering on one hand if this was really happening, and then on the other how to prolong every sensual second.

They fell back onto the bed with unleashed lust as Tamasin's expert tongue and hands explored and undressed the body of her young understudy. Ella lay back, happily submitting, taking in the overwhelming sensations. Tamasin stripped quickly and lay atop her as the two found a rhythm, writhing, awakening, fulfilling.

It was, Ella recalled much later in life, the moment she realized that rules were for sheep. And she would not join a flock. Fuck rules. Fuck tradition. Fuck Tamasin.

And she did.

They became partners, friends, lovers, inseparable for six glorious weeks, dreading the end of the season. Romantics, they'd lie on blankets under the stars, listening to Simon & Garfunkel wax poetic about the inevitability of endings.

"False promises are for fools," Tamasin told Ella. "Let's not make them."

So, they didn't.

The finality only heightened the experience.

Their last week at Williamstown, Ella gave Tamasin an antique pocket watch inscribed, *Waste not a moment.*

As a farewell gift in return, Tamasin feigned illness the night the Sylvan Light agents flew in to see her. "Fuck 'em," she said, "let them sign you."

They didn't. But who cared?

For on that night, Ella Gaddy was *In the Boom Boom Room.*

THE TAXMAN COMETH

MILLICENT

At a certain point we all have to pay . . .
—ONE WHO DIDN'T

1965–1969

Millicent immediately had understood the crucial mistake she had made at the high tea at Claridge's, and when she and Lucille were alone, had apologized, trying to course correct. She promised Lucille she would never ask any questions like that again. She didn't care what a bastard daughter was, she just wanted to be with her.

But Lucille was resolute, promising that the Lycée le Rosey was one of the most exclusive academies in the world and it was a wonderful opportunity that Sir Rodney was providing. They would be together soon, she promised.

A little over a year later, in a small civil ceremony, Lucille Baxter officially became the next Mrs. Goldstone. There were pictures in society columns and dinners thrown by Princess Margaret and Sir Antony Armstrong-Jones, but the squeaky wheel who had been sent away was not invited. Lucille had written, of course, about the engagement and the wedding and had sent a picture in a small silver frame that she instructed Millicent to put in her room as a temporary memento. *We'll take another with the three of us when we're together,* she wrote, promising that they would all spend the summer in Sydney where Millicent would meet Sir Rodney's three children whose names Millicent didn't know. Lucille rarely spoke of them. In a universe where history could be rewritten if not erased, those children, much like Millicent, were reminders of past mistakes, and impediments to Lucille's future.

On the plus side, Millicent had a new guardian, a new narrative, and a new pedigree. And pedigree, at least in the world she now inhabited, was essential. So was survival. While she could have written a letter, begging to come home to Aunt Fifi, Millicent understood this was an opportunity to not only forge her own path but perhaps, eventually, find her own patron.

With that in mind, she took stock of her situation. Her expenses, within reason, were rarely questioned, and were paid by a local accountant. She made a few friends, and on occasion, when invited to their homes, would contact said accountant for plane fare or clothing or anything else required.

The arrangement was comfortable as long as Lucille kept the coffers full. But what if she didn't? What if she fell so in love with her new life that she didn't want to be responsible for her old one? Millicent realized that she was a pawn in a game that Lucille was playing halfway across the world, threatening a truth Lucille wanted buried. Late at night Millicent wondered if Lucille might simply cut the purse strings one day, and then where would Millicent be? She needed security, some sort of guarantee that Lucille couldn't pull the rug out from under her again. And that's when it occurred to her: if Lucille feared the truth that much, then the truth, perhaps, had currency.

"It doesn't matter where we come from, Squeak," Lucille had once told her, "just where we're going." But where they came from *did* matter to Lucille, Millicent knew that now. Though she still wasn't sure what a bastard daughter was, she was certain that the facts surrounding her past might be the key to her future. And while she had no intention of sharing those facts, whatever they were, she wondered just what her silence would be worth.

Shortly after Lucille had written of her marriage, Millicent asked the local accountant for an airline ticket to London to go with one of her friends to her family home in Hampstead for the weekend. The accountant, after checking with Lucille, provided airfare and spending money—for a new winter coat, and gifts for her friend's family—reminding her that she was, after all, now related to Sir Rodney Goldstone.

"Act accordingly," the accountant said, quoting Lucille.

Millicent nodded, took the ticket and the cash, but instead of visiting a friend's family, made her way to Aunt Fifi, whom she had contacted via post telling her how much she'd missed her, how often she'd tried to get in touch, and explaining that Lucille, who controlled the purse strings, wouldn't allow it.

Fifi, guilt-ridden over what had transpired and furious at Lucille for keeping them apart, finally provided the truth that Millicent's sister had so desperately wanted hidden. Sitting in her parlor in her worn floral chairs, Aunt Fifi explained that at the age of thirteen, Lucille had relations with the taxman once, maybe twice, in his Packard, and that was where Millicent had been conceived. He was, Aunt Fifi thought, living in Wales now, but if Millicent wanted to make contact, Fifi believed she had a way to reach him.

There it was: the secret that had been buried and shrouded and scurried away to Switzerland, never to rear its ugly truth. Because if it had, it might just destroy the carefully constructed blueprint designed by the now royally celebrated Mrs. Goldstone. Millicent knew that Sir Rodney, who fashioned himself a family man, might think twice about having a wife who abandoned her child if not in responsibility, then in spirit.

And that made this truth priceless.

That night, while still at Aunt Fifi's, Millicent went to the cramped bedroom she had once shared with Lucille, memorializing the note she had been writing and rewriting in her head.

Dear Lucille, I have gotten clarity about my past, and apparently yours. I have no interest in sharing it, but I would like to stay at the Lycée until graduation, at which time I would like to discuss a monthly expense account to support me until I can support myself. I am staying with Aunt Fifi and look forward to hearing from you.

She mailed it that afternoon, half expecting Lucille to show up the next day or the day after. But she heard nothing until January of 1965, when Millicent Baxter, fourteen, the same age Lucille had been upon giving birth, was visited at school by a solicitor who explained that her tuition at the Lycée had been extended and prepaid for five additional years, along with an expense account of one hundred pounds monthly.

"But after that," the solicitor warned, staring her down, "you're on your own."

Millicent tried to compose herself, steadying her shaky voice. "I asked for my expenses to continue after graduation," she said, the words now sticking in the back of her throat, which was suddenly dry.

"*If* you agree to our terms," he continued, "you will receive a one-time-only payment of one hundred thousand pounds."

Millicent stared, aghast at the fortune her veiled threat had yielded. It was a great deal of money, more than most people have for their whole lives. The solicitor explained that this was all conditioned upon her silence. He pushed a "Separation Agreement" toward her and asked her to sign. After she did, he handed her a note from her sister.

For your future, Lucille had written.

And for yours, Millicent thought.

The truth had bought her time and freedom. But neither would provide long-lasting security. For that, she knew, she needed her own patron. And while she wasn't quite sure what a patron was or how to find one, she believed the zeros would lead the way.

(LITTLE) BIG MAN ON CAMPUS

BEANIE

It was the short men who caused all the trouble in the world.

—IAN FLEMING

1976–1978

Beanie Rosen loved Fisher Braverman in a way that defined and redefined her. For the first time in her life, life made sense.

She had first noticed Fish the summer of 1976. He was cute, like Donny Osmond cute, only Jewish, which when you're thinking about marriage was an important distinction, at least to the Rosens. Though only fifteen, in her mind's eye Beanie Rosen would one day become Beanie Braverman, living a life of marital bliss in Laurel Canyon because Fish said that was where all the cool musicians lived. She was sure of it.

He was a brilliant musician, or at least he would be, she believed. His dark thick hair framed a dimpled smile, and his *Keep on Truckin'* army jacket and black lowrider bell-bottoms were worn in all the right places. He was a year older than Beanie and several inches shorter, but since he had been held back a year, and she had skipped a grade, they were in the same classes and fell into a friendship.

He liked her name, he said, and so she suddenly liked it, too. He was smart, he was talented, and he was short. He liked to say he was five foot eight, but at five foot five Beanie was taller, so she started wearing flats. When she stood beside him, she felt tall—and not just because she was.

By the time they'd started school in the fall, people knew her as his girl, if not his girlfriend. The distinction only bothered her when it was pointed out.

And it was pointed out by one of her skinny stepsisters, Esther. "He's a dog," she told her. "He's messing around with two seniors."

Beanie rolled her eyes. "You wouldn't understand," she said, believing in truth that Esther wouldn't.

Of course, she knew Fish fooled around. Sometimes he'd even tell her with some casual remark that somehow made her feel closer to him. "Donna gives the worst head," he'd say, and she'd nod, dismissing it-slash-Donna as a random. That's what he called his hook-ups: "randoms." They weren't regulars like Beanie. They didn't mean anything to him like she did.

And though he never made a pass at Beanie, nor showed any kind of interest in having an intimate relationship, he did give her a stuffed animal holding a heart for her sixteenth birthday. It might as well have been a diamond.

He loves me, she thought. She was his watchguard, his bodyguard, and his constant companion until Shalom Rubin, a transfer from Fairfax, became the goddess of Fish's unending fantasies.

Her reputation, like her beauty, preceded her. She was a model and an actress and was legitimately famous. "Rumor is, she dated Barry Williams," Beanie told her friend Elise, who was both slightly cross-eyed and a bit pigeon-toed, which somehow lent her symmetry. It was as if each eye followed the opposing foot.

"Who?" Elise asked, not nearly as vested.

"Greg on *The Brady Bunch,*" Beanie told her.

"Wow," Elise said, impressed. "He's hot." Beanie nodded in agreement, but something was deviling her. "Fish looks a little like Barry Williams, only shorter, so . . ." Beanie trailed off, suddenly concerned.

"So, what?" Elise asked. "You think Shalom will go for Fish Braverman?"

"Maybe," Beanie said.

Elise looked cross-eyed at her friend, but then again, that's how she looked at everything. "Barry Williams is gorgeous," she said, "and Fish, well . . ." Elise let the silence fill in her feelings.

Still, Beanie decided the best defense was a good offense. The only way to prevent losing Fish was to become the architect of his desires. If he wanted Shalom *that* badly, she was determined to be the one to deliver. Like a cat who brings a mouse to his master, Beanie knew that if she could make him happy, Fish would recognize, if not how beautiful she was—that would come in time, especially now that she had lost *the weight*—but how valuable she was. It was a tactical move designed to reinforce the idea that he'd be lost without her. Even if he didn't *want* Beanie, he would *need* Beanie. *It's like the difference between a Snickers bar and air,* she thought. *You might want a Snickers, but you* need *to breathe.*

"I could get to know her," she offered one afternoon as Fish stood lusting at Shalom, who seemingly floated in slow motion across the quad, her long feathered blond hair blowing gently in the wind.

He was mesmerized. In truth, so was Beanie.

Shalom Rubin defied the stereotypical makeup of the student body at Sinai High. Everything about her was taut, tan, blond, and Waspy, except she was Jewish, which made her perfect. *She looks like Farrah Fawcett,* Beanie decided, thinking Shalom could be her younger sister. Her style was free and easy, favoring bell-bottoms and peasant blouses. Defying all dress codes, Shalom refused to wear a bra, proudly displaying her nipples like a Girl Scout badge. Or two. While Farrah's nipples spoke for themselves on every poster in every bedroom, airport, and mall, Shalom's—a little less global—announced their presence with equal authority and defiance.

"Fish," Beanie said, snapping him out of his reverie. He turned. "I could make friends with her. If you want."

She was half hoping he'd say, "No, Beanie. All I want is you."

Instead he screwed up his face into what she thought was a cross between gratitude and astonishment. "Would you do that?"

She smiled, nodded, and, gauntlet thrown, sought out the wave that was Shalom Rubin's friendship with the singular goal of making the boy she loved happy, even if it meant getting him another girl. She was, after all, her father's daughter.

SHALOM

It means piece . . . pun intended.

—BEANIE ROSEN

1977

"She's just like Marilyn on *The Munsters,*" Beanie told Elise as they watched Shalom Rubin from a distance.

"Wait," Elise said, sounding shocked and somewhat offended. "Does that mean that you think we're the freaks?"

"Uh, yeah," Beanie answered, wondering if her friend ever looked in the mirror.

Elise, understandably jealous, was annoyed at Beanie's singular obsession with this new girl. "What kind of name is Shalom?" she asked rhetorically, knowing exactly what kind of name it was.

"Hebrew," Beanie answered, adding that she thought it was beautiful and all-encompassing in that this one word meant hello, goodbye, and peace be with you.

"Then Shalom," Elise said, indicating that her new friend was coming as her old one was leaving.

It was easy for Beanie to get close to Shalom.

Getting her to notice Fish was a different story. Shalom was dating Leonardo Strickler, a blond, naturally tall (i.e., sans lifts), gorgeous college freshman who was away on a football scholarship to the University of Michigan. Shalom, who welcomed Beanie's friendship, had little interest and less time for a short high school junior with big ideas.

When Beanie dutifully reported her lack of enthusiasm for Fish to

Fish, he suggested she bring Shalom to The Hideout, his uncle's club where he played piano every Tuesday.

"Chicks love it when I play. It turns them on," he said. Most people would have found that comment narcissistic and obnoxious, but Beanie knew it was true. She could watch him sing for hours. And it did turn her on, but she kept that to herself.

The following Tuesday, she and Shalom went to The Hideout and watched from a back table as Fish played "The Long and Winding Road." Beanie thought he looked especially sexy with his long brown suede vest and platform shoes that served the dual purpose of saying *I'm cool,* and *I'm tall.* Or at least taller.

Shalom thought he was adorable. And perhaps because she had a boyfriend out of state, and everyone else had been too shy to befriend her, the two friends became three, and the three, for a while, were inseparable, tooling around the valley in Beanie's 1970 Dodge Dart Swinger.

Her father had gifted her his pale yellow two-door with a V8 engine for her sixteenth birthday, which Beanie had promptly, and as one of her skinny stepsisters had reminded her, *stupidly* decorated with pink bathtub appliques to look like the backdrop on *The Dating Game.* Thinking the flower power would make her cool, she was dismayed when the petals peeled away, leaving a pink polka-dot behemoth. But she was the only one with wheels, so the dotted Swinger became their chariot.

Their regular haunt was Bob's Big Boy on Van Nuys and Roscoe, where they'd sit for hours after school sharing a combo and Coke, talking endlessly about what they would do with their lives—or, more specifically, what Shalom would do. Fish loved listening to Shalom tell about being discovered at Pacific Ocean Park and becoming a model, or how she got cast in the role of Valerie Bertinelli's friend who died of bone cancer on *One Day at a Time.*

"You should be an actor," Shalom said to Fish one night at his house.

That's where they'd end up most weekends, in his converted garage/bedroom with the deep pile shag carpeting, the black lava lamp which cast the room in shades of red, and the macramé plant holder that Beanie had made for the ivy plant she had given him that encircled the room proprietarily, like prehensile fingers threatening to tighten their vines around anyone who came too close. There was an upright piano next to a low platform waterbed where Shalom would lie, her body undulating with the rhythm of the mattress.

"I'm serious, Fish," she said, leaning on her elbow as her body moved hypnotically. "You've got a magnetism like Brando."

"He wants to be a musician," Beanie told her, upset that Shalom was redesigning Fish's future. That was Beanie's job, and she didn't need nor require *her* suggestions for *their* lives.

"I can do both," he said, sitting down and playing a medley of new Billy Joel tunes from *The Stranger*, an album he knew Shalom loved.

When he got to "She's Always a Woman," Shalom jumped up from the waterbed and danced in the middle of the room with unselfconscious abandon.

Beanie watched Fish watch Shalom.

It was a triangle of unrequited love.

Until it was no longer unrequited.

"He's a great lover," Shalom casually told Beanie in late June 1977. They were in the bathroom during the school's nutrition break, and she was glossing her already glossed lips in the mirror. "He went down there," she whispered, screwing the cap back onto her strawberry Bonne Bell stick. "Leo never did," she confided.

"Never did what?" Beanie said, trying to pretend she didn't understand; to deny a truth she wasn't prepared to accept.

Shalom pointed to her nether regions and told her that Fish could do it for hours.

"We need to talk," Beanie said to Fish later in the day. She had been waiting for him outside his classroom.

"I have Spanish," he said.

"Skip it," she told him, more of a command than a suggestion.

They walked to a bench nearby. He sat. She didn't.

"Why didn't you tell me you and Shalom went all the way?" she asked, close to tears.

He just stared at her.

"I mean, I tell you everything," she said, getting angrier at his silence. "I didn't even know that Shalom and Leonardo had broken up."

Fish stood up. "They hadn't," he told her, clearing up the order of which came first, the fuck or the "Fuck you."

Beanie was angry beyond words. She felt left out. Worse, she felt cheated on. And that made Fish angry.

"What did you think was going to happen, Beanie?" he argued, which was a fair point. What *did* she think? That they would all be just friends? Forever? "Grow up," he said. "This is between me and Shalom."

And just like that, their threesome had become two, leaving Beanie no other choice but to say, "Fuck you."

Beanie, like her mother, had learned to keep score. And, also like her mother, she felt entitled to her fair share. She wouldn't return Fish's or Shalom's calls. She was too angry. Too hurt. She had gotten Fish what he wanted, and it wasn't that he'd forgotten to include her—that she could understand, perhaps even forgive. But he'd purposely *excluded* her, spitting her out, like a fingernail.

After two weeks of unreturned calls, Fish sought out Beanie at *her* home. They went into *her* room, where they sat on *her* bed, where he apologized profusely, and then slowly and seductively gave her a blow-by-blow rundown of what it was like to fuck Shalom Rubin.

What he did. What she did. How it felt.

Everything. It was sick and twisted and highly dysfunctional, but in that way Beanie and Fish were able to become sexually involved by proxy. After "the misstep," as she called it, she and Fish and Shalom resumed their relationship. They were inseparable, and when they weren't, Fish filled in the gaps.

But in the summer of 1977, Leonardo said goodbye to Michigan and put in for transfer to USC. Fish's converted garage and all it contained was no longer the draw it had once been for Shalom Rubin.

And Fish never saw it coming until it went.

Shalom.

THE PATRON SAINT

MILLICENT/MERCEDES

And if we go to hell, we will turn the devils out
of doors and make a heaven of it.
—JOSEPH SMITH, JR.

1970–1975

Millicent had learned from Lucille how to ingratiate herself to those who could help her rise, and using those tactics, sought out a friendship with Patricia Herrington, the girl who sat at the top of the top of the zeros at the Lycée. Patricia had a father worth millions and a mother who protected both their money and their reputation. Knowing that, Millicent weaved a narrative that, while not remotely accurate, gave her a pedigree that even Patricia's class-conscious mother would envy. Without providing specifics, Millicent implied that her parents had met an untimely demise in a car accident abroad and had left their vast fortune in trust for her and her older sister, Lucille. Strategically omitting the details lest they be fact-checked, Millicent focused instead on the role Sir Rodney Goldstone had played, stepping in immediately, first as a close family friend, and then falling in love with her much older sister, and now as her unofficial "uncle" by marriage. Given that Sir Rodney was well into his sixties, referring to him as "uncle" seemed more appropriate than "brother-in-law," which he would be if Lucille were her sister rather than her mother, which, in truth technically made him her stepfather. But those were just minor details, easily overlooked in the face of his legacy. Rodney Goldstone was not only knighted, but was one of the richest men in Australia, and that was good enough for the Herringtons, who began inviting Millicent for holidays at their summer estate in Bath where she could focus her attention on the monied friends of her monied friend's parents.

Millicent had learned enough from watching Lucille that patrons were people with more money than time: an older, dissatisfied lot, looking for something or someone new to jumpstart a second act; to level up if not in status then in youth. And since time was not on their side, they would choose partners who, by association, would lend them vigor if not years. And that gave young Millicent, at fifteen, a leg up. Now she just had to figure out how to use it.

Knowing that the secret to attaining patronage had to do with whatever happened behind closed doors, Millicent began opening them, taking advantage of her summer holidays with the Herringtons, and choosing a different local boy every summer to school her. But, by her eighteenth birthday, as her skills improved, there was nary a patron in sight. And that concerned her. Lucille's stipend would run out in less than a year, and then Millicent would be officially and legally on her own. There was an air of desperation to her search for a patron, and a fear it wasn't going to be quite as simple as she'd once thought. In the meantime she needed to be frugal, allowing her friends' families, who were always generous, to foot the bill for many of the bigger-ticket items.

"I could write Uncle Rodney," she'd always offer, but they'd stop her mid-sentence and tell her not to bother, it was their pleasure, et cetera.

Initially, she'd hoped that Sweet Uncle Rodney, still believing that Millicent was the beloved younger sister and only family member of his wife, would continue to send money separate and apart from Lucille, presuming he didn't know that there'd been a falling-out between them. But then she learned from Aunt Fifi that Sir Rodney and Lucille were "infanticipating," and she was advised that she shouldn't hold out hope for a reconciliation. *A legitimate child and an illegitimate lie cannot coexist,* Fifi had written, which was why Millicent paid special attention when Patricia let it slip that her very wealthy and very naughty uncle by marriage—Lord Shay Stapleton, the Earl of Sussex—was going to spend the weekend with them at the Herringtons' estate in Bath. Stapleton, who had just arrived with his wife and twin boys for Patricia's father's fiftieth birthday party, was an absolute sex fiend, according to Patricia.

While tall and thin and balding, Stapleton, Millicent thought, was not at all unappealing. *He is lithe,* she decided, as she stared at him through the window, *and debonair,* she thought, with a strong jaw and dimpled chin, reminding her of Prince Philip.

As Millicent watched from afar, Patricia took that moment to relay a particularly salacious rumor surrounding her uncle and a nineteen-year-old girl. Apparently her aunt, Lady Elaine Stapleton, a filthy-rich socialite who found validation if not in her marriage then in what others thought of her marriage, made a great deal of effort to squash those rumors.

"Which is why she keeps him on a short leash," Patricia told Millicent, confiding that while her aunt dismissed all gossip, Patricia didn't. "I think he's a frustrated sexual fanatic," she said, giggling.

Millicent looked out the window again. *Not for long,* she thought.

Over the next two days Millicent waited, watched, and when the opportunity presented, she presented back. It was the afternoon after the big birthday party and everyone, except Lord Stapleton, was by the river at a family picnic.

Feigning a headache, Millicent stayed back as well, hoping to casually run into Stapleton. Finally, after a light midday snack, she observed him making his way into the library.

It's now or never, she told herself, taking a deep breath, walking in, and closing the door behind her. The wood-paneled room with a large mahogany desk in the corner smelled of new polish and old money. Deep green overstuffed chairs flanked the fireplace, and floor-to-ceiling books, some first editions, were arranged categorically and alphabetically. It was impressive by any standards, the kind of room where you could stash your secrets between the prose and the poetry; the kind of room where you felt protected, and coddled, and safe enough for an illicit assignation.

Under the pretense of finding a book, Millicent acted surprised to find that she wasn't alone, and immediately apologized for intruding.

Stapleton looked up as if seeing her for the first time.

She smiled sweetly, reintroducing herself, knowing that he had little or no recollection of meeting her, though they'd been introduced at breakfast that morning.

"You go to school with Patricia, do you?" he asked, sizing her up. "You seem so much younger."

"I'm just petite, sir," she said coyly, adding, "but as my father used to say, 'Good things come in small packages.'" Again, she smiled.

His interest piqued; he watched as she walked over to the mahogany ladder.

"I'll be out of your way in a jiff," she told him, climbing to the highest rung, just below the fourteen-foot ceilings. Though she weighed just over a hundred and ten pounds, she acted a bit wary, tentative even, as if the ladder wouldn't support her weight, and asked, ever so politely, if he wouldn't mind holding it steady.

Stapleton, of course, complied, walking over and securing both sides.

Millicent, who was wearing a short pale blue polka-dot mini skirt, with white lace panties underneath, stretched on tippy toes and reached for one book, then another. Her legs were parted—just enough for Stapleton to steal a glance.

He looked away at first, until he realized he wasn't stealing anything.

Millicent, from the top rung, smiled down at him, then slowly parted her legs further, solidifying in one bold gesture that this was an invitation and not a mistake.

He could see the outline of her labia and a few curly pubic hairs peeking from the sides. His mouth was dry, and his cock was hard as she descended, swaying from side to side, as if she were waving a red cape in front of an angry bull. Finally, at the bottom rung, she slid right up against Stapleton's bursting loins. He had never wanted anything or anyone quite as much.

They fucked wantonly on the oriental rug at the base of the ladder. It was rushed, passionate, inarguably tawdry, and though or perhaps because she was still a schoolgirl, it fueled his ardor and determination even more. Surprised by both his good fortune and renewed stamina, he locked the door and fucked her again against the desk, vowing if this treasure was only an afternoon's fantasy, then he would take full advantage. But after their second romp, he was delighted to discover that Millicent was equally as insatiable.

In less than a week, Stapleton found a sudden need to travel to Switzerland, and by Christmas he'd already suggested that Millicent transfer from the Lycée to St. Bartholomew, an exclusive academy in London where he had strong ties with the school administration, and a convenient flat nearby in Chelsea. He promised her a future filled with wild adventure. But Millicent wasn't looking for adventure; she was looking for security. If Stapleton wanted more, it was going to cost him.

Explaining that Sir Rodney would never approve of a midyear transfer and that her trust was tied up with Goldstone until she was twenty-five, the besotted Earl of Sussex found himself pleading to Millicent to let him help find a solution.

It took her six weeks, but by January of 1970, Millicent Baxter had so deftly handled the negotiation that Stapleton was *begging* to subsidize her monthly expenses. Which meant that along with the money that Lucille was already depositing, he was going to give her additional funds. And the pièce de résistance: *he* felt the victor.

Shortly after her transfer to St. Bartholomew, Stapleton and Millicent, who were staying at his townhome in Chelsea, began looking at smaller flats in nearby Mayfair to purchase.

"But why do you need two homes?" she asked.

"I don't," he told her, smiling.

A few weeks later Stapleton presented Millicent with an early graduation gift of a large one-bedroom plus study in Mayfair which he promptly put in *her* name, along with a stipend to decorate it.

For the first time in her life she was absolutely speechless.

"Mine?" she asked, disbelievingly. He nodded, curiously moved by just how moved she was. After all, she came from money, and this was just a small flat in a nice neighborhood. But to Millicent it was a palace; new and modern and most importantly, it was hers. After school and on weekends she set about decorating it with orange, yellow, and white acrylic modular furniture.

No matter what, she thought, *I've a place of my own now.* That, combined with the pre-negotiated settlement of £100,000 that Lucille was due to deposit upon graduation, could, if necessary, set her up for life. But only if necessary. Millicent made certain that her future was secure, attending her school by day, and her patron by night.

For his part, Stapleton was both pleased and relieved. He didn't want to run the risk of his muse and his wife sharing space, even if only from a distance. While Lady Elaine spent most of her time at the estate in Sussex with the boys, she sometimes would spontaneously pop over to London for some shopping or dinner or an event they'd attend with mutual friends. If that were the case, it might require a bit of unnecessary juggling. In a don't-ask-don't-tell universe, he preferred to keep his arrangements tidy, and though it cost him £65,000, it was little to pay for his peace of mind.

Millicent graduated St. Bartholomew in the spring of 1970 and without ceremony or commemoration, Lucille made the last and final deposit into her account. Secretly, Millicent hoped for some sort of rapprochement—a note, a gesture—but there was nothing. Swallowing any disappointment, she turned her attention to her patron saint, with the singular goal of keeping him, and keeping him happy. When he wasn't in Sussex visiting the boys, they'd spend most days and evenings going to museums, films, having dinners primarily alone but sometimes socializing with friends of his who also had what Stapleton referred to as "side dishes." At nineteen, Millicent was the youngest and most consistent "dish." His friends, on the other hand, liked variety. And, with the constant rotation of partners, Millicent began finding it difficult to keep them straight. Finally she just stopped trying. "Really you should make more of an effort," he scolded. But she shook her head. It was impossible. Instead she told him that she did a "*Gilligan's Island* on them," explaining that it was easier for her to group everyone into the characters from her favorite television show.

"Most of the men," she explained, "are Thurston Howells, with a few

Skippers, and maybe one or two Professors, but that's only if I'm being kind."

"What's so special about the Professor?" he asked, his curiosity piqued.

"The Professor," she told him, smiling, "was sexy and smart and sophisticated. Like you," she added, coyly.

"Oh, so I'm a Professor?" he asked, bemused.

"Without a doubt," she reassured him.

"What about the women?" he asked.

She thought about that and decided that most of the women were Gingers or Ginger wannabes. "Sexy, stacked, and glittery." He nodded and smiled as she continued. "I'm guessing that the men are all married to Loveys," she told him, explaining that Loveys were like well-preserved old ladies who lunch. "Hats, gloves, that kind of thing."

"So, who are you?" he asked, charmed by his young muse and her musings.

"I'm the only Mary Ann," she said, puffed up with a pride and confidence that made him smile.

"I take it that's a good thing," he said. She nodded emphatically, explaining that Mary Ann was the wholesome gal next door who all the girls wanted to be, and all the men wanted to fuck. He laughed out loud, positively besotted.

"I don't know if I could love you more," he said, scooping her into a bear hug. She felt secure in his arms, convinced that she had finally found safe harbor—or at least enough zeros to keep her afloat.

For his forty-seventh birthday, Stapleton, a collector of vintage automobiles, flew himself and Millicent to France where he bought a 1957 Mercedes SL Roadster. "There's nothing more beautiful than this car," he told her, "except for my Millicent." As he said it aloud, he looked at her strangely, making her momentarily self-conscious.

"What?" she asked, wondering if he had suddenly changed his mind about the car, or her, or perhaps them. She panicked, but hid it well. "What?" she asked again, trying to quell her nerves.

"We have to do something about your name," he said more to himself than to Millicent. They were outside Paris, on their way to the Crillon

Hotel, and they had just stopped to get petrol. She nodded, unable to respond because she didn't quite know how to. Was it just her name? Or was there something else he didn't like? She felt unsure, nervous inside. But Stapleton, deep in thought, didn't notice. "You're exotic," he told her, "and mysterious, and classic. Much like this car," he said. Then he turned to her, an idea taking shape. "Mercedes," he declared. "What do you think of that name, my darling?"

She looked at herself in the dashboard mirror. "Mercedes," she said, trying it on. She liked it. More than that, she liked the idea of disappearing into a whole new persona. Millicent had been a sad creature who lived in a two-up two-down in the East End. But Mercedes was exotic and mysterious and classic. Mercedes had her own flat in Mayfair and a future yet unwritten. She smiled, hugged him, and Mercedes Baxter was born.

When they got home to London, Stapleton, who had bought a Polaroid, began asking Mercedes to model for him. "You're my muse," he'd tell her as she would pose in a variety of wigs, wearing pink-and-orange mini dresses and go-go boots with colored tights. She would paint fake lashes under her eyes like Twiggy, and then cover them with giant Jackie O sunglasses, doing a little peek-a-boo for the camera, puckering her lips, lifting her dress, showing her bum.

"What do you do with all these photographs?" she asked, lying on the bed thumbing through dozens of them. "Do you show them to your friends?"

"For my eyes only," he said, explaining that when he wasn't with her, he looked at them.

Turns out he wasn't the only one looking.

"Do you want to explain these, Shay?" Lady Elaine Stapleton asked as she flipped through the cheesecake Polaroids of Mercedes in a blond wig. They were in their elegant townhome in Chelsea, getting ready to attend a formal function together. Lady Elaine had come to London for the weekend and had found the pictures in Stapleton's valise.

Ever cool, Stapleton simply smiled, took them back, and shook his head. "They're Camillo's, darling," he told her, reminding her that their friend, the Italian film director Camillo Santorini, had recently used their flat in London while casting a film. "I put them in my valise to return them to him," he said smoothly, then asked Elaine to help him with his tie.

She clocked his answer but didn't comment further. To ensure she wouldn't, Stapleton had Santorini and Mercedes show up coincidentally at a restaurant where he and Elaine were dining a few nights later so she could observe them from afar.

"Shall I call them over?" he asked Elaine, who told him not to. She didn't care for Camillo and had seen quite enough of the young woman.

Mercedes, for her part, didn't mind the charade; it was the price she was paying for the life she was living. Besides, she liked Santorini who was, in truth, the only real *Professor* in Stapleton's crowd. He reminded her of an older Tom Jones dressed in his Yves Saint Laurent flowered shirt, unbuttoned at the top, revealing black and gray chest hair where two thin gold "S" chains nestled cloyingly.

Also, the farce gave Mercedes a chance to observe the woman who held the title.

But I hold the man, she thought smugly, allowing Santorini to order for her.

PLUS ONE

ELLA

Guess who's coming to dinner . . .

—ALICE LEE GADDY BOCH BEHIND CLOSED DOORS

1978

In the fall of 1978, Ella, who had graduated early with honors from NYU and would attend Harvard Law the following year, was summoned back to the farm to spend a week with the family.

The Senator, as Eve Lynn now singularly referred to her husband, insisting everyone do the same, had been feeling nostalgic for the gaggle again, and since Ella had gone to Europe just after graduation, he had made a personal appeal that she visit. It had been far too long since they'd all been together, and the family was expanding at a rate that made the Senator misty. After all, Knox had a new girlfriend, a Dupont, no less, and Alice Lee would be there with her new husband, Phillip Boch, whom she'd married the year before—fulfilling Eve Lynn's manifest destiny that the South, or at least her circle within it, would rise again.

The ultra-formal wedding had been held at the Gaddy farm: all the staff had been dressed in livery, with polished brass appointments, and it had been written up in the *Courier Journal* as the Event of the Decade, befitting the daughter of the senator from the fine state of Kentucky, and his wife Eve Lynn Knox Gaddy, one of the South's most celebrated ex-debutantes. The union of these two families solidified Eve Lynn's place among the fortunate 500.

A reluctant bridesmaid, Ella had been warned not to do anything to embarrass her sister, and certainly not to make a scene. So, instead, she made an impression. The once gangly and gawky redhead had somehow acquired sophistication and polish, and while Alice Lee was cautious when it came to all things Ella, others were smitten.

There was just something about the youngest Gaddy girl that made you look twice. Sitting next to her sister for a wedding portrait, she not only dwarfed Alice Lee, blond and petite in her custom-made ivory Christian Dior gown, but Ella pulled the focus, looking stately and elegant in her lavender duchess satin bridesmaid dress, with a floral wreath of baby's breath and violets crowning her long, curly red hair, which, while still untamed, seemed to halo her face in a most attractive manner.

"She's a real beauty," Boo had said under his breath, observing his two daughters from afar.

"Yes, she is," Eve Lynn agreed, but they were not looking at the same child.

The gaggle hadn't been together since.

"Honestly, she is always late," Alice Lee complained, annoyed that once again they were waiting on Ella. Alice Lee and her husband and Knox and his girlfriend had all arrived at the farm punctually for a noon lunch.

But Ella, who apparently still lived by a different clock, had not.

"Now don't you start," Eve Lynn warned, reminding her daughter that everyone else lived nearby, and Ella lived in New York City. "That doesn't matter," Alice Lee responded, resenting the special dispensation that her younger sister still received. "She is as rude as ever," Alice Lee declared in a huff.

Eve Lynn searched Alice Lee's porcelain face imploringly. "Please," she said. She didn't want arguments, certainly not in front of the Dupont girl, and she was genuinely looking forward to the family reunion. Eve Lynn had settled into the idea that Ella was finding her way. And as long as that way was at a good distance, Eve Lynn would make the best of it. She hoped Alice Lee would as well.

"By the way," Eve Lynn said confidentially, trying to change the subject, "she's bringing someone."

"Who?" asked Alice Lee.

"She didn't say," Eve Lynn told her. All Eve Lynn knew was that Ella had called the Senator from the airport and told him that she wasn't coming alone.

And that also annoyed Alice Lee. "Why do you let her get away with that kind of behavior?" she asked, chastising her mother for not only allowing but perpetuating Ella's rude sense of entitlement. "You are not doing her any favors," Alice Lee scolded.

"Well, I think it's that Jewish boy she was dating," Eve Lynn confided.

"Don't be so certain," Alice Lee said smugly. "After all, it could be a woman," she said, adding that there had been a rumor at her boarding school that Ella Joy was a lesbian.

"You stop that talk right now," Eve Lynn snapped, casting a look toward Knox's girlfriend, who was within earshot.

"I'm not making this up, Mother," Alice Lee told her, less trying to upset Eve Lynn and more attempting to reinforce her spot as the number one.

Ever since Ella had gone away to college, then gotten accepted on her first try to Harvard Law School, there was, Boo had noted, a bit of jealousy that Alice Lee exhibited toward her younger sister. Eve Lynn had dismissed the Senator when he mentioned it, saying that Alice Lee wasn't even a bit envious and had everything she'd ever wanted, but in truth, Alice Lee had everything Eve Lynn had wanted *for* her.

"Here she is now," announced the Senator, overjoyed as Ella walked toward them with her arm around Essie. It was hot outside, and she wore a poncho, shorts, and flip-flops. Her red hair hung long, and a pair of granny glasses covered her eyes.

"Here's our brilliant scholar," the Senator said, walking up to her expansively with Eve Lynn in tow, who was looking around for Ella's guest.

"I thought perhaps you'd be bringing Mr. Finklestine," Eve Lynn said, mispronouncing his name either due to some ancient anti-semitism so deeply ingrained she'd be insulted by the mere suggestion, or just a lack of familiarity with *-steens, -stines,* or *-stones.*

"We broke up ages ago," Ella told her.

"Well, I thought the Senator said that you said you were bringing someone?" Eve Lynn responded, confused.

"No, Mother," Ella corrected, "I said I wasn't coming alone."

"Well, what on earth does that mean?" interrupted Alice Lee, enjoying neither the riddle nor the riddler. "And aren't you melting in that heavy poncho?"

"I am," Ella said, taking it off and exposing her plus-one.

Ella Joy Gaddy was heavily pregnant.

. . . AND SCENE

BEANIE

Celebrate endings, for they precede new beginnings.

—JONATHAN LOCKWOOD HUIE

1977

Shortly after Shalom shalomed, Fish decided he wanted to try out acting. Beanie said she did as well, hoping that their time together and their mutual interest would bring them closer.

It did. They were doing an improv—a nonverbal exercise—playing strangers on a train who were attracted to each other.

From the back of the room, the teacher shouted instructions tasking them to adjust their performances in real time. "It's a crowded train," the teacher yelled, "you both keep trying to sneak looks." Standing on opposite ends of the stage, they pretended to subtly check each other out. Finally, he said, "Beanie, it's your stop, and you need to pass Fish to get out."

As she did, Fish grabbed her.

And kissed her. WITH TONGUE!

At first she was frozen, as the stranger on the train would naturally be, and as Beanie Rosen could only be. And then both she and her character melted, passionately kissing back.

And Fish was right there, grinding against her. She didn't know how far he'd take it, but she was willing to go the distance. She didn't want it to end. *Ever.*

It was the teacher who ended it.

"And scene," he said, indicating that the assignment was complete.

Like being awoken by a hypnotist, they snapped out of it, broke apart, and went back to their seats as if nothing had happened.

But it had. At least for Beanie. She wasn't sure how Fish felt. They didn't talk about it. Not during the break. Not on their ride home. But that night when she dropped him off at his house in her polka-dotted Swinger, Fish asked if she wanted to come inside and hang out.

"Sure," she said, turning off the engine, trying not to let her voice betray the quivering inside her. Since Shalom said shalom, they'd rarely hung out after hours.

She followed him into the converted garage, which had its own separate entrance, and stood by the door as Fish turned on the lava lamp, put on a Rod Stewart record, and sat across the room in "The Beanie Bag" chair, the one he'd named for her.

"Come here," he said, more a command than a request.

"What?" she said, unable to move.

"You heard me," he told her, leaning back, legs spread, cigarette lit.

She walked over as "Tonight's the Night" prophetically filled the room. It was so on the nose Beanie wanted to smile, or comment, or both, but stopped herself lest she break the spell.

"Take off the sweatshirt," he told her.

She took it off, dropping it by the waterbed.

"Turn around," he said, studying her.

She turned, instinctively putting her hands over her midsection.

"Put your hands down," he commanded.

She did. She was wearing a denim skirt and a T-shirt that said, *I'm a Pepper.*

Be cool, she thought to herself, taking a deep breath before meeting his gaze.

"What do you want me to do next?" she asked, trying to sound sexy, subservient.

"You show me," he said, challenging her.

Okay, this is it, Beanie girl. You can do it.

She kept her eyes on Fish as she took off her shirt.

Her quilted bra showed off her hardened nipples. Still staring at him, she played with them. She could tell he liked it. Truth was, she knew what he liked. She'd had a cheat sheet squirreled away with tidbits Shalom had shared. "He likes to watch me," Shalom had told her. So, Beanie, emboldened, let him watch her. She unhooked her bra and dropped it on the floor then shimmied out of her denim skirt. She stood before him in blue panties with pink flowers, wishing she'd worn the black lace ones she'd bought with her babysitting money.

"C'mere," he said.

She obeyed, walking over, holding his gaze.

"Get on your knees."

She did.

She was having a kind of out-of-body experience. Channeling Joel Schnitzer in the purple-hued peacocked garden at the Sportsmen's Lodge, she took the initiative, unleashing his cock, then skillfully adding her hands, then her mouth, letting instinct and his moans guide her to his climax.

But Fish never reciprocated, not the way he had with Shalom. In fact, he and Beanie never actually had sex, not the real kind. She was still a virgin that way.

He wouldn't, he always told her. She might get pregnant.

"What about condoms?" she'd ask.

But he dismissed the thought, like she was daft or stupid, or worse, uncool. "Might as well not do anything," he said.

She nodded in agreement, saying she was just kidding, but inside she worried she wasn't good enough, pretty enough, thin enough.

"We can do it another way," he said, grabbing baby oil and rubbing it on her backside. "You've got a great ass," he told her, reassuringly adding, "Everyone does it."

"Did Shalom?" she asked quietly.

"She wouldn't let me."

So, Beanie did.

They never discussed it. Any of it. It just became a part of their lives.

Like Hebrew school on Wednesday nights, just something else they did together.

A kind of release for Fish.

A kind of intimacy for Beanie.

Falling short for both.

. . . and scene.

SECRET AGENT

If someone stands between you and success, knock
them the fuck down and keep going. Next time they'll
be smart enough to get out of your way.
—SHEILA DAY, ON HER RISE TO BECOMING AN AGENT

1978

"Sylvan Light agents are coming," Fish said with the breathless excitement he'd heretofore only reserved for all things Shalom. It was a Saturday evening in early June 1978, and Fish was about to do a monologue for one of the showcases his advanced acting class was sponsoring. Casting directors, producers, and agents had been invited, but a Sylvan Light agent had RSVP'd.

Everyone backstage was excited. Nervous. There was no bigger agency than Sylvan Light. They had all the stars, all the connections—hell, if you were represented by the Light office, it was almost a guarantee that you'd make it.

Sylvan Light had been established in 1944 when Schmuel Lichtenstein, a small man with big vision, went to the William Morris board of directors in the New York office and suggested they send him to the West Coast. Frustrated booking nightclubs, Lichtenstein wanted to expand into the new area of television. After all, William Morris already had a small office in Beverly Hills, and he thought he could fit in there just fine. Unfortunately, the board disagreed. So Lichtenstein packed up his life and headed to California, opening his own office right next door to Morris. That way when clients and buyers came to their offices, he could run into them. And he did. Taking many of the tenants and clients from his old agency, he set out to build a better mousetrap, one that celebrated young men with both vision and ambition. Within the first year Schmuel Lichtenstein incorporated as the Sylvan Light Agency.

And man did they shine.

Everyone wanted to "come to the Light," so the idea that the Light was coming to Fish was humbling. "I mean, this is huge," he whispered. Beanie nodded, not exactly sure why it was huge, but understanding it was very important to Fish, so it became equally important to her. She wished Fish luck and went out front, studying the audience, wondering who the Light agent was and how she could somehow influence him to meet and sign Fish. There was an urgency to her search. Much in the way she had delivered him Shalom, Beanie needed to be the instrument of that introduction, otherwise, she feared, Fish might discover he didn't need her at all.

There were about fifty people in the audience, and they all looked regular, normal, unimportant. She studied them, trying to pick out the Hollywood heavyweight. *Maybe the Sylvan Light agent doesn't want to be noticed,* she thought, eyeing a man in the back who sat alone, slumped in his chair.

Suddenly the acting teacher brought her focus back to the stage as he welcomed everyone and explained that the ten actors who would be performing monologues had left their headshots at the back of the room. "Take one, leave a card," he told them, and then without further ado, he introduced the actors. "First up is Fisher Braverman doing a monologue from *Grease.*"

Beanie had helped Fish choose the material. It was either that or *Rebel Without a Cause,* but they chose *Grease* because John Travolta and Olivia Newton-John were coming out with a film version in a few weeks' time, and there was a coolness to it that seemed to speak to who Fish was.

Beanie felt her heart wildly beating as the smattering of applause subsided and Fish became a distraught Danny Zuko conflicted about Sandy, a girl he'd met over the summer. She had worked with Fish after school for months running lines, discussing character, motivation, and when he got tense and couldn't get into the right headspace, she'd let him fuck her up the ass. *It was all worth it,* she thought that night as she watched him disappear into the role. She believed Fish's performance was brilliant and layered.

Unfortunately, the Light agent didn't.

"Who cares?" Beanie said, pointing out that a few casting directors had left their cards in his box. But Fish cared. A lot. In fact, he was devastated. It wasn't just that Sylvan Light didn't want him: no agents had left cards.

"You don't get it," he said, taking a final drag off his Marlboro, and stubbing it out on the floor. "An actor needs an agent to get a job," he said, then asked if he could borrow a dime so he could call Shalom.

That sent Beanie into a tailspin.

"What's Shalom gonna do?" she asked in a panic, following him to the pay phone.

"Introduce me to her agent," he told her, depositing a coin and punching out numbers he'd obviously committed to memory. She reached out and grabbed his arm, stopping him.

"No," she said. "You can't call her. It will ruin everything."

He looked at her, confused. "What the hell does that mean?"

Thinking quickly, she blurted out that *she* was planning on introducing him to an agent. That was why she had been so flippant. "I'm going to help you," she assured him.

He studied her, trying to ascertain the level of bullshit. He knew Beanie was threatened by Shalom and suspected this was just a stall tactic. "You don't know any agents," he said.

"No," she agreed, "but Neiman Spitz does." That got his attention. Neiman Spitz, Dr. Spitz's cousin, was a world-famous composer. If Beanie could work that connection for Fish, he could really get somewhere.

Fish put the pay phone receiver back in its cradle. "You're going to ask Neiman Spitz to help me?" he said, still somewhat dubious.

"Already have," she told him, adding, "He said, and I quote, 'No problem, kiddo, happy to help.'"

Fish was flabbergasted. "No bullshit?"

"No bullshit," she confirmed. "It was a surprise. I was going to tell you after the show. That's why I said 'Who cares?' earlier. I didn't mean 'Who cares?' I meant who cares, you know?"

"Fuck," he said, running his hands through his hair. This was huge. Really huge. "Who's his agent?" he asked.

Beanie, thinking quickly, pulled the only agent's name she'd ever heard of out of thin air. "Sheila Day," she told him, adding that she wasn't sure if Neiman was introducing Fish to Sheila—using her first name as if she and Sheila were familiar—or someone Sheila recommends.

Fish nodded. It sounded legit.

Even Beanie was impressed with herself. That was quick thinking. Sheila Day, the senior vice president at STC and Partners, was considered the most powerful female agent in the business, and had been profiled on *60 Minutes* where she'd spoken about her "twinklies"—that's what she'd called her stars—and her meteoric rise as a female agent.

"Honeeeey," she'd said to the interviewer, "when I started, the men had the desks, and the women were under them." In the interview, she'd been acerbic, aggressive, wickedly funny, brilliant, charming when she needed to be, and had left enough of an impression on Beanie that it was the only name she could think of with her back to the wall.

But it worked. Fish was floored. Sheila Day, while not an agent at Sylvan Light, was still a fucking legend, so if Beanie was recommending someone to Sheila based on Neiman Spitz's request, well then, Jesus, it was way better than anything Shalom could do.

He looked at Beanie like she was some sort of wizard or goddess or both. Never mind that none of it was true, that she'd only met Neiman Spitz in passing, and that Sheila Day had just announced her retirement. Those were just details: little, small waves she'd have to navigate. Another time.

At that moment Fish was happy. So, she was happy. And that night they made out, which rarely happened since he didn't like kissing, and he dry humped her until *he* came, which was almost like regular sex.

Afterward they held each other, and Beanie told him how good an actor he was, how much his Danny Zuko had moved her, had moved others, she was certain. In her arms, he saw his greatness. And she would make sure others would as well. She was, after all, his secret agent, selling, prodding, coaxing, and convincing everyone else to fall in line.

Now she just had to find someone who believed in him as much as she did.

SIDE DISH

MERCEDES

If he strayed from his wife with you, what makes you think he won't stray from you with someone else?

—A GINGER

1978

By 1978, Mercedes was living the *Sex and the Single Girl* life. She had plenty of money, plenty of time, and while she didn't have plenty of friends, the regular Gingers—as opposed to those who were rotated out every few weeks—sufficed.

And it was one of the regulars whom she turned to for advice as her twenty-fifth birthday loomed. Worried that Stapleton would be looking to be reimbursed for the apartment once her trust kicked in, Mercedes—who had distanced herself from all family ties, including Aunt Fifi, lest her patron discover the truth about her inheritance, or lack thereof—needed help.

While she never offered the Ginger any specifics, she did share that she was supposed to reimburse Stapleton some monies he had laid out and was worried that she would be unable to do so, since her funds were tied up overseas. They were at a café in the West End splitting an apricot tart. The Ginger, packing a fresh box of Viceroy cigarettes against the table, was confused.

"You're supposed to pay *him* back?" she asked.

Mercedes nodded.

"Has he asked for the money?"

Mercedes shook her head no, but worried it was just a matter of time.

"The Earl of Sussex," the Ginger said, taking one of the cigarettes out of her pack, while signaling to the waiter that they were ready for the check, "is worth something north of forty million pounds. I wouldn't worry about whatever funds he's laid out." She studied Mercedes, lit the cigarette, and took a long drag. "But you need to be more forward thinking," she advised, explaining that Mercedes needed to worry less about debts owed, and more about a future secured. The check came and Mercedes reached for her wallet, but the Ginger paid. "I got this, luv," she told her, putting money down and standing to leave. The Ginger knew what she was talking about. While no beauty, the tall, curvy twenty-nine-year-old brunette did the best with what she had. She had been with her partner for less than eighteen months and already had a flat in Kensington that dwarfed Mercedes's tiny apartment in Mayfair, and a proposal of marriage, which she had yet to accept. As they walked home she confessed that she honestly wasn't sure she was going to. Unlike Stapleton, her patron was not nearly as well set, and she liked keeping her options open.

"Here's the thing," she told Mercedes as they walked, "if he strayed from his wife with you, what makes you think he won't stray from you with someone else?" They stopped at a corner, and the Ginger looked at her younger protégé. "Don't worry, darling," she said. "He's not going anywhere. Yet. But you need to be a little smarter." Reminding Mercedes that the good Lord of Sussex was twenty-six years her senior, she warned that the advantage belonged to Mercedes, and she shouldn't let him get too comfortable. "He needs to fear that *you* might start looking elsewhere, luv. Understand?"

Of course Mercedes understood, but the thought hadn't occurred to her. Not really. She had spent the last six years accommodating his every request. Even when he had suggested occasional threesomes with a rotating Ginger while an associate, some friend from Parliament who was barely a Thurston Howell, watched from the corner until he joined in. She recalled being both repelled and drawn to this strange grouping and groping with body parts intertwined like a game of Twister. It was comical and quizzical, but she liked the way Stapleton liked it, the way he looked at others look at her.

"It's time to make him work for it," she told Mercedes, adding that if she played her cards right, he'd never let her go.

They parted ways and Mercedes, contemplative, walked alone, unsure of the terms she wanted, but certain she had left too much on the table.

The next day when Stapleton, who had been in Sussex visiting the boys, arrived at her flat, Mercedes wasn't there. This was strange behavior. Usually she'd be home waiting, and they'd go out to eat or to a film or both. She always carefully planned for their first night back together. It had been this way for years. So, her absence was unusual. Perhaps, he thought, she had gone to her aunt's house, or possibly met a friend for dinner. But he realized he didn't know her friends or her aunt. He didn't even know the aunt's name or where she lived. The only relative he could contact was her sister, Lucille Goldstone, and they hadn't spoken since Mercedes refused to move back to Australia. The Goldstones, who now had a daughter of their own, had become estranged from Mercedes, and Stapleton, fearing their judgments, had encouraged the separation.

He felt suddenly helpless, and rather stupid. How could he not know where she was, and how could she be so careless and thoughtless not to check in?

He waited. Anxiously. All night long.

The next morning Mercedes came home without explanation. She greeted Stapleton with a kiss on the head and then went to shower and change.

"Where have you been?" he demanded, following her into the bathroom.

She told him she'd been to the theater the night before and had seen *Hair.*

"They're all naked," she said, smiling. She began soaping up in the shower, casually explaining that she'd had too much to drink and spent the night with a friend.

"I don't understand," he said, unable to process her cavalier statements.

Then she grabbed a towel and walked to the bedroom. "I'm sorry, darling, but I'm terribly late."

"For what?"

"A job interview," she said.

Stapleton's head was spinning.

"I've always wanted to get into interior design," she told him, slipping a colorful Pucci mini dress over her naked body.

"You're not wearing anything underneath," he said.

"I never do, silly," she said, winking. She grabbed her sunglasses and a bag before he stopped her, demanding to know exactly what the hell was going on. She calmly explained that a friend had recommended her for an interior design job, and she very much wanted to take it. It would involve some travel, she told him; the firm had projects in France, Italy, and the States.

He grabbed her by the wrist. "I forbid it," he said, "I absolutely forbid it."

She freed herself and looked at him, shocked, as he realized he had gone too far. He tried a different tactic.

"Darling, you don't need to work. I provide for you. If there's anything else you want, just let me know."

She stopped, kissed him gently, and said, "My independence."

She had changed on a dime.

He hadn't expected it and was both terrified and paralyzed by the thought of losing her. Vacillating between depression and anger, he tried to find his way in this new version of his life but already missed the old one profoundly.

"Have you fallen out of love with me?" he asked. It had been two weeks since she'd made her declaration of independence, and now he sat on the white leather swivel chair in her small flat, looking somewhat pitiful and broken.

"It's less about you and more about me," she told him, explaining that

Sir Rodney had invested much of her trust, and she was tired of being dependent on Stapleton or on anyone.

And that's when he told her that he wanted to take care of her. Forever.

The following week he went to Lady Elaine and demanded that the charade of their marriage end, confessing his love for someone else, someone he wanted to marry.

Mercedes Baxter, the bastard daughter hidden away in the bowels of life, a side dish no longer, was soon to become Lady Mercedes Stapleton.

GIVE ME TEN MINUTES . . .

BEANIE

. . . and I'll give you a star . . .

—BEANIE ROSEN WITHOUT TRAINING WHEELS

1977

If Beanie was going to get Fish an agent, she needed all the tools at the ready. She studied Fish's headshot, paid for with money she'd taken from Dr. Spitz's sock drawer. It was unconventional in that it was a full-body photograph with Fish leaning against a wall, cigarette in his mouth, his hair shaggy around his face. Taken from a low perspective, it was specifically designed to make Fish look tall. Or at least taller. Underneath, it said "Fisher Braverman," with his height, five foot eight (Zambonied), his hair color, eye color, and age.

"I'm not sure about it," Fish said, holding the headshot.

"I like it," Beanie told him, hoping she didn't have to take more money from Dr. Spitz's sock drawer to pay for more photographs. "It's sexy, and different enough that it makes you stand out."

Fish agreed, he did look hot, but something was off. "It's the name," he said, telling Beanie he'd been thinking of changing it for a long time. "Makes me sound like an old Jewish man," he explained, and she laughed because he was right. It did. "I mean, most people look at me and they think I'm Italian," he told her. He turned to Beanie and asked, "What do you think of Fish Campisi?"

Beanie made a face and shook her head, it wasn't right. "How about . . . Fish Zuko?" she offered, doubling down again on how good he was as Danny Zuko.

He said it aloud, then smiled. He liked it.

And so, *Fish Zuko* was born, and he would be bigger than Fish Braverman, if not in actual size, then in legendary stature.

"Sheila Day retired," Fish told Beanie the following week after he'd done some research.

Beanie, nonplussed, acted like she'd known. "Yeah," she said nonchalantly, "she's going to recommend someone else. Don't worry."

But Fish wasn't worried. Beanie was. At first. But then it occurred to her that maybe it was a blessing in disguise. She was never going to get Sheila Day to be Fish's agent. That was a fool's errand. But surely she could find someone else who would see how amazing Fish was, and they would scoop him up. There were hundreds and hundreds of agencies out there; she just needed one agent who believed in him as much as she did.

Beanie, who would start UC Berkeley in the fall, had only eight weeks to find the person lucky enough to represent Fish Zuko. And so, a woman on a mission, she went first to the venerable Sylvan Light Agency with Fish's old headshot and new name.

Confident that she could at least get him a meeting, Beanie walked up to the receptionist. "Hello, I have an appointment with Mr. Light," she said officiously.

"Try Memorial Park mortuary," the receptionist replied, referring to the cemetery where industry heavy hitters were laid to rest.

"Oh, I'm so sorry," Beanie responded, momentarily flustered. "I just need to see someone if you could let me in. Sheila Day personally recommended I come here," she added, thinking they'd believe her. But, of course, they didn't. These were new waves, and she needed to learn how to navigate them. Quickly.

Determined and desperate, she got a list of franchised agents from the Screen Actors Guild, about one thousand names in teeny-tiny print on both sides of the paper. Organizing them based on locale, Beanie would take the Swinger on her days off from her part-time job at a card store in the Northridge mall and hit the agencies on the fly: ten, fifteen, sometimes twenty a day with Fish's portfolio under her arm, trying to get in.

At each agency she went to, she gathered bits of knowledge, a shorthand, an understanding of the ropes. You had to get friendly with the receptionist to get to the secretary, and friendly with the secretary to get to the agent.

Six weeks passed, and she couldn't even get to a secretary. But nothing deterred her. Every day off, she'd drive to Hollywood, hitting makeshift offices off of Vine where photographs of famous people hung askew, intimating an association that was, in truth, as thin as the agency's shabby walls.

And every night she'd come home and lie to Fish, "The agents Sheila recommended are out of town, on vacation, on the moon . . ." She was running out of excuses, running out of time, and Fish was running out of patience.

"This is bullshit," he said, threatening again to call Shalom.

Finally, one day in August she went to an office in West Hollywood, the Drysdale McClaren Agency. She couldn't get past the receptionist and was about to turn away when she saw the agent behind a scrim.

Out of time, out of excuses, out of her mind, Beanie started jumping up and down, screaming the name of every short actor she could think of. "Excuse me, I have Al Pacino in this portfolio. Dustin Hoffman. Steve McQueen. Can I see you for one minute?"

The agent, curious, came out to the reception area. "What's going on here?" he asked.

Beanie opened the portfolio to Fish's old headshot with his new name. "Fish Zuko," she said. "He's what's going on. And he's brilliant," she told him, adding that he was young and hot and in demand. "And I swear to God if you don't meet him," she said with a conviction that only comes from truth, "you'll see his name on billboards, on stage, on movie posters and remember that you *could have* signed him. Once. Fish Zuko. The one that got away . . ."

He smiled.

She smiled.

It was like great sex. Or what she imagined great sex would be like. She could intuit the climax. He was right there. Get the yes. Get the yes.

"It's ten minutes of your time," she said. "What do you have to lose?"

"Ten minutes," he answered.

"But if I'm right, it'll be the most valuable ten minutes of your life," she responded.

He looked at her and shook his head in surrender. "All right, I'll see him."

Beanie zipped up the portfolio, extending her hand.

"You're welcome, Mr. Drysdale."

"I didn't say thank you," he said.

"You will," she told him, then left.

It was the beginning of Beanie's signature style. Knowing how to end a signing on a high.

And make no mistake, that day, in that office, she'd signed Roy Drysdale.

"She's good," Drysdale said, after Beanie had left. But he was wrong. Beanie Rosen was great.

Her heart was in her throat as she reached for the pay phone on Sunset and Laurel. "Roy Drysdale wants to see you," she said to Fish, never explaining how hard she'd had to work to get the meeting, or that Drysdale was more interested in Beanie than Fish. And though Fish was reticent, citing that Roy Drysdale was hardly Sheila Day, he begrudgingly took the meeting.

By the time Beanie had settled at Berkeley, Drysdale had signed and booked Fish in his first professional acting role playing a juvenile delinquent who takes on Ponch on *CHiPs.*

"*What are you gonna do about it, Pig?*" Beanie said, quoting and then requoting his one line to anyone who'd listen. She had watched it with reverence in her dorm and tried to call Fish immediately after it had aired. Ignoring the long-distance rates, she phoned in the morning, at night, during peak hours, trying to congratulate, celebrate, commemorate his brilliance, but Fish was never home, and never returned the repeated attempts.

She tried to see him at Thanksgiving when she heard he got a commercial for Big Thunder Mountain Railroad, the new "E" ticket ride at Disneyland, and again at Christmas after he landed a semi-regular role on *Happy Days,* playing Potsie's troubled cousin Josh, but her calls and letters and efforts seemed to fall away.

It's said that fish, like guests, stink after a few days. For Beanie it was more a matter of months, and while the sting and the stench ultimately faded, she never forgot the thrill she had in selling Fish not just to Roy Drysdale but to Shalom Rubin, and to anyone else who stood in her way, whoever questioned his talent.

I can do this, she thought, and after graduating early from Berkeley, she set her sights on a place too good for Fish, but not too good for her.

Beanie Rosen would be an agent at the Sylvan Light Agency.

It was, she decided, her destiny.

BEANIE IN WONDERLAND

BEANIE

So, the agent says to the studio head, "You need to cast my client in your film." The studio head shuts him down: "Sorry," he says, "we've cast this other actress." The agent looks at him like he's nuts. "You can't cast her," the agent says, "she has no talent, a huge ego, and her last gig was on Hollywood and Vine!" The studio head screws his face up in rage. "She's my niece," he sneers to the agent. And without missing a beat, the agent responds, "I wasn't finished . . ."

—OVERHEARD IN HALLS OF THE SYLVAN LIGHT AGENCY

1980

"I'm here for the secretarial position," Beanie Rosen told Debbie Hawkins, the receptionist behind the large polished mahogany desk, who was both signing for an incoming delivery and handing over another on its way out.

Beanie recognized her immediately from a few years earlier when she'd gone to the venerable agency seeking representation for Fish Zuko. Thankfully, Debbie didn't recognize Beanie. In fact, she barely acknowledged her, multi-tasking and supervising the incoming, the outgoing, the clients, the agents, the deliveries, greeting, chatting, directing with a choreography that would impress Fosse.

Ignoring Beanie, Debbie punched in an extension on her command-central phone with its three vertical banks of buttons, twenty down, four across, and a cord long enough to wrap around Beanie's ambitions.

It was almost noon on a Monday in June 1980, and Debbie was busily manning the reception desk at the Los Angeles branch of the Sylvan Light

Agency, greeting the guests in the lobby, and operating the complicated multi-extension phone lines like she was commanding an army.

"I've got a package for Mr. Khan," Debbie said into her headset, then looked up. "Hi, Cush!" she said, calling to a bald man in Gucci loafers and a knotted neck scarf who walked past, waving but never looking, his diamond-and-ruby pinkie ring catching the light.

"Hiya, Puss," he said, heading toward the glass doors that led into the inner sanctum of the first floor. He held out a hand, stopping a secretary in stilettos. "He in?" Cush asked, jerking his head toward a door, asserting his power with as few words as possible and implying a limited supply of vocabulary or patience for those who served.

"He's behind closed doors," Stilettos said, "in a meeting with Mr. Lonshien. But if it's urgent, Mr. Cushman, I can take in a note," she offered, smiling, providing an abundance of information, which further communicated subservience.

She might as well have bowed, Beanie thought, studying the exchange, memorizing every nuance. This was a new ocean and Beanie needed to understand the rules to negotiate the waves.

With great interest she watched as Stilettos, not only knowing her place but knowing Mr. Cushman's, offered up even more information. "I can ring you as soon as he's free," she said with deference and a smile, as if expecting a pat on the head, or the ass.

Cush gave neither.

"Thanks, Puss," he said, satisfied, and kept going.

This dance was subtle, a tacit understanding where power, words, and names were reserved for only those on the same level. For Mr. Cushman, all secretaries were "Puss," and mailroom boys distinguishable only by their willingness, nay enthusiasm, to live up to the moniker of "afternoon delight." Those that did were fast-tracked with invitations to private parties and promises of promotion, if not at this agency then at other companies with like-minded individuals who appreciated special services.

Stilettos, having completed her exchange, walked up to reception to collect the package for Mr. Khan, who Beanie knew was the president of the Sylvan Light Agency—which meant, she deduced, that Stilettos was his secretary.

Beanie studied her. She was Asian, beautiful, and looked like a movie star, Suzie Wong–like, or a model, or a very rich high-class call girl, with thick, straight black hair, elegant and delicate pink oval nails—long enough to make a point, but not so long as to make a statement—and just a hint of gardenia about her as she walked by. Breathtakingly beautiful, and immaculately put together, Stilettos, on closer look, was older, perhaps in her thirties, Beanie guessed. *A career secretary,* she thought, taking in the tight pencil skirt, silk blouse with matching peekaboo camisole, and the aforementioned black stilettos, showing off enough leg to make the straight men look twice.

And they did. Which Beanie guessed was the point.

Stilettos, though petite, comported herself with a dignity and import that put her atop the food chain, at least in the secretarial pool.

Beanie cut her a wide berth as she silently assessed her own outfit, carefully chosen that morning: a high-collared blue-striped shirt with tiny buttons up to the neck, puffed shoulders, and long sleeves, and a coordinating gaucho skirt that hit at mid-calf with Pappagallo pumps. She had bought the ensemble at Bullocks Fashion Square where everyone south of the Boulevard shopped, and had thought it looked smart and professional, just like the drawings in the J. Peterman catalog, only now she second-guessed herself and made a mental note about the gauchos. Still, she decided, it was smart to differentiate herself.

I don't want to be a career secretary, she thought, *I want to be an agent. Gauchos are both feminine and masculine,* she told herself, reinforcing her choice, since she had none other.

As Debbie and Stilettos chatted, Beanie took in the understated and elegant lobby of the Sylvan Light Agency, with a picture of its founder on the far back wall between the elevator and the staircase. The seating area was filled with beautiful women, she guessed actresses, auditioning for roles, or agents, or both, who sat cross-legged on curved couches facing each other, divided by a large round glass coffee table covered with the latest trades, news magazines, and business weeklies. Designed for men, it was all very feminine and circular.

Beanie looked at the glass doors separating her from Wonderland. She had to figure out a way to get in, to get through, and her first point of entry was reception. Debbie, the receptionist, was beautiful, black, and ballsy, with short cropped hair, large gold hoops, thick fake eyelashes, and long squared red nails. She wore a short purple rayon dress cinched at the waist, with shoulder pads wider than her hips. Four-inch heels put her well over six feet if she stood, which she did only for punctuation.

Beanie, who had tried not to be intrusive, caught the end of their conversation: "You remember Glo from Franklin Day's desk? She works at Bonwit's now. They're having a massive shoe sale." Debbie was urging Stilettos to go.

"Can't," Stilettos said, picking up the package for Mr. Khan. "Let me know how it is."

"I'm working through lunch," Debbie said, frustrated. "Glo's going to let me bring the shoes here, try 'em on. I thought if you were going, you could pick 'em up . . ."

"Sorry," Stilettos said, heading back to her desk.

"I can go," Beanie said, interrupting with an enthusiasm that finally got Debbie's attention.

She turned, seeing Beanie for the first time.

"To Bonwit's, I mean," Beanie said, clarifying. "I overheard your conversation, and . . . I'm happy to help out. If you want."

Debbie looked at her suspiciously.

"Who are you?"

Beanie smiled, handing over her résumé.

"Beanie Rosen. I'm here for a job interview. Secretarial. I have an appointment at two forty-five, but I got here early, so I'm happy, you know, if you need a hand."

Debbie was tempted.

"I love shoes, too," Beanie added, grinning, "so you'd be doing me the favor."

And that made Debbie smile.

"You sure, hon?"

Beanie nodded.

"Thanks," Debbie said, adding, "It's Beanie, right?"

"Right," Beanie said, and then repeated, "Beanie Rosen," just to make sure she'd remember. Then she turned and went to Bonwit's with the knowledge that she had dipped her toe into the Sylvan Light ocean.

Beanie was back in twenty minutes with a giant bag from Bonwit Teller filled with pairs of sample shoes. Debbie was like a kid in a candy store, or a woman at a sample sale where the sample sale came to her. She tried each on, modeled them, Beanie weighed in, and Debbie was thrilled.

"Glo, I'm taking the Ferragamos, and the Yves Saint Laurents," Debbie said into her headset. "I'll send the other ones back. Love them. Love you."

Now she looked at Beanie. "And you, missy," she said, "are going to the front of the line."

"What line?" Beanie asked, overjoyed that she'd not only gotten past the receptionist, but had perhaps made a powerful ally. Debbie looked toward the fifteen sexy girls sitting on the sexy couches.

"That line," she said.

"I thought they were actresses?"

Debbie shook her head no.

"They're all here for the secretarial job?" Beanie asked, hoping there was another group of frumpy girls behind them, hidden, so as not to sully the ambiance.

"Those are just the afternoon applicants," Debbie said, letting the full reality of the competition crash around Beanie, like dozens of stilettos piercing her over-starched, ultra-conservative outfit, which now, comparatively speaking, looked like a costume reject from *Little House on the Prairie.*

Just then an older woman, maybe late forties, came out holding a white paper bag. "This needs to be delivered to Dr. Israel," she told Debbie, "while it's warm."

Debbie nodded, shouting at a young man who was racing out, "Fred, wait up!"

Fred, who looked to be in his early twenties, wearing the Sylvan Light mailroom uniform—white shirt, skinny tie, black pants, black shoes—was either coming from or going on some errand, in a hurry, on the make, with business too important to waste on a receptionist or her assignment.

"Whatcha got, black beauty?" he said, leaning on the counter, cluelessly racist, flirting in the way men do when they think they're as charming as they are clever, and they are neither.

Fred was a bad boy in training, learning from the other bad boys how to act, how to hustle, how to bully, how to treat women.

Debbie held up a package.

"Mr. Kotlowitz's stool sample," she said.

"Fuuuuccck me," he told her, backing away. "Give it to the new guy," he said, heading out. "I'll owe you."

"You already owe me!" Debbie shouted. She had learned to tolerate and survive the boys' club with a sense of humor on the outside, but a deep resentment within. Debbie, like Beanie, had a just-in-case box, where all the secrets from all of those who'd bullied, profiled, marginalized, and discounted her were buried, or stored.

Just in case.

She picked up the phone, punching in an extension.

"It's Deb. I need the new guy. Stat."

She hung up the phone and turned back to Beanie.

"Which desk are you applying for, hon? Do you know?" she asked.

"I don't," said Beanie, pulling out the *Variety* ad she'd answered with a carefully typed cover letter and résumé. "Is there more than one?"

"Two," Debbie said. "One in television, one in motion pictures. Come back at two o'clock," she told Beanie, winking. "I'll send you up first."

Then Debbie looked beyond Beanie.

"You the new guy?" she asked.

Beanie turned and saw a trainee: tall, thin, with curly brown hair. He was almost indistinguishable from all the other trainees in his Sylvan Light uniform.

"Yeah," he said, "Barry Licht."

"Nice to meet you, Barry Licht. Mr. Kotlowitz has a stool sample that needs to be delivered."

"Umm, I'm at lunch," he said.

"Ummm, I don't care," she responded. "Neither does Mr. Kotlowitz." She handed Barry Licht the warm bag. "Take it to Dr. Israel in the medical office building next to Bonwit's," she told him, then grabbed the large bag of shoes. "While you're at it, drop these off in the shoe department."

"Are they for Kotlowitz, too?" he asked sarcastically.

"Yeah," she said, staring him down, "and now we're both full of shit."

They looked at each other. It was a standoff. Debbie, waiting for him to challenge her directive, and the new guy, unsure, standing with two bags each containing samples, of a sort.

"Let me help," Beanie said, opening the door.

"Who are you?" he asked.

"That's Beanie Rosen," Debbie said. "She'll be here longer than both of us."

Debbie, as it turns out, was partially right.

OLLIE WOOD

MERCEDES

Each meeting occurs at the precise moment for which it was meant.

—NADIA SCRIEVA, *FATHOMS OF FORGIVENESS*

1980

Lady Elaine Stapleton had agreed to an amicable divorce with one non-negotiable condition. "We hold off on any formal announcement until the boys graduate," she insisted, hoping to spare them, or herself, the shame of scandal while they were still in school.

Lord Stapleton, who called bullshit, was frustrated. It was just a power play, a stall tactic. His boys wouldn't graduate until June of 1981. That was fifteen months away. Elaine was hoping it would all disappear.

"But I'll show her," he vowed, moving into Mercedes's flat full time, and beginning the search for a larger place they could purchase together. Well into his fifties, he was acutely aware of their age difference, and so he suggested fun, young neighborhoods like Notting Hill. Her need for independence had so unnerved him, he was desperate to keep her interested and happy.

"We can go wherever you want," he told her.

"How about California?" she asked.

That stopped him. "The States?" he said, trying to figure out how and why and if it was feasible.

"Not full time," she reassured, "but as a place to go to! For fun."

He relaxed into the idea and understood that it would probably be easier there for Mercedes. Elaine had a powerful circle who, he was certain, would be less than forgiving, and Mercedes had fewer friends and less family to shield her from gossip and untoward suggestions.

A few months later while on holiday in Palm Springs, he suggested they drive up to Los Angeles for the afternoon, where he then surprised Mercedes with a half-million-dollar pied-à-terre in Beverly Hills. The luxe apartment, located on the Wilshire corridor, had a private elevator that brought you to a private landing that led to a private foyer giving entrance to a private paradise with wraparound views of all that was possible.

"This will be our first place together," he told her, suggesting she hire a decorator and make it over as the next Lady Stapleton would.

The gesture brought her to tears. This was really happening. They would start life fresh in the States where her new title would provide the pedigree her old background could not.

Shortly after he purchased the condo, Camillo Santorini, who was in Los Angeles screening his latest film, invited them to the premiere of *Urban Cowboy*, a new film starring John Travolta.

Since Stapleton had to visit his boys, Mercedes stayed back and took her interior designer, Nathan Jeremy, who claimed to have done work for the star. At the after-party, while the designer tried to get Travolta's attention, Mercedes wandered through the crowd. It was dank and crowded and some friend of a friend who'd had too much to drink and too little to do was getting handsy and loud and cornering Mercedes in a rather aggressive way, blowing smoke about his import, entrapping her with stale breath and bad clichés. Mercedes was looking for a way out when it presented itself in the form of an affable, rather nice-looking man who wore a lanyard instead of a tie.

His name was Oliver Burns, he said, introducing himself, and in one fluid motion got rid of the rube and moved Mercedes with him behind the velvet rope where the only thing blown was coke, or a lucky guy in a dark corner. Either way, no one complained. She liked the way he took charge, and though she didn't know who he was, she could tell that he was connected by the way people deferred to him. He was on the make, she was certain, but who wasn't?

"What exactly do you do?" she asked, studying him as he ordered two Tequila Sunrises and explained that he was the man who did all the staffing for the Sylvan Light Agency.

"That's a big job," she said, feeding his ego. "There must be a lot of people who want to work there."

"Hundreds," he told her, "but I can size someone up in thirty seconds to know if they're Light material." He looked Mercedes up and down. "Take you, for example," he said, studying her. "Born into money, private schools, the whole nine. Am I right?"

She smiled, giving nothing away.

"You're not married," he said, "but you are fun. And discreet."

She raised her eyebrows. "Is that what you're looking for in an employee?" she asked.

"Absolutely," he told her, seeing if she took the bait.

But she didn't, and that only made him want her more.

"Call me if you're ever interested in something secretarial," he said, making it clear that that was the job for which he believed she'd be qualified. He handed Mercedes his card.

"Olliwood?" she read aloud.

"It's where dreams are made, kid," he said, pointing out that his home number and service were on the back.

Later that night on her lovely terrace overlooking the Wilshire corridor, she studied Burns's business card, thankful she would never have to run to Olliwood to make her dreams come true.

SALAMI 'N' CHEESE

BEANIE

The sandwiches were beside the point.

—BARRY LICHT TO BEANIE ROSEN

1980

It was the place where the people who worked for the people gathered and talked and dreamed of the day when they, too, would be people.

"So, you're trying to get a job at Light to fuck him?" Barry Licht asked after hearing Beanie's story about Fish Zuko and her quest to get him an agent.

She hadn't really thought about Fish in a while. Like Darrin on *Bewitched,* they'd replaced Fish on *Happy Days.* They never said why, and no one other than Beanie seemed to notice that suddenly Potsie's troubled cousin Josh was another short, disgruntled wannabe. She pondered the question.

Without Beanie, Fish had gone belly-up.

"Maybe to show him," she said finally, biting into the pastrami sandwich they were sharing, careful not to get mustard on her high-collared shirtwaist.

They were at the Salami 'N' Cheese on Charleville, a little joint around the corner from the fancy agency in the fancy city where the people who worked for the people who ran it came to eat or smoke or gossip. Nestled between an overpriced boutique and a nail salon, Salami 'N' Cheese was a deli all the support staff went to for their requisite one-hour respite. Beanie, recognizing this was a whole new world, needed to learn the whole new world order.

Quickly.

"What do you want to show him?" Barry asked.

"That he missed the best there ever was," she said, eating the one pickle between them.

He liked her. She was funny. Ballsy. Outspoken. Driven. Everything he wasn't but hoped to be.

So, who was he?

Barry Licht, the great-nephew of Sylvan Light, Sr., was being fast-tracked through the training program.

Those around him knew he was connected, but no one knew quite how. And since Barry's grandfather had changed their name from Lichtenstein to Licht, as opposed to Light, the nepotism, while no less direct, was less apparent. Barry's father, William Licht, had tried his hand at the Sylvan Light Agency in the late '50s, only to hit brick walls, flop around for almost a year, and through an army buddy get a job in sports, which he considered a much more manly profession.

"The agency business is unreliable," he had warned his son, "full of fairies and fairy floss." He approved of neither. Rising to become the CMO of the NFL, he expected his son to follow suit, and Barry obliged, attending Northwestern and studying business. His only detour, if you could call it that, was his minor in cinema, which he kept under wraps along with his weekly outings to the midnight show of *Rocky Horror,* where he'd go, dressed in drag, with like-minded zealots. Privately, Barry rationalized his proclivities as simply having a flair for the dramatic. What's a little makeup and a boa say to the world except that you're hip, expressive, and idiosyncratic? After all, it was the 1970s, and punk and *Kiss* were the vibe. So, he lived this double life until his minor focus became his major obsession.

"I want to work at the Sylvan Light Agency," he told his father after graduating with an MBA. Barry had hoped to intern at Light during the summers when he was in college, but his father had always steered him away.

This time he couldn't.

"If I don't try, I'll always wonder," Barry said, trying to agent his way to at least an interview with the venerable agency. "If I don't become an agent in two years," he offered, "I'll come back to Chicago, and the NFL."

Bill Licht considered. *I'd have given him three,* he thought, more certain than ever that if this was a sample of Barry's negotiating prowess, he had nothing to worry about. The next day Bill put in a call to Harvey Khan, the agency president, and Barry was on a plane a week later.

"Wow, so you're related to the actual Sylvan Light," said Beanie, having digested the whole story and half the sandwich. She felt like she'd struck gold. Of all the mailroom guys she could have befriended, she'd found someone cute, Jewish, and *related* to the name on the door. "You've got an in," she told him.

"Everyone does," he replied, telling her that Harvey Khan, the agency president, was married to Adolph Zukor's daughter. "That's how he got started. Everyone knows someone," he continued.

"And now I know you," Beanie said with a smile.

He smiled back. He liked her, she could tell. And he was on his way, already out of the mailroom in less than four weeks, and in Dispatch, which was one step closer to securing a desk. But he despised Dispatch.

"In Dispatch," he explained, "you're essentially a messenger taking the company's piece-of-shit car, to deliver the agent's piece-of-shit script, or contract, or stool sample, all over Los Angeles, from Malibu, to Burbank, to Culver City, to La Cañada." And since he wasn't a native and didn't know the back roads, he had to drive everywhere with a Thomas Guide map. Grunt work, he called it. "But the worst part, by far, is that you're never in the office long enough to get to know the agents, or, more importantly, let them get to know you."

That, apparently, was the goal of the training program. You needed facetime with the agents, which was a conundrum, since messenger runs kept trainees out of the office. So, the trainees had to figure out a way, either before work, after work, on weekends, and/or holidays to make inroads, to make contact, to make connections. A trainee would do just about anything: read scripts, walk dogs, babysit children, mistresses, whatever it took to get an in, an edge, a leg up. A trainee just wanted to stay close.

Barry confided that he had found a way.

"How?" Beanie asked, instinctively understanding that, like herself, he was a strategist.

"I made friends with Ollie Burns, the head of Personnel," he told her, explaining that Burns, a quirky guy obsessed with Willie Nelson, had just lost a file clerk. So Barry quickly struck a deal that he would forfeit the morning Dispatch run and work instead in Central Files to help Ollie out. This was a temporary fix for Ollie until he could hire a full-time clerk, but it kept Barry in the office and close to Sydney Lonsdale, the agent he'd been targeting. Barry knew that Lonsdale's trainee was interviewing at Fox, and he was able to make inroads when no one else could. Naturally, it pissed off the other trainees who not only would be out of the office delivering packages all day, but also had to absorb Barry 's morning runs while he stayed close in Central Files.

"Is that allowed?" Beanie asked.

Barry shrugged. "You want to run the maze, you better study the rats."

She couldn't wait to study them.

"So, how does a secretary become an agent?" she asked.

"She doesn't," he told her, throwing away the wrapper and heading for the door.

"Never?" she asked, following him.

"Never," Barry said, adding that if Beanie told them that she wanted to be an agent, they'd throw her résumé in the garbage. This was confusing. How could she show them how good she was if they didn't want to see it?

"So, how do *I* do it?" she asked.

He looked at her, as if debating a truth he wasn't sure she could handle. "You really want to know?"

She nodded.

"You're not going to get this job."

They were on the corner of El Camino and Charleville, Sylvan Light's three-story stately brick building in their sights. She had fifteen minutes until her interview.

He could tell she was upset. "I'm not saying it to be mean," he told her, "I'm saying it to be honest. They don't want girls who look like . . . you."

Beanie wasn't bad looking, she knew it. Some would say she was pretty, with her long dirty-blond hair and brown eyes. She had great legs, too; you just couldn't see them in her midi-length gaucho skirt.

"What do I look like exactly?" she said, trying not to sound as offended as she felt.

"Their daughters," he told her. "Their sisters. Their first wives. Everything they're running from. Nice Jewish girls with smart mouths and thick ankles."

"My ankles aren't thick."

"You know what I mean. They want girls who like the catcalls, not the Shiva calls. Like her," he said, pointing to a woman in a short skirt and high heels with big curly brunette hair, and breasts that led the way across the street. "That's who they want answering their phones, serving their lunch, massaging their balls after their clients crush them."

Beanie nodded. "If their wives can't look like that," he told her, "then their sexitaries need to."

"Wait," she said. "What did you call them?"

"Sexitaries," he replied. "That's what everyone calls them. And any girl inside who isn't called a sexitary won't last," he said, watching as the tall woman in the short skirt and high heels walked into the building. She could even be interviewing for the same job Beanie was interviewing for. "But maybe a different position," he said, joking that hers would be on her back or her knees depending on the day.

Beanie was speechless.

"Don't look so glum," he told her. "She won't get it either. You know why?"

She shook her head.

"Too tall. Mike Barron likes spinners, you know, someone small, who—"

"Spins," she said. "I get it."

He shrugged. "But she *is* good-looking, so they'll keep her on file for someone else."

"Jesus," she said, exasperated, "it sounds like a fucking beauty contest!"

"It is a fucking beauty contest," he told her. Then immediately felt bad. It was a lot to take in. "Hey," he said, trying to look at the bright side, "you don't want to work for Mike Barron. He plows through sexitaries every few months."

"And this is allowed?" she asked, shaking her head.

"Technically, no," he told her, confidentially. "The agents get warnings, a slap on the wrist, but behind closed doors people like Barron remind the alter cockers what it was like when they could get laid three times a day by three different women."

When she made a face, he said, "You want the truth, Beanie Rosen? Here it is. They not only like it when he's bad: they dine out on it. Get it now?"

Sadly, she did. Mike Barron would never hire her. She shouldn't even bother interviewing.

"What about the other opening?" Beanie asked. "The receptionist said they were interviewing for two positions?"

Barry nodded. "Billy Zepnik, a TV agent, with a wife and four kids, specifically asked for a leggy blonde."

"Wow," Beanie said, facing a wave that was tidal. "It's like they're picking off a menu."

"They are," he said, matter-of-factly, "and if they hear that you're a college graduate, man, they run the other way."

"They don't like smarts?" she asked.

"Not in their women," he said. "They equate it with ambition. When a girl gets a job as a sexitary," he told her, "at least at the Light Agency, she has to say that's all she wants to do. She has to assure them that she's not looking for a promotion, or a husband, or even a raise. They want to hire you, admire you, and if they're unhappy—"

"Fire you," she said before he could.

"There's enough ambition and backstabbing in this building as it is, the agents don't need secretaries vying for their jobs. And by the way," he added, "same goes for the trainees. They'd be fucking furious, after working their way through the mailroom and Dispatch, if a sexitary got promoted to an agent. I would be," he told her truthfully. "A trainee is required to have a college degree; a secretary is encouraged not to. How's that for a double standard?"

"Fucked up," she said. "It's the eighties, for God's sake," she said, pointing out that the Equal Rights Amendment had nearly passed, and these guys were still living in the 1960s.

"They liked the sixties," Barry told her. "They miss the sixties."

It was a lot. Even for a strategist. How do you get into the mousetrap when you're not the cheese they like?

"Go somewhere else," he said. "Get promoted there. Make a name for yourself. Then come back if you want. Lots of places have women agents, we have women agents, but they had to leave to come back." He said it all with a finality that was hard to ignore. "You need a plan B," he told her.

But she didn't want one.

They were at the entrance to Sylvan Light. Barry had to go on messenger runs to the valley in an unair-conditioned car, and she had to go to a job interview upstairs that she'd never get. He gave her his number.

"Let's stay in touch," he said, walking toward the parking garage.

Beanie nodded, quickly working the tumblers in her head.

"There has to be a way!" she shouted to him as he walked down the street.

"There's no straight line," he shouted back.

Lucky for Beanie Rosen, life had already prepared her for curveballs.

THE CURVE BALL

BEANIE

The pessimist complains about the wind.
The optimist expects it to change.
The realist adjusts the sails.
—WILLIAM ARTHUR WARD

1980

"Are you humming 'On the Road Again'?" Ollie Burns asked Beanie Rosen, who sat in his outer office waiting to be interviewed.

She nodded, smiling as he invited her inside.

"One of my favorites," Burns said, escorting her inside.

Oliver Burns, head of Personnel, was an odd sort: friendly, officious, with an oversized desk that made him look small. There was a signed Willie Nelson picture on the wall just behind him, and a Willie Nelson bobblehead on his desk. He could have been in his late thirties or forties, hard to tell with his thinning hair and paunch Buddha belly, partially hidden by a white button-down, but instead of a tie he wore a lanyard, fastened by a large piece of turquoise at the neck.

She looked at the bobblehead on Ollie's desk. "I *love* Willie Nelson," Beanie told him, adding that she didn't know much about his music but would surely love to.

Beanie's father had taught her to always get the client talking about something they love. "And then hang on every word like it's gospel," he'd said, "like it's air, like it's the missing piece to a puzzle you've been working your whole life. And if you can," he'd suggested, "take notes, like you're memorializing every morsel."

And that is exactly what she did. For fifteen minutes she sat enthralled as Ollie Burns waxed poetic about all things Willie Nelson, which songs he loved the most, the least, which he recommended she listen to first, and which, while still worthwhile, were less important. "Hawkeye was right," Burns said, impressed. "You *are* special."

"Who?" asked Beanie.

"Debbie Hawkins, the receptionist. We call her Hawkeye," he told her. "She doesn't miss a trick. And she didn't miss you for sure."

Beanie smiled, hopeful, until he finished the sentence. "But I'm sorry, I mean I'm really sorry to say the two openings we have just don't seem like a fit. Besides," he said, "you went to college, you're not going to want to be a secretary."

Barry had been correct. Her résumé had betrayed her, and she hadn't had the time to change it. So instead, she pivoted. "I don't really have ambition," she said, "beyond working at the Light office." If Beanie was a pitcher, that was her windup. "What I really love," she said, throwing a perfect curveball, "is organization." She paused for effect, and then added, "And filing. I love to file."

He looked up, but she pretended not to notice, lost in the euphoria of a Dewey Decimal fantasy.

"I organize everything in my stepfather's medical offices: papers, invoices, *files*," she said, hitting the word, then circling back. "I really love to file," she reiterated, just in case he'd missed it the first three times. "In case there's no secretarial position available, I'd be open to doing something else . . ."

His eyes lit up.

And just like that, Beanie Rosen swam through the wave of *no fucking way* and landed a job at the Sylvan Light Agency.

She could not have been happier.

Barry Licht, on the other hand, was furious. "Fucking furious," to quote him. He hadn't even left for his messenger run when she sought him out in the parking garage to tell him the good news. Only he didn't see it that way.

"I take *my* lunch hour and give you crib notes, advice, good advice, all the things you'd need to know, things most people never hear, and what do you do? You take the one good job I'd found, the one job that kept me close to Lonsdale. Now they're going to have me doing runs from eight in the morning 'til eight at night, and all the work I've put in is going to fucking mean nothing."

He was mad. Spitting mad.

And she was sorry, genuinely, but he had laid out the odds so clearly that she didn't have a choice.

"If there was any other way," she told him, "I'd have done it, but I couldn't accept no. It's just not who I am. Which is why," she continued, "I'll be a great agent."

"Not here," he said, getting in the car to go on another Dispatch run. "You'll never get out of Central Files."

"I want to be friends," she said, ignoring the rules of a game she was determined to rewrite.

"Fuck you," he said, backing the piece-of-shit car out of the piece-of-shit space.

But when he drove past her, she saw a half smile that didn't exactly let her off the hook, but at least gave her an opening which Beanie knew she could noodle. Eventually.

Barry wasn't as cute as Fish, but he was taller, smarter, and her only friend at Sylvan Light.

"You're going to have to forgive me someday!" she shouted to him as he headed to the valley, flipping her off.

THE FAMILY WAY

ELLA

Conceived in love without pause or consequence.
Stay wild, my wild, wild child.
—ELLA GADDY, TO HER UNBORN BABY

1978–1979

"Just to recap," Senator Gaddy said, settling into the easy chair in his study, as he tried to get his head around the enormity of both the situation and his daughter. "The father of your unborn child is married?"

"Yes," Ella answered, almost smugly—at least it seemed that way to Alice Lee, who insisted on being included in all discussions. Also present was Eve Lynn, standing stoically in the corner along with Knox and his Dupont heiress, though neither said a word.

"And this married man doesn't know you're *with child*?" Alice Lee asked.

"I don't want him to," Ella said, holding her ground.

"Ever?" Alice Lee demanded.

"Ever."

"Because?" asked Alice Lee, pushing the point.

"Because it's none of your fucking business," Ella said.

Everyone held their breath as the Senator, realizing that Alice Lee's presence only exacerbated an already unstable situation, encouraged her and Knox, along with his silent but wide-eyed heiress, to excuse themselves and let him handle things.

And with that the family get-together blew apart, with Eve Lynn fleeing to her room due to a sick headache, and Alice Lee and her brother both making plans to cut the visit short.

Still, Alice Lee couldn't leave the room without imparting a few choice words to her mother, loud enough for all to hear. "Well, the good news is at least she's not a lesbian."

"Who said I'm not?" Ella countered, and then to her brother's new girlfriend, added, "If we don't get a chance to say goodbye in the morning it was lovely to meet you, Miss Dupont."

Very few details were revealed over the course of the next few weeks. All anyone knew was that Ella had gotten pregnant in her gap year, sometime in April or May. She had considered an abortion but felt that this baby was the very best of her and the mystery father and *needed* to be born. She told her father that she still intended on going to law school in September of 1980, but first wanted to make sure that her child would be raised in the right kind of environment.

Needless to say, the Senator and Eve Lynn were relieved.

"I'm not a martyr," Ella said. "I don't think I can do it myself, and I don't want it to be raised by you guys," she said matter-of-factly, which they found both offensive and a relief. She planned a home birth, which Eve Lynn reluctantly agreed to, and wanted to interview prospective families so *she* could choose who would have the honor of raising this special being, who was conceived in love and destined for greatness.

"I'll have my attorney get involved," the Senator said, arranging a meeting just before Christmas during which Ella insisted on an open adoption, so everyone could know each other.

"That sounds difficult," Eve Lynn said later that night, after the Senator relayed Ella's desire for continued communication after her child was placed. "She needs to put this behind her," she said, brushing her long ash-blond hair a little harder than necessary. The Senator walked over to her, trying to calm her frayed nerves.

"Nothing's changed," he told her. "Ella is still going to Harvard next year." Eve Lynn looked at him as he reassured her that they would take care of this matter with expedience and discretion, and no one would be the wiser.

"Besides, the lawyer assured me that open adoption never comes to much."

Eve Lynn nodded, took a Valium, and went to bed.

By the new year, the unfortunate situation, as Eve Lynn referred to her daughter's condition, seemed headed for resolution. Ella had whittled her baby's choices down to two families: one from Chicago, the other from Denver. And Eve Lynn had even purchased a few items for the baby as both a going-away present and a peace offering to her daughter, which touched Ella deeply. Eve Lynn finally was able to sleep unaided at night, but that all changed one afternoon when she overheard a phone call Ella was having with her attorney that ensured a lifetime of insomnia.

"Since my child will be biracial," Ella was saying, "I need assurances from each family that they will raise him or her to celebrate and embrace both the Caucasian and African American cultures."

Eve Lynn didn't hear much after that; she just walked to the library, shut the door, and stood in front of the Senator, who was working at his desk.

"Our daughter," she said, pouring herself a large tumbler of Gaddy bourbon, "is pregnant with the child of a *married black man*?"

"I know," he said. "Essie told me."

"Essie?" asked Eve Lynn, confused, and then aghast. "You don't mean her son . . ." She whispered, as if the thought of Harlan impregnating her daughter was too frightening to say aloud.

The Senator shook his head. "Darnell," he said softly. "Essie's nephew."

Eve Lynn struggled to remember. It had been years since she'd seen Darnell. "You mean the one that went to Howard University?" she asked.

The Senator nodded.

"But he's . . . so much older, isn't he?" Eve Lynn asked, trying to do the math while getting her head around it all.

"Darnell is twenty-eight, married, two kids," said the Senator. "He's a doctor," he added, hoping that would somehow lessen the blow. It didn't.

Eve Lynn sat, dumbfounded, as Boo explained that Essie had long suspected a romance between Ella and Darnell, revealing that Essie knew about the pregnancy months before Ella had told her parents. She'd guessed the paternity and confronted Ella, and while Ella didn't confirm, she didn't deny.

"Essie doesn't think Darnell knows," the Senator told his wife, whose head was spinning. "He's a well-respected doctor and she didn't want to upset the balance of his life. They had only been together once and apparently Ella had been the aggressor," he said with a certainty that left no room for further questions.

But of course, Eve Lynn had a question. "And we know this because?"

"Because Ella told Essie," he said softly.

"Essie has known about this for months and never said a word," Eve Lynn said, with an icy finality that left no room for a future.

The Senator and Eve Lynn Knox Gaddy dismissed Essie and James the next day. James was seventy-two, Essie sixty-seven. They had met as children on the Gaddy farm. Their parents had worked for Boo's parents.

When Ella heard, she was bereft and inconsolable. Within days, she went into early labor and delivered a baby boy three weeks prematurely.

She held him once.

LET THERE BE LIGHT

BEANIE

Life is a banquet, and most poor suckers are starving to death.

—*AUNTIE MAME*

1980

On July 16, 1980, nineteen-year-old Beanie Rosen, who had graduated college a year early, began her career in a windowless storage room adjacent to Personnel, filled with metal file cabinets, and tucked away in the furthest corner of the third floor of the Sylvan Light Agency. The room was bare but for a Wells Fargo Bank calendar from 1978, and in the upper left-hand corner, an air-conditioning vent, where a wad of dust and dirt stubbornly hung, refusing to be dislodged by the wisps of air.

"Barely enough to breathe," Ollie had said, promising to get the vent cleaned.

But Beanie didn't mind or notice. She had a job at the Sylvan Light Agency.

Still living at home, Beanie quickly fell into a routine, rising at 7:00 A.M., getting dressed and ready to go by 7:45, taking the canyons over the hill, fighting rush hour in the Swinger, and usually arriving by about 8:30/8:45, parking in the employee lot just off Wilshire.

She'd walk in her clogs the three blocks to the agency, and once there, change into Jelly high heels and neon-red opaque stockings. She'd quickly learned to raise her skirt length, tease her hair, show décolletage, and wear lip gloss.

"They like the lips shiny. And red," Hawkeye told her on that first day.

And though Beanie, who was practically in another zip code, rarely saw anyone who could appreciate her shiny red lips, she glossed them anyway, just in case, and buried herself in the mind-boggling minutiae of filing paperwork.

And there was a lot.

The motto at Sylvan Light, literally written on the bottom of each piece of stationery, was: "Put It In Writing." Light had taken that philosophy from his days at William Morris. It was the law of the land. And each agent obeyed the law. Every request, idea, suggestion, had to be typed and memorialized, with a copy sent to Central Files.

There were no exceptions.

Every morning she was greeted by a seemingly endless supply of interoffice memorandums; everything from travel requests to termination papers, all recorded in triplicate by secretaries using carbon copy paper in their Selectric typewriters. Anything she could want to know about anyone, not only in the building but in the industry, was laid bare in front of Beanie like a beautiful banquet of spin, with flowery words and hidden agendas, inside jokes and outside braggadocio.

TO: Staff Worldwide
FROM: Norman Seamus
SUBJECT: Well, hello, Dolly!
I am happy to report that after a brief visit with ICM, Carol Channing has found her way back home to us at Sylvan Light.

And then there would be the memos applauding the memos.

Nice to have you back where you belong,

or

Dolly is coming home again to stay!

One memo could spawn a hundred and thirty replies, all of which would be filed under the subject matter, in this case, "*Re: Carol Channing.*"

Four times a day, mailroom boys would do their third-floor runs, depositing close to five hundred interoffice envelopes, many of which came through the New York pouch, each containing correspondence that needed to be opened, sorted, and filed. On any given day, there were between one thousand to fifteen hundred memos, contracts, letters, that in order to be filed, first needed to be sorted . . . and read.

Which meant, to anyone with a functioning brain, that the Central File tsunami looming in front of Beanie Rosen held riches beyond her wildest dreams. All she had to do was dive in and swim through the mind-fucking, ego-stroking politics necessary to not only survive the boys' club, but to thrive in spite of it. "Every wave is another opportunity to learn how to get the yes," her father had told her. "If it knocks you down, learn the lesson, so the next one won't."

And the lessons, like waves on a beach, kept coming, washing up daily treasure.

It was a bonanza of information that told her who was most vulnerable and who was most valuable.

"If you need to navigate a maze," Barry Licht had said, "study the rats who are running it." This position that she'd co-opted out of desperation wasn't the dead end Barry had forecast, but rather a gold mine he hadn't seen. "Your biggest opportunity," her father had advised, "may be right where you are."

And it was.

Every morning she was greeted by the inner workings, the petty gossip, the personal and confidential exchanges between all the men in power; what they said aloud, what they whispered privately. It was an instruction manual, a behind-the-scenes glimpse of grandstanding, posturing, and survival. Beanie pitied the ignorant, studied the shrewd, and learned the game from the bottom up.

She'd spend days analyzing the idiosyncrasies of each agent, the jealousies between them, the hierarchies, the egos, and the backstabbing.

TO: Mike Barron

FROM: David Levy

SUBJECT: Hasselhoff

I heard Cush is losing him. Couldn't happen to a nicer guy.

It was a baptism less by fire and more by words. Everything was memorialized and filed, even the inside jokes.

TO: Phil Carter

FROM: Len Greenberg

SUBJECT: Five Easy Pieces

Six if you count Mike Barron's new girl . . .

No matter your position within the agency or what you were writing, everyone copied Central Files. It was almost involuntary. So, if the president of Sylvan Light, Harvey Khan—"King Khan" to those trying to curry favor—wanted to have someone fired or promoted or transferred, he'd *Put It In Writing.*

And if it was personal and confidential, his girl would put it in a P&C envelope and circulate. That way, only the sender, his secretary, the recipient, his secretary, and the file clerk were privy. Which meant that young Beanie Rosen, now a member of that elite group, was, by proxy and position, given instant access to the inner workings of the most powerful agency in the entertainment industry. And that was how she found out, a month into her job, that Sydney Lonsdale, head of the literary department and the person with whom Barry was trying to curry favor, was being fired.

"You need help," she told Barry the next morning at the food truck.

He always bought a breakfast burrito before the morning run, and she had been waiting there to talk to him since he hadn't returned her calls.

This was P&C information, and she knew she'd get fired for repeating it, but she had to pay him back somehow, recalibrate the scales.

She pulled him into the side alley, wet from being hosed by some gardener or janitor perhaps, washing away the night's secrets. It was, after all, Beverly Hills, where everything was beautiful on the surface.

"Lonsdale's being fired," she said quickly, spitting out the bad news, as if the words themselves couldn't wait to land. "I read it in an interoffice memo between Harvey Khan and Nate Rosenthal." Nate Rosenthal was CFO at Sylvan Light. If someone was being fired, he had to be notified. "They think he's a dilettante," she said. "Overpaid, not a team player. They're going to promote Fundtleyder."

"Fuck," he said, grinding his cigarette onto the clean asphalt. He had bet on the wrong horse. "Fuck," he said again. Beanie could see the wheels turning in his head, trying to figure out his next move.

"Hold on," Beanie whispered urgently, "there's something else, something better. Way better. But it's a secret, I mean, really, really secret."

"Go on," he said, annoyed at himself for betraying his interest.

Then she spilled the beans, or as her father would say, "the Beanies," telling Barry that Phil Carter, head of the rock and roll department, now called "Personal Appearance," was going to be given a trainee.

"It's part of his renegotiation," she explained. "They aren't going to tell him until his contract is up, November first. His lawyer asked for him to have a trainee, and they're saying no right now. 'If we give it to Phil, then we'd have to give it to everyone else,' *blah blah blah.* But that's just a ploy," she told Barry. "They've agreed amongst themselves to give him the trainee. He just doesn't know it yet." She let it sink in.

"So, he'll fire his secretary?" Barry asked.

"No," explained Beanie. "He's going to get a secretary *and* a trainee!" This also was big news. Huge. No one above the first floor had a secretary *and* a trainee. "They'll give it to him instead of paying more money."

He took this in. "Wow," he said, leaning against the building.

"So," she continued, "if you act quickly, you know, volunteer to read for him, or walk his cat, or whatever he needs, he can think that it's, you know, genuine, that you're that good a guy. I mean, how could you possibly know what *he* doesn't even know yet?"

Barry cracked a smile.

"I couldn't."

"Right," she said, letting the monumental news land.

Barry looked at her.

Damn, she was good. Beanie had already learned not only who the players were but how they played. But could she have made it up? Was she leading him down some wrong, twisted road, just to mess with him further? Perhaps she was an officer of his father's army, a foot soldier strategically placed to lure him back to Chicago, the NFL, and his loosely called fiancée Marci Goldklank, with her two-bedroom condo plus den that her zayde, who wanted nothing more than to see his shayna punim happily settled, had bought her as a pre-wedding gift. The thought made him shiver.

"How did you find this out?" he asked.

"I told you, I read it in an interoffice memo," Beanie said.

"Bullshit," Barry said, emphasis on *shit.* He knew there were thousands and thousands of interoffice memos, and the idea that she would happen to read the one memo that was about the one person that he most wanted to work for was too much of a coincidence. He walked away.

Beanie, not comprehending, followed. "It's true," she said.

"Really?" he asked, turning on her. "Out of the millions of memos, you happen to read one about Lonsdale getting tossed? Gimme a break," he said, heading for the food truck.

"No," she shouted. "I read them all."

And that stopped him.

Most file clerks, including Barry in his brief stint, just read the subject matter, filed the memo, and moved on. No one could possibly read every single memo.

Except Beanie Rosen.

And as remarkable as it sounded, he realized that it had to be true. This ball of genius energy, not yet twenty, who had graduated UC Berkeley early with honors, read every fucking memo she came across.

"Holy fucking shit," he said, smiling.

She let out a relieved breath. "Good, right?"

"No," he said. "Great."

Phil Carter's client list included everyone from Cheap Trick to Guns N' Roses to David Bowie to Blondie. And Barry Licht had six weeks before anyone else in the training program would know that Phil Carter was getting a trainee to work his magic.

Initially he went to Phil's office, introducing himself, telling Phil how much he admired not only his amazing client roster, but Phil himself, having done a deep dive on his background. He casually offered assistance should he ever need any help, any time. "Anything," Barry stressed. Phil, impressed, thought the young man was authentic, insightful, and had good taste. After all, Barry liked Phil, and Phil liked Phil.

"Sure, kid," Phil said, appreciating both the attention and the deference. "I'll be at the Troubadour tonight with some friends covering the Eurythmics. Show up. But not dressed like that," he added, smiling.

That night, Barry, dressed casually in Sergio Valente jeans, a T-shirt, and brown suede Ferragamos, did everything from bussing the tables to making sure Phil and his ever-expanding guest list had everything they needed.

The next night he did the same thing at The Roxy for Linda Ronstadt, that weekend at the Hollywood Bowl for Guns N' Roses, then the Whiskey a Go Go for the Ramones, and at the end of October, the Forum for Pink Floyd. Barry had a natural talent for making friends fast, greasing palms, working doors, pulling strings to make sure wherever Phil went, it was smooth sailing.

By the time Sylvan Light officially announced that Phil Carter was getting a trainee, the position had been filled.

The other trainees never had a shot.

Barry Licht found his way to a desk, and Beanie her way to redemption.

MOTHER AND CHILD REUNION

MERCEDES

"I did have a mother," said the baby bird. "I know I did. I will have to find her."

—*ARE YOU MY MOTHER?*, P. D. EASTMAN

December 1980

Mercedes had been carefully curating an image befitting her new title, accumulating a wardrobe of understated elegance, dressing in Chanel and Dior with pops of Halston and Armani. She made herself over as a different kind of Lady Stapleton: sophisticated, but with a style and panache telegraphing a new age.

Her future looked bright when, quite by surprise, her past and her present collided.

It was December 1980, six months before she and Stapleton could come out of hiding and officially announce their engagement. Mercedes was in London, packing up odds and ends from the Mayfair flat. Soon enough she'd meet up with Stapleton in California after his skiing holiday with his boys in Gstaad. That's where he and Elaine intended to break the news of the divorce.

But first Mercedes and Stapleton were scheduled to attend—separately, of course—a retrospective of Antony Armstrong-Jones's photography at London's Savoy Hotel. Mercedes would be accompanied by Graham Leeder, a business associate of Stapleton's, and a closeted homosexual who was having an affair with a married member of Parliament.

As the evening wore on, Mercedes, tiring of Leeder's endless complaints about his lover, slipped into the ladies' room to gloss, powder, and take a breather. She stared at her reflection in the mirror, grateful that this would be the last such event she would attend under such subterfuge. Her dark brown hair was cut short, in a bowl like Dorothy Hamill's. It suited her, she thought. Daniel Galvin, who had cut Twiggy's hair a decade earlier, had suggested it. "It's pert and young, like you," he'd told her, saying that not many women could pull it off. But she had the body and the face for it. Mercedes's figure was taut and athletic, and though she was twenty-six she easily looked five years younger, she thought, admiring her white, beaded Halston gown with a slit up the side that was a bit more daring than the event called for.

But she didn't care. *This is a stuffy crowd*, she thought, surveying the other women who stood nearby, checking for cracks in the veneer of their lives. Mercedes, anxious to make her own friends a continent away, closed the clasp on her matching beaded clutch and turned to leave when suddenly a group of beautifully appointed women walked in, dressed in Givenchy and Dior, their taffeta gowns whooshing by as they enjoyed the altitude their lives afforded.

She felt the presence before she saw it in the mirror's reflection, an apparition in Carolina Herrera staring back at her. It had been thirteen years and five months since she'd last seen Lucille, and now there she was, poised, coiffed, powdered, perfect—yet something was different.

It's the hair, she realized: it was flat-ironed and a shade darker than she remembered. At forty, Lucille was still breathtakingly beautiful, but around the edges Mercedes could see the wear. Her polished skin was beginning to show cracks, and her makeup, like her waist, was a bit thicker. But not so you'd notice.

Lucille had carefully constructed and then curated a reputation befitting a woman of influence and had at the ready a jigsaw puzzle of lies, should she need them, as to her early years. But she didn't need them because her reputation was sterling, beyond reproach. At least until she saw Mercedes two feet in front of her, threatening by her mere existence to unravel that reputation.

Familiar strangers in beaded gowns, Mercedes, eyes full, was inexplicably overcome with emotion. She wanted to ask how the baby was—Gloria, that was her name. She'd seen a photograph in *Newsweek,* but that was years ago.

She has to be close to twelve now, Mercedes thought, and suddenly wanted to know all about her. *Were they at all alike?*

Mercedes searched Lucille's face for an opening, a gesture, a kindness; some indication that said, *All is forgiven.* It's all she needed, it's what she wanted. Then she'd run to her, she thought, she'd apologize for the pain she'd caused, all the stupid and senseless words. She'd wrap her arms around Lucille and feel safe again.

Emboldened, Mercedes took a step forward. "Lucille," she whispered, open arms, open heart, and Lucille recoiled with not only hatred, but with repulsion.

Lucille looked around to make sure no one noticed, then whispered, "What are you doing here, Millicent?"

"It's Mercedes now," she said stoically, gathering herself up to her full five foot four inches (with heels). "I'm a guest of the Earl of Sussex. He's my patron," she added, smiling. "You know about patrons, don't you, Lucille?"

Lucille's cheeks reddened slightly, then she collected herself, turning to leave.

But Mercedes, not ready to let her go, reached for her arm.

"Don't touch me," Lucille said, spitting out the words with a venom masking something else.

She's afraid, Mercedes thought. Realizing that Lucille didn't want a scene, she stood her ground, threatening to create one. "What is it, Lucille? You don't want people to know that you're related to someone who, what, dates a married man? Perhaps you should take solace in the fact that Lord Stapleton was born into his title, whereas Sir Rodney bought into his."

The fine lines around Lucille's mouth cut through her porcelain skin, much like Mercedes's words cut through the lie she had so carefully crafted.

"Keep your voice down," Lucille hissed, her eyes darting around the room, conscious now that others were close.

"Well," Mercedes continued, raising her voice just enough so the restroom attendant and all the stalls could hear, "I learned from the best." She took her beaded clutch, and when passing Lucille, lips to ear, whispered, "Mother dear . . ."

THE ROLODEX

BEANIE

Size matters.

—A THIRD-FLOOR SECRETARY WITH A FIRST-FLOOR ROLODEX

1981

One Saturday in the spring of 1981, Beanie Rosen and Barry Licht were in Phil's inner office redoing his massive five-thousand-card Rolodex. It was a double-ringer, packed with the home numbers of every rock and roll legend, their managers, their roadies, the concert venues, the hotel owners.

"There's no ink in it," Barry said proudly, turning the wheels, showing off. He worked daily to keep it up to date.

Phil was meticulous that way. He expected every card to be typed single space, and current in terms of—well, anything particular to the designated person. If, for example, Blondie liked Ho Hos in her dressing room, that would be noted on her Rolodex card.

While Beanie had seen a Rolodex before, she had never seen anything quite like this. It was a treasure trove, a slot machine where every time you turned the wheels you landed on another jackpot.

"It's crazy," she squealed, reading aloud the names and addresses of artists such as Bruce Springsteen, Billy Idol, Kenny Rogers, Dan Fogelberg, Belinda Carlisle, Lionel Richie, Mac Davis, Gordon Lightfoot, Mick Jagger, David Bowie, and thousands of others. And it wasn't just their names, it was their birthdays, their social security numbers, the names of their kids, or dogs, or, in Keith Richards's case, his armadillo, and any other peculiar likes or demands.

"The only thing in pencil were the wives," Barry said. *Spouses didn't last as long as the pets*, Beanie thought as she pulled out a blank Rolodex card and carefully typed her name, her cat's name, and her social security number. "For future use," she said, smiling up at Barry, who laughed out loud as she slipped it in place.

It was a huge undertaking, laborious and tedious, but in the end would make for speedy access to clients and client information, and that made Phil happy, which made Barry happy, which made Beanie happy.

Since Phil was on vacation, Barry had brought the secretarial Selectric typewriter into Phil's office so he and Beanie could take turns typing while stretching, bullshitting, and smoking.

Barry, who had smoked in college, had picked it up again going to clubs and gigs. With his mustache, his longer curly hair, and Jordache jeans, which he'd wear only on weekends, he looked cool, Beanie thought. *Like Jim Croce.*

Beanie stood up and walked around. She loved being *inside* an actual agent's office, and Phil's was a vision in black lacquer. Front and center was an oblong black lacquer desk with a privacy panel to discreetly protect anything going on underneath; two mid-century modern chairs framed in black lacquer were in front of the desk, one of which Barry sat in when working alongside Phil, listening in on calls, taking copious notes, or rolling his eyes along with his boss at something stupid someone had said on the call.

There was a toggle switch on the trainee phone to allow Barry to listen without being heard, and to give his boss prompts should he need them. There were two guest phones on side tables, so that anyone could pick up an extension, and a black lacquer credenza behind the desk displaying photographs of Phil with famous friends and clients, cementing, by association, his own fame. There was also a large caricature of a man spinning vinyl, with a note: *For Phil*, it said, *The man behind the music.*

"It's a Hirschfeld," Barry explained. "Hirschfeld only does caricatures of famous people like Minnelli, or Sinatra, so this," he said, referring to the small cartoon, "is . . . really priceless."

Beanie nodded, made a mental note. One day she'd have a Hirschfeld, too, which would say, perhaps, *Unstoppable.*

Below the caricature and opposite the desk was a large deep green velvet couch, flanked by two black-and-gold Billy Haines deco swivel chairs.

Barry loved those chairs. To him they represented a defiance against authority, a confidence that no one can deter you from your destiny. "Billy Haines," he explained to Beanie, "was a Hollywood actor who, being homosexual, refused Louis B. Mayer's edict that he marry. Instead, he kept his boyfriend and left acting, becoming a top decorator. His career, legacy, and relationship lasted longer than anyone in Hollywood. Including the man who tried to change him."

Beanie understood that Barry's father, like Mayer, was trying to control his life, putting pressure on him to leave something he loved, to marry someone he didn't.

"Is it okay if I lie down?" Beanie asked. They had been at the Rolodex for a good few hours.

"Sure," Barry said, putting a mixtape into the cassette player.

Robbie Dupree's "Steal Away" filled the room as she closed her eyes, letting her hands dance along the back of the sofa. That's when she found the earring. It was sitting alone, waiting to be rescued, perhaps reunited with its twin. She picked it up. Studied it. It was a dangling clip-on, dainty, with little diamonds surrounding the tear-drop jewel.

"Phil's?" she asked with a smirk while holding it up.

Barry squinted, looked, and smiled.

"You look like the cat who swallowed the canary," she said suspiciously.

"I'm working here," he said, trying to shift the focus.

"Or *maybe* the real question is, who swallowed Phil's canary?" she asked, playfully walking over, dangling the incriminating evidence in front of him. "I thought he was going out with Phyllis Mitchell?" she said, referring to the newscaster on channel seven. Phil and Phyl had been an item for at least a few months.

They were a "new two you" in Army Archerd's column a few months earlier. Army Archerd wrote for *Daily Variety,* and he always reported potential couplings as "new two you." And there had been pictures of them in George Christy's "The Great Life" on the back page of *The Hollywood Reporter,* where rich and famous people were photographed looking rich and famous.

"You think it belongs to Phyllis?" she asked, walking around to the edge of Phil's desk, setting the earring down, and blocking the Rolodex and Barry's access to the cards. He'd have to reach around her.

He knew it. She knew it. It was a game. She liked games.

While no longer overweight, Beanie was still curvy, and dressed to emphasize it. That day she was wearing a pink jumpsuit with a wide white belt and white leather mid-calf boots with her pants tucked in. She coordinated with big white enamel hoops and a white headband tied in a bow on top of her head, just like she'd seen Lisa Whelchel wear on *The Facts of Life.*

Beanie had grown confident, if not in her body, then in her skill of knowing how to present it. And that made her sexy.

"I need to get back to work," Barry said, reaching around her.

"Fuck work," she told him, pushing aside the double-ringer, upsetting the stack of alphabetized cards.

They were toying with each other, veering dangerously close to something forbidden. Until that point, they had avoided intimacy and any talk of sex. She knew he had a girlfriend back home, counting the seconds until he failed here.

"Come on," she said, leaning in.

"It's a secret," he told her, smiling.

"I won't tell," she whispered.

They were inches apart, his mustache framing the curve of his top lip. It was intimate, titillating, charged.

"Okay," he said. "Every Wednesday, Phil brings in girls—"

"What does that mean?" she asked.

"Actresses," he said, explaining that they were usually brunettes, sometimes redheads, never blondes.

"And?" she said softly.

"And he 'auditions' them," he told her, making quotation marks in the air.

Beanie frowned. "But he's in rock and roll. He doesn't handle actresses." She was trying to apply logic to entitlement.

"He likes to help out," Barry told her.

"Unless they're blond?" she countered.

He looked at her and smiled. "Yeah. Now, can we get back to work?"

"No," she said, moving closer, sitting on the desk. "And does said audition involve them taking off their earrings?"

"Sometimes," he said.

"Does it also involve them taking off more?" The breath escaping her lungs belied her casual tone.

"Sometimes," he said again.

"And they do it?" she asked. Her heartbeat quickened. Her face flushed. She was growing moist.

"Always," he said. "And it doesn't take much persuading."

"How would you know?" she asked, gaining control. "It's not like you're sitting there."

Then he dropped the bomb.

"Phil lets me listen in."

Beanie, rarely at a loss for words, was dumbstruck.

Her eyes darted around the desk, the office. *How?* she wondered. *Could the room be bugged, was there a hidden microphone?* And then she saw the intercom.

Barry saw her see it.

Her voice locked in her throat. "The intercom?" she hissed, barely audible.

He nodded. Even though it was disgusting on every level, an invasion of privacy, ethics, and decency, and even though there were shades of blackmail and coercion, the intimacy of the confession Barry had made, and the fact that they were alone in the office where it had all transpired, was wantonly tantalizing.

"So, Phil switches it on, and . . . you hear everything?" Heart pounding, she looked at Barry, challenging. He held her gaze. She was simultaneously disgusted and turned on. She hated that she wanted to hear more. But she did. Badly.

"But why would he offer to have you listen, and why would you want to?"

"It'd be rude to say no," he told her.

He was defending the indefensible, he knew it and she knew it, but she wasn't going to call him out. She wanted to understand what happened behind closed doors, what was expected, and to stand in judgment would defeat the purpose. She wanted to know more. To hear more. She was too far in to turn back.

"What does Phil say to them?" she asked, urging him on, her warm breath close enough now for him to feel.

"He'd listen to their 'audition'"—again, the air quotes—"and then stop them after a minute, tell them he'd rather just get to know them, that he could spot talent a mile away. Then he'd get them talking about their lives, their dreams, where they came from, and ask them to make him a drink. 'Get yourself one, too,' he'd say. Loosen them up, you know?"

She nodded, envisioning the scene that had played out in that very office the Wednesday prior.

"Then he calls Dan Bazuka, a casting director friend of his. Big guy, he does all the TV shows. Phil met Bazuka through Mike Barron. They all run together on weekends."

She nodded. *Mike Barron. Phil Carter. Dan Bazuka. They all run together. 'Nuff said,* she thought.

"He'll put Bazuka on speaker," Barry continued, "and Phil would say that he had a pretty talented little actress in front of him. And Dan would say, 'What does she look like, you know, is she tall, sexy, fun?' And Phil would say, 'Well, Dan, she's tall and sexy, but is she fun?' And then the girl will laugh or say something, to prove she's fun, and it would . . ."

"Loosen them up?" Beanie whispered.

Barry nodded.

They were all in on it. Mike Barron who liked spinners, Phil Carter who liked brunettes, and Dan Bazuka, who liked them all. They passed around favors and girls and sometimes new memberships. Barry was being indoctrinated by Phil. Perhaps someday he, too, would be a member.

He watched her watch him. Was she judging?

Beanie smiled, trying to indicate that she was fine, enjoying it. One of the guys. Or one of the girls who gets the guys who get the girls.

"I mean it's legit, in a way," he told her, explaining that Bazuka always agreed to see the actresses for open roles, reassuring Beanie, or perhaps himself, that there was actual business being conducted. "Some of them even get hired," he said, as if their ass justified the means.

She wondered if they had to do repeat "auditions," all the way up the food chain, trading their bodies for a few minutes of screentime.

"Then what?" she asked, ready for the hard stuff.

He looked at her analytically. "Why do you want to hear all this? I mean, can't you sort of do the math?"

She shook her head, smiling. "No, I'm bad with numbers."

They were at a crucial point, not only in the story but in their relationship.

She leaned forward, lips to ear. "Please," she whispered, her hot breath urgent, sending shivers down Barry's spine.

He swallowed, not sure where this was going but quite sure he wasn't the one driving. "They'd have a drink," he told her quietly, not breaking her gaze. "Then he'd compliment them, you know, their legs, their eyes, their ass, and ask them to pull up their skirt a little . . ."

Beanie's face flushed with heat.

"Does anyone ever say no?" she asked.

He shook his head.

Quietly, she asked, "And then?"

"Depends," he said, staring at her sitting on the edge of the desk, her lips moist, parted. "Sometimes he asks for a massage. Other times he massages them, tells them how pretty they are, how sexy, how much he wants to help them, until . . ."

She held her breath in glorious agony, wanting and never wanting this to end.

"Until he asks them to strip for him," Barry told her, his voice sticking in his throat. "And masturbate."

She swallowed thickly, adjusting, wanting to herself at that moment.

"Then he tells them to walk over to him," he continued, "with their shoes on, he always wants them to keep them on, and they sit on his lap and . . ."

"And?" she said, leaning in.

"And fuck," he told her, as if the word completed the symphony.

They stared at each other. Inches apart.

"Any other questions?" he asked.

"Just one," she said, as her eyes went from his face to the bulge in his Jordache jeans, and then back. "Were you as hard listening to them fuck as you are now, telling me?" Point. Beanie.

Nothing had prepared Barry for this, and everything had prepared her.

She stood up close to him, parting his legs with hers. "Do they always fuck?" she asked, hitting the hard "k." "Or do they do other things?" she said, kneeling between his spread legs, her mouth inches from his crotch.

Barry swallowed, unable to speak, as she ran her mouth up and down his bulging zipper. His eyes were closed, his head tilted back. Beanie, on her knees in front of him, was driving. For Barry, this was uncharted territory.

For Beanie, it was her comfort zone. "Like this?" she whispered, moving her mouth up and down his crotch. Either because of Joel Schnitzer and Fish Zuko, or in spite of them, it not only turned Beanie on when she talked dirty, it made her feel in control and powerful.

"I bet they got on their knees in front of Phil and asked if they could suck his hard cock. Didn't they?" she said as she unzipped Barry's pants, stroking him.

It was only the third penis she had ever seen, the second she had actually handled, but it was huge—*magnificent,* she thought. It had a mind of its own as it stretched and yearned for her touch. She complied, grabbing the shaft, running her lips the length, over the head as she'd been taught, never taking her eyes off Barry's, deep-throating him.

It was the best head he'd ever had. In less than a minute he exploded in her mouth.

She swallowed a little, let the rest drip down her face, unzipping her jumpsuit, rubbing it onto her heavy breasts still harnessed in her bra, as Shalom had once instructed.

"It's primal," Shalom had counseled. "It says *You're mine.*"

And though Barry belonged to someone else, Beanie hoped that he understood she was willing to share.

AFTER BIRTH

ELLA

Not all those who wander are lost.

—J. R. R. TOLKIEN

1979

Ten days after her son was born, Ella left in the middle of the night and got on a bus heading west. She planned on staying with her old friend Tamasin Sullivan, whom she hadn't seen in over six years but had kept in touch with intermittently.

Tamasin had offered her a room in her apartment in Studio City, but at the last minute she'd rented it out after taking an offer to understudy Lucie Arnaz in a national tour of *They're Playing Our Song.*

Ella was mad. Not because she'd lost the apartment, but because the offer was beneath Tamasin. She had been a star at Yale Drama. She should have been a star anywhere. But give her a choice, and she'd usually make the wrong one. In 1975 Tamasin had passed up an opportunity to star in a new Broadway show and instead moved to the coast with a hot young actor from *The Deer Hunter.* The show that got away was *A Chorus Line* and the hot young deer hunter cooled. Tamasin, for her part, got some jobs in episodic television and finally landed that agent at Sylvan Light, but she was having trouble getting him on the phone. Her career, once so full of promise, petered out as real life interceded.

But like Ella, Tamasin took it all in stride.

On the bus westward bound, Ella was unsure of where she was headed, but quite sure of where she no longer wanted to be. She wouldn't go back to Kentucky for twenty years, and by then, she would be one of the most powerful women in Hollywood.

But first she had to meet Beanie Rosen.

THE FINK FILES

BEANIE

At some point we have to stand together.

—YESINIA RODRIGUEZ

1981

Barry had long ago suggested that once Beanie got into Central Files, she needed to devise a plan to get the hell out. "It was a dead end," he had warned, and though it provided a treasure chest of information, the "dead end" no longer justified the means. It was time for her to make a move. "But where?" Barry had asked.

"I'm working on it," she told him, smiling with a confidence he had to admire. He liked Beanie. He liked her gumption, her drive, and her ability to illuminate the darkest corner at the Light Agency. She was unlike anyone he'd ever met.

And for her part, Beanie felt similarly about Barry. He meant the world to her and was one step closer to being a real boyfriend—though he still had a fiancée, or the idea of one. Because of that she kept herself in check. The extracurricular activities were just some fun they'd have every Saturday, going to gigs, then ending up in his studio apartment in Westwood with a hot plate and a view of a cemetery. They'd get high, have sex, but mostly lie in bed and dream of a future where they would both conquer Hollywood. "We'll rock and roll this agency," she'd tell him, and he'd lie closer if only to catch the dream.

"I think I'm going to be Ollie's secretary," she said to him one night as they shared a post-coital joint. She felt particularly good that evening because he had completed the act. Most nights he didn't, claiming he was too high or too tired, which always left her feeling unsure. Sex with Barry was the only "real" sex she'd had, so it was important to her that he was satisfied. It made her feel validated and somehow whole.

"I thought he didn't want a secretary?" Barry asked.

"That's only because he doesn't know he wants one," she said with a mischievous grin, explaining that becoming his secretary was just a means to an end to becoming a floater. "Wait, so now you want to be a floater?" She nodded, hoisting herself onto her elbow as she explained that a floater was someone who could seamlessly fit in whenever a secretary was on vacation, allowing the agents as few disruptions as possible. Sylvan Light usually had three or four floaters on staff and the requirements were less stringent on appearance and more focused on skill and discretion. So, if she showed Ollie what a good secretary she could be, then when there was an opening in the floater pool, she would convince him to allow her to fill it.

Surely once an agent saw how good she was, how smart she was, how loyal she was, they would want—nay, *demand* that she be their permanent hire. "And then over time," she told him, "they can help me become a trainee, and one day, if I'm good, really good, which I will be," she added with confidence, "an agent." While some might have called this multi-tiered plan at worst a pipe dream, at best a long shot, Beanie had good aim. And besides, she was used to long shots.

And so, without invitation or decree, Beanie Rosen moved her Central Filing duties to an empty desk outside Personnel where she began answering Ollie Burns's phones, typing his correspondence, and even doing pre-interviews on secretaries when he was otherwise occupied. After about a week working the two jobs, Ollie, who didn't object to Beanie being there, realized she had totally reorganized his files.

"When did you do all this?" he asked, unsure if he should be grateful or annoyed.

"After hours," she told him, explaining that everything was sorted now by appearance, showing him the Polaroid pictures she'd attached to each résumé. She had divided everyone into categories and subcategories. "I mean, let's call it what it is," she told him, opening the file cabinet, and flipping through the folders. "We've got curvy, thin, long legs, big boobs," adding that there was a subdivision within each category of blonde, brunette, redhead, etc.

His face was a blank. She couldn't tell if he was pissed or impressed.

It was a gamble, she knew. The suggestion that secretarial hirings, especially for specific agents, were based on anything else was a farce. No one said that Matt Saperstein wanted a curvy redhead. Aloud. But until he found one, Ollie's job wasn't done.

"This way it's easier," she said. And without irony or judgment she went to the curvy section, then the subsection of redheads and—*voila!*—produced three possible candidates.

"Shall I set up appointments?" she asked.

There had never been a discussion of a raise or even overtime, she simply began doing her work and his: screening the applicants, the agent requests, the personnel complaints, the workman's comp filings, the unemployment paperwork. Finally, after two months, Ollie hired a full-time Central File clerk and Beanie became his full-time secretary.

And that was when she found out about the Fink files.

They were in a separate file cabinet containing information about Mike Barron, Stu Geller, and other bad boys who'd had numerous complaints lodged against them. But no one got more complaints than Randall Fink. A television packaging agent who had taken credit for inventing the miniseries, putting together such shows as *Rich Man, Poor Man, The Thorn Birds,* and *Roots,* Randy Fink held the record of thirty-three complaints lodged against him. In September of 1981, Beanie witnessed the thirty-fourth.

Yesinia Rodriguez, a secretary who had worked for Fink for eleven months, accused him and a manager, Charlie Folder, of attempted rape.

"Fink held me down," Yesinia said, "and he told Charlie to go first."

Yesinia had apparently escaped by kicking one party and throwing a Rolodex at the other, then running to the ladies' room where a secretary from Business Affairs advised that she go home and file a formal complaint.

Fink, for his part, was happy to be rid of her. He came into Personnel with an attitude that seemed to put all the blame on Burns. "Do me a favor," he instructed Ollie, "get me someone who's not crazy next time . . . like Greenberg's girl," he said, referring to another secretary who was much more accommodating. "This last one was a hysterical fucking mess." He claimed that Yesinia's work had fallen off and that she'd concocted much of the story because she knew he was looking to replace her.

But when Yesinia appeared in Personnel two days later to officially file a complaint, she was neither hysterical nor a mess, presenting a plan to move forward. She wanted to work for another agent, preferably a woman, she told Ollie, saying that she would float until the right position became available, as long as she didn't have to work for Fink again.

Ollie told her that, unfortunately, there were no openings in the floater pool, and more importantly that they take formal complaints quite seriously. "We need to investigate this," he said, adding that right now it was her word against theirs.

"And what are *they* saying?" she asked.

"That it was a joke," Ollie said, "albeit a bad joke that obviously had gone too far."

"A joke?" Yesinia repeated. "Fink held me down while Charlie Folder went up my skirt, tore off my panties, and put his fingers inside of me. So, tell me, please, really, tell me, what about that seems funny?"

"Nothing," Ollie said quietly.

Beanie could feel the blood rushing to her face. She was angry. For the girl. For the situation. For the inertia that was settling around them, like the aperture on a camera, slowly closing.

Why was there no action? Beanie wondered. This girl had been violated. A line had been crossed. Surely, there were lines, even there. *Hadn't a law been broken?*

"I promise you we'll get to the bottom of this," Ollie said. "In the meantime, we want to offer you this." He pushed an envelope her way.

She opened it and pulled out a check for $932—two months' pay.

"Hush money?" she asked.

"Severance pay," he corrected.

She looked at him, slack-jawed. "So, I'm gone?" she said. "From the agency? That's it. You squawk, you walk? You can't be serious?"

"Mr. Fink said your work had fallen off, and that you were so dismayed you . . ." He didn't bother to complete the thought.

Yesinia stared at him, daring him not to feel like the phony bastard he was—that they all were.

"It's probably better this way, Yesinia," he told her, passing her a paper and pen. "Sign the paper. Take the money. Get a job somewhere else."

"And what does the paper say?" she asked.

"It simply absolves you and the agency from any responsibility," he told her.

"What exactly am I responsible for in this scenario?" she asked rhetorically.

"Do yourself a favor, Yesinia," Ollie said gently, "put it behind you."

"Until what? Somebody else takes my place?" She looked at Beanie, sitting silently on the sidelines. "At some point," she said to her, "we have to stand up for ourselves and stand together."

Yesinia got up to leave, pushing the envelope and the unsigned agreement back toward Ollie. "Save it for the next girl he 'plays a joke' on."

And she left.

Ollie shook his head, looked at Beanie, and sighed. "These girls," he said sadly, "they act like they weren't part of the tango."

"Didn't sound like they were dancing," Beanie said.

But Ollie, who had walked back into his office, didn't hear. "Let me know when the new girl gets here," he said. "She's here at Fink's recommendation."

Beanie felt dirty, complicit. *Maybe we all are,* she thought. *Every man who allowed it, every woman who knew, who turned a blind eye, we're all part of a system that makes it possible.*

Thirty minutes later a leggy strawberry blonde walked into Personnel.

"Hi," she said, extending her hand. "I'm Ella Gaddy, and I have an appointment with Ollie Burns to interview for Randy Fink's secretarial position. And you are . . . ?"

That made Beanie smile. No one asked her name. But this confident, gawky, and unselfconsciously direct young woman had a friendliness and genuine curiosity, along with a slight Southern drawl, and legs that folded under her as she sat—like a crane or an accordion.

"I'm Beanie."

Ella nodded. "I figured it was somethin' cool. Short for Barbara?"

"Bernice."

"It's a fine nickname," Ella said. "My daddy used to call me *Egad* on account of our last name, Gaddy, and the fact that I was always in some kind of trouble. Kinda wish that had stuck, but my mother . . ." She drifted off, unfolding her long legs and walking over to a signed picture of Clint Eastwood that hung on the wall. "He a client here?"

Beanie nodded.

"You'd think Clint Eastwood wouldn't need an agent," she said, then turning to Beanie smiling, added, "but, thankfully, he doesn't think so."

They both laughed.

Ella Gaddy was charming, refreshing, and authentic. Beanie instantly liked her.

"Where's your résumé?" Beanie asked.

Ella shrugged. "I don't have one," she said, explaining that she'd just met Fink the day before on the set of *Hill Street Blues.* "A friend of mine got me a small part," she told Beanie, sitting back down. She wasn't an actress, she clarified, but thought it might be a hoot to try it out. "Turns out it wasn't," Ella said. "Just a lot of standing around."

Beanie looked at her, momentarily impressed.

"Who's your friend?" Beanie asked, once again aware that this was a business based on connections.

"Veronica Hamel," Ella told her, explaining that Veronica was friends with one of Ella's exes. Beanie nodded knowingly. Randy Fink represented Hamel. "He said I might like being a secretary," she told Beanie. "It might be fun."

Beanie looked at this gawky birdlike creature with her idiosyncratic beauty and wondered if she could tell her the truth. Beanie's job was to help Ollie fill the holes, not to warn incoming applicants to circumnavigate them. But something was different about Ella Gaddy. Or maybe it was Beanie who was different, changed by Yesinia, and all the other girls in the Fink files who'd come before her, replaced by complicity and ease.

"Send the new girl in," Ollie said over the intercom.

Ella unfolded her legs and stood. "Nice to meet ya," she said, extending her hand to shake.

"Tell Burns you want Accounting," Beanie told her, holding rather than shaking her hand.

"What?" Ella asked, looking from Beanie's hand to her face.

"We have a position we've been trying to fill in Accounting. Tell him you're great with numbers, that you've done accounting before. You thought about it, and you'd rather be in Accounting than be a secretary for Randall Fink."

Ollie buzzed again.

"I'm not particularly great with numbers," Ella told her, "and I haven't done accounting before."

"Lie," Beanie whispered, squeezing her hand for punctuation.

Ella could see the panic in Beanie's eyes.

"Why?" she asked.

"At some point," Beanie said, "we need to stand together."

And they did. For the rest of their lives.

THE SLIPPERY SLOPE

MERCEDES

You know the nearer your destination the more you're slip slidin' away.

—PAUL SIMON

1981

For New Year's Eve 1981, Mercedes had planned a beautifully catered dinner on the terrace of their newly decorated pied-à-terre. The twinkling lights from the Hollywood Hills would be the backdrop to their future. But Stapleton, who was scheduled to arrive on December 29, sent a telegram saying that he had to pop over to Geneva to deal with banking issues and would be there by the first.

Initially frustrated, she rationalized, what's a day when you're planning a life? This was their time, and if they had to begin it a few days into the new year, so be it.

But by the third of January when Stapleton still hadn't shown or sent word, Mercedes began to worry. What if something had happened? Now the conundrum was hers. Who to call?

She started with Graham Leeder, who certainly knew Stapleton and Elaine well enough to reach out. But Leeder was on holiday with his married lover. Then she tried a few of the Gingers to see if they'd heard anything, and even left a message with Santorini's answering service.

Finally, she thought she'd just call Elaine. They were adults, after all. But again, she had no way to reach her.

Graham finally called her back with the news on the fifth of January: Shay Stapleton, while skiing in Gstaad, had hit a tree, and broken his neck. He had been in a coma for six days on life support. On the seventh day, Elaine had him unplugged.

"He's gone," Graham told her.

She hung up the phone and stared at the twinkling lights, which now seemed to mock her. Halfway across the world, with only a flat in London and a paltry nest egg that hadn't been feathered in years, Mercedes Baxter, at twenty-six, felt quite alone.

She looked at the picture of Stapleton. Smiling. Hopeful.

Dead. Fuck. Dead.

This wasn't supposed to happen. Not before she was installed or inducted or whatever ceremony one needs to do to become a Lady.

"Make sure he puts the apartment in California in your name," the Ginger had told her. But he didn't. It hadn't seemed necessary. Perhaps Elaine would let her keep it. As a token.

She didn't cry.

It wasn't that she didn't want to—it was just, what's the point? Crying was for people who had the luxury of time. And she had run out.

Most people in this situation would panic, but not Mercedes. When her back was to the wall, she stood straighter.

She needed a new blueprint.

And she needed it quickly.

She walked over to the desk and found her little black Filofax and pulled out a business card, which read: OLIVER BURNS, THE SYLVAN LIGHT AGENCY.

WE NEED A THIRD . . .

Always trust your gut. It knows what your head hasn't yet figured out.

—SOMEONE WHO DIDN'T

1982

"We need a third," Ella told Beanie after looking at a one-bedroom-plus-den in Los Feliz.

Beanie didn't love the idea. While she and Ella had gotten close, finding a third roommate could be tricky. Other than Hawkeye and Barry, she didn't really know many people at the agency, and Ella primarily kept to the crowd in Accounting, who were quite a bit older—and to Sam Lesser's trainee, Garry Sampson.

Sam Lesser was the most powerful agent in Hollywood and worked in the corner office on the first floor. His trainees, always Waspy, and by proxy, powerful, usually kept their circles tight. But, for whatever reason, Garry Sampson had let Ella Gaddy in. They'd bonded shortly after she got hired.

"It's a Southern thing," Ella told Beanie, who guessed it was more than that. But Garry was too powerful, too discreet, and too private to be their third roommate, which meant they'd have to get a stranger.

"Try the new girl," Ollie Burns suggested one morning, referring to a new "executive floater" he'd hired. Mercedes Baxter, petite, pert, and English was, Beanie guessed, six or seven years older than she and Ella.

"I think she's sophisticated," Ella said.

But Beanie wasn't sure. There was something she couldn't put her finger on, something she didn't like about the new girl. She and Ella watched her from a distance as she waited in line at the food truck.

"She looks like Beverly Sassoon," Ella said, referring to Vidal Sassoon's beautiful brunette wife. Vidal and Beverly had a talk show, which Ella had watched religiously before getting her job at Light.

Beanie studied Mercedes. "Yeah, only not as pretty."

Five foot two, with hair cut short like a boy, Mercedes was dressed in an immaculate Perry Ellis blouse with a Peter Pan collar and tailored pants with matching pumps. Her jewelry, unlike the chunky black and silver rings, bangles, and earrings Beanie wore, or the turquoise rings Ella favored, was minimal and understated.

"I'm open to it, if you are," Ella said, heading back to Accounting.

Beanie, undecided, headed back to her desk as well. She wasn't against Mercedes, per se, but what did they know about her? Nothing. She had not gotten hired traditionally, which wasn't that unusual. Often, agents or executives ran into girls, usually models or actresses or wannabes, and traded desk jobs for blowjobs. Ollie called it an off-book hiring.

"It happens," he'd say, and then they'd figure out where to put them.

But with Mercedes it was Ollie who had hired off book. He'd waltzed in a month earlier and announced they had a new executive floater.

"A *what*?" Beanie had asked.

"Someone who floats exclusively for the executives."

They had never had the need for such a position, and now suddenly they had both the need and the girl. Maybe it was coincidental. Maybe not. But Beanie wanted to be a floater and this girl had potentially taken her job.

Curious about her backstory, Beanie went to retrieve her file. Only there wasn't one.

"I must have misplaced it," Ollie told her.

Another coincidence? Perhaps. But Beanie smelled a rat. With an English accent. And she wasn't ready to invite that rat into her home.

"I'm not sure," she told Ollie when he asked again.

"She's a good kid," he said, adding that she needed to get out of her situation. "She's been living with a patron," he told her, "and she can't any longer."

"What the fuck is a patron?" Beanie asked Barry that weekend.

"Don't know." Barry shrugged. "I guess someone who sponsors someone."

They were at her desk in Personnel going through "personal and confidential" memos from the week prior. Since Beanie had left Central Files, she'd trained the new girl who'd replaced her to leave all personal and confidential memos for her review. That way she was still able to monitor agency secrets.

"I think Ollie's fucking her."

"Who cares?" said Barry, reading yet another kiss-ass memo from Mike Barron to Sam Lesser.

"She basically invented her own position," Beanie said. Or Ollie had invented one for her.

Barry looked at her, shaking his head. How could Beanie not see the irony? He held up Beanie's new nameplate on her new desk for a new position that had not existed until Beanie invented it.

"Sounds familiar," he said.

Beanie reddened. He was right, of course. Mercedes and Beanie were similar in *that* way. Maybe that's what annoyed her. They'd both found holes in the system and filled them.

Or in Mercedes's case, Ollie filled it. She had fucked him, Beanie was sure, and then convinced him that the agency had a need that only *she* could fill. But maybe Barry was right: maybe Beanie was splitting hairs, and they were just two sides of the same coin, women trying to rewrite a rulebook for a place that didn't recognize them as players.

She decided to give Mercedes a try.

"If you lean out the window, you can see the MGM sign," Beanie said excitedly, making room for Ella and Mercedes to look. There it was, within spitting distance, with the roaring lion in the center, just down the block from the apartment Beanie had found in Culver City.

Beanie and Ella had agreed to ask Mercedes to be a third. A half a block from the fabled studio, the apartment—a two-bedroom, one-bathroom with an eat-in kitchen and a small balcony—was huge and empty, waiting to be filled with the details of three lives waiting to be lived.

"I love it," Beanie said.

"We should grab it," Ella seconded.

"Where exactly are we?" asked Mercedes, who didn't know Los Angeles, didn't drive, and would have to share a ride or rely on the bus to get to work.

"Beverly Hills adjacent," said Beanie, who had learned from her mother to fit truth into reality. "We can't afford anything closer." Ella agreed this was a steal, and while costly at $450 a month, it would be split three ways, making it affordable.

"We're going to have great times here," Beanie said, in an all-for-one kind of moment.

Ella agreed, hugging her. "I'm in!"

Mercedes, however, stood away from the two and just smiled.

She's cold, Beanie thought. *Icy.* And then, trying not to be so negative, waved her over. "C'mon, group hug, " she said, drawing her in.

They called the landlord and told him they wanted to put down a deposit. "Ella and I will share the bigger room, and then you can get your own room for an extra forty dollars a month," Beanie said to Mercedes, reconfirming the agreement they'd made earlier.

"Hmmm," said Mercedes, looking around, reconsidering. "I'm not sure that's fair."

Beanie and Ella stopped. *Uh-oh.*

"If I'm providing all the furniture, cookware, and dishes," Mercedes told them, "it's only right that I'm given some sort of dispensation."

Beanie and Ella looked at each other. *Holy shit,* Beanie thought, *she's negotiating.*

"Then I think it's only right that we see what we're getting," Beanie countered.

So that night, after work, they met Mercedes at her luxurious high-rise on Wilshire and Selby, which *was* Beverly Hills adjacent. There was a doorman, a concierge, and more orchids than either girl had ever seen. And that was just the lobby. They took an elevator up to the twenty-third floor and stepped into a private foyer.

"Jesus," said Ella. "It's the only apartment on the floor."

"What the hell?" said Beanie.

Mercedes, in stocking feet, but still head-to-toe Perry Ellis, invited them into a spectacular one-bedroom-plus-den apartment with southeast-facing views showing a panorama of Southern California, from the Hollywood Hills to Century City to LAX, and beyond.

"Damn," Ella said, "and we thought the MGM sign was something special. Would you look at this?"

The sun was setting and there was a bit of a glare, so Mercedes pressed a button and electronic silk drapes closed soundlessly.

"It's like something out of a movie," Ella said.

Mercedes offered them Perrier, then showed them around the chic, beautifully appointed apartment. It was a vision in pastels. Tasteful, feminine, perfect. There were two pink loveseats facing each other and lavender club chairs on either side, making a perfect square.

Beanie and Ella, who had taken off their shoes, let their feet curl on the white fur throw rugs placed over the carpet. "Are these coming, too?" Ella asked.

"Everything," Mercedes confirmed. In the dining room was a white marble dining table with a chrome base and four white chairs accented in turquoise with a turquoise vase on the center of the table filled with fresh calla lilies. "I love calla lilies, don't you?" Mercedes asked.

Beanie and Ella, speechless, just nodded.

There were chrome swivel bar stools at the white kitchen counter, and a black teakettle with a pop of turquoise on the spout, tying the whole room together. The den had a sleeper sofa and a large new color television with a Betamax.

"Jesus," said Beanie, "you can actually watch movies at home?" It was less a question and more a statement as she looked around in awe. But it was what lay beyond the Betamax that took their breath away. There were all sorts of futuristic gadgets like a portable microwave, and a new answering machine that came with a beeper so you could get your messages remotely.

"I read about these," whispered Ella, holding the cunning small beeper in her hands.

"I don't get it," Beanie said, asking Mercedes, "Why leave?"

"Because he needs it back," said Mercedes.

"Who?" asked Beanie, trying to sound more curious than bitchy.

"My patron," Mercedes told her. She opened up a piece of Louis Vuitton luggage and began to pack.

"What the hell is a patron?" asked Ella, sitting on Mercedes's perfectly made bed.

"A patron," she explained, "is like an uncle, except you're not related. Really he's just an old family friend who offered to let me stay until I could find a place of my own."

"But you're keeping everything?" Beanie confirmed. "Dishware, cookware, underwear, *everything*? Right?"

Mercedes nodded. "He's very generous," she said, her icy veneer giving away as little as possible. "So, now you see why I suggest we split the rent equally."

"Hell, I'd almost pay *you* to get the Betamax," Ella told her.

Two weeks later the three women moved in together, with furnishings and gadgets that were much more Beverly Hills than adjacent.

Beanie and Ella had found their third.

THE DANCE

The lion is most handsome while looking for food.

—RUMI

July 1982

"Do you think they're happy?" Beanie asked, as they watched an ABC special commemorating the one-year anniversary of the marriage of Princess Diana and Prince Charles.

Mercedes, sipping her tea in her striped pink pajamas that her "patron" had gifted her from the Beverly Hills Hotel, shrugged. "I think they chose well," she said, blowing on her tea. "There were rumors that Prince Charles had a torrid affair with Camilla Parker Bowles and might still be involved, " Mercedes said, off the cuff.

"Do you think Princess Di knows?" Ella asked.

Mercedes smiled smugly. "The wife always knows," she said.

Beanie wasn't sure, but Ella completely agreed. "Just like Grace Khan," she said. "Grace has to know about her husband."

"Who?" asked Mercedes.

"Harvey Khan's wife," Ella told her, explaining that Harvey Khan was the president of Sylvan Light, and he was having a torrid affair with his secretary.

Beanie shot Ella a look. Mercedes caught it.

"I won't say anything," Mercedes said, claiming that she knew few people to tell. But that wasn't good enough for Beanie. If Mercedes wanted to know more, then she had to share more.

Quid pro quo.

"Fine," Mercedes said. "Ask me anything you want."

"Okay," Beanie said. "Are you and Ollie Burns having an affair?"

"Yes," said Mercedes.

"Well, that was easy," said Ella, smiling.

"Your turn," Mercedes said, turning to Ella, who looked at Beanie, who gave a small nod.

"Okay," Ella said, folding her long legs under her. "Stilettos—that's Beanie's code name for Harvey Khan's secretary because she always wears the highest heels—has been having a hot affair with Khan for almost two years. And she's, well, head-over-stilettos in love with him. And he with her. At least we think he is. But she's like thirty-five, and he's like older, much older," Ella said, getting up to make some Sanka.

"How much older?" Mercedes asked, a bit too curious for Beanie's comfort.

"Sixty-seven," Ella said, explaining that she had access to everyone's real birthday through her job in Accounting. "Though he tells people he's sixty-three."

"Why doesn't he leave the wife?" Mercedes asked, presuming of course, that he wanted to.

Ella turned to Beanie, who considered the question and the questioner. Maybe she was being too harsh on Mercedes Baxter. After all, Mercedes was just trying to get the score like anyone else. And she had told them the truth about her affair with Ollie Burns. *Why not share the wealth?* she thought as she leaned forward, punctuating the confidentiality, and explained that Harvey Khan was a gambler, highly leveraged, and it was his wife's money.

Mercedes, both impressed and thoughtful, wondered aloud how Beanie could possibly know such details. Beanie just smiled, not revealing that she and Debbie Hawks, the veteran receptionist who had befriended her on day one, traded information daily, filling in the blanks for one another so that neither would ever be caught by surprise.

"I make it my business to study people," was all Beanie said.

Same, Mercedes thought, but remained silent.

"Get to the good stuff," Ella told her.

"Okay," Beanie said. "Stiletto's real name is Rose Liu. She was a secretary at Twentieth when Khan brought her over to Light in the late '70s. Ever since, she lived for the guy, totally devoted, and he for and *with* her, at least three days a week—"

Mercedes raised her eyebrows, enthralled.

"—on Bedford, just around the corner from the agency in a sweet little setup that he pays for. Meanwhile, he and his wife have a house in Bel Air, up Stone Canyon, and a spread out in Malibu, which is where she stays normally. So, three nights a week he tells her he's at the Stone Canyon house—"

"But really he's with the rose?" Mercedes asked, less a question and more a puzzle she was working.

"Yeah," said Beanie. "Until recently, when someone told Grace that they saw Harvey coming out of an apartment on Bedford with a gorgeous Asian woman every single Tuesday. Now Grace is no idiot, and to your point, she could only turn her back so many times. She knows her husband. She knows his secretary."

Mercedes nodded as Ella took over, adding that Grace couldn't pretend not to know what her friends suddenly knew. "So, now, Grace is on the warpath," Ella said, "stopping by Harvey's office unannounced, staying in Bel Air, sending in Cheryl, their daughter, for drop-ins. And apparently refusing to pay his latest debt unless he ends it with Stilettos."

"It's a standoff," said Beanie.

"It's a dance," Mercedes corrected her, with what Beanie thought was a summation born of experience. "Getting back to your original question, does the wife know? Of course the wife knows. And the husband knows that the wife knows. So, it's just a dance between suspicion and confirmation separating those who stay married and those who don't."

Beanie had the feeling that Mercedes understood the dance better than most.

"This isn't about fidelity, ladies," said Mercedes. "It's about power. And subtext. Grace Khan let this continue until she'd had enough. Perhaps she sensed his feelings for his secretary were getting too strong. Or perhaps she felt that his secretary was getting too comfortable. But when facts become public and truth can no longer be covered by subterfuge, then it's time to remind people who's in charge." With that, Mercedes stood, said goodnight, and went to bed.

"I think she's gonna be a great roommate," Ella said.

"Me too," Beanie told her, trying to believe it.

The next day Mercedes, who was floating for Stu Lonshien, the CEO of the agency visiting from New York, stopped by Khan's desk, introducing herself to Rose Liu, and dropping off a chopped salad from La Scala.

"I noticed you work every day through lunch," she said, "and I thought you might be hungry."

Rose smiled. It was a lovely gesture. "Thanks, what do I owe you?"

"It's fine," said Mercedes. "You can buy me lunch another day."

A few days later, Mercedes offered to run packages to the mailroom for Rose.

"I'm going there anyhow," she said. The next day she asked if she wanted the extra copy of *People* magazine that had been left for Stu. By the end of the week, the two were having drinks after work at Hernando's Hideaway, a bar up the street in the Beverly Wilshire Hotel.

Mercedes never broached the subject of Harvey Khan, she just got to know everything there was to know about Rose, her family, where she came from, which designers she liked—every single thing except who she was fucking. Mercedes shared bits of her own story as well, growing up in England, never knowing her father, and the fact that she was a very private person who selected friends carefully.

Rose, who felt similarly, liked her immediately. They were the same age, sophisticated, and well-traveled.

The next week Mercedes, who was floating on Cushman's desk, dropped off a bottle of Giorgio perfume. "A late birthday gift," she said, remembering that Rose's birthday had just passed. Rose, in turn, invited Mercedes to a screening that Mr. Khan had gifted her because he was out of town.

That weekend the two of them made a day of it shopping on Rodeo Drive, and having a late lunch at the Bistro Garden before they went to

Twentieth Century Fox to see a screening of a new movie, *Arthur.* After the film, they walked a bit down Pico Boulevard, talking about the likelihood of a shopgirl like Liza Minnelli marrying a rich man like Dudley Moore, and if fairy tales like that were even possible. And that's when Mercedes told Rose that her life was anything but a fairy tale, confessing that she'd had a brief affair with Ollie Burns and was trying desperately to end it.

Rose understood and told her that she would never judge, and then confessed her own love affair with Harvey Khan.

Mercedes was impressed, less with the confession and more with the accuracy of Beanie's details. Rose told her she loved Khan, but his wife was an alcoholic, in and out of rehab and relentless.

"He'd divorce her, but it's complicated," she said, explaining that Grace wanted Khan to fire her.

"No!" said Mercedes. "You can't leave. We'll figure something out."

A week later Mercedes had a plan and a solution. "Ollie is going in for back surgery," she told Rose, confidentially. "He was going to let his secretary, Beanie Rosen, run things, but she really isn't qualified," Mercedes said. "I mean, she'd kill me for saying that, since we're roommates, so you've got to keep it between us."

Of course Rose agreed and listened as Mercedes explained that Rose should fill in for Ollie, who'd be out for at least two months, and *she* would fill in for Rose on Khan's desk. That way, Harvey's wife would see that Rose was gone and take her foot off the gas. And Mercedes would be the eyes and ears to let Rose know when it was all clear. After all, Mercedes was an executive floater, so it made sense. There would be no suspicions.

Rose looked at Mercedes like she was an angel, a savior, more than a friend: a sister. "How are you going to get Ollie to hire me over your roommate?" Rose asked.

"Let me work on Ollie," Mercedes told her, knowing that it would take a few blowjobs, and perhaps an overnight to rework the plans.

It was the overnight she dreaded most. His West Hollywood apartment—crammed with knickknacks of country-western heroes—was a claustrophobic dust trap, an homage to his great-auntie Dale Evans, who'd been married to Roy Rogers. Mercedes hated everything about it, but there was a brass ring in sight, and to get that she'd suffer through his stories and the music and the small man with big dreams for the two of them.

Three weeks later, Rose Liu temporarily took over for Oliver Burns who was out on sick leave while Mercedes Baxter was asked to float on Harvey Khan's desk. No one blinked an eye except Beanie Rosen.

"I thought I was going to fill in for you?" Beanie asked Ollie when she visited him after surgery.

Ollie, on heavy pain meds, explained that this made more sense as he had decided he was going to hire Beanie full time as a floater.

Beanie, elated, finally saw her way out and up. She would float from desk to desk until someone powerful and smart and fearless recognized how good she was. Happy with this plan, she wished Ollie well and went back to work as a secretary, temporarily, for Rose Liu.

Meanwhile, on the first floor Mercedes kept a lookout for Grace Khan, dutifully letting Rose know when she or her children came by. Since her goal was to calm the storm, Mercedes was formal, polite, and deferential to Mrs. Khan, accommodating her, making sure she was comfortable. It was all about recalibrating the scales. Meanwhile, when Grace wasn't there, Mercedes would let Rose know and Rose would come downstairs and spend precious time with Harvey in the apartment they kept around the corner. And Mercedes would make sure they weren't interrupted.

It was a sweet setup, and the best part was, after a month, Grace no longer suspected a thing. Believing Harvey had moved on, Grace's visits became less frequent. They settled back into a routine of mutual understanding and separate lives. For his part, Khan was not only relieved but elated.

"It was," he said, "a genius idea." There was no longer drama nor guilt, and all debts were paid. And he was still able to see his Rose on the side. More and more he began to rely on Mercedes, appreciating her thoroughness, her professionalism, and her discretion.

And then one Sunday night in early November, just before Ollie was supposed to return from his sick leave, Harvey suggested that Mercedes come to Stone Canyon and help him prepare for a board of directors meeting the next day. She came to the grand Arts and Crafts stone house around three o'clock, served him dinner at seven, sat with him dutifully listening to Sinatra, and then took him upstairs and fucked him like he hadn't been fucked in quite a while.

"He likes oils," Rose had told her, so Mercedes rubbed them all over her body and then his.

Who knew? he thought, surprised and turned on that this prim English girl had such a wild erotic lust inside of her. Unlike curvy Rose, Mercedes was small, athletic, built more like a gymnast. He liked the newness of her, the fact that she was so proper on the outside and wanton on the inside. He had grown tired of Rose and her tears, and the associated drama. *This one, this Mercedes Baxter, is low maintenance, and smarter,* he thought. She'd befriended Grace, and Grace liked her. Trusted her. He trusted her too, he decided. And he preferred this new arrangement. He could still have his cake, and Mercedes would be his icing. And the best part was, Grace was happy, and the purse strings, once again, became unconditional.

In early November 1982, Ollie Burns, a loyal Sylvan Light employee for almost fifteen years who took pride in every company signing and every extraordinary deal, was fired without cause, as Rose Liu was promoted with a significant raise to become the new head of Personnel.

"We'll still see each other," Khan promised Rose. Though they began seeing each other less and less.

Mercedes Baxter was not only a cunning opportunist, but an expert strategist; someone who survived by sniffing out the holes, using them for leverage, and then filling them in afterward without leaving a trace. Much like Lucille, she had climbed her way out of the two-up two-down, becoming whoever she needed to become to reach the next level in the game of life.

It didn't matter that Rose had devoted her life to Harvey Khan, that Ollie had devoted his to Sylvan Light, or that Beanie had devoted hers to becoming an agent. They were casualties of a war Mercedes had waged against a world that had shorted her from the get-go. It was a game of musical chairs, beautifully conducted with all the players scrambling for different seats. And when the music stopped, Mercedes had found a new patron, Rose a new position, and Beanie a new boss.

Citing that she needed to be closer to work, just in case Harvey needed her, Mercedes Baxter moved out. She gave no notice but left the furniture, agreeing to sell it to the girls at a discount, if they paid monthly.

"Wow," said Ella, "we lost a roommate and gained a Betamax." And then it occurred to her, "I never got to ask if she was fucking the patron."

"She was fucking the patron," said Beanie, adding, "She fucked everyone. Including us, and I'm going to let her know that I know."

"I know what you did. We all do," Beanie whispered.

Mercedes, who was standing to the side of the food truck, turned to find Beanie standing a tad too close. Several inches shorter, and many pounds thinner, Mercedes moved away.

So Beanie inched closer. "Ollie Burns loved this agency," she hissed. "He gave his life to it, it's all he cared about, and you stepped on him and shredded him and left him with nothing. You used him," Beanie continued. "Like you used me and Ella, Rose, and, I'm guessing, that patron who you cleaned out from your soup to his nuts."

The man at the window handed Mercedes two hard-boiled eggs. She thanked him and walked away, never acknowledging Beanie Rosen or her blistering words.

"I'm onto you," Beanie shouted, as others, curious, turned. "We all are."

Mercedes never looked back.

In retrospect, Beanie wished that she had said something smarter, more pointed, but anger and frustration had tripped her up. She had wanted to imply that she might just tell Rose the truth, and then perhaps Rose would tell Khan, and Khan would see her for who she was. But she didn't. And she wouldn't. And she felt silly standing at the food truck having made a scene. But now all gloves were off. She had made an enemy, and though she wasn't threatened per se, she realized with a sad and sickening clarity that no obstacle at Sylvan Light would be more challenging to her future than Mercedes Baxter, who understood the dance from the first step to the last.

WIGGLE ROOM

When all else fails, wiggle, baby, wiggle.

—HUGH HEFNER

February 1983

"It's all my fault," Beanie told Barry a few weeks later when they happened to pass in the hall. She no longer saw him for playdates—or after playdates—since Marci Goldklank had moved out to Los Angeles and upgraded the studio in Westwood facing a cemetery to a one-bedroom in Marina del Rey with a view of the Pacific, and an eye toward a commitment.

"Ollie was going to make me a floater," she said, sadly, "and now I'm working for a woman who got played by a woman who played us all."

He wanted to hear more, to console her, to help, but now that Rose was in charge, Beanie was required to clock in and out each time she left her desk.

Suddenly there were regimens and rules and lunch hours that allowed no time for wiggle room, not even the kind the agents liked to joke about when they'd watch the girls rush back to their desks from Salami 'N' Cheese. "Hey hon, do you want my pickle?" they'd shout, and the girls, some flattered just to be noticed, others playing along not to be judged, would giggle and wiggle and rush back to their desks. "All in good fun," the agents would say, slapping an ass when they could, taking a rain check when they couldn't. There was always time for wiggle room when it came to agents, secretaries, and the boys-will-be-boys club. And whether you were the secretary they had staked their pickle on, or just a friend whose wiggle was more waddle, you learned to laugh because it was all a game, and the game didn't change. But the players did. Sometimes. And then you had to adjust to their rules.

Like when Rose wanted to hire her own "girl."

Rose told this to Beanie without apology, without emotion, and without waiting for a response, because, honestly, there was none. How could there be? A job Beanie had created would soon be filled by someone else. All the work she had done to forge a way in, to plot her way through, to become a floater and then finagle a desk that somehow would lead to agent was now moot, meaningless, someone else's dream to fill.

A hangnail from the archives, Beanie was swept up in Ollie Burns's backwash while Burns became an afterthought, a footnote, a pink slip with two weeks' severance and a handful of stories about famous people he once knew.

Sure, the agents noticed his absence. For five, maybe six minutes they stopped, made note, even protested. Mildly. But then life went on. The world reset, and Rose Liu became the girl who got the girls who got the coffee, with a wiggle.

Beanie Rosen was put on a ticking clock.

Lucky for her, she had a friend in a high place on a low floor who kept the clocks wound, serviced, and perpetually running.

THE HAWKEYE

Always be on the lookout for the presence of wonder.

—E. B. WHITE

1983

Hawkeye was all bull and no shit, less a greeter and more an enforcer, and she'd been the face and staple of the Sylvan Light Agency since 1977 when the NAACP began questioning the hiring practices within the entertainment industry.

Before then, Sylvan Light would strategically place their African American employees on the first floor as evidence of their inclusion, most especially when their clients of the African American persuasion were dropping by. Yvonne Ash, for example, who worked in Payroll, could always be counted on to bounce from third to second to first floors whenever Belafonte, Poitier, Flip Wilson, or Bill Cosby were paying a visit, ensuring that their agency, to whom they'd shell out 10 percent of their income, was inclusive, open-minded, and diverse. It was a blanket practice used by many in the industry until the NAACP peeked underneath and began publishing articles citing the business as being "so white." The Light board, concerned that their rotating support staff might be seen for the sham that it was, realized that the agency needed a facelift.

And that face could not be white.

Debbie Hawkins didn't apply for the job of reception. She was recruited, hired, and celebrated with a worldwide memo welcoming her to the family. Negotiating a fee more suitable to a junior agent than receptionist, an expense account, and a car allowance, she became a stalwart and trusted employee who had power and influence with first-floor decisionmakers. All who entered or exited were assessed and filed under her careful hawk eye. Her instincts were impeccable, and her integrity beyond reproach. She knew who was getting fired, who was getting hired, which clients were thinking of leaving, and was even brought in to help save a few. The agents feared her. The clients loved her. It was whispered that Steve McQueen gifted her a pearl necklace one Christmas, and Brando a Bengal tiger. She returned the necklace, but the tiger, it was rumored, was kept at a reserve in San Clemente that Brando subsidized, and she visited via helicopter with the great man himself. Hawkeye collected friends, enemies, and information, and if you crossed her, you could never get your way back. But if you were a friend, she was the one person you'd go to for help, or advice, or inside information.

Beanie Rosen was a friend.

"You need to get out of Personnel," she told Beanie at lunch.

Beanie had gone to Liu's, the Chinese restaurant around the corner, and brought them back dumplings and duck sauce. They ate together on the bench across the street while one of the mailroom drones covered reception. "You stink of Burns," said Hawkeye, expertly utilizing the chopsticks that Beanie found a waste of time.

Honest, smart, shrewd, and on the outside of a club that secretly resented them both, the two women found comfort and familiarity in their overlap. They'd formed a bond, if not a united front, but Beanie, unlike Hawkeye, was expendable—which was why she listened when Hawkeye told her she had a plan.

"You know who Jamie Garland is?" Hawkeye whispered, clocking the people going in and out of the building.

Beanie nodded. Of course she knew. Everyone knew. The biggest casting director in the industry, Jamie Garland was a legend. She had an eye, and everyone wanted her to cast it their way. If Jamie Garland believed in an actor, she'd find a way to make him a star. Brilliant, witty, devilishly flirtatious, and diminutive, there was no one bigger. Jamie, four foot nine, in heels, made up for in charm what she lacked in size, and her talent for discovering talent was legendary. Her ex-boss, David Mastro, an old-time casting director threatened by her eye, her wit, and her ambition, would often refer to her as "The Little No One" when directors like Peter Bogdanovich or William Friedkin requested that Jamie be assigned to their films. When Bogdanovich heard the reference, he was not only insulted, but offered to back Jamie in her own company which she pointedly named "The Little No Ones," so she would never forget from whence she came, and Mastro would never forget what he'd lost.

The Little No Ones would dominate the film and television industry for the next decade, and Jamie would be heralded as the new Carl Sagan by *Life* magazine; discovering more stars in the universe than the renowned astronomer.

"She's a legend," Beanie said to Hawkeye, giving her the last dumpling from Liu's.

"Okay," she said, pausing for dramatic effect. "Only a handful of people know what I'm about to tell you."

"I won't say a word," Beanie promised.

"Jamie Garland's coming over to Sylvan Light to run the talent department."

"WHAT?" Beanie said, her face like a Richter scale, registering the shock wave. This was huge. It wasn't just that Jamie Garland had relationships with all the biggest stars, it was that she had discovered a lot of them. If she could bring some of them over . . .

"This is big," Beanie said, listening as Hawkeye told her that they'd sealed the deal last Thursday after hours in Sam Lesser's office and he'd had her order in champagne.

"She's going to be head of the motion picture talent department," Hawkeye told Beanie.

It was a game changer on many levels. First of all, Mike Barron, the boyishly handsome and charming bad-boy agent who some called "a narcissist in search of a lake," had been lobbying to become head of the motion picture talent department despite the secretarial turnover on his desk and accompanying complaints. Barron had been a favorite of the boys on the first floor, and had it all locked up, or so he thought.

"Barron's going to be pissed," Beanie said.

"Doesn't matter," Hawkeye told her. "Garland's a bigger get. And Beanie," she said, leaning in. "She's going to need a secretary." She let that land a beat, then added that it should be someone who knows the ins and outs of the agency.

Beanie's mouth went dry. Holy shit. Maybe she could work for Jamie Garland. "How do I do it?" she asked. "How do I get her to hire me?"

Hawkeye, standing in her Balenciaga heels, which made her well over six foot, straightened her skirt. "Babe," she told her, "all I can do is lead you to water. You've got five days before anyone else drinks."

Beanie had a new wave, and its name was Jamie Garland.

OVER THE RAINBOW

Be fearless in your pursuit of what sets your soul on fire.

—JENNIFER LEE

May 1983

Jamie Garland liked to say that Judy took *her* name. Frances Gumm was performing on the vaudeville circuit when George Jessel asked Jamie's father, a stagehand, "Who's up next?" "The Gumm sisters," her father replied. "What kind of name is Gumm?" Jessel snarled to himself, and then, turning back to the stagehand, asked, "What's your name?" "Henry," her father said, "Henry Garland." It had been Jamie's brush with greatness, until she'd found her own.

Nicknamed "Gidget," for her tiny countenance and adorable face, Jamie Garland was not to be discounted. And Beanie certainly wasn't discounting her. This wasn't just a desk: it was a gift, a sign, providence dressed as a miniature ballsy ex-casting director who had been hired to become not only an agent, but the head of the motion picture talent department in search of a secretary to help her navigate. And that, Beanie believed, was her destiny; to work for a woman of influence who could influence the world to see Beanie not just for who she was, but for who she could be.

While Beanie was supposed to have kept it confidential, everyone needed an inner circle whom they could tell the things they weren't supposed to tell, and Ella was hers.

"Maybe if I make some kind of welcome packet," she said that night, thinking aloud. "Like nothing anyone has seen."

Ella nodded, focused, driven. "We'll do it together," she told her.

At first, Beanie neither expected nor anticipated Ella's assistance. But oddly, given her access to accounting information, and commissions paid, her roommate was able to provide insider information that few outside the board of directors even knew about. Ella quickly and easily projected the agency's top money earners for the rest of '83 going into '84, and also provided historical context for legacy clients, filmmakers, touring groups, and broadcast journalists, giving a simple and clear overview of who's who, who's where, and how much they're fucking worth to Sylvan Light. Clients like Dionne Warwick, for example, might actually mean more to the agency than red-hot Steve Guttenberg. Ella's report was succinct, enlightening, and one of a kind.

"It's a work of art," Ella told her proudly.

Beanie just had to figure out if Jamie was a collector.

That Monday, Army Archerd announced that the old guard was ushering in a new decade with the hiring of Jamie Garland to the Sylvan Light agency. Change, even for the good, can be unnerving. While the corridors of power at the other agencies and the studios shook with gossip and intrigue, the corridors at Sylvan Light shook with fear and uncomfortable silence. There was speculation as to which office she'd occupy, which clients she'd bring, which agents she'd fire.

But most of the internal gossip centered around Mike Barron, who kept his mouth shut and his door closed, signaling his displeasure. This was a position he had been promised. There were already rumors he was meeting with the head of ICM, a competing agency.

For Beanie, the news meant that she was now in a race with any other secretary smart enough to pay attention. She needed to implement her plan quickly.

"I have a welcome manual," she told Rose Liu, presenting her the booklet just after the news about Jamie Garland's hire went public.

Rose, sitting behind what once was Ollie's desk in what once was Ollie's office, stripped now of all things Willie Nelson and decorated in floral chintz with pictures of hummingbirds, took the booklet, thumbed through it, and then looked at Beanie who, holding her breath, braced herself for judgment, or criticism, or total rejection.

But to her surprise and relief, Rose smiled and looked at her anew. It was almost as if the Burns stink had finally lifted and Rose was able to see Beanie's brains, fortitude, and her willingness to help.

"*This* is remarkable," she said. "How in the world did you know to do it?"

Beanie, prepared for the question, explained that she did one for Ollie and had been keeping one current for Rose. "I could walk it over to Ms. Garland's office, as a gift from Personnel," Beanie offered, "if you can spare me?"

Rose, excited, not only jumped on the idea, but made it her own.

"Yes, yes," she agreed. "Let Ms. Garland know that this was something I prepared. Go now. I don't need you here." Instantly regretting her words, she apologized and told her she didn't mean it that way.

Beanie nodded, smiled, took the booklet, and headed out.

Of all the scenarios that had played out in her head, she never anticipated one where Rose would be nice, let alone grateful—in fact, Beanie had toyed with the idea of calling in sick and flying solo, seeking out Jamie on her own. But that was too risky and could result in instant termination, should Rose find out. It was much more cunning to bring Rose in, making it her idea.

The Little No Ones casting offices on North Beverly Drive had a small, nondescript reception area filled with actors, some of whom Beanie recognized. Up-and-comers, she'd call them, and they were all obviously waiting to audition. On edge, they stared at Beanie.

She stared back. *Someday I might be representing one of you,* she thought as she walked up to the receptionist and told her that she had papers from Sylvan Light that needed to be hand-delivered to Jamie Garland.

A few minutes later, Beanie was ushered into Jamie's elegant office, currently unoccupied. Beanie looked around. Everything was white, new, and modern: the couch, the desk, the walls, the upholstered expensive-looking chairs—all white. There were pops of red and orange in the pillows and artwork. A few Nagels hung on the wall, along with a cartoon of a crying woman with the caption, *Nuclear War, there goes my career,* signed by artist Roy Lichtenstein. *To Jamie,* it read. *Not even a war could stop you.*

But most overwhelming to Beanie were the avalanche of flower arrangements, also all white, that kept arriving every few minutes, from well-wishers who wanted to be counted as well-wishers lest they fall out of favor.

The industry was paying homage.

A few minutes later, Nancy Barlow, Jamie's attractive, long-standing secretary, walked in. Nancy was, Beanie guessed, twenty-six or twenty-seven. She was slim, pretty, blond, well-dressed in a fitted burgundy skirt just above her knees and a Perry Ellis blouse. Honey-brown shoulder-length hair was tied with a Burberry ribbon, pulling out the burgundy in her skirt and matching pumps. Her only jewelry was a Cartier watch. She was perfectly and elegantly appointed.

Beanie, in clogs and a red sweater, which she thought made her look thin and secretarial, felt self-conscious and dumpy next to Nancy. She chastised herself silently for believing that she could actually get to meet, much less work with someone like Jamie Garland. What was she thinking? That they would have lunch? Chat? Do each other's nails? Of course, Jamie would want a secretary that looked like Nancy, if not Nancy.

That thought sickened her as well. Nancy was probably a part of the package. *Well, it was fun for a minute,* Beanie thought, pulling out the manual and showing it to Nancy who, instead of dismissing Beanie, asked if she could stick around and go through it with her in a bit.

"We have one more role to cast in *The Big Chill,*" Nancy told her, explaining that Lawrence Kasdan, the director, was in the other room with Jamie, and she needed to take notes.

Beanie, who was happy to be out of Personnel, even if this was a bit of a fool's errand, followed Nancy to her office which, also white, was a smaller version of Jamie's, except instead of original artwork on the walls, there were eight-by-ten glossies with the cast so far, Beanie guessed, of *The Big Chill.* Glenn Close, Jeff Goldblum, Tom Berenger, Kevin Kline, and Mary Kay Place all hung in wait for the call to action.

"We just have to find the guy who dies," said Nancy, ordering Beanie a salad from La Scala and promising it wouldn't be long.

Forty-five minutes later Nancy, who was walking an actor down the hall, popped her head into the office, telling Beanie that they had cast the film, and she would be right back.

Beanie, recognizing the actor, extended her hand. "Beanie Rosen. Sylvan Light," she said to him, smiling, "Congratulations."

He smiled back. She melted.

Kevin Costner was one of the up-and-coming hot actors that Sylvan Light had targeted. If Beanie could sign him, she thought, maybe they'd promote her.

"They're lucky to have you," she told him, pouring on the charm, as he thanked her and headed out.

Nancy looked at her, cocking her head. "Do you want to be an agent?"

Beanie nodded. "Yeah, but I'm not even on a desk," she told her, explaining that she was stuck in Personnel.

"You should work for Jamie," Nancy said, casually, as if it was no big deal, as if she was asking if she wanted cream cheese with chives or plain?

Huh? Beanie thought. Feeling like she had entered an alternate universe, she replayed Nancy's words in slow motion. "Youuuuuu shouldddd work forrrrr Jaaaaamiiieee." She shook her head to clear it. "What about you?" she asked Nancy, once she had come back to earth.

Nancy explained that she was on track to be a casting director. "It's one thing for Jamie to change careers, but I don't want to," she told her, explaining that she'd be starting from zero if she moved with Jamie. She just couldn't get her head around doing that. "I'm actually looking for someone to replace me," she said, and then added, pointedly, "Someone like you."

It was like a cosmic game of musical chairs, only this time, for the first time, Beanie had a seat. But still, she held her breath, expecting it would be pulled out from under her.

Then she heard this: "Would you consider working for Jamie?"

Rarely speechless, Beanie Rosen stood slack-jawed. Finally, somehow, she was able to give a small nod.

"Great!" Nancy said, telling her to come back at the end of the day, and she'd introduce them.

But Beanie, not wanting to move a muscle, decided to stay, and called Rose explaining that Jamie's secretary was sooooo grateful to the Personnel department and specifically to Rose and asked that she stick around to review the welcome manual with her.

Rose, of course, agreed.

It wasn't a win-win, it was a win windfall.

Jamie Garland sat curled up on one of the white chairs in her white office next to a garden of white orchids. She was dressed in a pair of navy high-waisted Calvin Klein pants with very high strappy heels and a cute sailor top. She was tinier than Beanie had imagined, and younger. Maybe because of her size or her petite countenance, she seemed childlike. With blond hair, cut short like a boy's, and small gold hoop earrings, and several diamond tennis bracelets lazily wrapped around her gold Rolex, she reeked of style, class, and accomplishment.

Beanie, standing awkwardly in front of her, wanted nothing more than to bask in her approval. *Please God, let her like me,* she prayed.

"How long have you been at Light?" Jamie asked, giving her the once-over.

"Almost two years," Beanie said, trying to stop the quivering in her voice.

"So, why hasn't anyone else hired you?" she wondered aloud, lighting a Benson and Hedges menthol cigarette.

Beanie, smart enough to be honest, looked from Nancy to Jamie, and told her plainly. "My wiggle is more waddle."

Jamie laughed.

Beanie was in.

It. Was. That. Easy.

By the end of the week Jamie Garland had offered Beanie Rosen the job.

The plan was that Jamie, finishing her casting obligations on *Footloose* and *Sixteen Candles,* wouldn't officially start at the agency until January

1984. Beanie, expected to help her transition, spent most of her days updating Jamie's Rolodex, setting lunches, and overseeing the renovations to Jamie's new corner office on the second floor, next to Mike Barron's—rubbing salt into his already festering wound.

Barron had made his dissatisfaction known and was waiting until the year-end bonus to see how the board would handle it.

"What's Barron like?" Jamie asked a few weeks after Beanie had been officially hired.

Beanie, knowing that Barron was a monster, but also knowing that gossip reflects badly on those who spread it, gave a somewhat neutered response. "He's charming," she said, which wasn't a lie.

"Is he gay?" asked Jamie.

"No," said Beanie a little too quickly, and then realizing her answer needed further explanation, added, "He dates a lot. Mainly actresses."

Jamie nodded, considering. "He's attractive," she said, explaining that she'd seen him recently at Morton's, a favorite eatery on Robertson. "Kind of a cross between Warren Beatty and Dean Stockwell, don't you think?"

Beanie nodded, really thinking, *He's a guy's guy who wants to fuck women so he can dominate them.* But she kept her mouth shut until Jamie asked, "What aren't you saying?" Beanie took a deep breath.

"He's ambitious," she said, choosing her words carefully. "You should know that *he* wanted to be head of the Talent department." Had she said too much? Perhaps. Still, she reasoned that Jamie needed to know the score, and Beanie needed to spell it out to her in a way that communicated honesty and loyalty.

Jamie studied her for a minute. Beanie couldn't tell if she was grateful or angry, or worse, reconsidering the hire. Finally, thinking aloud, Jamie said, "Costner's looking for a new agent. Maybe you should let Barron know."

Beanie shook her head. "Maybe you should," she said, adding that Mike Barron wouldn't want to hear that news from Jamie Garland's secretary.

Jamie, surprised, studied her. *The kid's smart,* she thought.

"Okay," she said, stubbing out her cigarette. "Get him on the phone for me."

Beanie got Mike Barron on the phone and Jamie charmed him and flattered him, and though she was eight and a half years older, flirted shamelessly. Jamie let him know that she would call Costner and give him a nudge Mike's way. They kibitzed, they gossiped, they set up a lunch, and in that way, Jamie Garland signed Mike Barron, and Beanie Rosen signed Jamie Garland.

THE JACARANDA TREE

Where there's a will, there's a Rosen.
—HARRY ROSEN TO HIS DAUGHTER

August 1983

Beanie Rosen, answering to no one, divided her time between the casting offices on North Beverly where Jamie was closing out accounts, and the Light Agency two blocks away where Beanie was training a new secretary for her old job. At Rose Liu's insistence, Carol Lesak, the girl Rose had hired to replace Beanie, was told to learn how to do everything just as Beanie did. The irony was not lost on Beanie that Rose had been trying to replace her and now suddenly Beanie was someone of value, not just in Rose's eyes, but in the eyes of other employees who began to seek her out. Even if they didn't know her by name, she was now *Jamie's girl,* and that gave her a sense of purpose and import, a cog in the wheel of the Sylvan Light Agency.

As the conduit to all things Jamie Garland, Beanie had a temporary line installed in Personnel and had Carol Lesak answer when Beanie was running errands for Jamie, making Carol her de facto secretary.

"Beanie Rosen's line," Carol said one morning in September '83, then covering the receiver, asked, "Do you know a Moze Goff? He says he met you at Berkeley."

Beanie took the phone as the voice on the other line explained that they'd had classes together, and he'd heard that she was working there.

"This is she," Beanie said, sounding officious, "but I don't remember you. Are you not memorable?" she asked boldly.

Laughing, he said, "Apparently not." He explained that they shared an English class, but never actually were introduced. "You read a story called 'Love Less,'" he told her, "and I never forgot it."

Neither had Beanie. It had been a wry, barely veiled story about Fish. "Did you like it?" she asked.

"No, but I liked you. I liked your confidence and your heart, and I liked that you wore them both on your sleeve."

She twisted the phone cord around her finger and circumnavigated the backhanded compliment, demanding instead to know why he didn't like the story.

"Because your conclusion that love was a lie was wrong. The asshole who'd hurt you was the lie. Love is everything," he told her, and then said if she was ever free he'd love to meet up.

Beanie scheduled the appointment for the following week when she knew Rose would be off site. She chose a black power suit with shoulder pads and a pencil skirt that hit above the knee to show off her slender legs, adding a wide white belt to accentuate her waist.

She was nervous as Carol Lesak escorted Moze Goff, a tall glass of Brooklyn water, into the office where Beanie sat behind Rose's small desk.

Moze was cocky, dimpled, smart, self-effacing, and, as she'd presumed, sexy. A cross between Tony Danza and Paul Michael Glaser, whom she'd always loved from *Starsky & Hutch,* Moze was earnest, funny, and whip smart.

"How did we *not* meet?" she asked, regretful that she had been so caught up in her heartbreak with one Fish, she'd failed to notice the others in the sea.

But Moze explained he'd only been there for a year before he had to go back to Brooklyn and attend Brooklyn College because his father was ill. "But I got out here as soon as I could," he told her.

Presuming he wanted a job, she asked, "You're interested in working in the industry?"

"I'm interested in a lot of things," he said, smiling provocatively. It had been a minute since anyone had flirted with Beanie Rosen. Barry and she sometimes still got hot and bothered at lunch when she'd feel his cock and get them both worked up without release, but that was just Beanie keeping a toe—or in this case, a hand—in, as a reminder, primarily to Barry, of what could have been. She still resented the fuck out of Marci Goldklank, and whenever Barry invited Beanie to their Marina del Rey apartment with a crappy view of the dirty lagoon, she begged off with other plans.

Beanie and Moze spoke for an hour, about life, about jobs, about school, and then, afraid Rose might return, she offered to take him on a tour of the Beverly Hills Flats.

"Hold my calls," she said to Carol as she and Moze left the building and walked the pristine streets of Beverly Hills. Immune to traffic noises, they strolled the white sidewalks as automatic sprinklers clicked on and off regardless of weather or water shortages, and Mexican gardeners tamed any leaf that dared to grow its own course, their faded red trucks the only momentary intrusions of life outside the wide empty streets.

Moze hadn't seen the homes, the wealth, the scale, not up close. He marveled at the yawning oak trees kissing in the middle, offering shade and protection from harsh sun, and buried secrets.

"They're transplants," Beanie said, referring to the trees whose prehensile roots wrapped around the earth, defying anyone to challenge their right to claim it as their own. "Nothing you see is native," she told him. "Even the palm trees, they came from somewhere else." When she was little, she said, her teacher had told the class that the jacaranda tree outside their school, the one that dropped huge purple flowers every spring and left a line of sticky sap impossible to get off the car roofs, had been there for centuries, that they were native to Southern California, and people had no right to complain. "But that was a lie," Beanie said.

Her father had told her they were from Brazil or somewhere tropical in South America, and her teacher had just made it up. She'd asked her father why the teacher would lie, and her father said that maybe the teacher didn't want them to know the truth, which was that Los Angeles had all been a desert once. There were no fruit trees or exotic flowers, or deep green lawns all geometrically squared, just a vast wasteland with a bunch of cacti growing wild.

"Were you upset?" he asked, referring to the jacaranda tree.

"Hell no! I was excited," she said. "It meant if they could turn a desert into a paradise . . . so could I."

She smiled. He smiled.

"Where there's a will . . . there's a jacaranda tree," he said.

"Exactly," she responded, taking his arm, and adding pointedly that LA was a city of transplants. "Once you set down roots, a person can thrive here."

They spoke with an ease neither had felt before, as if they'd known each other a lifetime instead of a few hours.

Moze told her that he had no idea what he wanted to do, he just had a hunch it would be away from the shtetl, as he called the Jewish community that had both embraced and raised him his whole life. But without a plan, his father was nervous. "Children of Holocaust survivors carry a unique burden," Moze told her.

She nodded, not sure exactly what that burden was, but understanding there was a lot to unpack. His father, Moishe Goffenburg, a dentist, had lost his first wife and child in Auschwitz, and met his new wife, Moze's mother, at a relocation camp after the war. They made their way across Europe, doing odd jobs until they could afford passage to America, where Moze was born ten years later in 1957.

All their hopes lay with their son.

It was a lot for him to carry.

He told her that he was temporarily staying with friends of friends in Studio City.

"South of the Boulevard?" Beanie asked, little bits of Miriam creeping in as she explained the line between the Hills and the Hills Not.

"Hills not," he told her. "But lines are for people who keep score."

"Like my mother," she said bitterly.

"Don't judge her too harshly," he said pragmatically. "Just try not to be her."

Jesus, she liked this guy, and though they'd just met, she thought about offering him the spare room in her apartment.

It had been Ella's idea that she and Beanie continue to share a room while renting out the spare on a weekly basis to actors, actresses, directors, and anyone who came to town for a short stint. And if the landlord or any assignee were to show up, they'd say that so-and-so was a guest, a friend, a family member on holiday. Given their network of friends and associates—secretaries and assistants to people who knew people—they were quickly able to spread the word that a fully furnished room for rent, clean, safe, and close to the studios, was available, but only with references upon request. They put the condition less for security and more for exclusivity. Everyone wanted what few could have, and this little gem, a stone's throw from the MGM lot, became a must-get for anyone who could get.

As soon as they rejected a few people, and waitlisted others, it seemed to be the room everyone wanted. It was, after all, a sweet setup, with a white lacquer platform queen-size bed, a color TV, and a mini fridge stocked with soda, snacks, and cream for the Mr. Coffee that sat on top. Six weeks after Mercedes left, they had a rotating group of regulars, charging as much as five to six hundred dollars per week when the tenant was flush, allowing them months when they had no need to rent it out at all.

This was one of those months.

HOLY MOZE

I have been deceived.

—ELTON JOHN

September 1983

Ella wanted Beanie to win in every way. So when she learned about Moze—or the potential of Moze—she was all in.

"Do you like him?" Ella asked, and Beanie, shrugging, gave a small smile. Moze Goff was someone Beanie *could* like. Really like. There hadn't been anyone since Fish. Even Barry was a drive-by.

But Moze had sought *her* out. He'd thought about her for years, remembering her story, wanting her to know that love wasn't a lie.

"I'm going to call Garry and tell him I'm going to stay with him for the week," Ella told Beanie as she headed for the blue phone with a cord long enough to wrap around Beanie's trepidation.

"You don't have to do that," Beanie told her. "Moze can stay in the spare room, and we can stay in ours."

But Ella was already dialing. "I wanna give you guys some time to get to know each other," she said, winking, "and some space."

Beanie smiled. She loved watching Ella float through life, casually calling the most powerful trainee, not just at Light, but in the industry, and telling him, not asking, that she was coming over. Beanie guessed that Garry Sampson would be thrilled. She knew that Garry wanted more, but Ella didn't. Which no one, least of all Beanie, understood.

Garry Sampson, as Sam Lesser's trainee, had power by proximity, a guaranteed future as an agent, and people killing just to get *him* to return their calls, never mind Lesser.

But Ella had him so turned around that he'd drop whatever he was doing just to be with her.

"Thanks, El," Beanie said, as Ella, heading out the door, reminded, "Anyone would be lucky to get you, Bean."

Moze and Beanie ordered in Chinese from the Kung Pao Palace and had a carpet picnic on the fur rug in front of the fake fireplace where he informed her that he had been born Jacob Goffenburg, and he went by Jack until he was seven when his father Americanized their last name to Goff.

"That's when the teasing began," he said.

"Jack Goff," Beanie said, then covered her mouth.

"Funny, right?" he said, not laughing. So, he took his middle name, Moses.

She asked, "You're going to lead us all to the promised land?"

"I'd rather follow you," he said, smiling. And she melted.

She spoke about her parents' divorce and the new life her mother had made with Dr. Spitz, pushing him to first become a plastic surgeon and then to take a loan and move his offices from Sherman Oaks to Beverly Hills. "Poor guy," she said. "He thought all he needed to give her was a house south of the Boulevard."

He laughed. And she felt relieved.

They were lying on what once was Mercedes's pink couch, both wanting each other, but enjoying the divine complicity in not acknowledging it.

"You know what I think?" Beanie whispered. He shook his head, brushing the hair from her cheek. "I think you should get into the mailroom at Sylvan Light," she told him. "Even if you don't want to be an agent," she explained, "you could meet studio heads and producers and network executives. And that way," she said, pressing into his hard cock, "we can work together."

He smiled, enjoying the tease, then brought her back to reality by reminding her that he never actually graduated CCNY, and a college degree was necessary for a mailroom guy. "So, say you did," she told him nonchalantly. "I mean, they check, but not rigorously. Not like they used to."

He stood up, breaking the spell of the moment. "I don't lie," he told her, walking toward the kitchen.

Beanie, confused, followed him. "What if I do it?" she said.

He turned to look at her. What didn't she understand? "I don't want anyone to lie for me," he said.

"It's not a lie," she said, "it's a Zamboni."

He looked at her blankly as she tried to explain the difference. "You're what, a couple credits shy of graduation?" He nodded. "My mother changed our zip code for less."

He smiled, but still shook his head.

"Everyone Zambonies," she reasoned. "Actors do it on their résumés, executives do it on their tax returns, when you tell someone their baby's cute, and it really looks like a Potato Head. That's a Zamboni. It's not a lie," she said, "if it's almost the truth."

"Almost-truth isn't truth," he told her, sticking to his moronic moral guns.

Beanie stood her ground. "I'm sorry," she said, "but you're wrong. Almost-truth can be nudged to truth, polished. Like a Zamboni machine on the ice."

"You really believe that?" he asked.

She did, she told him. Completely.

"There is truth," she argued. "'Two plus two is four.' There is a lie. 'I did not kill your cat,' as the cat lay underneath the car you were driving. And there is the Zamboni. 'I graduated college.' You've got to see the difference," she pleaded.

He scratched his head and smiled just enough for her to worm her way in.

Get the yes. Get the yes.

"I mean, we're talking, what, six credits shy?"

"Four," he told her.

"And you're going to let that stop you from a job you might love? A job that can change the course of your life? Four. Measly. Credits. You know what I say?" He shook his head. "I say, that's worth a Zamboni." He laughed hard, and as he did, his whole body relaxed.

"You're impossible to resist," he told her.

"Then don't," she smiled, knowing she had won.

She wrapped Moze Goff around her vision, urging him to see a future by her design. He would sail through the trainee program, she decided, and she, as Jamie Garland's secretary and perhaps someday a trainee herself, would sail beside him.

"Please, please let me help," she begged, explaining that this would be absolutely no problem. She didn't wait for his answer, instead describing the process of working in the mailroom, then going to Dispatch, then hopefully getting a morning desk, then a real desk, and then becoming an agent.

"You're something," he said softly.

"You are," she whispered back.

He leaned over and finally gave her a long, deep French kiss that sent shivers down her spine, and left her wanting more.

The old Beanie would have mounted and dry humped him like a dog in heat, as Fish once jokingly said. But something inside gave her the foresight and wisdom to pull back.

"We have time," she whispered, taking control of their narrative, because it was one she hoped would last forever.

THE ZAMBONI

A Zamboni is a gentle urging of dull facts toward a shinier truth.

—BEANIE ROSEN

October 1983

Getting Moze into the trainee program wasn't quite as easy as Beanie had represented. While she still technically worked in Personnel, Personnel no longer handled the trainees. Mike Barron did. The board had given him purview over the trainees as a consolation prize for not getting the Jamie Garland job. Abusive and vindictive, he used his new position for his own gain, asking trainees to perform menial tasks while they tried to curry his favor. And he was the wave Beanie had to swim through to get Moze the position.

The first thing she did was falsify Moze's college degree. That was the easy part. She then needed to handwrite two letters of recommendation on good, bonded stationery, carefully changing her cursive for each, hoping that the personal touch would overshadow the fact that neither was typed on business letterhead. She chose names important enough to give Moze a pedigree, but not so top-heavy that they could be questioned. Short of nepotism, the tumblers did not easily fall into place at the Sylvan Light Agency, so Beanie needed to be smart *and* strategic.

Given that Moze was from New York, she decided to write a letter of recommendation from Bernard Warbler, an alumnus of Sylvan Light who was now a manager looking after most of the talent on *Saturday Night Live.* Knowing that Warbler had ruffled feathers when he pulled John Belushi from Light and delivered him to the Alliance Group, a red-hot agency full of Sylvan Light defectors, she assumed he wouldn't be someone Barron would readily call. She wrote that Moze had interned for a summer in Warbler's New York offices, and Bernard, impressed by his integrity and hustle, thought he would be a great fit for the Light boys. The second letter, she decided, would be from the theater world. Again, she chose a non-client, Joseph Papp, who, being a Russian immigrant from Brooklyn, she stated, was a longtime family friend. Again, she wrote of Moze's determination, loyalty, and diligence, all qualities the board, if not Barron, admired.

With Moze's application packet complete, she needed to figure out a way to slip it into the folder of preapproved trainees that sat on Mike Barron's desk. The applicants in that folder had already been vetted, interviewed, and listed in order of preference by the trainee committee before getting the final sign-off from Barron. Moze, who had neither the credentials, the references, nor the inclination to lie about any of them, would be taking a shortcut.

Just before lunch, when Barron was in the motion picture meeting, Beanie asked Hawkeye to call his secretary to reception, giving Beanie enough time to go into Barron's office and slip Moze's application packet into the folder with the other preapproved applicants. Believing that Barron would look at the list and question the placement of number one and number two, Beanie strategically retyped the list, putting Moze Goff third, after Howie Mishkin, referred by Rodney Dangerfield, and Joe Portola, Norman Lear's nephew.

Later that day she went back into Barron's office and, introducing herself as Jamie Garland's new "girl," told him that Jamie personally wanted to recommend Howie Mishkin, a trainee candidate that Jamie thought could be a winner.

Barron looked at Beanie and then opened the trainee folder, looked down at the list and saw that Howie Mishkin was the first name. He pulled out Mishkin's application and perused the letters of recommendation. He told Beanie he'd see what he could do but added that there were only two positions open, and there were a few other outstanding applicants that he was also considering.

Half an hour later, Barron's secretary came into Personnel to tell them to ready the paperwork for two new hires: Joe Portola and Moze Goff.

Howie Mishkin had been waitlisted.

"You are fucking amazing," Ella said at the food truck later that day, absolutely gobsmacked that in less than twenty-four hours Beanie had gotten Moze a job that would take most applicants months if not years.

Beanie shrugged, explaining that once she told Barron that Jamie Garland preferred the first choice, she knew that he'd choose numbers two and three. "It was his only way of exerting power," she said, making Ella swear not to say anything to anyone.

She didn't want Moze to know that this wasn't just a simple Zamboni about a college degree. This had been a full-frontal attack in which Beanie had gambled not just his future, but her own.

"Poor Howie Mishkin," Ella said, realizing his fate had been shuffled by Beanie's agenda.

"I know," Beanie told her, "but Barron will hire him. You'll see. He just wants to make Jamie sweat."

That night Beanie and Moze were watching *Valley Girl* on her Betamax. It was one of the few Mercedes perks that Beanie could appreciate. They were cuddled on the couch when Beanie leaned over to Moze and asked if he had a white dress shirt pressed and ready.

"Why?" he asked.

"You got the job," she said, smiling.

He reached for the remote and paused the movie. "Wait," he said, "what are you talking about?"

"You start tomorrow," she said triumphantly.

Moze was astonished. "Are you kidding?"

She grinned ear to ear, shaking her head. "Not kidding."

Moze stood up and began pacing. "How is this possible? I haven't met anyone or interviewed or anything."

Beanie shrugged and said, "We just got lucky, that's all."

"You dreamed this up last night, and suddenly, poof, I'm a trainee?"

Beanie shrugged again. "Sometimes dreams come true, and when they do, you shouldn't question them," she said, getting up and bringing over the wine that Rabbi Kirschenbaum, the new rabbi at the new temple Miriam and Dr. Spitz now attended, had gifted them. "When I want something, I figure out a way to get it," she told him.

"Me too," he said, grabbing the bottle, taking a swig, and then giving her some.

Droplets of wine dribbled down her chin, and he caught them with his finger, bringing them to her lips. *Oh my,* she thought. *Here we go . . .*

He opened her mouth and ran a line of red wine from her lips down her chin to her chest, unbuttoning her periwinkle blouse tucked into her form-fitting Guess jeans, which Ella had insisted she wear. "Men like junk in the trunk, and you've got some junk, girl," she'd told her.

Beanie reached over to turn off the light.

"Don't," he said. And then stroking her cheek, repeated, "Don't hide the thing that's most attractive about you."

She looked at him questioningly. "Your confidence," he told her. "From the first time I saw you, I thought, what must it be like to be with someone so sure of themselves?"

Fuck, she thought. All she wanted to do was hide her tummy and position herself in a way that at the very least elongated her torso, but Moze didn't want to see that. He wanted the girl that stood up in class and exclaimed that love was a lie and lust was a detour. He wanted someone who loved themselves warts and all, or in her case, with a fat ass and a pot belly. And so, inhibitions be damned, she took a swig from the bottle, and turned on the light.

He looked at her with lust and took the wine bottle, dragging it down her chest, unbuttoning her blouse and slipping it off her shoulders. She shivered as he began kissing her neck, expertly unclipping her front-clasped sheer black bra, and releasing her heavy breasts. "Beautiful," he said and then dragged the bottle around her areolas, following with his tongue as her nipples hardened to his touch. She moaned uninhibitedly as the bottle found its way down her tummy. He kneeled over her, pulling down her jeans, and though her belly jiggled, she didn't care. She embraced her curves and her shape and her wanton sexuality and arched her back as he took the bottle and ran it down one leg, and then the other, opening them wide, and then gently moving it over her crotch, massaging her through her drenched panties.

She had a new appreciation for the new rabbi and the new temple.

Finally, Moze set aside the bottle, replacing it with his mouth, nuzzling her most private area with his nose, his lips, his tongue, breathing hot air inside of her until she was ready to explode. No one had made love to her this way. She wanted him inside her, and pulled at him frantically, undoing his belt, taking his pants down, releasing his penis which stood at full attention. All at once she was kissing him, inhaling his sex. She ran her hot tongue up and down his shaft, expertly deep-throating him as she'd been taught by Fish, and then taking it in her hands she guided him inside of her, as he took over, moaning, plunging deep.

They had sex twice that night, and once the next morning, and then drove to work, where he reported to the Sylvan Light mailroom and started a whole new career, never knowing how rough the ice had been, or how intense the Zamboni.

SCALING HILLCREST

There is nothing more difficult to take in hand, more perilous
to conduct, or more uncertain in its success than to take
the lead in the introduction of a new order of things.

—MACHIAVELLI

November 1983

"Good morning," Mercedes Baxter said to Harvey Khan, rolling off him, post-sex, pre-coffee. She loved when he stayed overnight and they could start the day together, discussing clients, agency politics, industry trends.

Mercedes wanted to make sure Khan knew that in her he had a partner, perhaps someday a life partner. But she never pushed, nor questioned, nor complained. Unlike Rose, she stayed friendly with the wife and made herself an ally. She had seamlessly assumed the role of mistress, secretary, and confidante to both husband and wife, who equally sought her counsel.

She was careful never to criticize Grace to Harvey, choosing rather to support her position, her beauty, her style. And when Grace would call and complain that her husband was working too hard, too long, too thanklessly, Mercedes would sympathize, listen, but always reinforce how often he tried to get out of the office. Then she'd encourage Khan to spend time with her in Malibu on the weekends.

"What will you be doing when I'm there?"

She'd smile and change the subject, which kept him anxious enough to hurry back. She had learned well.

The Spanish duplex she'd purchased through an offshore account he'd set up was just around the corner from the agency, off Charleville. Completely renovated, it was a charming two-bedroom, two-bathroom with a small terrace tucked behind walls of red and purple bougainvillea. Rose never owned the pied-à-terre they'd shared for years, trusting instead that Khan would provide.

Mercedes had learned otherwise.

"Do me a favor, doll," Khan said, slapping her ass as he walked into the steamer shower, "call Jamie Garland's new girl, Beanie Rosen, and have her set lunch with Jamie."

Almost tripping on the white shag carpet, which, like Mercedes, had just been laid, she was flabbergasted that Harvey Khan, the president of Sylvan Light, would know Beanie's name, much less her new position. She resented his familiarity almost as much as she resented that Beanie was still there. She had spoken to Rose about her, and Rose had agreed to replace her. What the hell?

But Mercedes was flawless in her reaction. "Absolutely," she said, and then decided to shower with him.

"Hi, Mercedes, you called?" Beanie asked innocently, after dialing her up at the end of the day. Carol Lesak had told Beanie that Mercedes had called first thing that morning, but Beanie purposely waited until day's end to return the call, not because she had to, but because she didn't.

"Several hours ago," Mercedes said, pretending not to be as irritated as she was.

"How can I help you?" Beanie asked.

Mercedes, uppity, bristled at the implication that Beanie could do anything for *her*.

"By doing your job," she said tersely, adding that Mr. Khan wanted to schedule lunch with Ms. Garland.

"Oh right," Beanie said, as if it had slipped her mind. "He mentioned it last Sunday when we were at Hillcrest," she said, letting it slip that she, too, flew in circles above her station while omitting the fact that she had been there with her parents.

It was a dinner arranged to introduce Moze to her family. She had spoken of him several times, and they had suggested and then insisted on meeting Beanie's "fella" at Hillcrest, the exclusive Jewish country club on Pico in Beverly Hills. Hillcrest had been established in the early days of the motion picture industry when Jews were not permitted to join the existing and quietly "restricted" country clubs that barred them from membership. So moguls like Louis B. Mayer, the Warner brothers, Harry Cohn, and Adolph Zukor got together and formed their own. They'd come, usually a few nights a week, and have dinner with George Jessel, Eddie Cantor, Al Jolson, and then as years went by George Burns, Milton Berle, Joey Bishop, Sammy Davis, Jr., and sometimes Sinatra, who was an honorary Jew, and later became a member. Everyone who was anyone, at least in the Jewish community, knew that Hillcrest was the club to join. And so, Miriam Spitz, once again angling for a better zip code, had urged that her new husband abandon their old club, and pay the hefty dues to socialize with a "better crowd."

Once they'd joined, Beanie began bowing out from the requisite Sunday-evening dinners, fearing that she'd run into one of the Sylvan Light heavyweights there, not because they'd know her of course, but because they wouldn't. And that would irritate her mother. She didn't want Miriam or Dr. Spitz to know how unimportant she was in the bigger scheme of things. But Moze wanted to meet her family, so she finally and begrudgingly agreed.

Beanie watched her mother watch Moze as he approached the table. He shook hands with Dr. Spitz, made small talk with Miriam, smiled at Esther, and had a comfortability that put everyone at ease. He said something amusing that Beanie couldn't hear, but she could tell that Miriam, that everyone, was instantly charmed. She relaxed into the moment. Her parents seemed happy. And she realized that she was happy, too. "You look good, Bean," Dr. Spitz said, winking at her. Beanie felt good. She had started wearing short skirts and wedge sandals to show off her legs, and perhaps because she was happier than she'd been, well, ever, she was less bothered by Miriam's judgments.

Miriam scrutinized her daughter. "It's your skin," she said, studying her. "It looks healthy. What have you been doing?"

Swallowing, Beanie thought.

"Doesn't she look pretty, Esther?" Miriam asked.

"Um-hmm," Esther said, with the enthusiasm of a gnat.

"He's handsome," Miriam whispered, then added, "What do we know about his people?"

Beanie looked over to Moze and shouted, "Mother was just asking about your people, Moze." Miriam was aghast. But Moze, immediately disarming, put everyone at ease and told them about his mother, his father, growing up in Brooklyn and the ultra-religious life that he both embraced and rebelled against. He had so much integrity you couldn't not like him.

"You'll go far, son," Dr. Spitz said, causing Moze to change the focus to Beanie.

"How about Beanie? Quite a job she's gotten herself."

Miriam dabbed at the corners of her mouth. "Four years of college, two years already at that fakakta agency, and she's just now becoming a secretary," she bemoaned. "Why don't they make you an agent already?"

Beanie rolled her eyes to Moze as if to say, *I told you so . . .* and then, looking beyond him, caught sight of something that made her stop short. Harvey Khan had walked in with his wife, his son, his daughter, and a few family friends. While the fact that Mercedes Baxter wasn't with him did give Beanie some momentary relief, it was short-lived, as Dr. Spitz saw Khan as well.

"That's Harvey Khan, the head honcho at Light," he announced. Miriam craned her neck. "Go over and say hello," she urged.

"No," said Beanie, practically screaming, and then, softening, added, "He doesn't know me."

"How can he know you if you sit with your head in your soup? Lenny," Miriam said, turning to her husband, "call him over."

"I'll go!" Beanie said, immediately jumping up.

She was on autopilot as she walked past the giant potted trees in the pink room with the round tables to the one farthest in the back, where Harvey Khan sat holding court. "Oh, hello Mr. Khan," Beanie said, interrupting his story, "I'm Beanie Rosen." He looked at her, confused, trying to place the name or the face. "Jamie Garland's new girl," she added.

He nodded, smiled, and relaxed, introducing Beanie to his wife,

Grace, his son, Todd, his daughter, Cheryl, and their friends. They made some small talk, and before she left he suggested that she set up a lunch for him and Jamie. "It's long overdue," he told her.

From Miriam's point of view, Beanie was making headway. From Moze's point of view, she was fearless. And from Beanie's point of view, she had just navigated a wave and come out the other side victorious.

And now she was reaping the rewards of the encounter. "He was with Grace and the kids," Beanie told Mercedes pointedly, "celebrating Grace's birthday." Then she added, "Grace asked me to join them for cake. She's so kind."

Beanie heard a small intake of breath on the other end of the phone, and, feeling momentarily triumphant—*Point, Beanie*—began to suggest potential lunch dates for their respective bosses.

Beanie had hoped Khan's interest in Mercedes would wane and she'd be gone in a month or two. But Hawkeye gave her a reality check. "They're closer than ever," she said, adding that Mercedes was playing it brilliantly. It got to the point where Beanie didn't want to hear about her anymore. "She's in the rearview," she told Hawkeye.

But Mercedes, however, had Beanie in her sights.

THE MORNING GUY

Oh, what a beautiful morning . . . guy.

—GIL AMATI

November 1983

Beanie was feeling insulated and empowered, not only because she was going to be Jamie's girl, but also because she had a loyal group of fellow travelers who watched out and protected each other. She and Ella were a twosome who became a threesome with Moze, who became a foursome when Ella introduced Moze to Garry Sampson, and then they were five whenever Barry could free himself from Marci.

Though it was quite the Zamboni, Beanie had done a good thing in getting Moze into the agency. Everyone liked him. Instantly. And he was learning the ropes. Quickly. He had been in the mailroom for nearly four weeks when Gil Amati noticed that there was a young man reading books and scripts and newspaper articles and suggesting them for his clients. Amati, who next to Sam Lesser was one of the most powerful and certainly most colorful agents in the industry, favoring Versace and entertaining barefoot, was famous for working hard and playing harder, but never so hard as to ignore a call from one of his clients.

Amati had a wall-size photograph of superstar Richard Gere taken by legendary photographer Herb Ritts in front of his bed. It was the first thing he saw in the morning and the last at night. The rest of his clients, like stars in the galaxy, were scattered about his Hancock Park Regency home in Tiffany silver frames, always facing out so people could either stargaze or star worship. His clients were his children, and he nurtured and pampered them to superstardom. So when Moze began making smart suggestions for Gere, Amati began taking notice and liking what he saw, inviting Moze to work his famous Friday-night parties, where his "nephews," blond and hairless, would answer doors and serve drinks or themselves.

"Love to," Moze told him, appreciating and, Beanie feared, perhaps encouraging the overture. She had warned Moze that while it would be great to work for Amati, he needed to draw some lines so people wouldn't presume he was gay.

"Who cares?" he told her, reminding her that he didn't like labels. But Beanie, now referring to him as her boyfriend, did.

Two months into his tenure at Sylvan Light, Moze had landed Amati's morning desk, with an eye to becoming his full-time trainee, since Guy Hooper, the trainee on Amati's desk, had been officially informed that he would not be an agent at Sylvan Light.

But someone else would.

In November '83, Samuel Lesser casually notified Garry Sampson, as he was leaving for Palm Springs with Johnny Merritt, his longtime personal assistant, that Sampson was ready to be promoted. He made the remark in passing, neither expecting nor desiring any kind of demonstrative response.

Garry, familiar with Lesser's discomfort around intimacy, kept his feelings contained as Lesser informed him that he intended to share a few of his top clients, starting with Scott Westman.

No one in Hollywood was hotter than Scott Westman. He and Tom Cruise, both in their early twenties, were the two breakout stars on top of everyone's list in 1983, standing beside Ford, Stallone, and Travolta.

Lesser liked to compare Scott Westman to a young Paul Newman, saying that when he saw him in a revival of *Equus* in '79, he was not only mesmerized, but invigorated, wanting to know more about this young man. "It was like watching Brando in *Streetcar,*" he told Westman, who knew that Lesser had been Brando's attorney before becoming his legendary agent.

Sam Lesser, who preferred that talent seek him out, vigorously pursued Westman, flying back and forth to Baltimore where the revival was running until the young star agreed to sign with him.

"I just have to let my agent down easily," Westman told him, saying that he was a single practitioner who had signed Westman when he was starting out.

"Tell him I'll split the commission."

Westman, relieved, asked, "For a year?"

"For life," Lesser told him, shaking his hand and never looking back.

Over the next few years Sam Lesser guided Scott Westman from one film to another to become one of the biggest box office stars in the world, and while he knew Westman was not looking to leave, he also knew that he wasn't impervious to being poached. Sam Lesser was fifteen years older than his competition at the red-hot Alliance Group, many of whom he had trained and trusted, only to have them betray him when they'd left, poaching his clients, and circling the agency. Lesser began to worry that perhaps he was just too old, or too old-school. Either way, he knew he needed backup at Light from someone he could trust.

Garry Sampson had been on his desk for almost three years and Lesser knew that Garry and Westman had become friends, good friends, and confidantes. It was time to give Garry his wings, and allow Sam, a loyal soldier at Light, to fortify his army.

"Thank you, sir," Garry said as Sam left for the day.

"Find somebody good to replace you, or you'll be back working for me," Sam warned, and then left.

Garry waited until Sam was out of the building before calling the only person he wanted to share the news with, Ella Gaddy.

"Holy shit," she said later that evening, letting the enormity of it all settle. They were basking in the afterglow of the news as they finished a bowl of ramen noodles at an outdoor café just off Washington Boulevard.

"I want you to be my wingman," he told her, insisting again that she leave Accounting and work for him.

She shook her head. "I don't want to be your secretary," she told him, but he pressed her, explaining that she'd be less a secretary and more a touchstone.

"Whenever you read a script at my place, you have amazing instincts on how it can be better, or which actor should do it," he argued.

"I'll still have them in Accounting," she told him, realizing she liked the distance her job provided.

Garry was insistent, so they agreed to table the subject for the time being and celebrate the big news. "You're not just going to be some junior agent like Barry," she said, pointing out that Barry Licht, who had also finally been promoted, wasn't going to fly like Garry would. Barry was going to be a junior agent running errands for big rock groups. "You're going to be representing Scott Westman and Goldie and . . ."

"Warren," he told her, knowing that Lesser expected his help with Beatty. This news was huge, and Garry, excited, nervous, and a bit scared, was only worried about one thing: "I don't think the guy on my morning desk is good enough," he told her, knowing that if Ben Fleetwood, his morning guy, didn't make the grade, Sam would expect Garry to go back to being his assistant.

That was a problem, Ella agreed. Fleetwood, who was average at best, couldn't hold a candle to Garry, and by comparison might disappoint Sam enough to pull Garry back. They walked in silence around the periphery of the MGM lot.

"What about Moze?" asked Ella.

"He's got a morning desk," Garry told her, adding that it wouldn't work anyway because Moze was Jewish.

"Who isn't?" asked Ella.

"You," he said, "me, and whoever works for Sam next."

Ella didn't understand. "But isn't Sam Lesser Jewish?"

"Yeah," he told her, "but none of his trainees are."

Ella thought about that. "Just because none of his trainees are, doesn't mean they can't be," she said, asking if Lesser had ever specifically said no Jews. Garry shook his head. "Well, that's your problem there, boy," she told him. "Stop overthinking. Get him the best man for the job, and you'll never look back."

That was one of the many reasons Garry loved Ella. Her common sense cut through the bullshit. She was right. Moze Goff had more integrity, smarts, and gumption than anyone in the mailroom or Dispatch. He was the kind of guy you wanted on your team, the kind of guy you could trust to make smart decisions and keep confidences. With a great deal of relief and excitement he realized that, thanks to Ella, he had found his replacement. He just needed to make it right with Gil Amati, whose Versace feathers were easily ruffled.

That Monday, Garry called Amati and asked him if he wouldn't mind parting with his morning guy. Amati was taken aback, but Garry, full of praise, said that he and Sam—he always dropped Lesser's name when he wanted to emphasize a point—thought that if someone was good enough for Gil Amati, then maybe they had earned the stripes to work for Sam.

Amati was flattered but troubled. He needed someone to take over when his trainee left. Garry suggested Ben Fleetwood, who was experienced and ready to move up to full-time trainee.

"No one is better at training people than you, Gil," Garry said, "and both Sam and I will be indebted."

Ben Fleetwood was transferred to Amati's desk as Moze moved down a floor to work with Sam Lesser.

Garry Sampson, one step closer to agent, had found his morning guy.

THE CHEESE

High, ho, the derry-o
The cheese stands alone . . .
—"THE FARMER IN THE DELL"

December 1983

"1984 is going to be a great year," Ella told Beanie. More a declaration than a wish, they were sitting together quietly on a Sunday morning, in the living room of their apartment with the MGM lion hovering outside the window, like a reminder that they too would roar. It was three days before New Year's, and they both felt at peace. Beanie, eating a scooped-out bagel with low-fat cream cheese, looked over to Ella, who was working the *New York Times* crossword puzzle, and smiled. "What's up?" Ella asked. But Beanie didn't have words. She just felt happy, relieved, grateful. Moze, who had easily become her project if not her obsession, had landed the most coveted desk in the industry. And it never would have happened without Ella's help.

"You're like the sister I never had," Beanie told her.

"Ditto," Ella said, shuddering at the thought of the sister she did have, the one she hadn't spoken to or about in years. Ella Gaddy had wiped away her past and escaped to Hollywood. It wasn't the fact that it was glamorous or beautiful or twenty-five hundred miles away from home; it was the fact that in Hollywood you could be anyone you wanted. And Ella wanted to be someone who could start over, erase the Eve Lynns, the Alice Lees, and the rules about decorum and manners and having a child out of wedlock. The ole Kentucky homestead was part of a world that informed everything she didn't want, and to share it even with her best friend was to give it life. The only life from her past she cared about was now being raised by a family in Chicago that she'd handpicked and secretly wished had raised her. Ella wasn't dishonest about her past. She was oblique.

And Beanie was smart enough not to pry. None of it mattered, not really.

So, she kept her distance regarding Ella's past, and focused on their future. Together, they decided, they would be the team of the '80s, especially now that Ella had finally agreed to work for Garry as his secretary. Beanie couldn't believe she'd hesitated. This was a choice job, and Garry Sampson as a conduit to Sam Lesser would be working with the biggest stars in the world. Which meant Ella would be working with them.

Everyone was moving up—Garry, Barry, Moze, Ella—but no position among this upwardly mobile and ambitious group was more eagerly awaited than Beanie's, who would work for Jamie Garland, the new head of the motion picture talent department. She had found a woman to mentor her, to help her push through the waves of "no secretaries allowed" and maybe perhaps, one day, become an agent. Beanie was so excited, she even let Miriam buy her a purple Anne Klein tailored suit, which was sleek and slimming with removable shoulder pads, held on by two Velcro strips, so she could be either imposing or demure.

"It's very Linda Evans," Ella told her, surveying her friend as she finished off the outfit with a chunky gold chain necklace, matching gold medallion earrings, black Pappagallo pumps, and a new briefcase courtesy of Barry, Ella, Garry, and Moze. "Next stop: the world," they had told her as they celebrated the New Year together.

January 3, 1984, Beanie Rosen, a shoulder-padded vision in purple, walked straight to her new desk in front of Jamie's beautifully appointed new offices decorated in blue and white by none other than David Hicks. She was greeted by Nancy Barlow.

Beanie, confused at first, thinking perhaps Nancy had forgotten something, asked why she was there.

Nancy took a deep breath and opened the door to the office. "Why don't we go inside?" she said, guiding Beanie into Jamie's beautiful blue-and-yellow office, now stuffed with flowers, cards, and blinking lights on the multiple phones that Beanie had installed and silenced.

Though she had a sinking feeling she knew the answer, Beanie asked the question anyway. "What's going on?" she said, listening as Nancy guiltily admitted that she'd had a change of heart.

"I don't want to leave Jamie," she told her, explaining that she'd tried to deny her feelings, but the more she thought about it, the more it made sense that she give Sylvan Light a try.

"What about your casting job?" Beanie asked, referring to the extra's job on John Hughes's *Breakfast Club.*

"He's using someone local in Chicago," Nancy told her, explaining that she had called Jamie two days earlier to talk it over. "She wanted me to make sure you were okay with it," Nancy said. "So, are you okay?"

Beanie, mouth dry, just walked away.

"I'm sorry, Beanie," Nancy said as she left the office. "You made agenting seem so exciting, I wanted to see what it's like. Who knows?" she shouted to Beanie, halfway down the hall, "maybe we'll be agents together!"

For the first time in three years, Beanie had nowhere to go. She was out of ideas, out of gas, and out of time. She sat in Ella's secretarial chair while Ella, dumbfounded, threatened to scratch Nancy's eyes out.

"Let it be," Beanie told her sadly, explaining that it wasn't Nancy's fault. She'd had second thoughts; Beanie didn't blame her. You don't leave someone like Jamie Garland and expect the world to let you fly. Nancy needed protection just like Ella did, and Barry did, and Garry did, and even Mercedes Baxter. They had all worked the system one way or another to get ahead.

Except Beanie. She had failed.

"At some point in some game," Beanie told Ella, "the cheese stands alone." Beanie, the cheese, typed up a resignation letter.

"Maybe you can float for a while," Ella said, desperately searching for a solution.

But Beanie knew there was none. She had gone too far announcing her position with enough authority that the absence of it would leave her only one option.

Still in shock, she walked down to Personnel to officially resign when a beautiful redhead, complete with a short red skirt, legwarmers, and a headband, burst in ahead of her, weeping that Mike Barron had called her a slut for not doing the splits in front of him.

"I can't do this anymore," she told Carol Lesak, who tried to calm her down, as she'd been taught, especially when it came to one of Barron's sexitaries.

Beanie watched the familiar scene unfold, and then something clicked inside of her.

This wasn't just a random complaint. It was a unique opportunity disguised as an Olivia Newton-John workout video. On autopilot, she marched straight into Mike Barron's office.

Barron, who was at his desk, turned around. "Yes?" he said in a tone that was more annoyed than curious. "What do you want?"

"I want to be your secretary."

He laughed.

She didn't.

"You think I need a secretary?" he asked, amused and perhaps a bit impressed by her chutzpah.

"No, Mike Barron, I think you need me," she said, and then packed up the redhead's bags. "Now, let's get to work."

And just like that, Beanie Rosen was no longer the cheese.

THE ART OF WAR

My enemy's enemy is my friend.
—MERCEDES BAXTER, BY WAY OF SUN TZU

January 1984

Mercedes Baxter listened as the board deliberated via speakerphone on how to fairly compensate Mike Barron, who had already gotten quite a generous year-end bonus, but was still burned that Jamie Garland had been given the job and, more importantly, the title he'd been promised. Mike's father, Leo Barron, who like Joseph Kennedy ruled his son from a distance, had made it known that his boy was still not happy, and expected the board to do right by him. "Otherwise . . ." Leo warned, letting his words trail off with the veiled threat implied. Leo Barron, an old-time movie producer, had been a close friend of Harvey Khan's. They shared a past and rather dubious business associations that kept Leo out of the limelight but allowed his son to shine.

Harvey Khan had a gun to his head. He knew it. And Leo knew it.

This pissed Khan off even more. He couldn't afford to lose Mike Barron, despite the secretarial turnover and complaints against him. In less than ten years, the Alliance Group had not only caught up to Light but had surpassed them. Khan was cornered.

"We'll take this up next week," he told the board, disconnecting the speakerphone and leaning back in his chair, thoroughly frustrated.

Mercedes walked over to him and began massaging his shoulders. "Close your eyes, sweetie," she told him. "It's not worth the aggravation."

He knew she was right and tried to let it go. "I just hate that this kid and his fucking father have us over a barrel," he said, finally relaxing into her hands.

"I don't think they do, my love," she whispered, which brought him out of his reverie. Khan opened his eyes and looked up at her. "I've been thinking about this situation," she continued, still rubbing his shoulders. "I may have figured out a way for you to trump Mike Barron and his father."

Khan sat up, more amused than annoyed. "Oh, I see," he said, "so you've solved something on your own that the board cannot?"

"Yes," she told him stoically, "I think I have."

He shooed her away. "Stop the nonsense. You don't understand how it works." He picked up his reading glasses and reached for the mail.

Mercedes, offended, pulled the mail back. "How do you know what I do or I do not understand?" she asked.

He sighed; he wasn't in the mood for an argument. "It's complicated," he said gently, reaching his arms out for her to come to him.

"Don't patronize me," she told him, walking away.

Khan, who had been hoping for a quickie before lunch, was exasperated. "There are politics here I couldn't possibly explain," he told her.

She stared at him. Hard. It was a mistake to underestimate Mercedes Baxter. After all, she had been weaned on the art of leveraging private information for personal gain and had pieced together a good amount of information on the bad-boy agent. She had a deep understanding of who he was and, more importantly, what he was hiding. Mercedes Baxter had done her research.

Mike Barron, who started in the Sylvan Light mailroom in 1978, had, thanks to his father's associations with Harvey Khan, been able to quickly leverage his way into a choice position working for Bryan Forester, a red-hot television packaging agent.

"You keep your mouth shut and your ears open," Leo had told his son on his first day as Bryan's trainee. Since there was a toggle switch on the phone of any agent who had a trainee, the trainee could listen in on phone calls and learn the art of negotiation. A good trainee, knowing that he shouldn't listen when the door was closed, used discretion.

Mike Barron was neither good nor discreet. He was an opportunist sitting outside the office of a man many believed was being groomed for the future at Sylvan Light.

And then another future called.

His name was Steiglitz.

Forester listened.

So did Barron.

"Matt Stieglitz is courting my boss," Mike dutifully told his father, reporting that Bryan had agreed to meet on the condition that they also meet his East Coast partner Kevin Lewis. Though located on different coasts, the two agents, one from Baton Rouge, the other from Yonkers, had equal parts integrity and ambition. Sharing not only clients but philosophies, they agreed early on that if one left, the other would as well. "They're meeting at Shipp's house Friday afternoon," Mike told his father. David Shipp was the good cop to Matt Stieglitz's bad.

"Okay," Leo said. "Don't say a word. I'll take it from here."

At 9:15 Friday morning, Mike Barron stood in front of Harvey Khan, Sam Lesser, Stu Lonshien, and Gil Amati, telling them about the pending meeting with Steiglitz and Shipp, and adding, as his father had advised, that though he didn't personally hear it, he wouldn't be surprised if the two agents had already started calling clients.

It was like a knife to the gut as the senior agents, saying little, sat stunned. Stieglitz and Shipp had already wounded the venerable agency when they along with five other top young men walked out three years earlier and formed the Alliance Group, claiming that the old guard at Light were too stodgy, too set in their ways. The board of directors belittled them at the time, and tried to pretend it was business as usual, but Alliance began making not only headway but inroads, signing many of Light's bigger clients, and now, apparently, key agents. If this was true, what young Mike Barron had heard, then history was repeating. Homegrown young men were jumping ship; worse, they were jumping to the mutineers. Where three years earlier they had ignored the rumors, this time they could not. Immediate action was required, and two hours later, though they had yet to take the meeting, nor call a client, Bryan Forester and Kevin Lewis were escorted out of the building.

It was assumed someone had snitched. People were pointing fingers, but no one pointed them more aggressively than Mike Barron.

Calling Bryan Forester at home that evening, Mike told him he wouldn't rest until he found out who'd betrayed them, but he confided, confidentially, that he'd heard it had come from someone inside Alliance. He volunteered that along with Bryan's personal effects, he was going to sneak him his Rolodex.

Nothing was more important to an agent than the spinning wheels of little white cards containing precious personal information. So the gesture Barron made was not only germane, but it was his way, he believed, of successfully covering his tracks, showing his loyalty, and creating an opening, should he need one, with the competition.

"We have to close that opening," Mercedes said, after recounting the facts to Khan as she knew them.

Khan was surprised, not just with the information she'd gathered, but the accuracy.

When had she done this research? he thought. *And why had she done it?*

He looked at her, astonished, as she took a seat on the other side of his desk. It was both presumptive and annoying that she thought she could help.

"We can't let the competition hire him," she said, snapping Khan back to reality.

He sighed. "Okay, so, what? I call Stieglitz and tell him not to hire Mike Barron?" he said, pushing his chair back, signaling an end to this nonsense.

But Mercedes was just getting started. "In an industry where talent is rewarded, betrayal is punished," she told him, adding that Mike Barron had snitched on Bryan and Kevin and pointed the finger at everyone else in order to exonerate himself.

"That was five years ago," he reminded her. "No one cares."

Mercedes disagreed. "Disloyalty has no expiration date," she said, referring to Benedict Arnold. "Maybe it's time to let it be known that Mike Barron, like his father, is a man of questionable character."

Khan shook his head, growing annoyed once again. "What don't you understand? I'd be eating my own," he said, adding that he didn't want to destroy the boy's reputation; after all, Mike Barron was a valuable asset to the company.

"His reputation as an agent has nothing to do with his reputation as an employee," she argued, saying that while clients wouldn't care about whether or not he had snitched, agents would, most especially those whom he'd snitched on. She leaned on the desk and drove her point home. "Mike Barron has gotten by because no one has confirmed a truth many have suspected." She stared at Khan hard. "It's time to confirm it," she said, then outlined a plan that was cunning in its simplicity. "I'll schedule separate lunches with Barry Hirsch, Skip Brittingham, and Tom Pollack," she told him. "It'll be a catch-up, no specific agenda, but at those lunches you should casually ask what they think of Barron. Tell them you're considering promoting him, but that you're worried about his loyalty, letting it slip that after all, he was the one who snitched on Forester and Lewis. Say it matter-of-factly, as if you assumed they knew," she said. "They'll do the rest."

It was a genius idea.

Hirsch, Brittingham, and Pollack were widely respected top entertainment attorneys who had relationships with all industry leaders. They would, of course, tell all the heads of all the agencies, staining Mike Barron's reputation enough to make them think twice, but not so much as to affect the clients he serviced.

Khan stared at his muse with both awe and fear.

"You will wound him enough to maim, but not kill," she said, walking over to his side of the desk and standing before him. "And in that way, keep him on a short leash for life."

Harvey Khan was flabbergasted. Mercedes Baxter had demonstrated that she not only understood the rules but could twist them to her benefit, and as long as she was on his side, to his benefit as well.

Kneeling in front of him now, Mercedes unzipped his fly and took out his penis, flicking her tongue over the tip. "My enemy's enemy is my friend," she said teasingly.

Then she stopped talking.

BLOODY RED BARRON

The way to gain a good reputation is to endeavor
to be what you desire to appear.
—SOCRATES

February 1984

"Why would you want to work for that asshole?" Ella asked Beanie in the bathroom a few hours after Beanie had convinced Mike Barron to give her a week to show him what a real secretary could do. It wasn't that Ella didn't want her to have the job; it was that no one thought she would last. But no one knew how hard Beanie had fought to get there.

For his part, Barron had said yes less because he liked the idea and more because he thought the redhead might file a complaint. Harvey Khan had already spoken to his father about the number of complaints lodged against him, saying that he worried if any of the young women filed a complaint beyond Personnel, to, say, the law, the agency might have to take disciplinary action, which they didn't want to do for a multitude of reasons. Khan had been candid about the boy's future, reiterating that Mike could go all the way if he stopped dipping his pen in company ink.

"He's got a lot of fucking nerve," Mike said to his father when he called. "Khan's fucking his secretary when he's not fucking the head of Personnel, and I need to watch *my* pen?"

His father, infuriated, spit out his words like pellets penetrating Mike's bravado. "Until and unless you have Harvey Khan's title, you use a pencil, and you use it off campus. Understood?" He hung up, not waiting for an answer. The conversation had put Mike into a foul mood. His father was mad at him, Khan was watching him, and some dumpy girl was sitting outside at his secretarial station, while the hot redhead was in Personnel, filing another fucking complaint. He didn't need this. Not now. Not on top of the rumors that had begun circulating again about him being "the snitch."

He didn't understand how they had resurfaced. It had been over five years. *Who gives a fuck?* he thought, knowing that Bryan, Kevin, and probably all of Alliance did.

"Beanbag!" he called to the girl at the desk.

"It's Beanie," she said.

"Come in here."

She did.

He wanted to know what the hell she thought she was going to do for him.

"Glad you asked," she said, sitting on the obligatory black leather couch where she imagined many a woman had sat before, only her legs were closed, and her eyes were open.

Beanie, laser focused on the Mike Barron wave that rose before her, knew that this was her do-or-die moment. Poised, she would either swim through to her future, or be caught in an undertow that would dump her with the thousands of other nameless sexitaries who'd failed miserably on his desk.

But at least they had been on his desk. Beanie was still hovering somewhere above it. She took a deep breath and with articulate precision outlined her plan for *their* future, which included Mike becoming head of the motion picture talent department, with Beanie as a motion picture agent.

She knew that she was taking a calculated risk revealing her personal ambition, but she also knew that he'd smell bullshit if she kissed ass. Most importantly, she knew that he knew that she knew exactly who he was, and what was expected of his secretaries. Therefore, it was her job to set herself apart not only from the spinners whom he usually hired, but from any other secretary he might want to hire.

Which was why she opted to tell him about her long-range goals.

"You want to be an agent?" he asked, looking at her in amazement. "You know the rules," he said, reciting, "Secretaries can't be trainees, much less agents."

Silently he thought, *Especially ones that look like her.*

"We don't believe in rules," she told him, again aligning the two of them as one, as she went on to explain that Jamie Garland would tire of the position that Mike had wanted. "So, if *we* play our cards right, you can have it in six months."

He looked at her, unable to hide the incredulous grin on his face. "And how are *we* going to do that?" he asked. He wanted a plan.

Of course, she didn't have a plan, because twenty minutes earlier she hadn't known she needed one. So, she put on her dancing shoes, tapped for a future that was still forming, and explained that for Barron to become head of the motion picture talent department, he needed to first reduce the number of complaints lodged against him, which by virtue of the fact that she was now going to work for him would not only ameliorate but obfuscate anything that came before.

"I'm well liked," she told him, not at all sure she was. "I can let it be known that you've changed your ways."

Barron looked at her. "Oh, so *you* are going to help me?"

She nodded, ignoring the astonishment and sarcasm behind the comment. "Yes," she said with absolute certainty. "You need someone who believes in you, and I need someone who believes in me," she told him, doubling down that it wouldn't hurt if he stepped it up and signed a few hot stars on his own.

Of course, she knew his client list, but most of them had been signed by Amati, so no matter how much work Barron did, he'd be the number two and Amati would always get the credit. "They can never see you shine if you're in someone else's shadow," she told him. She was aware he had signed Robby Benson and a couple of the kids from *Fame,* but that wasn't enough. She was talking about signing someone hot. Someone who could perhaps become as big as Scott Westman.

This loony bitch has some fucking balls, he thought.

"Who do you have in mind?" he said, sitting back in his chair, both insulted and intrigued.

"Nicolas Cage," she told him.

It was the first person who'd popped into her head. He was the prototype, the young actor that young Hollywood admired. Everyone was talking about Nicolas Cage and Sean Penn. Penn had exploded in *Fast Times at Ridgemont High,* and Nicolas had just come out in *Valley Girl,* which had propelled him to the top of the hot young stars. They were both in demand. Everyone wanted to meet them, to know them, to work with them.

"How am I going to do that?" he asked.

"I'm going to introduce you," she said matter-of-factly, "and I'll tell him how good you are. How smart you are. You don't just play with a catcher's mitt like most agents," she said, stroking his wounded ego. "You build careers. And someone like Nicolas," she added, using his first name for familiarity, "needs an architect. We're architects."

Again, the *we.*

He looked at her. *Jesus, this kid talks a lot,* he thought, but still: what she was saying was intriguing, if it wasn't bullshit.

"How do you know him?" he asked suspiciously.

Trying to stay as close to the truth as she could, Beanie explained that her stepfather's cousin was Neiman Spitz, a famous composer who had done some work with Francis Coppola. And Nicolas was Coppola's nephew, so . . .

"So?" he asked.

"So," she explained, "that was how we met, through Neiman, and then we just became friends."

While the first part was true, Neiman Spitz *had* done some work with Coppola, or so she'd heard, the second part was as big a lie as she'd ever told, but Barron bought it. She added that it was Coppola who'd gotten her into the agency. As long as she was lying, she figured she'd swing for the fences.

Before he could drill down, she stood up, reminding him that the motion picture meeting started. Handing him the casting folder, she told him that she had lots of ideas, and that they would strategize later.

Five minutes earlier he'd have tossed her on her ass just for presuming there would be a later. He'd have asked for someone with long legs and no last name, and not thought twice about this crazy loon. But Barron, an opportunist, recognized an opportunity. This dumpy girl might be exactly what he needed. Harvey Khan and, more importantly, his father would approve. He looked at Beanie, took the folder, and left, his silence signaling that she had earned the right, at least for that afternoon, to stay.

It happened so fast that Beanie hadn't had time to process. And though Ella, Barry, Garry, and especially Moze were shocked when they'd heard that Beanie was suddenly working for a misogynist who passed his sexitaries around like loving cups, they were more shocked that she was happy to be there.

In a stunning turn of events, she had lost a desk she'd been promised for several months and taken a desk that no one had lasted on for more than a few weeks. In survival mode, she'd gone on autopilot, looking for a place to land. That it had been with the man who was most degrading to secretaries, the one she had originally hoped to work for, didn't seem odd. It seemed somehow providential.

That night, lying on her side next to Moze, Beanie knew one thing for sure: Mike Barron was enough of a narcissist that if you were willing to devote your life to his, he'd keep you around.

Beanie Rosen was willing.

Now all she had to do was figure out how to meet Nicolas Cage.

THE ABRACADABRA GIRL

Look at things not as they are, but as they *can* be.

—ANONYMOUS

March 1984

Quirky, clever, and whip smart, Ella Gaddy was making her own life on her own terms and was forming a loyal group of friends who had become her surrogate family. Few remembered her as the long-legged strawberry blonde from Accounting, with skirts too short and hair too yellow, and blouses with polyester ruffles. Now she was the girl on Garry Sampson's desk. The girl he deferred to, took to premieres or lunches and even signing meetings. People knew that Garry relied on Ella, but only Beanie knew that he was in love with her.

Unfortunately, it was one-sided. Ella, a free spirit, didn't want commitment, at least not with Garry Sampson. In fact, now that she was working for him, she had started to carve boundaries, especially after hours, when she preferred to be a lone wolf with multiple options.

Shortly after becoming his secretary, Ella laid down a new set of rules and encouraged Garry, who was growing frustratingly confused, to lay down his own. Specifically with other women. "You're a catch," she told him, encouraging him to date. She made it clear that while her devotion to him would not wane, she wasn't traditional, and quite clearly Garry was.

After a good amount of back and forth, they became more partners than lovers, dedicated to protecting one another and building and servicing Garry's growing client list, most especially Scott Westman, one of the agency's biggest clients. Scott had grown more and more reliant on Garry for his advice. And since Garry was reliant on Ella, Scott, too, began to seek her out. Ella was smart, and funny, and without an agenda, and Westman found her refreshing. He'd come by the office to hang, to chat, to schmooze, and if Garry wasn't there, he'd spend time with Ella. They'd go into Garry's office, throw back a scotch, order a sandwich from Salami 'N' Cheese, turn on the TV, and shoot the shit.

Naturally, it raised eyebrows, but if Westman was happy, the agency was happy, and the eyebrows were irrelevant.

Named *People* magazine's "Sexiest Man Alive" for 1983, Scott Westman's fame was a double-edged sword that only made him more insular. It was Ella who kept him real, and he became dependent on that reality check.

Often Beanie would come home and find Ella on the phone with Westman, laughing and talking intimately. There was a plethora of rumors about Garry Sampson's secretary and the biggest star in Hollywood, but Beanie never addressed them, even as Ella was spending more and more time with him.

Besides, Beanie was preoccupied with trying to figure out a way to meet Nicolas Cage. She hadn't shared the condition of her employment with Ella—or anyone. It was too embarrassing. She had made up a lie to keep a job no one else had wanted. Now she was on her own, needing to figure out how to meet Cage, befriend Cage, and then, *hello,* convince Cage that he needed a new agent even though his career was skyrocketing.

To make it worse, Mike Barron had announced at the motion picture meeting that he was inside-tracked to sign Cage, and every week thereafter would anxiously await news from Beanie.

The first few weeks Barron was almost nice to her, letting her make casting suggestions on projects and listen in on calls, but when after a month there was no Cage progress, he began to grow angry, calling her into his office where he would grill and shame and berate her.

"Beanbag!" he would shout, and she would go in, close the door, and listen to him call her a "fucking moron," or a "loser" or a "retard," all the while questioning her capabilities as a secretary and doubting the authenticity of her claim. "If Cage is a friend, how hard is it to introduce me?"

Beanie would calmly and logically explain that this wasn't about an introduction, it was about a signing, and it needed to be finessed. "It's all about timing," she would say, reminding him that Nicolas's career was on fire, and she didn't want to waste an introduction only to get a no. Beanie's strength, or one of them, was that she never sounded as desperate as she felt. Her advice was sanguine, and her lie, now almost two months old, had grown to enormous proportions. She didn't know how long she could quell Barron's suspicions or silence his questions. Beanie was not a liar by nature. She was a visionary, seeing something before it manifested, willing it into existence. Just because something wasn't true didn't mean it couldn't be. Her father had called her the abracadabra girl, explaining that the magic chant translated literally to, "I will create as I speak."

Say it. See it. Be it.

Abracadabra.

And that became Beanie's mantra.

Get the yes. Get the yes. Or in this case, at the very least, get the fucking intro.

It wasn't until early March, almost two months after the inciting incident, that she confessed the truth to Ella. It was after eight o'clock, and they were both home, sharing a pizza on what once was Mercedes's pastel couch.

"What fool says they know someone they don't just to keep a job?" Beanie said, with tears of shame and embarrassment.

"The same one who said they'd get their loser high school boyfriend an agent when they didn't even know what an agent was," Ella reminded her. Ella, who'd hated that Beanie had taken the job, hated it more when she beat herself up. "Let's figure this out," she said, getting up and pacing.

"Figure out what?" Barry asked, coming in the front door. Barry, who had become an agent and split from Marci the same week, had moved into the third bedroom, which made sense since Ella and Beanie both liked him, and Barry could afford the higher rent.

Moze thought it was a fine idea, too. Beanie, of course, had never told Moze that she and Barry had fooled around. It didn't seem relevant.

Moze didn't live in the past; in fact, Beanie knew little of his prior entanglements. And when she became curious, she was strongly advised by Ella not to ask. "Do not press him," Ella had warned. "None of it matters." Of course Ella would say that, not wanting to be pressed herself. But still, when it came to Moze, Beanie needed guidance. He was, she feared, quite suddenly out of her league.

Nine months earlier he had been a college dropout looking for a gig, and now he was on Sam Lesser's desk with industry insiders seeking him out, relying upon him for advice and confidences. While it wasn't lost on Beanie that she had been the architect of his meteoric career, she never flaunted it. She didn't want Moze to resent her, or worse, reject her, as Fish had years before once he started getting jobs on his own. Moze's rise in both the agency and the industry had been astounding, and she feared, much like Fish, his need for her might diminish. She believed this relationship was different than any relationship she'd had, and while it wasn't traditional, it was special, and she wasn't willing to let that go, no matter the compromise.

And there were compromises. Shortly after they'd begun sleeping together, Moze had told her that monogamy was against nature, and he didn't believe in it. Honesty was important to him, and he didn't want in any way to paint a picture otherwise. And with that, Beanie understood the rules which he—and she, if she chose to stay in the relationship—would have to live by.

"He fucks around," she'd confessed to Ella at the time.

"Who doesn't?" Ella had replied.

"Me," said Beanie.

"Then fuck around," Ella said cavalierly. "It's the eighties, for God's sakes. Sex won't kill you."

Ella, neither possessive nor proprietary, thought like a guy, which was probably why she was catnip to most of them. But Beanie wasn't, and so she decided to accept the irregularity of her time with Moze and try not to focus on her time without him.

Ella caught Barry up on the whole Nicolas Cage debacle, then asked if he knew him.

"I saw him once," Barry said, "at The Roxy when the Ramones played. That's the best I got."

Beanie sighed. "This is impossible."

Ella stood up and walked to the phone. "I'm gonna ask Scotti," she said decisively, referring to Scott Westman.

Beanie, alarmed, just about jumped out of her skin. As much as she appreciated the offer, she did not want Ella to tell anyone, *much less one of the agency's hottest clients,* about the lie she was perpetuating.

Barry agreed that that would be dangerous.

"Too late," Ella said, punching in his number on their powder-blue phone with the extra-long cord.

Beanie, nervous and embarrassed, paced.

"Chill," Ella warned as Westman answered.

They chatted a while about the idea of him doing an adaptation of his favorite book, *Zen and the Art of Motorcycle Maintenance,* before she broached the forbidden topic, simply saying that Beanie needed to reach Nicolas Cage.

Turned out, Scott didn't know him. But he'd done a film with rising young star Adrienne Seabergh, who apparently knew him well. "She's cool," he told Ella, "I can call her. Maybe we can all meet for a drink at the Formosa Café later if you want."

Beanie. Was. Floored.

Could it really be that easy?

She stared at her beautiful kooky friend with gratitude and love. Nicolas Cage had been an albatross around her neck for nine weeks, and while this date didn't guarantee, well, anything, it put her in striking distance.

She now knew someone who knew someone who knew Nicolas Cage. And for Beanie Rosen, she was riding the wave.

CAGED

A journalist to Bette Davis: "What's the easiest
way to make it in Hollywood?"
Bette's response: "Take Fountain."

March 1984

Twenty minutes after that phone call, Ella and Beanie—sans Barry, who as a new agent didn't want to get more involved in this mess—were driving her Swinger to the Formosa Café just off Santa Monica Boulevard. Truth was sometimes the best ally, and Beanie had decided to just tell it straight up, soup to nuts.

"Hell, she'll either think you're crazy or brilliant," Ella said, laughing.

Turns out Adrienne thought Beanie was a little of both. But so was Adrienne.

An ambitious writer, director, and actor who was an adorable, voluptuous, petite blonde, Adrienne Seabergh was a cross between Belinda Carlisle and Blondie, with a sparkling personality and a raucous laugh.

"So, you told this asshole you knew Nickie?" Adrienne asked, ordering one more round of shots.

Beanie smiled stiffly, trying to downplay the fact that Mike Barron was an asshole.

After all, Scott Westman, one of the agency's hottest clients, whom she'd only met in passing, was sitting across from her. A company girl all the way, Beanie didn't want Westman to think one of his representatives was a jerk.

"You got balls, girl," Westman told her.

"Giant ones," Ella laughed, and then, hugging Beanie, added, "She's my fucking hero."

Westman, who wore a leather jacket, a CBGB T-shirt, and jeans, was huddled in the corner so people wouldn't notice him. He smiled at Beanie. "Then you're my hero, too."

Adrienne slammed back a tequila, grabbed her vintage shoulder bag, got up and said, "Well let's go . . . hero."

"Where?" Beanie asked.

"Nickie's place," she said.

Located just off Rossmore, the El Royale apartments in Hollywood were built in 1929 by the same man who'd built the Chateau Marmont. The original apartments were large with living rooms, dining rooms, studies, and terraces. By the mid-1980s most of the apartments had been cut up and subdivided, except a few on the top floor. One of those was occupied by Nicolas Cage.

It was after eleven o'clock by the time Beanie followed Adrienne to the exclusive address. Scott Westman and Ella had stayed back at the Formosa, leaving Beanie to do the deed or die trying. It was all so surreal that she had neither time to panic nor think.

"Welcome," Nicolas said, greeting Beanie and Adrienne in his smoking jacket and slippers. His hair, wet from a recent shower, Beanie guessed, was slicked back, and his droopy brown eyes seemed kind, she thought. Welcoming.

He swept Adrienne into his arms.

He's so handsome, Beanie thought, *like an old-time movie star.*

"Look at him. He loves Bela Lugosi," Adrienne said, laughing.

Beanie laughed too, unsure who or what Bela Lugosi was.

Nicolas and Adrienne went into the back room while Beanie waited in the vast empty living room with high ceilings crisscrossed by wooden beams.

Adrienne had told her earlier that Nickie was temporarily house-sitting at the El Royale for a friend who was hoping he might purchase the luxe penthouse that had been on the market for over eleven months. Nicolas, just twenty, was looking for a place to park his treasures; a retreat away from Hollywood and into what Beanie quickly surmised would be a world of macabre antiquities. There were mounted and framed spiders, some propped upon scripts, and others leaning against the thick white stucco walls, which she assumed belonged to the young Lothario. Otherwise, the room was sparse, with highly polished wood floors and a distant view of Los Angeles. There was an aubergine velvet couch and some side tables, but the main point of interest was a large terrarium against the back wall, ten, perhaps eleven feet long. It was filled with plants and rocks and a giant python.

The evening, already surreal, was unfolding into a triptych of the impossible, improbable, and bizarre. She waited in the empty living room, staring at the python, who had uncoiled and then recoiled, as if Beanie wasn't worth the effort of his stretch. Other than the distant sounds of street traffic, the penthouse was so silent that she began to wonder if Nicolas and Adrienne had slipped out the back, leaving her alone with the snake and spiders, frozen in eight-legged repose. Finally, about forty-five minutes later, Nicolas, his hair still wet, and Adrienne, hers now wet too, emerged from the back.

"That's Louise," Nicolas said, referring to the python. "You want to hold her?"

"Less than anything in the world," Beanie said, deadpan.

He smiled, sat down, and listened to Beanie tell him the truth about her lie.

"So, I'm the bounty here?" he said, less a question and more a strange concept he was trying on for size. It was after midnight, and they'd been talking for about half an hour.

Beanie's goal had been twofold. In the immediate, she wanted to set a lunch, a meeting, hell, she'd take a phone call, anything to prove to Barron she knew the young star. But for the long play, she wanted Nicolas to know that Sylvan Light, a company she loved and believed in with all her heart, was a force to be reckoned with. It was the place to be. It was the place he *had* to be.

To her surprise, he was surprised. "They want to represent me?" he asked, reminding Beanie that movie stars, even those as hot as Cage, were still one job away from anonymity.

"More than anything," she told him. It felt like ten minutes ago he was a no one, kicking around for bit parts, and now agents whose names he'd read about, legends like Sam Lesser and Jamie Garland, wanted to meet *him.*

"What do you get out of it?" he asked.

"She gets to keep her job with the douchebag," Adrienne told him.

Beanie jumped in. "While some might call Barron a douchebag, he's also an amazing agent. I mean, they're not mutually exclusive," she explained, adding that when it came to getting a client hired, he was in it to win it. "At the end of the day," she said, "that's who you want on your team. Someone who will stop at nothing to get you the job."

Nicolas put an unlit pipe in his mouth, flipped it from side to side, and explained he wasn't really looking for an agent.

Beanie told him she understood but added that it couldn't hurt to see who was out there.

He nodded. "Would a lunch or a meeting in the office be better for you?"

She looked from Adrienne to Nicolas. Was he kidding? She hadn't hoped for anything like an in-office meeting. But if he would, if that was possible, then everyone would see him come into the big conference room on the second floor, and people might even get wind that *she* was the reason. If Nicolas came into the office, it might be enough to make Mike Barron head of the motion picture talent department, and Beanie a trainee. It was one thing for Mike to have a lunch and hope that others saw him with a star, but to reel in a tuna like Nicolas Cage and walk him down the halls—that was a fucking trophy.

And it would be Beanie Rosen who baited that hook.

"Nothing would be better than you coming into the office," she told him, quickly adding, "Except of course, if we signed you."

He laughed. "How long before you're an agent?"

"I'm not even a trainee," she said.

"Call me when you are," Nicolas said, handing her and Adrienne a flute of Dom Pérignon.

"Let's make a toast," Adrienne suggested.

"Abracadabra," Beanie said, raising her glass and pinching herself. "Abracafuckingdabra."

THE SWEET'N LOW HIGH

At first, it burned . . .

—BEANIE ROSEN

March—April 1984

Mike Barron took Beanie into his arms and kissed her deeply, putting his tongue in her mouth, and wrapping it around hers. He pressed himself against her, and she could feel how hard he was.

She hadn't had time to react, it had happened so fast. She had gone into his office the Monday after the fateful meeting and told him that she had spent the weekend with Nicolas and Adrienne, dropping tidbits about the Formosa Café, the El Royale, the spiders, Louise, providing enough detail and authenticity to fill in the blanks she'd previously left opened.

"He's coming into the office to meet you, Thursday," she told him casually. "Four o'clock. I'll reserve the second-floor conference room."

Mike, feeling overwhelmed and grateful, decided he'd fuck her. It was the greatest gift he believed he could give. Nothing excited him more than when someone loved him as much as he loved himself. And Beanie, he thought, not only loved him but could help him. None of his other secretaries had meant anything. Not in the long run. They were decorations, toys who always seemed willing and then, in the end, complained. "They couldn't take dictation or a joke," Mike would say to Personnel in answer to the inevitable summons that would come about the way he treated "his girls."

But Beanie could, he thought. She might be the key to his success, helping him break away from the pack, the Randall Finks, the Stewie

Wolfs, the agents he considered competition rather than teammates. He hated them all. "There's no 'Mike' in 'team,'" his colleagues would whisper. But there wouldn't have to be if he brought in Cage. A signing like that could push him ahead, maybe he'd even become one of Lesser's boys. Barron knew Lesser didn't like him and had been forced to watch as the senior agent bestowed his time and his clients on other agents, most recently Garry Fucking Sampson. All the people Mike hated shared the same middle name; Jamie Fucking Garland, Randy Fucking Fink, and now Garry Fucking Sampson. Garry had been an agent for five minutes and already had more A-list clients than he did. But something like this could turn it around for him. Sam Lesser's approval was very important to Mike, just as Mike Barron's approval was very important to Beanie.

"I want to fuck you," he said, his voice thick with lust.

And though she'd never admit it, not to Ella nor anyone, she momentarily considered fucking him right there on the floor of his office. She pressed against him, giving over to the feel of what she had elicited, and momentarily considered showing how great she was with her mouth, how fun she could be as both co-conspirator and lover. Maybe it was the fact that she wanted to be like the girls he'd chosen, the spinners, the pretty ones who'd made him look sexy just by being there. Regardless, she savored the truth that Mike Barron was hard because of her. And that gave her power.

It also gave her pause. If she fucked him, she'd be like everyone else, only thicker in places and more self-conscious in others. It would give him something to make fun of, to demean when the Nicolas Cage meeting had run its course. Her strength, she knew, would be in the wanting, not in the doing. And so, instead, she pulled away.

"Let's get ready for Nicolas," she told him, suggesting they call a meeting of high-powered agents to prepare.

"First, we're going to need a little help," he said, smiling, and locking the door.

She was confused as he guided her to his desk chair, sat her down, and opened the thin middle drawer at the top of the desk, revealing a mirror, a tightly wound bill of some denomination, and remnants of white powder.

"You know what that is?" he asked.

"Sweet'N Low?" she said.

"Sweet and high," he corrected. Laughing, he took a razor blade from a box of paper clips and gathered the Sweet'N Low into a small pile. Dipping his index finger into the powder, he brought it to her lips. "Open," he commanded quietly, and she obeyed.

With his hard cock pressed against the back of her head, she parted her lips, allowing him to rub his finger across her gums. "Like it?" he said, as he repeated the action on himself.

She could feel a tingle, reminiscent of her trips to the dentist, sans cock, and rubbed her tongue across her gums, trying to decide whether she was actually enjoying the sensation. Before she could answer, he produced a small vial from his pocket and tapped a good amount of the white powder onto the mirror, using the razor blade again, but this time to form six thick white lines. When she looked up at him, he smiled. "You're going to love it," he promised as he put his hand where his cock had been and gently pushed her head down toward the mirror until she was inches from the lines. "Inhale," he commanded, taking the rolled-up bill with his other hand and placing it under her nostril.

There was something base about this, and wrong, and part of her wanted to run. She didn't want to take drugs. She never had. Even when Fish had wanted to get high, she had pretended to inhale but never did. The idea of control was too important, and nothing appealed to her about ceding it.

But sitting at Mike's desk, with his hand firmly on her head, she began to yield. There was a divine complicity; a sexually charged understanding of submission and dominance that felt both intimate and forbidden. She steadied the money straw and inhaled the thick powder. It burned at first and was uncomfortable. She sniffled, trying to clear her nose, moving it around, and then seconds later, almost instantly, felt a kind of euphoria.

"Again," he whispered, positioning the bill in front of the other nostril.

She repeated the action, inhaling deeply, anticipating the burn, then, seconds later, heaven.

Now it was Mike's turn. He leaned down, his face inches from hers, and expertly inhaled his lines. "More?" he said, offering her the money straw.

"Fuck yeah," she said, "that's a Sweet'N Low high," and he laughed.

They finished the vial in a few hours. No longer needing assistance, she waited her turn with the anticipation of a child at an amusement park going on the same ride over and over.

She was flying, invigorated, empowered. "You feel the drip at the back of the throat?" he asked. She nodded. "That's my favorite part," he told her.

But for Beanie it was impossible to choose. She loved everything about it. The insidious vial kept hidden yet readily available for a little bump, the preparation, the anticipation, the complicity. It was like an invisible door had opened to another world, and she never wanted to leave.

What was interesting about cocaine and what surprised her most was that she never felt out of control; in fact, she felt more focused, more invigorated, and more alive than she'd ever been before.

"We can go all night with this," he told her.

And they did, sharing stories about the things that drove them, and drove them crazy: his father, her mother, his plans to run a studio, and hers to be an agent. He told her that being an agent was a waste of time. He hated chasing after 10 percent of someone else's salary and saw Sylvan Light as a mere way station, a jumping-off point. Barron wanted to be the guy the agents courted, the buyer, the boss, the money who pushed the button, who made the light green and the cash flow.

But Beanie wanted to be an agent, she said. It was what she was born to do.

He promised he'd help her get promoted, and once she tired of it, she could be his right hand at the studio. "We'll do it together," he told her, as they worshiped at the altar of the almost empty vial.

Beanie Rosen was great on a normal day, but on a cocaine-infused binge, she was a goddess. Or at least she felt like one. No longer looking at this as a one-off to pacify the beast she'd created, she now wanted Barron to sign Cage, believing that this was only the beginning for the two of them. All week long she and Barron strategized by day and Sweet'N Low'd by night.

They were on fire.

She just had to make sure the right people knew that she was the conduit to Cage—specifically Jamie Garland, Sam Lesser, and Gil Amati. If Barron, who was head of the training program, sanctioned it along with the three of them, she could move from secretary to trainee. That's all she needed.

Fearing that in some way it might diminish his power, Mike, at first, hesitated with the idea of telling anyone that his secretary had arranged the meeting. But Beanie wisely pointed out that Nicolas might mention her in the meeting, and she didn't want the fact that Barron hadn't to reflect badly upon him.

Besides, it wasn't that she wanted or needed the world to know what she'd done—she needed the people who ran the agency to know. What Beanie was attempting to do was controversial. After all, if one secretary became a trainee, what's to stop the rest of them from trying? And then the system of mailroom to Dispatch to desk would be circumnavigated by some "ambitious female," as Mike called them, referring to Beanie or Jamie or any woman who thought she could do better.

But if Beanie found a loophole, she could make certain the other trainees wouldn't resent her for it. She had to convince them that she was the exception, not the rule. Sure, there'd been female agents, and yes, there had been the occasional female trainee, but never had a secretary crossed over.

Until me, she thought.

Thursday, March 23, 1984, Hawkeye called up to Beanie to tell her that Nicolas Cage was on his way to the second-floor conference room to meet with Mike Barron. It had been decided that a few senior agents would stop by to say hello, and that after the meeting Barron would personally bring Cage down to Sam Lesser's office for a private meeting. The group had rehearsed their parts, and even prepared, thanks to Beanie, an audio-visual presentation of where they projected Cage's career could go in the next five years. While citing the major stars and filmmakers they currently represented, they differentiated themselves by showing the actor how little direct competition he'd have at Sylvan Light, versus how much he'd have elsewhere.

The agents were proactive rather than defensive, smart, self-effacing, and generous, gifting Cage a small Basquiat.

"Token of our esteem," Mike said proudly. The practice of giving gifts to lure or to keep clients was new to the agency, but ever since the Alliance Group began upping the stakes, Sylvan Light felt they needed to keep pace. And since Adrienne had told Beanie that in addition to rare centipedes, Nicolas favored neo-expressionist art, Mike had lobbied the board to let him purchase the small painting. "It will remind him of us," he'd said, doubling down with the assurance that signing Nicolas could be a watershed for the agency, opening up the possibility of attracting stars like Matt Dillon, Timothy Hutton, or Debra Winger, none of whom they represented. Cage was a get, and certainly worth the price of a Basquiat.

While the meeting had been inconclusive, it had buoyed Barron both in the eyes of his colleagues and his potential client. Nicolas assured Mike, and more importantly Sam Lesser, that he would revisit the discussions after shooting his next film.

For Mike, it was a win. For Beanie, a triumph. He had kept his word and told Lesser and Garland and Amati that he'd met Cage through his secretary, and that she very much wanted to be a trainee.

"Give it a few months," he told Beanie. "Let them get their head around the idea of a secretary moving into the trainee pool."

She agreed, of course. This would be precedential, and it had to be carefully done. But she wanted that trainee position more than she'd wanted anything else. If she could break through, it might reinforce her worth and silence the noise, the doubt, and the endless screaming about rich relations who lived south of the Boulevard. Beanie would be good enough. Getting the yes. Getting the approval. Getting the client. It was all about getting the love. Until it faded. Then she'd find another wave to swim through, another mountain to move to prove herself worthy.

Amati was the first to seek her out. "Good work, kiddo," he said, adding that they were all impressed. He sidled up and whispered that if she had any relationship with Sean Penn, he was a big fan. Beanie nodded, hoping to give the impression that she was connected to all of young Hollywood. Jamie Garland, with whom she'd had limited interaction since losing her desk, went out of her way to say how impressed she'd been. "We're going to be discussing your future, young lady," she told Beanie, smiling. And Moze made certain that Sam Lesser knew it was Mike Barron's secretary who had secured the Nicolas Cage meeting.

Now it was just a matter of time.

LEOPARDS AND BARRONS

When someone shows you who they are, believe them.

—MAYA ANGELOU

July—September 1984

"So, what the hell is going on with your promotion?" Ella asked in July.

It had been nearly four months since Nicolas had come into the office, and the world had reset, people had moved on, and Cage wasn't returning Barron's phone calls.

Ella was concerned. She'd heard Mike Barron from down the hall scream at Beanie, calling her "a fucking moron."

"How do you let him treat you that way?" Ella asked.

Beanie just shrugged. "I poked the Barron," she joked. That's what they used to say in Personnel when he'd spew his bile. She knew that Mike didn't mean it. "It's just his way of blowing off steam." What she didn't tell Ella, or anyone, was that after that outburst, he'd brought her into his office, sat her down, shoved his cock against her head, and gave her a bump, or seven.

He felt guilty and it was his way of saying "I'm sorry" without saying "I'm sorry." And it was then, between lines of blow, that he'd offered a status report on her promotion, telling her that it was a bit trickier than they'd anticipated but it was going to happen. In confidence, he shared that while the committee liked her, there had been complaints lodged.

"About me?" she said, sobering up.

He swore her to secrecy, then confided that there were legitimate concerns, primarily from trainees, but also a few agents who didn't want to change a system that had been in place for years. If you could become an agent by being a secretary, then who the hell needed to go to the mailroom, or Dispatch?

Beanie volunteered that she'd go into the mailroom if they'd let her. She'd do whatever she had to do, she told him, rubbing the remnants onto her gums. But again, he assured her that that wasn't necessary.

"Relax," he told her. "It just needs to be finessed."

She just had to trust him and promise that she wouldn't discuss it with anyone, including her leggy friend who worked for Garry Fucking Sampson.

Mike Barron could feel that Ella Gaddy didn't like him and was wary of her friendship with Beanie. They fucking lived together, for Christ's sakes. It was all too incestuous for him. Calling her Sampson's white-trash hookup, Barron mocked Ella often and loudly.

Extracting a promise that Beanie wouldn't discuss any of this with Ella or anyone, he reassured her again that it would all happen in time. He did say it wouldn't hurt if she could help him in bringing in a few other people.

So, over the next few months Beanie got him a number on Eric Stoltz, who'd just been cast as the lead opposite Cher in *Mask,* and Lea Thompson, who had just come out in the sequel to *Fast Times at Ridgemont High* called *The Wild Life,* and was set to star in a new time-travel film called *Back to the Future.* Beanie didn't bring her promotion up again, lest he get annoyed, but in September Barron brought it up to Beanie one Saturday when they were at his house in Malibu.

"Fucking Jamie Garland," he volunteered apropos of nothing. "She's on the fence about making you a trainee." He was straightening the lines of cocaine on his mirrored coffee table and had said it so nonchalantly Beanie barely had time to process.

"I thought the delay was because of protocol, or politics or some trainee lodging a complaint?" she said. "I didn't realize it was one of the four members of the committee who were hesitating."

He inhaled a line and shook his head. "She's the one dragging her feet, but that's confidential," he said, enjoying the high of the first bump.

"But, why?" she asked, honestly baffled. It had been six months since the Cage meeting, and Mike, as frustrated as Beanie, held up his hands.

"I wish I could tell you, Hoover," he said, jokingly using the moniker he had bestowed upon her as a term of endearment and a reference to her love of the powder. He speculated that maybe Garland was just being cautious in her new job, maybe she didn't want to ruffle feathers. "I don't fucking know," he said, offering Beanie the money straw and encouraging her to take a hit.

Beanie and Barron had become inseparable, working late every night, and usually at his house in Malibu on weekends where they would do blow, watch porn cassettes, his entertainment of choice, and talk about who else they could sign. "This could drag into next year," he told Beanie, saying that Jamie Fucking Garland was a pussy, but he would work on her.

She nodded, trying to be stoic, and turned her attention to *The Dildo Nurses of Santa Fe,* which he had just put into his VHS machine.

The following week Beanie was at the bathroom sink during lunch when Jamie Fucking Garland walked in and smiled at her.

"Hi, Beanie," she said, turning on the tap to the sink adjacent and dabbing a spot on her pale pink Christian Dior blouse.

Beanie had seen Jamie a handful of times in the hall, in the garage, on the street, but other than a hello or a nod, Beanie always looked down or away, never engaging. She'd been told not to ask any questions, and since she knew Jamie had been heading the committee to decide her fate, didn't want to do anything to upset the applecart.

"How are you doing?" Jamie asked.

"Good. I'm good," Beanie said, and then, before she could stop herself, added, "and anxious."

Jamie stopped with the blouse and looked at Beanie, confused. "Anxious about . . . ?"

Beanie looked at her, surprised. Was she kidding? How could she not know why Beanie was anxious?

"My promotion," Beanie said. "Into the training program. I mean it's been six months, so I'm just wondering if you think you're going to decide this year." Beanie searched Jamie's face for an answer, or compassion, or at least an indication as to when this torture would end. It wasn't fair what they were doing to her, keeping her on tenterhooks.

And Jamie technically had done it twice.

She owed her.

"I mean, is there something more I can do?" Beanie asked, frustration creeping in.

Jamie seemed surprised. "I thought you knew," she said, genuinely confused.

"Knew what?" Beanie asked, trying to quell the rising panic.

Jamie, noticeably uncomfortable, explained to Beanie that while they appreciated everything she had done, the decision to promote her hadn't been unanimous, and, unfortunately, without unanimity they weren't able to move forward in getting her into the training program.

Beanie shook her head. "Wait. It was decided?"

Jamie nodded. "Back in March. I thought you knew," she said again.

Beanie shook her head again, trying to clear it more than give an answer. None of it made sense. How was this possible? She knew she had Barron's vote, and Amati had told her he thought she'd make a better agent than half the agents there. Moze had assured her that Lesser was in, so it could only mean one thing. Jamie had dissented.

Her eyes welled up. "What did I ever do to you?" she asked loudly, her voice echoing. People, curious about the commotion, began to gather, coming out of stalls. Beanie didn't care. She was raw. Tears were falling over her purple Anne Klein suit, which due to her seventeen-pound cocaine-induced weight loss, hung on her much thinner frame. After all she'd done, and all she'd been through, to come once again this close and get the fucking door slammed in her face, it was all too much to bear.

Jamie tried to calm Beanie, who was crying now, broken, but Beanie rejected the gesture. She was mad and didn't want to be placated, nor let Jamie off the hook.

"Women helping women was all bullshit," she said, hating the fact that she'd ever trusted Jamie Garland in the first place.

Finally, Jamie understood that Beanie wasn't just distraught by the situation. Beanie was blaming her. And that was unacceptable.

"It wasn't me," Jamie said, truthfully. "It was Mike."

Beanie heard the words, but they didn't land. Not at first.

"We all said yes," Jamie continued, "immediately, as I recall, but Mike dissented. He didn't feel you were ready. He was adamant that he would tell you himself. I had no idea that he hadn't . . ." Jamie said, flummoxed.

See, the thing about truth is that when you hear it, it crystallizes in a way that leaves no doubt. And that's how it was for Beanie. The world wasn't against her, Mike Barron was. Sadly, it all suddenly made sense. He had knowingly, selfishly, and sadistically strung her along, making her believe that a promotion was possible when, in fact, it was he who had prevented it. In some twisted scenario, he probably resented that she'd wanted to leave him, and feared that with autonomy she could gain power, and, given what she knew about him, she had the potential to become a threat. Mike Barron was using her for everything she was worth and then would toss her out like so many others.

Leopards and Barrons don't change their spots, she realized soberly.

AN AUDIENCE

And the king said to the maiden fair, "You truly are a loyal servant."

—KING ARTHUR

October–November 1984

Without revealing what she knew or how she knew or even that she knew, Beanie Rosen reported to work every day, did her job, waited, and watched. But inside, she boiled. Mike Barron hadn't just blocked her promotion, he had told the committee—and, she suspected, others—that she wasn't good, that she wasn't Sylvan Light material.

That's what she'd found out after she'd collected herself and gone into Jamie's office, closing the door, and apologizing not only for her outburst, but for the accusation. She'd assumed it was Jamie who'd blackballed her because Jamie had hired her initially and then let her go without a fight, without apology or explanation.

Jamie had been surprised by Beanie's reasoning. Nancy had assured Jamie that Beanie was not only fine but had been scooped up by Mike Barron. "I thought it was a win-win," Jamie had said, "and it never dawned on me to question it." Jamie apologized, but Beanie waved it off.

"Ancient history," she told her.

"I was as surprised that Nancy stayed as you were," Jamie continued, adding that it was actually Harvey Khan's secretary, Mercedes Baxter, who had convinced Nancy to give the agency a try.

Beanie drew in a breath as Jamie explained that Mercedes had pursued Nancy, taking her to lunch, drinks. "I think they even went to a screening together," she told her. "Mercedes really took a personal interest in Nancy and worked hard to convince her to stay."

Beanie's stomach fell, but her face never registered a change. She simply nodded, working the tumblers in her head. Mercedes Baxter was like a virus in a host's body. Once she got in, she took over. She had been the reason Beanie wasn't working for Jamie. It made sense. Mercedes didn't need anyone to remind her (or Khan) where she'd come from, or what she'd had to do to get there. But Beanie knew. And Mercedes knew that Beanie knew.

"We wanted to promote you," Jamie continued, "but Mike worked overtime to convince us that . . ." Then she stopped. "It doesn't matter," she said.

But it did to Beanie. She needed to know exactly what was said about her so she could understand exactly what she was up against. "It's not ego," she told Jamie, "it's survival."

Jamie looked at her hard and nodded. "Okay," she said. "He said you lacked the finesse, sophistication, and smarts to ever be an agent, much less a trainee, and that you were barely holding your own as a secretary." Beanie's eyes filled involuntarily. "I'm sorry," Jamie said, regretting the disclosure.

"No, I needed to hear it," Beanie insisted. "And I'm grateful. Is that all?"

Jamie shook her head. "He also said that you'd made unflattering comments about me and my ability to lead the department." Beanie nodded.

"He wanted you to hate me," Beanie told her.

"That's impossible," Jamie said. "I couldn't admire you more."

That night, Ella, after hearing the ugly truth, assembled the troops. It didn't matter that it was almost nine, she told Barry to leave his dinner, and Moze to leave the office. She even recruited Garry Sampson. It was all hands on deck as once again, Beanie Rosen was out of moves.

"I could see if I could get you into ICM," Barry offered. Apparently, they'd been courting him.

"You wouldn't leave Light?" Moze asked, upset in a way that should have alarmed everyone, if anyone was paying attention.

"Excuse me, but can we all fucking focus here," Ella said, referring to their friend who was sitting on the couch, distraught and lost. "We'll figure this out, babe," she said, walking over.

But Beanie shook her head. She had two powerful enemies. "It's not just Mike," she said. "It's Mercedes."

"Who?" asked Moze.

"Mercedes Baxter," Ella told him, "Harvey Khan's secretary. We all lived together for like five minutes."

Moze seemed surprised. "She's always nice to me," he said.

"She's always nice until she doesn't need you," Beanie told him. "Who knows what she would say to Harvey Khan if push came to shove? No one can overrule the president of the Sylvan Light Agency," Beanie said sadly, the reality of her conundrum sinking in.

"Sam Lesser can," came a voice from the kitchen doorway.

It was Garry Sampson, who had been standing apart from the rest of the group, quietly listening. "Khan yields to Lesser," he told them. "So, if you could pull another Cage out of your bag of tricks, bring someone directly to Sam Lesser, not to Mike Barron, Lesser would recognize how good you are," Garry explained.

"How's she supposed to do that?" Ella asked, worried that her friend would be frustrated.

But Beanie was anything but. "What if it *is* Cage?" she asked, an idea forming. "Would Sam Lesser still want to represent him?"

Garry's eyes narrowed. "In a heartbeat," he told her. "It was Barron he didn't want to work with," Garry confessed, explaining that Sam tried to keep his distance from the agent. That made sense to Beanie. Mike Barron had long suspected that Sam didn't like him and blamed his colleagues for poisoning the well. It never occurred to him that he *was* the reason.

"Okay," she said, pacing, putting the pieces together. She knew that Nicolas had been enamored with Sam, his reputation, his legacy, and had been genuinely excited to meet him. "I'm gonna call him," she decided.

"Who?" Ella asked.

"Nicolas," Beanie said, reaching for her Filofax.

Ella stood with her mouth agape, watching her friend take charge. Beanie knew it was a long shot, but it was also the only shot. And hell, if it worked, if Lesser signed Cage, or maybe even if he didn't, even if they just had lunch, surely Lesser would see how valuable Beanie was without prejudice from Mike Barron or interference from Mercedes Baxter. Garry was right: the world yielded to Samuel Lesser.

Everyone stood silently as she reached for the half-moon pale blue phone. Punching in the numbers for Nicolas Cage, she listened as the phone rang through. Sometimes he answered, but often in the past when she'd called, she got the service, as she did that night.

Unruffled, she left her name, home number, and a message saying that Sam Lesser had asked that she set a meeting strictly between the two of them. It was ballsy and brilliant. Barry looked to Ella, who looked to Garry, who looked to Moze. They were impressed. Not only was she smart and resourceful, but she was also fearless.

Twenty-five minutes later, Nicolas Cage returned the call. Beanie answered, listened, thanked him, and hung up.

"He's in," she said, smiling, exhilarated.

Ella screamed, Barry high-fived, but Garry stood very still, watching.

"If this girl doesn't become an agent, then it's our loss," he said, turning to Moze and instructing him to schedule a meeting for him and Sam the next morning. Garry knew that his name was one of the few Moze could pencil in without checking. The plan was to tell Sam that Mike Barron's secretary, Beanie Rosen, who should be an agent, had been doggedly nurturing the relationship with Cage, and knowing that Cage wasn't feeling Barron, had approached Garry to see if Sam might do a private sit-down.

"I just want to prepare you," Garry told her. "Mike Barron's going to freak."

Ella and Barry clocked Beanie for her response.

"You say that like it's a bad thing," she said, grinning, invigorated, and empowered.

Ella clapped. "Okay, then, let's do it!"

Beanie nodded, feeling the enormity of what was about to happen. And for the first time that day, she felt something else. Hope.

The following Monday, Samuel Lesser met Nicolas Cage for lunch at Hernando's Hideaway at the Beverly Wilshire Hotel.

After that lunch, Mike Barron's phone rang. Beanie picked up. "Mr. Lesser would like an audience," Anita Lejos, his long-time secretary, said to Beanie, and then added, "with you."

Beanie's heart was pounding as she stood up.

"What did Lesser's office want?" Mike asked, coming out of his office. He'd seen the readout on the incoming line. Lesser never called for him.

"Wrong number," she said.

He looked at her suspiciously. "Where are you going?"

"Bathroom," she told him, and walked away too fast for him to say anything else. Beanie chose the stairs rather than the elevator, taking the long way around so she wouldn't pass Mercedes Baxter. She couldn't risk Mercedes's shenanigans, not now.

Everything downstairs was plush, quiet, and powerful. Even the phones, observing the solemnity of the floor on which they were located, rang in muted tones. People seemed to move in slow motion as Beanie approached Sam's corner office.

Sam Lesser wasn't just an agent. He was a legend. The giants of the industry all sought him out for guidance, friendship, and advice. He was discreet, compassionate, strategic, brilliant, and never raised his voice.

"True power," he was quoted as saying, "means you never have to." She and Moze had read a profile on him in *New York Magazine.* His face, on the cover, stared off into the distance, hazel eyes crinkled at the corners, showing both kindness and foresight. The writer who profiled him compared him to a mythic Western painting, much like the Remingtons that hung in his office. The article had alluded to the fact that Sam had been briefly married when he was in law school, glossing over his "assistant," Johnny Merit, who lived with him on his sprawling estate in the Malibu hills. It was, Beanie decided, a well-manicured puff piece about a man at the top of his game.

But in between the puff lay smoke: thick, opaque, carefully curated by an army of individuals trained to protect the man while polishing the myth. And it was that army who now were on Beanie's side, urging her forward. Garry, Moze, even Anita Lejos, Lesser's longtime secretary, she believed, all wanted her to win. She walked past Anita, smiling, and then without revealing familiarity, glanced at Moze.

"They're waiting," he told her.

She nodded and went inside.

The office, rich in hues of forest green and wood, looked like something out of a Ralph Lauren showroom and smelled of Polo perfume. Sam Lesser, dressed casually in cowboy boots, Levi's, and a suede blazer, stood up and walked around his large mahogany desk, greeting Beanie with hand extended.

"So, you're the secret weapon," he said.

"I prefer secret sauce," she replied.

He smiled. His eyes were kind and warm. He asked her to sit as Garry Sampson told Beanie that Sam Lesser had signed Nicolas Cage.

Beanie's eyes nearly popped out of her head. She wanted to jump up, to scream, to hug Garry, to hug them both, but instead she said, "Good. That's good. It's good. Right?"

"It's great," said Garry, who described how amazing Beanie had been, how tenacious, how brilliant, and how she'd fought her way to be in that room.

Sam listened, nodded, and smiled. "I love an underdog story," he said.

"Oh well, then, you're going to love mine," she told him, taking him through her journey from Central Files to Personnel to Jamie Garland to Mike Barron. Of course, she'd left out anything incriminating or scandalous, just the adventures of Beanie in Wonderland.

She won him over.

"So, what's next for you, Beanie Rosen?" he asked.

She looked at Garry, who nodded, and taking a deep breath, told him flat out, "I want to be an agent at the Sylvan Light Agency more than anything in the world. But first, I need to be a trainee."

"Let's make her one," Sam said, turning to Garry.

"Great," said Garry, "I'll let Jamie Garland know." Garry turned to

Beanie, thinking that she'd be thrilled or at least grateful, and while she was both, she was also pensive.

She'd been thinking about the Mike Barron problem and had come up with what she hoped was a solution. She looked at the two men, took a deep breath, and told them both that since it was unusual for a secretary to go into the training program, she was thinking, with Mr. Lesser's approval, that she could become a departmental assistant, doing coverage for all the agents, filling in when they needed help on signings or servicing or supplementing. She didn't want to take an available trainee desk away, and she wanted to differentiate, on those rare occasions when secretaries became trainees, that there was a place for them to go next.

"A departmental assistant," Lesser said, letting the words and the idea settle. Then he smiled. He liked it. It would be an entirely new position that wouldn't infiltrate the trainee program, but a landing pad for someone exceptional. "How about a departmental trainee?" he suggested, explaining that it would be an option for anyone outside of the program, so the two could coexist without conflict.

"Even better," she said. She jumped up, wanting to hug him, and then, remembering her place, shook his hand vigorously.

On November 4, 1984, Beanie Rosen became a departmental trainee at the Sylvan Light Agency. It was the second time that she had invented a position out of thin air.

She spoke it. She saw it. She got it. Abracadabra.

A NEW DAY

The picture I will keep is of her seated on a sofa at a party shortly before the Oscars two years ago, her hair and dress perfect, a vision of serenity until you got close enough to hear her intone the word "cocksucker."

—ANNE STRINGFIELD, *THE NEW YORKER*

1985

The first staff meeting at the top of every year was less a strategic exchange of information and more a call to arms to renew, reinforce, and reinvigorate the troops. A catered breakfast from Nate 'n Al's would be served as agents, trainees, and secretaries gathered to hear an inspirational speech from CEO Stuart Lonshien projected from New York via the new telecom system onto a giant screen in the second-floor conference room.

Lonshien addressed the staff worldwide like Moses from the mountain, proclaiming that they were not just the chosen people, but the chosen family; brothers and sisters united to support and help one another. It was important to reinforce familial unity at the beginning of the year in order to wipe away the stink from the year-end bonuses given a few weeks earlier.

Most agents, bruised and underwhelmed, felt like the agency always gave them enough to keep them there but never enough to make them happy. A choice few got perks such as stock options or new cars with official initials on the license plates. Sylvan Light had adopted that practice from Alliance. HK SLA was Harvey Khan in his Cadillac, GA SLA, Gil Amati in his Jaguar, SL SLA, Sam Lesser in his Mercedes 450 SL Coupe. Sylvan Light was the only company to purchase cars, but lease furniture.

"Leave the car, take the client," competitors would chide, referencing the famous cannoli line in *The Godfather,* when Sylvan Light clients began jumping ship to Alliance at an alarming rate. While Lesser had signed Cage, thanks to Beanie, he'd lost Swayze, Ackroyd, and Stallone. It was a bloodbath, and the industry held its breath to see how Sylvan Light could stop the bleeding.

There were rumors about a merger, which put everyone on edge since mergers meant redundancies and redundancies meant casualties. You couldn't have two heads of the television department, for example, so one would have to go. Mergers bred in-house competition, suspicion, and gossip, but they also seemed the only way to stay alive in a business that was quickly consolidating.

So, when Lonshien asked Sam Lesser, who was fond of neither speechifying nor hyperbole, to make an announcement at the worldwide staff meeting, the worldwide staff held its breath.

"The Sylvan Light Agency is legendary," Lesser said, his voice strong, his eyes piercing. "So it makes sense that a legendary agent has agreed to join our ranks as my partner."

There was palpable relief and excitement as the staff realized it wasn't a merger after all. It was a new hire. But it had to be someone big enough to make a difference.

People sat up straighter, leaning in. All that was missing was a drumroll as projected across the giant screens in New York, Memphis, London, and live in Los Angeles, Sam Lesser proudly announced that the one and only Sheila Day had agreed to come out of retirement and join him as co-head of the Sylvan Light Agency.

At first there was stunned silence, and then, with microphones on, resounding cheers from around the globe. This wasn't an announcement; it was an earthquake, a seismic shift in the bedrock of the industry. Short of a merger between Light and Alliance, nothing seemed bigger. And the best news was, no one would be fired.

Or so they thought.

The Light Agency was back, thanks to a five-foot-four-inch blond ballbuster who didn't play fools and didn't mince words.

"The Messiah has come," Sheila Day said as she waltzed into the room, dressed head to toe in Chanel, with heels high enough to lift their spirits.

Beanie Rosen was in awe. This was the woman she had seen on *60 Minutes,* the one who'd ignited the flame inside her. "She's a legend," she whispered to Ella, who while curious, wasn't quite as enamored.

Sheila Day, fifty-three years old, had essentially been Sam Lesser before her retirement four years earlier. She was brilliant, funny, flirtatious, strategic, and irresistible. Everyone in the industry worshiped at the altar of Sheila Day. To get a phone call from her was a treat. To get a lunch, a prize. And an invite to one of her exclusive dinner parties was an honor you would talk about for the rest of your life. With an impeccably cast guest list seated and served, her dinners were elegant, interesting, and the best seat in town. They were filled with "twinklies"—her famous word for stars, dignitaries, and scholars.

And to get her to come to one of your events was like entertaining royalty. Her approval, doled sparingly, meant everything, and her criticisms, plentiful and sharp, could cut to the core.

"Honeeeey," she'd say to an agent who wasn't dressed appropriately, "next time we're signing schleppers, I'll be sure to invite you." There were no comps when it came to Sheila Day. She put men on a pedestal and women on alert. "We want to play in their pen," she'd say. "We gotta look prettier, be smarter, and make them think that whatever we want was their idea." There was only one way with Sheila, and it was hers. If you tried to block her, she'd tear you up, mow you down, and never look back.

Born in 1931 in Düsseldorf, Germany, Chavala Gittleman immigrated with her mother, father, and baby sister to New York City. Chavala became Shavala who became Sheila. Her father chose the surname Day to distance himself from what he feared was global anti-semitism.

"But we're still Jews," he reminded his children, lest they forget from whence they came. He'd intended to move the family to California, but they never got farther west than Washington Heights. He wanted to give his daughter the world. Instead, he gave her his dreams of who she would be in the world.

"You can do anything," he told her.

And she believed him.

Her father never made it to Hollywood, but his daughter did.

In 1955, Sheila Day got a job as a file clerk in the New York office of the Sylvan Light Agency where she met and charmed producer Billy Rose. He taught her how to dress, talk, and what real style was. "He had class," she recalled in later years. She became his secretary, his wife, his ex-wife, then his agent.

"Honeeeey," she'd say, "I tried on a lot of shoes until I found the one that fit." Sheila Day Incorporated, a one-woman operation, opened its doors just off Broadway and Forty-fifth Street in October 1957 with a roster of mainly comedians and nightclub acts, all whom she'd met through Billy.

People in the business were rooting for her to win. They loved her moxie, her humor, and her fearlessness as she charmed her way to a reservation at the hottest restaurant, or a booking at the swankiest club. By 1959 she'd built a roster impressive enough to have one of the biggest agents on the West Coast call her when he was in town.

His name was David Schwartz. They had dinner. She signed him by dessert.

Sheila, whose ambition often eclipsed her client list, and sometimes her talent, was suddenly moving to "the coast," and working alongside Schwartz at STC saying *she* represented Judy Garland, Jackie Gleason, Gregory Peck, Liza Minnelli, and every other client on Schwartz's roster.

"Team player," she'd say, when he questioned her motives, and he'd laugh.

They became friends and ultimately partners. He signed Alana Campbell King, multitiered Grammy, Tony, Oscar–winning singer, actress, and director who was an industry within the industry.

He asked Sheila to help him. Instead she helped herself.

The two women became inseparable, unstoppable, redefining the female triple threat. Schwartz held up his hands in surrender.

"I give," he said. And Sheila took.

With Alana as her number one, she became a partner at STC and built a client list that was unparalleled. Even bigger than Sam Lesser's. Those she didn't represent, she'd court with not-so-innocent invitations to one of her legendary dinner parties, always strategically cast.

A voracious reader, Sheila would invite a writer or two, and then mix up her dinners with politicians, artists, socialists, socialites. People like Ryan O'Neal, Jackie Collins, Henry Kissinger, Jack Nicholson, Tom Wolfe, Bella Abzug, and the pièce de résistance, Jacqueline Kennedy Onassis.

The mere fact that someone with that pedigree would come to her home, someone so beautiful and well bred, and Waspy, made Sheila, by proximity, pedigreed, well-bred, and, she hoped, Waspy.

"A gal can dream," she would say.

She was ballsy and loud, with a sharp wit and a sharper tongue; quick to make judgments and slow to make apologies unless it got her the client.

"If you don't sign with me, I'm going to blame him," she'd say, pointing to a random agent, "and he's going to blame her," she'd say, pointing to someone else. "And we'll all tell each other what we could have done better. So, spare them the blame and just let us know: How do you like me so far?" The potential client would laugh and relax and sign.

Always.

Sheila had the golden touch until 1980 when Alana left her for Sam Lesser.

"Honeeeey," she joked to anyone who asked, "it ain't over until the fat lady sings." Then she'd put on one of Alana's albums.

She retired a few weeks later.

She was done.

FUCK 'EM

It's like changing deck chairs on the *Titanic.*
—SHEILA DAY, UPON GETTING AN OFFER
TO WORK AT SYLVAN LIGHT

1985

It had been Jamie Garland who'd first suggested that Sheila come out of retirement. Jamie wanted Sheila badly, not only because she revered her, but also because Jamie had put all her eggs in the Sylvan Light basket, and now that Sam Lesser was under attack, *she* felt vulnerable. It was a selfish decision on her part so that she wouldn't go down with the sinking ship. Sylvan Light was under attack from CAA, Morris, and Alliance, and they needed something, or, more specifically, someone, to change the narrative.

Jamie, believing that someone was Sheila Day, convinced the board that Sheila's reemergence would be a game changer, a kind of proclamation to the industry and a checkmate to the Alliance Group.

Persuading Sylvan Light to hire Sheila had not been difficult.

Persuading Sheila to take the job was.

Sheila had been devastated after Alana left, and now she went back and forth as to whether she wanted to jump back in the pool—or, as she called it, the cesspool. Jamie Garland and Gil Amati had enlisted Sam Lesser in a campaign to convince her that this would be the cherry on top of her career.

"Everyone needs to reinvent," Sam told her, convincing her that she'd been away enough time to create a sensation in her return.

"I promise you, Sheila," Jamie had said, "this will be a second act like no one has ever seen."

"More like a second coming," Sheila said, as she took a deep breath and finally agreed. Stating that her terms were non-negotiable, she asked for an unprecedented five million dollars for five years, with a mutual option for five additional years at one million two hundred and fifty thousand dollars per year, increasing each year by an additional fifty-thousand-dollar bump, making the entire deal worth more than twelve million dollars. Additionally, she wanted the A stock, a car of her choosing, unlimited first-class travel, and the brass ring, a seat on the Sylvan Light board of directors.

The board was stupefied by the request; Jamie Garland, astounded.

"No one gets a seat on the board," she told Sheila. "Not even Samuel Lesser, and the fact that a woman is asking, it's too much."

"Grow a pair," Sheila told her. "They scare you into thinking you deserve less. And I'm not scared."

There was only one thing that Sheila was afraid of, and that was failure. Once Alana had left, she knew it was only a matter of time before she would be the food in a feeding frenzy, pulled apart, while all her "friends" watched. The thought was paralyzing, which was why she'd retired. So, for her to go back into the ring, they had to offer enough security that she'd be set for life. She knew the score. Sylvan Light had become a dinosaur; a relic of the past with little old men standing on their pedestals holding the purse strings.

They wanted her, sure. They needed her, absolutely. But to get her, they were going to have to pay. The truth was, she'd retired before she'd made real money, the kind of crazy money that top agents were being paid now. So, this offer, while well timed, needed to be greased. And the Light board, who were in a bind, needed to dip their hands deep in the Crisco. They gave her the money she asked for, plus an optional five years with the bumps, and the autonomy to hire or fire any agent east or west. But they shot her down on the board seat.

So, she passed.

It was a standoff.

For months they considered other possibilities. Meanwhile, they were losing clients at an alarming rate and felt backed into a corner.

"Honeeeey," Sheila said when Harvey Khan called her to plead his case. "I'm looking for a lifetime appointment," she said. "Like the Supreme Court with dollar signs, and chicer robes." But the board at the Light Agency, much like the board at William Morris, was a closed book. There were seven seats and they all belonged to men. No negotiation. "If Mr. Light were alive he'd die," said Stu Lonshien, absolutely frustrated by the stalemate.

But Sheila Day wouldn't give.

Finally, after months of waiting, the board had no choice but to grant her a seat with the caveat that it would not be effective until the beginning of the tenth year of her tenure. They reasoned that by that time, January 1995, she would have either proven herself or be long gone.

It was a tremendous victory on every level. A woman had broken through the glass ceiling and would be sitting next to the men on the Sylvan Light board of directors, making crucial decisions and loads of money, and while Sheila didn't give a fuck about being a feminist, she did give a fuck about the money and the power that equality afforded.

Sheila Day was back in action.

Fuck 'em if they resented her ask. She would finally have a seat at the table.

HONEEEEY AND THE BEA . . . (NIE)

The worst way to get a mentor is to go find one. The best way is to see the one that is already there.

—JEFF GOINS

1985

Though Sheila Day had a secretary, and an assistant, Beanie, as departmental trainee, was asked to help her with her transition. Naturally, Beanie was nervous. She had heard that Sheila was tough, especially on women, and feared that all the progress she'd made in getting this far could be easily and suddenly taken from her.

Sitting on the temporary couch in her temporary office, Sheila Day took a long drag off a French cigarette and assessed Beanie Rosen in her brown trundle skirt and silk blouse with a bow tied at the neck.

"Honeeeey," Sheila said, "when God gives you hips, you shouldn't add more."

Beanie nodded, making a mental note to throw away the skirt.

"So," Sheila asked, "what the hell is a departmental trainee?"

Beanie began to explain her duties, but Sheila was bored five minutes into it.

"Let's get to the good stuff," she said. "You wanted off Barron's desk, didn't you?" Her eyes narrowed as she studied this young woman whom Jamie Garland had raved about.

"Yes," Beanie admitted.

Sheila nodded, taking another long drag. "Why?"

Beanie was noncommittal, and Sheila was growing bored.

"Honeeeey," she said, "speak now, or forever hold his piece."

Beanie laughed. Sheila didn't.

The Mike Barron debacle still paralyzed Beanie with fear.

Initially Barron had felt double-crossed, submarined, and thanks to an overabundance of cocaine, deeply paranoid.

What had Beanie said? What had Beanie done? Why had they all betrayed him? And the most crippling thought of all was whether she had spoken ill of him to Sam Lesser.

Fucking cunt, he thought, spinning out on the realization that not only had he been excluded from the Nicolas Cage signing, but from any discussion about her promotion. They took her off his desk without his permission, as if he didn't matter. Then the thought crept in: *What if they were going to take away his title, take away the training program? What if they were going to fucking fire him? Could they? Did they have cause? What if she talked?* She might make up stories about him. "I'll fucking show her," he'd said to himself as he worked through an entire eight ball alone in his Malibu retreat.

Mike Barron began bad-mouthing Beanie around town, implying disloyalty and a disregard for truth. He told people that he'd wanted her off his desk and even made an untoward association between her, Ella Gaddy, and Garry Fucking Sampson, insinuating that they were all fucking each other as they fucked him over. He had a small cadre of like-minded bullies, in and out of the agency, people who thrived on gossip, especially happy when others fell, and he made sure they'd spread the Beanie Rosen poison. Barron even went so far as to warn Gil Amati to be careful, saying that this new departmental trainee was not to be trusted, and he asked his father to say the same to Harvey Khan, urging him to convince Khan to put a stop to this promotion.

But Khan wouldn't override Lesser's decision and told Barron's father that Mike should focus on his own business. And that made Mike more paranoid. *What did he mean by that? Did Khan think Mike wasn't focused? What fucking lies had Beanie Rosen told them all? And who had helped her?* He instantly suspected Jamie Fucking Garland, who'd given Beanie a party after the promotion and had the balls to invite him.

Eat me, he thought, and never responded nor, obviously, attended.

Sheila pressed the intercom. "Get me an iced coffee," she told her male secretary. She liked men to work for her; to answer her phones, type her letters, get her coffee. "It's my own little Planet of the Apes," she had said to Rose Liu, who'd offered her every female executive secretary she'd had. "I like to switch it up," Sheila told her, plucking Eric out of the mailroom.

"Honeeeey," she'd told him, "you'll write books about this one day. And I'll sue."

"What the hell do you have over Mike Barron?" Sheila asked Beanie, telling her that he wanted her gone. "He's saying it all over town."

Oh no, Beanie thought. *Now Sheila Day isn't going to like me.* Beanie, whose eyes filled, felt stupid for crying. "I'm sorry," she said, trying to get control of her emotions. She didn't want to look weak, not in front of a woman who was so strong. But surprisingly, Sheila was compassionate, empathetic even. "Honeeeey," she told her, "Mike Barron running around trying to get you fired only makes you more interesting to me." She patted the seat next to her and said, "I know what *he* wants me to think of him. Now, tell me exactly who he is."

And though Beanie worried she would look disloyal or disgruntled, she also understood that with Barron there was no middle ground. It would be a fight to the death. And Beanie Rosen was not prepared to die.

Sitting next to Sheila, Beanie recalled every sordid detail, from the abuse, to the complaints, to the way he would leave clients' phone numbers with different agencies so that the client would leave Sylvan Light, making the responsible agent vulnerable, and making Barron, who held on to his own clients, more valuable. Beanie held nothing back.

And Sheila took it all in. Finally, she stubbed out her cigarette, stood up, and said, "Okay, we're done."

Beanie didn't know whether it was a test, and if so, had she failed? Ella had warned Beanie not to trust Sheila, confiding that both she and Garry

Sampson were wary of her, but Beanie liked her, believing that Sheila, much like Jamie Garland, was on her side.

The following week Beanie was asked to lunch with Sheila Day in a private room at Hernando's Hideaway, the same place where Sam Lesser had signed Nicolas Cage a few months earlier. Sheila asked her to come promptly at 1:15 that afternoon, and when Beanie arrived, this time in a power suit that showed off her legs and slimmed her hips, she saw Sheila tucked away in a corner with Mike Barron.

Barron noticed Beanie immediately, shooting daggers her way.

For her part, Beanie didn't know if this was a setup or a send-off.

Maybe Ella had been right. Maybe Sheila was going to punish her for speaking badly about Mike. She wanted to turn, run, or bypass them both and go to the restroom, but Sheila, seeing her, waved her over.

"You two know each other," Sheila said, gesturing for Beanie to sit beside her.

Beanie, confused, stiffly sat down next to Sheila, opposite Mike, who had a strange kind of crescent smile on his face. As she subconsciously wrapped her hand around the butter knife, Beanie, whose heart was in her throat, listened to Sheila explain that they were in the middle of discussing some of Mike's hopes for the future, and some of the stars he'd been targeting.

"Go ahead," Sheila said to him encouragingly.

Mike looked from Sheila to Beanie. "I'm sorry," he said finally, "but what is *she* doing here?"

Sheila apologized, explaining that she presumed he knew that Beanie Rosen was not only a brilliant departmental trainee but her protégé, and that she had found her to be honest, smart, and deeply informative as to the inner workings of the agents and the agency. "I've asked her to join me on certain lunches," said Sheila, staring directly into his eyes, "to help me decide who should stay and who should leave."

Then she ordered the chicken piccata.

Mike, already paranoid when invited to the lunch, was off the charts after it. Deeply shaken, he left the Beverly Wilshire Hotel, went straight to his main suppliers and bought all the cocaine they had, then went on a three-week bender, calling buyers, clients, making crazy accusations and nonsensical rants until even his coterie of like-minded bullies began to worry.

Drugs at the agency were an open secret and everyone, from Gil Amati to Phil Carter to the rich trainees who had access and means, dabbled. But this was on a different level. There were rumors that Barron was freebasing heroin, and while never substantiated, they served to fuel and expedite an ultimate decision.

"I think Barron has a drug problem," Sheila told Lesser, who told Lonshien, who told Khan, who told Leo Barron, who recommended his son go to rehab.

One month after the fateful lunch, Mike Barron took an extended leave of absence that turned into a hiatus that turned into a mutual understanding that there might be a different career in his future. And like an Olympic diver, Mike Barron went down without a splash. There was no fanfare, no big announcement, just a whiff of powder then *poof*! He was gone.

THE ENEMY WITHIN

Do I not destroy my enemies when I make them my friends?

—ABRAHAM LINCOLN

1985

Mercedes Baxter sat in her office just outside Harvey Khan's executive suites, sipping tea and looking through the latest *People* magazine, when she glanced up and saw Beanie Rosen, the new departmental trainee, standing before her.

She'd been furious when she'd heard that they not only were keeping Beanie but promoting her to some ridiculous new position.

"What the hell?" she'd said, immediately appealing to Khan, who had little interest in Mike Barron's secretary. There was enough on his plate, and he dismissed Mercedes's complaints as petty jealousy, which was so deeply insulting and fundamentally true that she didn't know how to respond.

"Lesser said she's a keeper," Khan told her, doubling down and adding that apparently it was Beanie who had been the lynchpin in signing Cage.

That, of course, made Mercedes's head spin. She hated that Beanie had earned some exalted position to both Lesser and now Khan, effectively wiping out all the nasty rumors about her that Barron had tried to spread. Neutered, Mercedes was helpless to do anything more than watch as Beanie navigated a system designed to keep her out. Mercedes didn't trust her. She never had.

And now Beanie Rosen was standing in front of her. To gloat? Perhaps. But there was something about her manner, her face, that made Mercedes let down her guard. A little.

"I'd like us to be friends," Beanie said humbly. She had timed this visit with precision, asking Hawkeye to let her know when Khan had left for lunch, so there wouldn't be an audience in case there was a scene.

Mercedes looked at her strangely, cocking her head from side to side like a parrot. "I thought we *were* friends," she said, not at all sounding friendly.

"I hope so," Beanie told her, earnestly adding, "and I'm sorry for anything I've done to make you think otherwise."

Mercedes clocked Beanie for insincerity or sarcasm. "You said some pretty awful things."

"I did," Beanie said, solicitously. "And I'm sorry. I was angry about Ollie, and I blamed you. That was unfair. I really am sorry, Mercedes," Beanie said.

They held each other's gaze.

"Okay," Mercedes said, and went back to her magazine.

That night Beanie felt utter and total relief. While she and Mercedes would never be friends, she believed and hoped that she had neutralized the threat and was finally out of her crosshairs.

"Honestly, it's all because of Sheila Day," Beanie said reverentially as Ella was eating a bowl of cornflakes. "She made me see that enemies from within can do more damage than anyone else."

"Spare me," Ella said, galled that Beanie was paying homage to a woman who had countless enemies everywhere. And Ella was one of them.

"What did she ever do to you?" Beanie asked.

Ella shrugged. "I don't like her," she said, recounting a call she'd heard where Sheila referred to Scott Westman, Garry Sampson, and Garry's girl as the "Goys R Us" trio, telling Garry that they needed to get some "Jew" in there.

Beanie laughed. "She was kidding."

"No, she wasn't," Ella countered. "She wants to represent Scotti."

Beanie shrugged. "So? What's wrong with that? She's a legend."

Ella picked up her bowl and walked away, saying it would never happen. "I don't like her and neither does Scotti."

Beanie was mortified. "You should not disparage Sheila Day to a client, much less Scott Westman," she said, following Ella into the living room. "She was just making a joke."

"Yeah, well, I don't like her humor," Ella said, relaying that Sheila came into the office the day before and told her that her skirt was so short she could almost see her cooch. "So, you know what I did?" Ella asked. "I spread my legs and said, 'This any better?'"

Ella and Sheila had resented each other from the start. Sheila thought Garry's girl was acting above her station and should be more deferential, and Ella thought Sheila, obnoxious and judgmental, was another form of all the women whom she'd rebelled against.

The feelings of dislike and distrust between these two women would not only grow but inform a trajectory that neither could have predicted.

SIGNING SUNDANCE

It was the tipping point. The game changer. The one signing that could change the course of her life.
—AN ANONYMOUS OBSERVER, REFERENCING BOTH SHEILA DAY AND BEANIE ROSEN

1985

Six months into her tenure, Sheila and Sam were on the cover of *Los Angeles Magazine* with the title, "We're baaack," signaling to the industry and the city built upon it that once again Sylvan Light was, if not on top, then within striking distance.

While the Alliance Group still reigned supreme with Stieglitz and Shipp, the top two agents in the land, Sheila Day and Sam Lesser went on a signing spree unlike anything the town had seen in years, bringing in stars when they could, coming close when they couldn't, but more importantly changing the narrative in such a way that it turned the tide, making everyone root for them. In a town where the best story wins, nothing was more compelling than an ex-champion coming back into the ring.

There was a fire underneath Sheila Day, and the competition, no longer laughing, were beginning to feel the heat. Funny, acerbic, self-effacing, and brilliant, people couldn't wait to see what she was going to do next. Agents like Gil Amati and Jamie Garland huddled close to her, but it was Beanie Rosen—tucked away in her small office across the street in the brand-new Sylvan Light Plaza—with whom she strategized.

Maybe Sheila was drawn to Beanie because she saw a version of herself in her—certainly less chic and sophisticated, but a rough-around-the-edges protégé, who with polishing might just be a lifetime devotee and a reflection of her own professional largesse.

Or maybe it was because Beanie never argued back. Anxious to please and to prove herself, Beanie became Sheila's de facto confidante. Though technically a departmental trainee for everyone, Beanie was literally the on-call girl for Sheila.

The only person who had an issue with it was Ella, but even she understood that Sheila Day might just elevate her best friend in a way no one else could. So she kept her disdain to herself. Or tried to.

"Sundance has agreed to a meeting," Sheila told Beanie one Tuesday morning in late September 1985. Sundance was the code word for Robert Redford, and the mere fact that he had agreed to a meeting with Sheila Day and Sam Lesser was an absolute sign that they had pierced the heart of the competition. And if they could dislodge him, if he agreed to sign, it would be a mortal wound. Redford was not only a legendary actor, Redford was an anchor to Alliance. Cut him loose and that ship might sink. This was seismic. In truth, it was less about the man, and more about the idea of the man; what he stood for. Signing Sundance became some sort of holy grail for Sheila Day. "I need this," she confessed to Beanie in a moment of vulnerability. Sheila knew she'd been flying on fumes and false bravado, camouflaging the pain of losing Alana years earlier, and the fear that others might follow. But if she signed Sundance now, that could carry her into a whole new version of herself. It would signal to an agency that had marginalized her value and an industry that had written her off, that Sheila Day was not to be discounted. It was in that moment that Beanie understood how frightened Sheila had been to start anew, and that signing Sundance was a door to a second chance she desperately needed.

"You'll fly to New York with me," Sheila informed Beanie rather than asking, assuming she would comply. Beanie always complied. That's what she liked best about her. "We'll stay the week, work out of the New York office. Sam's coming in on Wednesday or Thursday."

The plan was for Sheila and Sam to meet Redford in Connecticut on

Friday where he was shooting, and then she would stay the weekend with Gore Vidal, who had taken a cottage in East Hampton. Sam would stay with Redford at the Newmans' in Greenwich.

After being informed, Beanie, trying not to show how insanely excited she was, simply nodded, left, and headed back to her cubicle to cull through articles, unpublished books, screenplays, anything that might convince Redford that no one would work harder for him.

She practically skipped across the street. It wasn't just the trip, which, given the fact that she'd only been east once, was thrilling; it was the idea that she, Beanie Rosen, had not only been taken into Sheila's confidence but was an integral part of something bigger, a cog in a wheel that might change the future of the company.

And . . . since Sam Lesser was going, Moze would be there, too.

She and Moze barely saw each other anymore, and this could be an opportunity to spend time together, see a play, take a walk, hell, just stay in the hotel and order room service. They didn't have to have sex. They hadn't in a while. And she was frightened that his lack of interest was due to her, rather than the overwhelming amount of work he now had on his plate, which is what he claimed.

Devoted to Sam, Moze worked night and day, but Beanie knew that if she played her cards right, they might reconnect. She presumed they'd have the weekend in New York off, so she was going to gently suggest that maybe they could have it off together. She just had to wait for the right moment to bring it up, so it didn't seem contrived or desperate or demanding. Fortuitously, she and Moze had a date to see each other that evening and celebrate his birthday, which had been six weeks earlier and postponed twice.

"Sheila's asked me to fly to New York with her on this Sundance thing," she said casually that evening at his place, as if the thought had just occurred to her.

"Wow, that's great," Moze said, knowing how important this meeting was, and acknowledging that Sheila's trust in Beanie solidified Beanie's import. He was making them scrambled eggs in his small studio apartment just off Sunset in West Hollywood. She had helped him furnish it with a dining table which doubled as a desk, and an Eames chair that was losing its stuffing but still had its pedigree. "So, I thought maybe we could hang out on the weekend, since Sheila will be in Long Island and Sam in Connecticut." She looked at his face, illuminated by the yellow blinking sign from nearby Tower Records, trying to gauge if he was annoyed, if she'd gone too far. "I mean, if you're not busy."

He brought the eggs over to her. One plate, two forks. "I was going to see my folks," he said, "you know, reconnect with the shtetel."

She nodded, took a breath. He had plans. Of course. She should have figured. "Okay," she said, no longer interested in food . . . or life. "No worries."

He looked at her a moment, considering. "I mean, you're welcome to come. If you want. They'd fucking love you," he said matter-of-factly, piercing some eggs with his fork and bringing it to her mouth. "Open," he commanded.

She did, but the rest of her stood paralyzed. Had she heard him correctly? He was offering to introduce her to his parents. His tribe? The innermost circle of his heart. It was too much to hope for and yet, at this moment, it seemed possible.

"Chew," he said, smiling, and she smiled back.

They were the best eggs she'd ever eaten.

While Sheila and Sam were off trying to sign Sundance, Beanie and Moze took the subway to Flatbush. Moze showed her around his old neighborhood: his yeshiva, the butcher, the fishmonger, the matchmaker.

She inhaled every second. Everyone thought she was his girl, and the best part was, he let them. At first she protested self-consciously, but then she stopped. *If he doesn't mind, why should I?* The finest table at Delmonico's couldn't have lured her away from that early fall afternoon deep in the borough of Brooklyn.

"Tell me darling, how is Moze doing out there?" Esther Goff asked Beanie confidentially as they sat on a loveseat in the living room she called the parlor, crammed with a lifetime of worn furniture, ancient photographs, and all their hopes for their prodigal son. On the mantel of a non-working fireplace sat pictures of Moze at every stage of life with an empty frame left for the next generation.

"He's doing great," Beanie said. "Amazing, actually."

Esther leaned in. "But he's a secretary? Answering somebody's phone. Typing their letters." She whispered so her husband and Moze, sitting nearby at the Formica kitchen table, watching a Mets game, wouldn't hear. "My husband doesn't know the details. He wouldn't understand," she confided.

Beanie took her hand, reassuringly. "Mrs. Goff," she said, "Moze has one of the most important positions not only at Sylvan Light, but honestly in the whole entertainment industry. You don't need to worry, I promise." Esther Goff studied Beanie Rosen and decided she liked her. She liked her a great deal.

"You'll stay for dinner. No arguments," she told her.

Initially, Moze and Beanie had planned to spend only the afternoon in Brooklyn, have lunch, walk around, and then grab a bite in the city. But there was no arguing with Esther Goff. They were staying for dinner.

That night, Beanie met more of his family and some friends who may or may not have been related. The shtetl embraced her as their own. Moses had come home, and with a Rosen no less. She felt like she was one of them, and Moze's parents made sure their son knew they hoped she would be.

"Bring her again!" his father told him.

"Don't be a stranger," said his mother, looking deeply into the eyes of the young woman she hoped would be her future daughter-in-law. Just before they left, she had one last request. "Let's take a snapshot of the two of you." She pulled an Instamatic camera off the shelf and posed them together.

Beanie stood self-consciously stiff, but Moze lazily draped his arm over her shoulder.

They held hands all the way back to the city and stayed in Moze's room at the Lowell all weekend where they ordered room service *and* had sex. Three times. Any doubts she'd had about their relationship or his feelings for her had been allayed. While untraditional, they had something special and deep, and she felt certain that if she could be patient it would develop into something more permanent.

Just before Christmas, Samuel Lesser and Sheila Day announced that Robert Redford was now a client of the Sylvan Light Agency. But the biggest holiday gift, at least for Beanie Rosen, happened a week later when she learned from Moze that Mr. and Mrs. Goff had put her picture on their mantel.

Though it was winter, it felt like spring.

Both she and Sheila had signed their Sundance, giving each a peek into a world of possibilities.

A STRANGE FLU

Man is not what he thinks he is. He is what he hides.

—ARISTOTLE

1986

By Christmas 1985, the agency had reemerged as the powerhouse it had once been. Sheila and Sam were an unbeatable team, and Beanie, though not directly working for either, felt connected to both. It was a great way to end the year and kick off the holidays.

Ella was housesitting in Malibu for Scott Westman and invited a few friends to spend the holiday weekend at the breathtaking estate, built on a bluff overlooking the Pacific Ocean. In addition to the main house, there were three separate casitas, enough to sleep six couples comfortably. Of course, she'd invited Beanie and Moze, but Sam had come down with the flu and Moze felt he had to stay close. Barry also begged off due to work, but Garry Sampson and his new fiancée, Meghan, said they'd come, and Veronica Hamel and her boyfriend also accepted.

"You're *my* date," Ella said to Beanie, "at least until Scotti gets here."

There was an unspoken understanding in their small circle that Ella and Westman were together. No one questioned exactly what that meant, especially since it seemed to be sanctioned by Garry Sampson. How Ella had managed that Beanie wasn't sure, but from his former lover and current secretary she had morphed into his best friend, trusted adviser, and love barometer, even when it came to Sampson's search for a soulmate. Ella lived a life by her own design, never giving fuel to the many raised eyebrows or whispered innuendos about her affair first with her boss and now with the biggest star in the world.

She doesn't give a hoot what people say, Beanie thought, *and that gives her immunity against them.*

Beanie, who had put in for vacation time, planned to stay the whole week between Christmas and New Year's with Ella, hoping that Moze would join on either one of the weekends, but as soon as she arrived and beeped into her answering machine she began repacking.

"Is this because Moze didn't come?" Ella asked, hurt and a bit offended.

They'd planned this for almost a month, and she'd even given Beanie the guest room in the main house, with the new queen bed overlooking the Pacific.

"No, I swear," Beanie said, adding that it was an urgent work matter, but she would be back on Christmas—or the day after, at the latest.

"What is it that can't wait?" Ella asked, not settling for the oblique excuse offered. Beanie took a deep breath.

"Sheila Day was invited to Bette Midler's house for Christmas," Beanie told her.

"Who gives a fuck?" Ella said, her suspicions confirmed that Beanie's abrupt departure had less to do with an emergency and more to do with kissing the ass of a woman Ella detested.

"She called me personally. I mean it was her voice on our machine, asking me to make a list of potential projects for Bette so she could try to sign her. I need to get back to the office today to access the database and prepare everything for tomorrow." Beanie picked up her overnight bag and again reassured Ella that she'd be back as soon as she was finished.

"It's Christmas fucking Eve," Ella said.

"According to Sheila," Beanie told her, "the holidays are the best time to sign. Actors get end-of-the-year jitters, and Sheila likes to take advantage of that."

"That's the spirit," Ella muttered, resentful that Beanie was a party to this manipulation.

While Beanie felt bad for letting Ella down, she also felt a bit emancipated, secretly hoping that she and Moze could get together for a day, maybe two. She would deal with Ella's disappointment later.

It took her less than an hour to drive to Beverly Hills.

She immediately went downstairs to see if Moze was in the office doing something for Sam, but he wasn't. Given that it was Christmas Eve, the whole building was pretty empty. *He's probably at Sam's house,* she thought, leaving him a message that she, too, was working in town all weekend and maybe they could hook up.

Back in her office, she spent a few hours going through all the databases and pulling synopses of all the scripts that could be right for Bette, including those with male leads that could be switched to female. She didn't finish until after seven, and then took the signing binder to Sheila's home, stopping first at a pay phone and leaving another message for Moze saying that she was going home to shower, then maybe they'd grab dinner.

"Come out, come out wherever you are," she said playfully into his machine.

And he did.

Twenty minutes later she found Moze lying on what once was Mercedes's pastel couch in Beanie's apartment getting deep-throated by Barry Licht. She had never seen two men having sex, oral or otherwise, and except for the fact that one of them was her current lover getting blown by her ex, she did think it was kind of hot.

For a moment they all stupidly stared, paralyzed mid-blow—or was it suck? She wasn't sure.

Finally, she said to Moze, "I guess you should have kept working for Gil Amati after all," and then walked out.

Moze, putting on a pair of shorts, followed, shouting for her to wait up.

"You like guys?" she said, turning on him.

"Yeah," he told her. "What's the big deal?"

"I mean," she started, unsure how to answer, "you introduced me to your parents." She was leaning against the Swinger, shaking her head laughing.

"So . . . ?"

"Never mind," she told him, getting into her car.

He held the door open. "What did you think was going to happen? We'd get married? Raise little agents?"

She slammed the door. "Fuck you!" she screamed.

"What don't you get?" he shouted back, pacing in front of the car. She had never seen Moze so out of control. He shook his head and balled up his fists in utter frustration. Finally, he walked up to the car door and opened it.

"What don't you get?" he asked again, only this time gently. "I'm not traditional," he said.

"Yeah, I know," she replied, starting the engine. "You told me." She was broken-hearted, less for what she'd lost and more for the idea of what she'd lost.

Christmas and New Year's came and went. They didn't talk again, not really. If they saw each other in the hall at work, they'd nod or smile, but he seemed preoccupied, distant. In truth, he was.

For the first two months of 1986, Sam Lesser had been in and out of Cedars-Sinai, exhausted by a strange flu he couldn't shake. He came back to the office in early March, but only for a few hours each day, dozens of calls left unreturned, many of them from star clients.

Moze did his best to juggle, enlisting and entrusting Garry. The two would send scripts, make appointments on Sam's behalf, and try to handle as much as they could without sending up an alarm. But on April 15, the alarm sounded regardless: Redford sent a termination letter firing the Light Agency and returning to Alliance. He stated that he'd barely heard from Sam, and while Sheila was a lot of laughs, he'd signed with Lesser.

Trivialized and marginalized, and once again frightened that others might follow, Sheila Day never showed how hurt she was. Instead, she brushed the whole thing off. "Hubbell Gardiner, he's not," she'd say to anyone who asked, and focused her attention on her new client Bette Midler and her other stars that needed tending.

But acutely aware that, like it or not, Redford had been correct in his claims that Lesser had been absent, Sheila worried that something was wrong, terribly wrong. Lesser signed the superstar, then disappeared.

She asked Moze, she asked Garry, but both just said he had a strange flu.

By May, Sam Lesser stopped coming in altogether; by June, he'd stopped returning calls to the board of directors, his friends, and all but a few of his clients.

Moze Goff became the conduit to everyone in the agency and the industry, claiming that Sam was recovering from a bronchial infection. But taking Garry's advice, Moze had confided to both the board and the senior management, including Sheila Day, that perhaps they should temporarily reassign Sam's clients until he recovered.

Suddenly Sheila Day, Gil Amati, and Jamie Garland were handling or trying to handle the massive list of stars and filmmakers who were beginning to feel Sam's absence. But no one other than Moze and Garry knew just how bad it was.

Together, they braced themselves for a truth neither wanted to face.

On July 25, one year to the day that Rock Hudson's publicist had announced to the world that the matinee idol, with his gaunt appearance and slurred speech, did in fact suffer from AIDS, Sam Lesser, whose face had aged twenty years and body had withered to 147 pounds, died from the same disease.

Disgusted that Hudson's publicist had gone public after Hudson had specifically instructed otherwise, Sam, upon learning the truth of his own diagnosis, leaned over to his companion Johnny Merritt and to Garry Sampson.

"Never tell," he told them.

The announcement was made official July 26, 1986.

Samuel Lesser had died from complications of pneumonia . . . and a strange flu.

GOOD MOURNING

Hollywood is a place that wishes you well when you are terminally ill.

—NED TANEN

1986

The largest chapel at Westwood Village Memorial Park was overflowing with heads of state, filmmakers, movie stars, Pulitzer Prize–winning authors, studio chiefs, foreign dignitaries, and the powerful men who ran Hollywood. Swifty Lazar, Lew Wasserman, Frank Yablans, Matthew Stieglitz, Stephen Ross, David Schwartz, David Shipp, and Freddie Fields offered condolences to the Sylvan Light board of directors.

It's like a scene out of The Godfather, Beanie thought, watching from the cheap seats. All five families were paying their respects while silently divvying up the spoils.

A little after eleven o'clock, everyone took their seats. From a distance Beanie observed the dance as the once powerful old guard gave way to newer, younger versions of themselves; all running too fast, laughing too loud, spending too easily to notice that their futures were sitting just across the aisle. The ex-agents, the ex-studio heads, the ex-wives, were now nothing more than footnotes in a chapter of a book nobody had read for ages. Beanie watched Sheila, who was watching Stieglitz, who was watching Stallone, who was offering condolences to Johnny Merritt, who was weeping openly.

It's a dance of knives, she thought.

Almost everyone at the memorial had been represented by Sam or Sheila or both, and a good majority of them had left the agency. Or were planning to. It was brutal, but Sheila put on a good show, never betraying how frightened she was.

But she was frightened. She didn't need this. She didn't want it.

"They're not paying me enough," she had told Jamie Garland after she'd heard the news about Sam. She'd come out of retirement to put a cherry on top of her career, and now she had a target on her back. She did everything she could to act like it was business as usual, but inside she was terrified. It was just a matter of time before the friendly smiles and reassurances turned to clandestine dinners and letters of termination.

She tried her best to prepare herself and the board, calling an emergency meeting a week after the memorial, and asking Beanie to take notes.

Gathered in Sam's offices alongside his longtime secretary, Anita Lejos, and Moze Goff, were hand-selected senior agents, including those from the East Coast who'd flown in to join Harvey Khan, Jamie Garland, Gil Amati, and Garry Sampson, in figuring out next steps.

It seemed disrespectful to Anita to hold the meeting in Sam's space, but Sheila, trying to lighten the mood, said, "Honeeeey, it was disrespectful that he died. Besides," she told her, "we need access to his files, his Rolodex, and his magic." Her voice cracked, more from fear than from sadness.

Moze, who had been praised for the way he'd handled things, had been quietly promoted to agent in the hopes that he, under the supervision of Garry Sampson, could keep a few of the hotter, younger clients like Nicolas Cage and Matthew Modine—who'd been a recent signing.

"We can't lose them," Sheila said to Moze, less a concern and more an edict.

Moze plus Garry equaled Sam, in Sheila's eyes, and that was how they had to sell it.

The irony that Moze was not only an agent, but now in the inner circle while Beanie, on the periphery, was still taking notes, had not been lost on her. But the whole company was in survival mode, and Beanie had to put aside all personal issues. It was as if she and Moze never were.

Perhaps we weren't, she told herself. But then her thoughts would drift to the way he'd become a staple at holiday dinners with her family, the way Miriam would look with pride at him, and by association, at her daughter.

Landing Moze had signaled that Beanie wasn't a loser who would end up alone with a hot fudge sundae and a cat—or seven. And it wasn't just her mother who'd embraced "her fella"; Dr. Spitz invited Moze for golf at Hillcrest, and even the skinny twins sought him out for advice. They were all awaiting a formal announcement or proclamation cementing Moze as one of their own. And she would disappoint them. Again.

Beanie supposed she could have granted their wish, as long as she closed her eyes when he fucked the caddy or the pool boy or any random port in the storm that suited his fluidity.

"Whatever makes you happy, darling," she should have said when she'd walked in on him and Barry. Or maybe she should have been nonchalant and simply put a sheet down so they wouldn't get lube on what was once Mercedes's pastel couch. Moze had told her, after all, that he was untraditional, and she had moved her lines as best she could. But this line was outside any picture she'd imagined of a life, even one with blurry lines. And then to add insult to blow jobs, after the *Beanie interruptus,* Barry moved out from Beanie and into Moze, so to speak, falling into his life as if he'd never leave.

But he would, eventually. Everyone did.

Moze was a live-by-the-seat-of-your-pants kind of guy, and there were a whole lot of seats and pants on the horizon. Barry, like Beanie, would find out the hard way.

Sheila's rising voice snapped Beanie back to reality.

"Clients either take meetings or take advantage, asking for reduced commissions, which is unacceptable." It was a pep talk that had turned into a tirade. Sheila had seen this before. Turnover, defections, deaths: it was all low-hanging fruit to the competition.

In the immediate, the agency was able to hang on to their anchors, the clients that kept the lights on. But the trades and gossips, and even the nightly news, were spinning a different tale. "An Agency Under Siege," they reported, as they lay in wait for their stories to self-fulfill.

"What the hell?" Harvey Khan said to Mercedes Baxter as he read article after article, throwing them across the room in frustration. After

Redford, no one had left the agency, not yet, but with this kind of scrutiny they would. The press was presuming and perhaps craving a bloodbath, and it was only a matter of time, he feared, before clients, perceiving their agency was in trouble, would look elsewhere to find a more stable home.

Khan was worried about the future of the agency, and Mercedes was worried about the future of Khan. Eight years older than Lesser, he was starting to have issues with his blood pressure. Mercedes had already been the accommodating lover of a wealthy man in an unhappy marriage, and didn't want, God forbid, to end up again with the short end of a wife's vitriol.

This time she tended to both the husband and the wife, monitoring Khan's stress levels and Grace's growing addiction to drugs and alcohol. She had neither conscience nor guilt that she had been the person to whom Grace had turned when seeking advice. Having been burned years earlier, Mercedes angled to be on the inside; guiding, advising, solidifying all ends toward her means. And after she'd checked Grace into the relatively new Betty Ford Center for drug and alcohol abuse, she was able to be with Khan practically every night, all the while encouraging his wife to focus on herself.

Sam's passing had been a reality check, putting Harvey's life and life choices top of mind. Mercedes, wanting to calm the seas, urged Khan to work in tandem with Sheila Day to help steady the ship, pointing out that Sam, brilliant as he was, had marginalized Khan, often keeping him outside of his deals and away from his clients. But Sheila wanted to include Khan, and Mercedes believed they could work together in a way that Harvey and Sam never had.

"It's going to be better in the long run," she told him.

And handing the reins to Sheila, at Mercedes's behest, he began to think so, too.

With Khan's endorsement and support, Sheila went to work changing the narrative. "They have the young turds," Sheila would say to the press, purposely mispronouncing "Young Turks"—the name given the newest crop of

Alliance agents. "We have the old broad," she'd add, turning their criticism of her on its ear.

Her humor saved them from bleeding out. She knew she couldn't beat the competition in terms of aggression or youth, so she leaned into legacy, experience, and wit, making the oldest agency in the world the underdog. People not only began rooting for Light, but they also began rooting for Sheila. They wanted her to win.

Reinforcing that narrative, Sheila advised that agents take clients into their confidence, asking for time to prove they could do the job. That tactic not only made the clients stand with the agents, but it undercut the sincerity of their other pursuers. The competition looked like bullies, picking on the beleaguered agency, trying to sign everyone and anyone, less out of passion and more out of a need to destroy. It became a sign of solidarity to stand with the old guard.

Sheila and her inner circle worked tirelessly, meeting each client, and each client's demands, empowering her lieutenants, encouraging them to take on more. Moze Goff seconded Garry Sampson on many of Sam's stars, while Sheila partnered with Gil Amati on the legacy clients such as Goldie Hawn, Stanley Kramer, and Warren Beatty.

Additionally, Sheila and Jamie Garland reinforced Candice Bergen's representation, which had been in question and, equally significant, they managed to secure the representation of Debra Winger, one of the biggest female stars in the world, signaling to the industry that Light wasn't just playing defense.

Sheila had magnificently steered the ship clear of danger, but with blinders on; she failed to recognize other obstacles—namely, the competition's pursuit of her key agents.

GO WEST . . . MAN

The king is dead. Long live the king.

—THE ROYAL SUBJECTS

1986

Less than five months after Sam died, Garry Sampson—a person whom Sheila had begun to rely on and also a person whom she had really begun to enjoy—asked if they could talk.

It was never a good sign when an agent asked to talk. It usually meant they wanted a raise or wanted to leave. For a stalwart like Sampson, Sheila assumed it was the former.

She assumed wrong.

Garry sat across from her and told her he was a bit lost without Sam and that he'd been made an offer to run Orion Pictures, and had, after much deliberation, decided to take it.

"You can't," Sheila said, as if her vote or her voice mattered. "You can't," she said again, waiting for her vocabulary to catch up with the terror rising from her gut.

Garry smiled and shook his head, which gave her an indication that maybe he hadn't made up his mind. Not completely.

It was an in, and she clawed at it with the will and the might of a person hanging on for dear life. Because that's how she felt. If someone like Garry Sampson left—someone who had been so close to Sam, who had taken on many of Sam's clients, and had, himself, the biggest star in the world with Scott Westman—that would be devastating, communicating that Sylvan Light hadn't been good enough to keep him; that *she* hadn't been good enough to keep him.

"Give me a year," she pleaded, reasoning that moving a client once was tricky, twice was death. They were barely getting back on their feet. "Please," she said again, her eyes filling with tears of desperation. "I can't make it without you."

Garry felt bad, and for a moment reconsidered. *I could put it off for a while*, he thought. *Make sure the clients are solid; the agency on terra firma.*

Sheila watched him wrestle internally with the dilemma.

"This is your agency," she said, trying to push his decision over the goal line. "Don't kill us while we're down on one knee."

She almost had him. She could tell.

"Name your price," she said. "Everyone's got a number."

And that's how she lost him.

There's a balancing act in a negotiation, a moment where the other party might yield; a tipping point that you can feel, where you can gain the advantage. In this instance, Sheila, miscalculating her opponent, not only lost the advantage but solidified his decision.

Garry Sampson couldn't be bought.

It was a mistake she made both in judgment and in character, and one she'd make again later, resulting in her own demise. He didn't want to work for someone who valued money more than loyalty. And nothing she said after that would convince him otherwise.

She took a guess in the game of chance and guessed wrong.

Garry shook his head sadly and told her that his heart was no longer in it. Without Sam there, he was rudderless. It wasn't just the offer; it was the echo of what and who had come before. He couldn't do it. He couldn't walk the halls without the man who had taught him how.

He told Sheila that he respected her and all she'd done to right the ship, but it was time for him to try something new: He would be a buyer, the head of a new studio, fat with money and opportunity . . .

Sheila didn't hear the rest. She was in a full-on panic as he explained that he would do his best to keep almost all his clients at the agency.

That snapped her back to reality.

"What do you mean, '*almost*'?" she asked, eyes narrowing, trying to understand what he wasn't saying.

And that's when he dropped the second bombshell: Scott Westman would not be staying.

The air left the room as Garry admitted that Westman had already had preliminary conversations with David Shipp at Alliance.

She didn't hear the rest. Not clearly. She knew Garry apologized again, and he made some attempt at reassuring her, but he left a few minutes later.

For a minute, everything slowed down. Then she went into hyperdrive.

She was mad, spitting mad, and called an emergency meeting in Khan's office, summoning Garry downstairs and asking him to repeat it all for the executive committee.

Garry swore to them that he had done everything he could to try to keep Scott Westman at the agency. He apologized to the group of agents Khan had assembled, including Amati, Jamie, Moze, with whom he shared many clients, Randy Fink, who'd once been accused of raping his sexitary and was now head of the television department, and a few of the heavyweights on speakerphone from the New York office.

"Have Westman meet with us," Sheila said to Garry. "It's the least you could do." It was more a command than a request.

But he shook his head, explaining that Scott didn't want to meet.

"Why not?" Sheila asked, adding that Scott didn't know her enough to hate her.

But even her humor couldn't mask her pain and then rage when Garry explained that Scott had been quite certain that with Sam and Garry gone, it was time for him to move on.

That was when Sheila lost it.

"Why the fuck would you tell him you were leaving before you told us?" she screamed.

Everyone shifted uncomfortably.

Harvey Khan tried to calm things down. They needed Garry's

friendship now more than ever, and until the rest of his clients were reassigned, they couldn't afford to alienate him.

But Garry shrugged it off, and said simply that he and Scott were friends, best friends, and their relationship was such that he couldn't keep something this big a secret.

"Honeeeey," Sheila said, lighting a cigarette and gathering her wits, "they're not our friends, no matter what you think. Just ask Alana."

Garry apologized and promised he'd call the other clients when he was back from New York.

"Fuck me," Sheila said after he'd left.

Stu Lonshien—on speakerphone—told her that they needed to cut their losses and make sure everyone else was secure.

But Sheila wasn't giving up on Westman. Not by a long shot. "If one leaves, they all leave," she said. They couldn't just lay down like that. They couldn't allow it to happen. Not without a fight. To lose someone as valuable as Scott Westman would open the floodgates. He was too big a star, too much an icon. She looked around the room accusingly. How was it possible that no one else had a relationship with him?

Everyone shrugged, looking at each other.

Finally, it was Amati who spoke. "He was a recluse, only close to Lesser, and Sampson," Amati said, admitting that he'd invited him to countless dinners, Oscar parties, and that Westman only showed once to a private screening of a Bertolucci film, and then left before the lights came up.

"You should ask Ella," Moze said, standing in the corner by the door.

Sheila looked at him blankly.

"Who?"

"Ella Gaddy. Garry Sampson's secretary," he explained.

Sheila screwed up her face. "That long-legged giraffe with the ruffled skirts up to her ass and the bad dye job?" she asked disbelievingly. Ella had always been disrespectful to Sheila, and the thought that *she* would ask *her* for help absolutely galled her. She looked at Moze like he was nuts, but he explained that Ella and Scott were close.

"Define close," she said, narrowing her eyes.

He shrugged and said he wasn't sure but told her they spent weekends together, vacationed, and spoke almost every day.

Sheila was astonished. "That tacky broad who walks around with her tits hanging out is the only other person at this agency who this guy listens to?" she asked, aghast. "Fuck me," she said, taking one last drag off her cigarette.

The next day Sheila stopped by Garry Sampson's office, where Ella Gaddy was packing up files. "I hear you're close to Scott Westman," she stated, trying to sound nonplussed.

Ella looked up without deference or surprise. "Yes. Very."

Holy fuck, Sheila hated this broad. "Good," Sheila said, adding that she knew Scott wanted to leave the agency and would appreciate the opportunity to meet with him. "Please," she hissed, not masking her anger. Sheila turned to walk away, then turned back. "Oh, and honnneeeeey," she said, "remind me to give you the name of my hair colorist. Maybe he can help." Then Sheila left.

Two days later, after she hadn't heard anything, she summoned Ella to her office.

"Did you do what I said?" asked Sheila.

"No," Ella told her, unafraid and unintimidated.

"Are you going to?"

"Nope," said Ella.

Sheila nodded and Ella left.

If Ella Gaddy wasn't going to work with Garry Sampson in his new position, she'd have fired her right there. But Sheila was smart enough to realize that with Ella that close to Westman, firing her would only solidify his resolve.

Still she was floored and in truth a bit intimidated by Ella's arrogance.

"Self-righteous *kooze,*" she said to Moze, whom she called immediately. "Least she could have done was lie and say she'd tried," Sheila told him. "But this fucking bitch wants me to know she's not playing."

"You can ask Beanie Rosen to ask Ella," Moze said, explaining that they were best friends and roommates, and Beanie was one of the only people that Ella really listened to.

Sheila was momentarily stunned. "Roommates?" she said, turning the concept over in her mind.

She had no idea they were even friendly. After all, she'd considered Beanie to be part of her inner circle; a loyalist, a protégé, so to learn that Beanie was that close to someone so disrespectful, so arrogant, genuinely threw her.

Moze explained that Beanie was the hub of a wheel to which many people were connected, and that it was probably the only chance they had.

Five minutes later Sheila was demanding that Beanie get through to that cheap tacky numbskull roommate of hers and convince her to convince Scott Westman to have a fucking meeting.

Beanie could tell that Sheila wasn't just angry, she was embarrassed. Her vulnerability made Beanie sad.

"Honeeeey," Sheila said, eyes full of emotion, "you're my last shot."

That night Beanie reasoned and pleaded and practically begged Ella to help.

But Ella was resolute, telling her that the reason Scott Westman wouldn't consider staying at Sylvan Light was *because* of Sheila. Garry had been too polite to tell Sheila the truth and he'd asked Ella not to as well.

"He fucking hates her as much as I do," Ella said.

Which made no sense to Beanie. Scott barely knew Sheila Day. In fact, Sheila only met him once at the memorial. No, Scott hated Sheila because Ella hated Sheila.

"You haven't even given her a chance," Beanie said.

"Why should I?" asked Ella.

"Because she gave me one," Beanie told her honestly. "And I owe her."

And that was the one thing that Ella couldn't argue away. All Beanie was asking for was a meeting with Scott Westman, just so the agency could save face, if not save a client.

"Please, ask him to think about it," Beanie said. "Please."

. . .

The following week Scott Westman came into Harvey Khan's office. It had been decided that meeting in Sam's office would feel disrespectful, and in Sheila's might feel uncomfortable, and Amati was not important enough.

Mercedes Baxter walked Scott, Garry Sampson, and Ella Gaddy down the hall.

Upon seeing that Ella was joining the meeting Sheila thought, *Sure, he brings the kurveh with him.* But she smiled and welcomed them all, thanking him again for making time.

"I appreciate it," she said directly to Ella, who nodded and looked away.

Fucking cunt, Sheila thought, hating the fact that this secretary would be witness to the groveling she knew was to come.

Stu Lonshien had flown in from New York, and Jamie Garland, whom Scott had met and liked, was also there. Noticeably nervous, Sheila chain-smoked while Harvey regaled Scott, who was a big Elvis fan, with stories of the early days when he used to look after the King and the Colonel. Garry was helpful in filling in the blanks for Scott on who everyone was, and Scott seemed engaged and interested, and he even laughed a little at some of Sheila's jokes.

Finally Sheila got down to it, thanking Scott again for taking the meeting and telling him she understood he didn't want to be there if the two people who'd represented him were no longer at the company. But she pointed out, both of those men loved this agency, and if he was going to start over, the question was: Would he be open to starting over at Sylvan Light? "If only to honor the legacy of what came before," Sheila said, asking for three months, and assuring him that he could pick any one of them to be his agent.

"If it doesn't feel right, if you're not happy, then you leave," she told him. "We might cry a little," she joked, but then quietly added, "but we'll never forget it."

She had openly and earnestly begged for a fighting chance. It was a powerful plea, and Scott, deeply moved, looked around the room at the anxious faces, most of whom he'd never met before, and made an instant decision.

"Okay, I'll stay."

Then he added, "On one condition." Everyone held their breath.

"All right, I'll sleep with you," Sheila joked, breaking the tension.

Everyone laughed. Except Ella.

"Tell us, son, what do you want?" Harvey Khan asked.

Scott got a kind of crooked smile on his face, as the thought became an idea and the idea caught fire.

"I want you to make Ella Gaddy my agent," he told them.

Once again, Sheila felt like the air had been sucked out of the room.

This was a joke. A cosmic joke. Surely Allen Funt would pop out from behind the rubber tree and tell her it was a goof, that Ella was a goof. No one in their right mind would choose that tacky long-legged bird over one of the most powerful female agents in history.

Yet he had.

And he wasn't joking.

"Who?" Harvey asked, confused.

"Garry's secretary," Jamie whispered.

"Ella," Scott said, politely correcting Jamie, while walking over to Ella and extolling her virtues. He told them that she was the smartest person in any room, brilliant with material, and beyond reproach in terms of her ethics and her word. He swore if they made her his agent, he'd stay. And he wouldn't be counting the months. This would be his home.

He'd never leave Ella.

"But she's going with Sampson to Orion," Sheila said, the words sticking in her throat.

Scott turned to her. "Would you stay instead?" he asked.

It's like watching a proposal, Sheila thought, aghast. *If he gets on one knee, I'm done.*

Ella looked at him, then at Garry, then everyone in the room, and broke into a big smile.

"Heck, yeah," she said. "That sounds fun."

Harvey, overjoyed, jumped up, shook Ella's hand, and said, "Welcome to the club, Ella Gaddy!" Lonshien seconded it, as did Jamie, who hugged her as Sheila sat frozen, swallowing the bile that had risen in her throat.

"Good. Good," Sheila said, finally finding her voice. "You're tough and shrewd and you'll be a fine agent. But we'll need a backup, obviously," she told them.

Amati quickly agreed, explaining that every star had two agents. Jamie added that since Ella was new to the position, it made sense that there should be two agents, so nothing fell through the cracks. Amati gladly volunteered, as did Jamie, but it was finally Harvey Khan, acting as a kind of referee emeritus, who decided that Sheila Day made the most sense.

"I think with two strong women behind you, you'll be well covered," he said, pointing out that with Ella's moxie and Sheila's expertise they would be an unbeatable duo.

Scott nodded, looked at Ella and asked what she thought, which annoyed Sheila to no end. *Does she hold his dick when he fucking pees?* she thought.

But surprisingly Ella agreed with Harvey Khan. She thought that two strong women were a great idea, but instead of Sheila—respectfully, of course—she suggested Beanie Rosen join her, telling everyone that Scott already knew Beanie. "And honestly if y'all think I'm smart, you'll just be blown away by the Bean. Wait 'til you see what we can do together," she told the group, with a twinkle in her eye.

Twenty minutes later Beanie Rosen was summoned to Harvey Khan's office with pomp, circumstance, and a glass of champagne.

Served to her by Mercedes Baxter.

And just like that, the Southern girl from Accounting and the Valley girl from Central Files became agents at the Sylvan Light Agency, representing one of the biggest stars in Hollywood.

THE RISE OF THE SECRETARIES

Behind every successful executive is a loyal and
diligent secretary. Until she gets promoted . . .

—UNKNOWN

1987

"Beanie Rosen's office," said the familiar voice with a confidence, nay, pride that comes only from a true friend or fellow traveler. In this case, both.

Hawkeye was now Beanie's secretary, which surprised the hell out of, well, everyone. She had been a fixture at reception for almost ten years; a well-paid, well-regarded, trusted employee who answered to no one. So this new position, working for a junior junior who got in on a pass, looked like a demotion, a bad decision, a misstep.

But to Hawkeye, it was a springboard to a future no one else would guarantee. Not even the boys on the first floor. Sure, they liked her fine to be the greeter, the one they'd make passes at, make jokes with, off-color, about color, and then take liberties because, hey, she was one of them.

But now it was time for her to test the limits of those liberties by piggybacking onto the jet stream of a woman who would reinvent the standard. Hawkeye had had plenty of offers to work for more senior agents. But what the men never understood was that it wasn't the status of the agent that had held her back from a job change, it was their ego—namely, would they be threatened by her ambition?

Beanie Rosen would understand Hawkeye's need for more, and she believed, if she tied her strings to Beanie's feathers, together they'd fly higher than either would alone. For many years, Hawkeye had been looking for someone she could trust to carry her over a line she couldn't reach because of the color of her skin. In the history of the big three agencies, there had only been one African American agent, and he'd lasted less than a decade.

Wally Amos started in the New York mailroom of the William Morris Agency in the late 1950s and quickly rose through the ranks by discovering a heretofore unknown folk duo from Queens called Simon & Garfunkel. As a talent magnet, he brought in acts like Marvin Gaye and Sam Cooke. His expanding and exploding roster was undeniable as rock and roll legends sought him out. He believed he had found his calling. But when Amos's bonus didn't increase with his client list, he knew his calling was elsewhere, and in 1967, he quit New York and the Morris office, heading for the West Coast where he was given a new moniker, Famous Amos, and went about making his fortune in cookies.

Now it was Hawkeye's turn. She wanted to be the first African American female agent and believed that Beanie Rosen—who had a fire inside fueled by the rejection that had come before; an eternal flame, burning down the barriers she'd spent her life resenting—would help her get there. Hawkeye predicted that Beanie Rosen would be one of the greats, gaining a reputation for breaking ground, breaking rules, breaking ceilings. And she also believed that, if she worked for her, Beanie would clear the way for her as well.

"Ella wants to know where you want to have lunch," Hawkeye said, interrupting Beanie, who was surveying her newly decorated office.

"I don't care. Maybe the Ivy," Beanie told her, taking in her new surroundings. She had been in temporary offices in the plaza across the street and was pinching herself to think this was all hers. She felt a sense of pride and accomplishment. As a starting agent they had given her a generous budget of $7,500 for furnishings, art, and accessories. It had taken her two months to decide on a style, and four months to get it all done.

Ella, who had assumed Garry Sampson's old office, had no interest in redecorating it. Frills and fuss were a part of a past she had long since buried, and the mismatched furniture and chaos reinforced her individuality, and that gave her comfort. But Beanie, less concerned with individuality, was more focused on appearance, and had taken note that the way you curated your office informed not only who you were but more importantly, at least at Sylvan Light, who you wanted others to think you were.

In an abracadabra universe, it was all about perception. Say it. See it. Be it.

From Phil Carter to Samuel Lesser to Jamie Garland to Sheila Day, Beanie had watched as they carefully constructed images from the outside in, portraying themselves to be chic, manly, glitzy, hip, famous, classy, irreverent, or all the above.

In Beanie's case, she decided that the shabby-chic vibe would show people that she was both cozy and Bohemian. Her office was filled with everything from an overstuffed floral chair that appeared both new and worn, an ecru loveseat that was slipcovered with mismatched floral pillows, and a distressed wood coffee table with books on English country cottages, though she'd never been to England nor anywhere near a cottage. Her desk was an old barn door, sanded and whitewashed, which coordinated with the reclaimed pale blue wood floor-to-ceiling bookshelves against the back wall. With the remaining funds, the decorator bought old books from the Rose Bowl flea market, picture frames, and knickknacks, giving the office a warm, homey effect. It was, thought Beanie, the most beautiful space she had ever been in.

But the pièce de résistance was that the office they'd given her used to belong to Mike Barron. She and Hawkeye had burned sage before the demolition.

Beanie had naively assumed that the agents who had once been fans when she was a departmental trainee would welcome her, if not as their partner then perhaps as a second, a junior on their teams. Instead, they guarded their turf against Beanie and Ella, as if they'd been hoodwinked by two women circumnavigating a system designed to keep them outside at the secretarial desks, or inside under theirs.

"It's the circumstances by which you were promoted," Barry Licht told her. "Once a secretary always a secretary," he said, pointing out that disgruntled colleagues not only resented their promotions, but the accolades and attention from the industry. "They don't like it," he warned as article after article came out characterizing them as the girls against the machine. Usurping the news that Garry Sampson had left to run Orion was the revelation that Scott Westman had chosen two secretaries to be his representatives.

Sheila, forgetting that Beanie had once been her protégé, lumped Beanie and Ella together with her spiteful dissatisfaction.

But never publicly.

When *Los Angeles Magazine* wrote an article entitled, "The Rise of the Secretaries," saying that one of the biggest stars in the world who could have been represented by Sheila Day or Matthew Stieglitz chose to be represented by two former secretaries, Sheila, conscious of the eyeballs hungry for drama, praised them both publicly, and giving an exclusive to Liz Smith, embraced the "girl power" angle. With that endorsement, the optics, already hot, caught fire. Suddenly Beanie Rosen and Ella Gaddy were symbolic of a kind of Horatio Alger success story with a feminist twist.

Jane Pauley, who was a client, requested an interview. "From apron strings to boardrooms," her segment producer pitched, saying that Beanie and Ella would be featured as a new generation of female entrepreneur who might just reach or at least scratch the glass ceiling. "Here's a debutante from the South and a yeshiva gal from Pacoima making room for themselves in the boys' club," the producer said, giving them a preview of how they'd be featured. "It would be a six-minute interview," she continued, but neither Beanie nor Ella heard the rest of the pitch.

No one had called Ella a debutante, even when she lived at home. It disgusted her and was antithetical to everything she stood for, everything she wanted to be. So the fact that someone had researched her background and found that out was appalling. Beanie was equally as mortified. Like her mother, she had erased all mentions of Pacoima from her bio and was deeply offended that they had somehow been able to reveal the truth beneath Miriam's Zamboni. And even though Harvey Khan personally represented Pauley, both women firmly refused to participate. Finally, the producer of the segment came to see Beanie personally and apologized, saying they would omit all mention of both ladies' backgrounds and urged them to reconsider, reassuring them both how much it would mean to Pauley. And that made Beanie soften.

"She's a client," she told Ella, suggesting they just do it and get it over with. "They won't say anything about where were from, or any of that," she told her. In truth, Beanie had been surprised to have learned about Ella and her lineage, having no idea that she came from money, much less pedigree. But Ella was resolute, saying that she'd walk if Sylvan Light insisted. Beanie, under no illusion that Light would keep her without Ella, knew that they had to say no to the interview.

But Khan wouldn't accept no. "Tell them to just fucking do it," he told Mercedes, who called Rose Liu and tasked her to be the messenger.

Rose, who had long ago forgotten that she and Mercedes had once been friends, accepted her subservient role, but she still got nervous when Mercedes Baxter called, especially since Mercedes's position in Harvey's life had become somewhat elevated. Ever since Grace Khan's untimely death on the French Riviera, Mercedes had stepped in on behalf of the family to ensure that the police investigation surrounding her accidental drowning was free from scandal.

Several tabloids, circling, implied that Grace, fresh out of rehab, had fallen off the wagon and into a pool, but Mercedes skillfully buried the headline and the innuendo. It was important to Cheryl and Todd, Grace and Harvey's children, that their mother's reputation remain unsullied, and it was important to Mercedes that her reputation with Cheryl and Todd remain the same. But the children stayed measured and distant. Respectful, they kept their gratitude in check. While they knew for years that Mercedes Baxter had been their father's companion, and they understood that their parents had been living separate lives, something about this woman seemed obsequious and inauthentic.

Perhaps it was the fact that less than four months after Grace's passing, Mercedes quietly moved into Stone Canyon, and not so quietly redecorated the entire home, wiping away any trace of all that came before.

Including them.

"Hi, Rose, I hope you're well," Mercedes said, not waiting for a response, and plowing ahead relayed Mr. Khan's insistence that the Jane

Pauley interview take place. Mercedes asked Rose to make sure that Beanie and Ella complied. The relationship between Mercedes and Rose was polite but frosty. Rose understood that she was there by Mercedes's grace, and in that way was able to keep her job, which paid extremely well, if not her man, while Mercedes was able to maintain control over a situation that, had Rose left, she might not have been able to manage. It was a symbiotic relationship with a benign acceptance between the two; an implicit understanding of each woman's turf that kept the scales balanced. "Please let them know that Mr. Khan is insistent," Mercedes said, and then hung up.

So Rose, choosing the path of least resistance, informed Beanie that Mr. Khan requested that they do just this one last interview. Then they would put it all to bed. Everyone knew that Ella marched to her own drum, and that while Beanie tried to curry favor with the hierarchy, Ella didn't.

"Please pass that on to Ella," Rose said, knowing that Beanie would cushion the blow better than she.

"What do I do here?" Beanie asked Jamie Garland, explaining that she was caught between a rock and a Gaddy. "If I ask her to do the interview again, she might just walk out of spite," she said. "Do you think you can speak to Mr. Khan and tell him that we shouldn't push this interview on Ella?" Beanie asked Jamie. But Jamie shook her head and told her that Khan loved Jane Pauley, and the only person who could influence him to shut it down was Sheila Day.

"You need to speak to her," Jamie said.

Knowing that Jamie was right, Beanie approached Sheila with trepidation. Ever since the double promotion Sheila had been cool, and not just to Ella. Beanie, feeling her anger by association, had kept her distance.

Now she stood before Sheila, asking a favor for a woman who had been disrespectful and dismissive toward her.

"What the fuck is she so afraid of people finding out with this interview?" Sheila asked, staring daggers at Beanie. "Is she hiding something?"

"No," Beanie said, honestly believing that wasn't it. "She just wasn't expecting this publicity. Neither one of us were," she told her.

But instinctively Sheila called bullshit. "You don't dress with your cooch hanging out, then shy away when people look," she told Beanie, sucking the life out of her cigarette.

While others cut a wide berth around Ella, Sheila cut to the quick, stating that she thought Ella was full of crap on a multitude of issues, starting with the fact that she was publicity-shy. "She wants people to look," she told her, circling back to the idea that Ella was, in fact, hiding something.

They all are, Sheila thought, suspecting a collusion between Westman, Ella, Beanie, and perhaps even Moze.

She didn't buy that Scott Westman had come up with the idea of Ella being his guardian agent on the spot. Sheila believed that it had all been premeditated and choreographed. *They were all fucking in on it,* she thought, and kept her distance as best she could. Sure, she worked with Moze because she had to. He had taken many of Lesser's clients and some of Sampson's, but Sheila didn't trust him. The Westman decision had been a slap in the face, an insult she'd tried to shrug off. But her gut told her that she'd been played.

And that it was the lanky goy with the bad bleach job who'd been the mastermind.

And now Sheila Day was being asked to do *her* a favor.

"What's in it for me?" she said finally.

"Anything," Beanie replied. "Name it."

Sheila smiled, turning over a myriad of possibilities in her head.

"All right," she said finally. "Invite me to the Costner dinner."

Beanie blanched. How the hell did Sheila know about the Costner dinner? It was all happening in real time. They had just planned it. Costner and Westman were friends, and Westman had been the one who had set up the meeting. He wanted to help Beanie and Ella build their profile, if only to reinforce his decision.

"Okay," Beanie told her, "I'll see what I can do."

By the time Beanie walked back to Ella's office, the Pauley interview had been shelved.

But Ella, rather than grateful, was annoyed. "How the hell did she know about the Costner dinner?" she asked, suggesting that perhaps their phones were bugged.

Beanie told her that Sheila had probably heard from Costner's business manager or lawyer. "People talk," she said, and then, pivoting, told Ella straight out that they should invite Sheila to the dinner. "Kevin will probably like her," she said. "Most people do."

Ella thought about it. Beanie was probably right. They were all on the same team, ish.

But that woman rubbed Ella the wrong way. Maybe it was shades of Eve Lynn, who'd tried to control the way Ella looked and spoke and acted.

"Let's start with a lunch," Ella said, "then we can talk about a dinner."

Beanie hugged Ella hard, believing that finally they were moving forward.

Baby steps, she thought.

THE POLIO LOUNGE

There's no such thing as a free lunch.
—ELLA GADDY, UPON REFLECTION

1987

The Polo Lounge was located inside the Beverly Hills Hotel and decorated in shades of pink and green with tropical wallpaper, and little lamps on horseshoed tables. There were unwritten rules when it came to where one was seated. The best tables, outside on the terrace, flanked with bougainvillea, honeysuckle, and night-blooming jasmine, were tucked away to allow privacy, but visible enough to leave an impression. Sheila Day's table was on the southwest corner booth, allowing unobstructed views both coming and going.

She was nervous and excited for this lunch. It wasn't just about the perception of "girl power," she needed these women on her side. With Lesser gone and a younger generation coming up, where did that leave dinosaurs like Sheila Day? The world was not kind to women who reinvented, especially women in their fifties. But Sheila was far from throwing in the towel. That seat on the board meant millions, and it was only a few years away. She wasn't going to let some long-legged shiksa get the best of her.

Enough noise had been made about the promotions that you could feel the energy in the room when the two former secretaries were escorted onto the outside terrace where Sheila Day awaited them.

What became instantly clear, to Ella at least, was the strategy behind this "simple lunch." It wasn't so much about a truce as it was about a public statement and a public display. Sheila Day wanted to put to rest any gossip that she had been bested, showing the industry that she not only supported these young female agents but would mentor them.

Beautifully wrapped gift baskets stuffed with sterling silver picture frames from Tiffany's, Elsa Peretti jewelry, candles, and gift cards were presented to both women, trumpeting their arrival into the boys' club.

"Two more have broken through," Sheila said to Dawn Steel, who stopped by their table to offer congratulations. Steel, the head of Paramount, who was rumored to be headed to Columbia, was the first woman to run a major studio.

As Sheila introduced Ella and Beanie, Ella realized that the choice of restaurant, the day, and the time had all been carefully choreographed. That's why Sheila had waited so long to tell them where they were going. She wanted the most bang for her buck. And she got it. The room, that day, was packed with heavyweight producers, actors, and studio executives all stopping by Sheila's table to pay homage.

"A few months back people started calling this place the Polio Lounge," Sheila confided, scanning the surroundings like they were her domain. "It was filled with alta cockers on their second martinis and third wives. But today," she said expansively, taking credit for the crowd, "we kicked it up a notch."

Ella guessed that Sheila, and perhaps a few other senior agents, had some ties to the eatery, and certainly knew in advance who had reservations and where they'd be seated. *She's using this lunch to her advantage,* she thought as Sheila continued her outward display of love.

"My two female secret weapons," she said to Julia Phillips, the first female producer to win an Academy Award for Best Picture. "Who would have thought I was a feminist?" she said, positioning herself between her two protégés.

More like an opportunist, Ella thought, watching her in action. But the thing about Sheila that was undeniable was her wit and her absolute charm.

Benevolent, gracious, and insanely funny, Sheila regaled both Ella and Beanie with stories of her past, who she fucked, who she didn't, who she wished she would have. She told them about the time she had been on a plane that was being hijacked. The hijacker wanted an audience with Golda Meir. Sheila had offered up Alana Campbell King.

Even Ella laughed.

"She's trying to sign us," Beanie whispered as Sheila spoke to Warren Beatty, who had come by the table to say hello.

Ella knew that Beanie was right. Sheila was working overtime to correct her past mistakes, and very much wanted them to like her. And Ella, at last, began letting her guard down.

"I think we three should target someone together," Beanie told them, just before she got up to go to the bathroom.

Sheila watched Beanie walk away. "She's a good kid," she said.

"The best," Ella agreed.

Sheila gestured for the waiter. "Honeeeey, another pack of Marlboro Lights," she told him, taking the last two cigarettes out of her case and offering one to Ella. "You smoke?"

"Sometimes."

"Want one?"

"Nope."

Sheila lit her cigarette, inhaling deeply as she considered the tall gawky bleached blonde with prehensile legs so long that she was able to cross them once then snake them around again for punctuation.

We get it, you got long legs, Sheila thought, shaking her head at this strange creature, who, for Sheila at least, defied all sense of style. But she had to admit there was *something* about the arrogant little hayseed that could be appealing. Part Will Rogers, part Ginger Rogers, Ella had a prizefighter's chutzpah mixed with an overly ruffled Southern style that while Sheila found cheap and tacky, others, for whatever reason, found appealing. She truly hoped that this lunch would not only repair past damage but demonstrate to Ella the power a friendship with her could yield.

"You think maybe we can start over? Straighten things out?" Sheila asked, packing the cigarettes the waiter had brought over.

"Maybe," Ella said, considering.

"I'd like that," Sheila told her, going on to explain again that having friends in high places can take care of a multitude of situations.

"I appreciate that you killed the Pauley interview," Ella said, extending an olive branch.

"That was easy," Sheila said, "but there's other things I can offer," she told her, removing an envelope from her purse and sliding it across the table. "Like protection."

Ella looked at Sheila confused, and then, opening the envelope, pulled out a small wallet-size class photo of an eight-year-old black boy, smiling big, missing his two front teeth.

"His name is Milo. Apparently, he's very willful," she said, and then whispered, "Like his mommy."

Ella looked at her, absolutely stupefied. It was a sucker punch to the gut that immediately took the air out of the room. Ella's eyes filled.

"No one has to know," Sheila continued, misreading the stunned silence as fear or shame or both. "Secrets are only as good as their keepers," she told her. "We all need someone to protect us. I'd like you to consider me a friend."

Ella couldn't breathe. She felt trapped in the corner booth, all the eyes from all the vantage points on her, and began to perspire.

"It's all right, Ella," Sheila said, reaching for her hand, trying to calm her down.

But Ella withdrew it. Fast.

Fuck. Sheila hadn't counted on this reaction. Was Ella upset because she'd seen her son for the first time in eight years, or was she upset that Sheila knew? After all, Sheila had gone to a great deal of trouble to uncover this secret Ella had been hiding, and she figured that if she aligned herself with the thing that Ella most wanted to protect, the two of them could protect it together. It was insurance, that was all. Why didn't Ella see that?

But again, Sheila had failed to take into consideration the character of the person with whom she was negotiating. Much like she'd done with Garry Sampson when offering him money to reconsider leaving, she had made a blunder from which she would never recover. She had misjudged Ella Gaddy and her motives for keeping things quiet. Ella didn't want insurance or protection. She wanted respect for her privacy and didn't want it slid across the little pink table at the southwest corner of the Polo Lounge.

Ella Gaddy took the picture, putting it in her bag, downed the remainder of wine in her goblet, looked at Sheila and said "I quit" as she slid across the booth, getting ready to leave.

"Please," Sheila said in a panic, blocking her exit. *This had gone wrong. Terribly wrong.* "I didn't mean it," she told her.

Ella called bullshit. To her, that photograph was a warning, a chit, a leveraging tool Sheila could and would use whenever she wanted to have power over her. But Ella wouldn't give her the satisfaction.

Big fucking deal, Sheila knew that she'd had a kid. She wasn't ashamed of her child. Not by a long shot. She was ashamed of herself and what she'd allowed people to talk her into.

"I'm going to Alliance," she said calmly, "and I'm going to take Scott Westman with me. Then," she said, with a stare so icy it cut through the bullshit like a cold, double-edged knife through hot butter, "I'm going to go after every single client you have. And even if I can't sign them, I'll make certain they leave you."

Sheila, devastated, was trying to catch her breath. She looked around the room. Everyone she knew was there. She didn't want to make a scene, but this had gone way off course. "I honestly thought that if I showed you how easily secrets can be uncovered, you'd recognize that having someone like me in your corner would only do you good. I was doing it to show you that I would be your friend."

Ella rolled her eyes.

"Please," Sheila begged, no longer caring who was looking, "I'll do anything." She desperately tried to keep her composure, but tears formed, nonetheless.

Ella saw Beanie in the distance, stopping at a table to talk to someone.

"Please," Sheila said again, pleading with every ounce of her being. "It was stupid of me. I fucked up. Don't leave. We need you," and then added quietly, her voice cracking, "I need you."

Ella looked at Sheila, steely-eyed. "Okay," she said, "here's the deal. We will never work together. You will never speak to my clients, and you will never mention that photograph to anyone, anytime. Understood?"

"Completely," Sheila said.

Two weeks later Ella and Beanie met and signed Kevin Costner. Sheila Day, neither informed nor invited, found out about their newest superstar in an interoffice memo addressed to staff worldwide. The two former secretaries now represented two of the biggest stars in Hollywood without Sheila Day's help, input, or association.

Beanie understood that in spite of their lunch, the rift between Sheila and Ella had somehow grown disproportionate in size. But since neither Ella nor Sheila spoke of it, she, too, kept silent, playing by rules she had neither set nor understood.

Caught in a web she couldn't see, Beanie was nonetheless cautious of the two spiders on different ends of the same floor.

A SEAT AT THE TABLE

Rewriting our history is how we deal with the horror of our truths.

—SOMEONE IN HOLLYWOOD

1988–1990

Power erodes, amplifies, emboldens, and changes, and like a drug, it seeds itself, creating a yearning, a need for more. But power can't be owned, transferred, or even bought; rather, it's something that is given, and conversely, something that's taken away.

The shift, at first, is imperceptible: a call dropped, a dinner missed, an accidental oversight. "How did that happen?" "Please forgive us." "We'll have to do it again, soon." But "soon" is a nicety, something to say until the new reality takes hold. It can take weeks, sometimes months, but eventually, the oversight becomes the norm, requests for meetings go ignored, underlings ask if they can help, invitations to dinners are no longer extended until quite suddenly you are an anachronism, living in a world that has shifted just enough to put you on the outside of it.

"It's not kill or be killed anymore," Sheila once joked, "it's kill or become irrelevant." And irrelevance for Sheila Day was not an option. In a business hungry to marginalize women, Sheila believed that a female agent was only as valuable as her proximity to power. "Lose the power, lose the dame," she'd say, citing the fact that while the boys' club protected their own, there was no girls' club in Hollywood to stand together, to look out, to huddle close against the dicks. Sheila knew that if she lost her clients, or worse, if she kept her clients and they lost their heat, she'd just be the shell of a person who used to represent people who used to be famous. On her rise, she hadn't thought twice about pushing aside those who were hanging on to a memory of who they'd once been. "Honeeeey," she'd say, hugging them, "you're a legend!"

And then, out of earshot, "At the Motion Picture Home."

Sheila had been ruthless, dismissive, and ageist, never considering that one day she might be on the other side of that coin, which was why she intended to play defense in anticipation of the inevitable. Fuck anyone who tried to kick her to the curb. She had seen the future splayed out at lifetime achievement ceremonies, where ancient powerbrokers who missed the deference that their power once yielded put on fancy jewels and sat like wax figures, if only to remind the world or themselves that they still mattered.

But Sheila Day, who would not go easy into that glittery night, intended to chart a different course, but not by signing stars. Clients were fickle, and fame was fleeting; to rely on either was a fool's whimsy.

Sheila was no fool.

She sought the power and security that came with a seat on the Sylvan Light board. Once you had the seat, there was no need to sign new talent. "Clients are for pishers," she'd told Jamie Garland when Garland and Lesser had approached her to join the agency. And she'd held out until she got it. It was the carrot they had dangled, the pot of gold at the end of the bullshit.

But she wouldn't get it until 1995. The board had bought themselves time. Namely hers.

But by 1989, she reasoned, circumstances had changed. Sheila Day had presumed that Sam Lesser would still be alive to co-pilot, co-lead, and share the burdens if not the spoils, and his right-hand Garry Sampson would be there to take up the slack. But they were both gone, and this was a whole new set of balls she was juggling.

As such, she wanted to be rewarded with an accelerated board seat. "I want that board seat next year," she told her attorneys.

Worried that her expectations were too ambitious, they counseled her to be patient.

She decided she'd rather be smart and found new lawyers, demanding a new deal before the tables turned, as tables do, and she would find herself in her sixties, free-falling without a parachute, golden or otherwise. She knew that the double standard for women was never clearer than when it came to ageism, money, and power. While men in their sixties were still in their prime, women in their sixties were dried-up grandmas. And grandmas did not sit on the board at the Sylvan Light Agency. But shrewd businesswomen might. She needed to claim that seat before they pulled it out from under her.

Her new attorneys went to the board, pointing out what she had done for the agents and the agency. "Without her, the agency would have sunk," they told them. The board effusively expressed their wholehearted gratitude but were inflexible on accelerating the board seat—until they heard the attorneys say something that gave them pause.

"The agents love her too," they said. "They'd follow her anywhere."

It was a highly calculated statement; a veiled threat with the power of absolute truth behind it. Sheila Day had been curating less a client list, and more an agent list, endearing herself to the power behind the power, and—save for Ella Gaddy—building an army of loyalists who with each day were becoming more devoted for one reason.

She overpaid them.

By contract, Sheila had been entitled to determine the salaries and perk packages of every agent in the motion picture and television departments, and she always added more than the board recommended, making sure the agents knew what the board had wanted to give them, and what she was going to pay in spite of their recommendation.

"I'm overruling them," she'd say. It was a strategic move intended to build both a singular loyalty to Sheila, and a division between the boys on the first floor and the woman holding the purse strings.

With a wink, a nod, and a "Honeeeey, I got you," she solidified her troops, giving them pep talks, advice, and loads of cash. She'd help them sign, always taking second position so the agent got the credit and she'd get the agent. Oblivious to her motives, the board had granted her, if not the kingdom, then at least the keys to it; and she had used those keys to turn the villagers against them.

"You wouldn't want her to leave," her attorneys said, doubling down and backing the board into a corner.

In April 1990, the board agreed to accelerate her seat by three years, giving it to her at the end of 1992. While it wasn't what she wanted, it was, finally, within reach.

All she had to do was keep the agents happy.

GETTING BIG

Be careful what you tell people. The friend
today could be your enemy tomorrow.
—BEALEADINGLADY.COM

1987–1989

A few months into his tenure as an agent, Moze Goff had lunch with Sheila Day who, wanting to solidify his loyalty, said four words that changed the course of his career.

"You represent Burt Reynolds."

Never mind that Biff Abrahamson was his agent at Sylvan Light and guarded all Burt Reynolds intel like state secrets in enemy hands, Sheila advised that a smart agent represented the whole client list, not just those people he was responsible for.

"That way," she explained, "a call from Moze would be as good as a call from Abrahamson. And trust me," she continued, "they'd rather speak to you."

Since Samuel Lesser and Garry Sampson, his two mentors, were gone, Moze had to find his own way. Sure, he represented some of the stars they'd left behind, but without protection he needed to make a name for himself by himself.

Though he didn't trust it completely, he accepted Sheila's friendship and advice and began to forge his own path, trying to put together films much like Sam had, representing filmmakers and actors. So, when he heard that Harrison Ford had dropped out of the lead role in *Big* after Steven Spielberg had dropped out as director, he suggested to Sheila, who was close to Penny Marshall, that they slip Penny the script for her to direct. He knew that Penny only had an attorney who might not have access to the material or up-to-date information. This was all happening in real time, so there was an urgency to the information and how it was relayed.

Sheila, who rarely read anything in its entirety, wanted to know what it was about.

Describing the script as a fantasy about a boy who just wants to be a grown-up, Sheila was instantly charmed, and called Marshall, who had just had a huge commercial success with Whoopi Goldberg in *Jumpin' Jack Flash,* and urged her to read it.

"I'll have someone hand-deliver the script to you," said Sheila.

Two and a half hours later, Marshall called her back, telling her how much she loved the material, and notified her attorney that she wanted Sheila to get her the movie.

Forty-eight hours after that, Penny Marshall had the offer to direct *Big.*

The following week Marshall, who was still not an official client, came into Sheila's office to discuss potential actors who could star. Travolta had passed on it that morning, and her feeling was that Eddie Murphy would as well.

Sheila, still not having read the material, invited Moze to the meeting.

"Tom Hanks should do this," he told them, explaining that he had been invited to an early test screening of *The Money Pit,* Hanks's next film. "It scored through the roof," he said, adding that the director, Richard Benjamin, an ex-client of Lesser's who had invited Moze, said it was the highest-testing film in Universal history.

Marshall, who had known Hanks for years, loved the idea, but was concerned that his last film, *Nothing in Common,* directed coincidentally by her brother Garry, hadn't been quite the smash critically or commercially and that the studio might be hesitant.

"Not if they see *The Money Pit,*" Moze said. But the question was how could the executives from one studio be persuaded to show the executives from another studio a film that was not being released for six months?

"Easy," said Sheila Day, who picked up the phone and expertly charmed Tom Pollack, the new head of Universal, into showing *The Money Pit* to Leonard Goldberg, the new head of Fox.

An hour after that screening ended, a firm offer was made to Tom Hanks, who read the script, loved it, and accepted.

While Hanks may not have known that Moze was the engine, Marshall did. Four months after the film wrapped, she signed with Moze Goff and Sheila Day, in that order.

Sheila, looking for an ally in Moze rather than a client in Marshall, never stood in the way.

Moze Goff, meanwhile, continued to target filmmakers, actors, and writers, once again leveraging the in-house client list, signing others he didn't represent, then selling "the package" to the studio. Within a year he established himself as a packaging agent.

Like his mentor Sam Lesser, Moze, affable, honest, and with a great deal of integrity, began to attract people in power. Jason Wolf and Henry Dunn who, some say, hijacked SONY, then hijacked Moze, began flying him on private jets to Aspen and introducing him as one of their own. Taking a liking to the New York kid who had authenticity and hustle, they steered clients his way. By 1989 he was representing heavy-hitting directors such as Miloš Forman, Robert Benton, and Richard Donner; ironically, even Richard Benjamin, who had directed *The Money Pit,* called Moze, asking him to be his representative.

Moze quickly became one of the youngest and most important packaging agents at the company. He soon moved to New York, where it was rumored he was living in the Village and dating Cher.

On the occasion when someone asked how he got started, Moze would always reference Beanie—who had, over time, gained both weight and perspective. Yes, she'd gotten him in the door, but not because he'd asked. It was the only way she could control and perhaps intertwine their destinies. She'd put him on the path to greatness and hoped he'd take her along. She didn't feel so much used by him as abandoned. And though they were both agents at the same agency, he was in a different stratosphere now, a part of a boys' club that had sought him out.

Moze had gotten *Big.*

He was the next generation and iteration of who *they* wanted to be.

Beanie, like Sheila, was marginalized; reduced to a stereotype: a know-it-all Jewish girl with a big ass and a big mouth who might have pushed her way into the job, but not the club. Never the club.

For Beanie to succeed, she needed to do what she'd done her whole life: circumnavigate them, climb over them, somehow ascend in spite of them.

"Study the wave, Beanie girl," her father had once told her, "and ride it all the way into shore."

THE SHIT

Rule number one: Never be number two.

—THE NARCISSIST'S GUIDE TO A HAPPY LIFE

1989

Beanie Rosen was the shit. And not in a good way. While she was the agent for Scott Westman and Kevin Costner, she wasn't the agent that the heavyweights called. She was the number two; the shit, the agent who did the work for the agents the heavyweights called. They were the ones who got the notoriety and the praise and the year-end bonuses with lots of zeros. They were the number ones.

Still, Beanie rationalized, she was thrilled to be an agent. It was all she ever wanted. And while Sylvan Light didn't give her a car like they did Ella, who got a new Rabbit Cabriolet convertible, or Moze's Alfa Romeo, she was, thanks to Sheila, making $75,000 a year, with an expense account and gas allowance.

She didn't expect a car. Besides, Scott Westman had once told her that the Swinger made her cool. You don't trade in cool for a set of wheels that belongs to someone else. At least that was the lie she told herself to insulate against the harsh truth that Beanie had gotten in on a pass. The girl from Pacoima who was told to say Arleta, who'd moved to Sepulveda but admitted to Northridge and then wiped them all away for a life south of the Boulevard, had always had to finagle her way in. This wasn't new. She'd never felt good enough, or pretty enough, or thin enough, so, this promotion hadn't been the exception, it had been the rule. Known as the girl behind the girl who signed Westman and Costner, Beanie felt both anonymous and codependent, and though she was grateful to Ella for all she had done, she would sometimes complain about not being recognized or singled out.

And that made Ella resentful. She had done everything she could, and if it weren't for her, Beanie would still be a departmental trainee. Beanie knew that, of course, and it wasn't that she didn't feel grateful, it was that she didn't feel seen.

"Like if you weren't here, they wouldn't want me," Beanie said to Ella six months after they'd been promoted. They had just gotten out of a motion picture meeting where everyone had been congratulating Ella for a deal she'd made based on an idea of Beanie's. It was a *Vanity Fair* article that Beanie had shown to a writer who had come up with a take for Westman. He liked the pitch, and TriStar had optioned the piece and put it into development.

"I said it was your idea," Ella told her, annoyed at the agents for ignoring Beanie's role, and annoyed at Beanie for this constant need to be recognized. "They know we're a team," she reiterated as they arrived at Ella's office where she sat on what was once Garry Sampson's couch. "No one knows what I can do on my own," Beanie said.

"Then fucking show them," Ella replied, sick to death of the constant complaints. "Go out and sign someone," she said, as her secretary informed her that Gil Amati was waiting downstairs.

Beanie, clocking Ella's tone, retreated into work mode. Standing up to leave, she suggested two scripts she'd read and liked for Westman, and an article she thought they should explore for Costner.

"Bean," Ella said, softening, "don't go."

"Amati's waiting for you," Beanie said, hurt by Ella's lack of empathy and embarrassed by her own neediness.

"I'm sorry," Ella told her. "We can talk about it later tonight. Okay?"

Beanie smiled, nodded, and walked away, knowing they wouldn't.

Though she still paid half the rent, Ella spent most of her time with Scott Westman, leaving Beanie alone in the large two-bedroom with views of the MGM lion and five years of memories. Ella was clearly making her own way. Maybe it was time for Beanie to stop bitching about being seen and step out of Ella's shadow so people *could* see her.

"I think I want to buy my own place," Beanie told Dr. Spitz and Miriam shortly after her conversation with Ella. They were having dinner at Chasens, and Miriam for once was counting chits instead of calories, measuring how important her daughter was, at least compared to others.

"Mrs. Koppelman's son is an agent at Gersh," she told Beanie, Dr. Spitz, and the skinny twins, both of whom had joined them. "But he's a pisher," she said, "not like our girl who represents Scott Westman."

Beanie smiled and nodded, reminding her mother that it was both her and Ella who represented Westman, and Costner, and anyone else of value.

But Miriam, good at reworking truth, had Zambonied Ella out of her narrative. Her daughter, though fat and single, was successful. And that trumped Mrs. Koppelman and her loser son.

"You should get your own place," Dr. Spitz said, and offered to help with a down payment. "You're a Maher now," he said proudly.

Beanie, embarrassed, dismissed him, but Miriam agreed, hugging her daughter while slipping diet pills into her purse.

"When you run out," she whispered, "I'll have Lennie get you more."

Two months later, Beanie said goodbye to her Culver City apartment with the distant view of a roaring lion and put an offer on a chic two-bedroom, two-bathroom west-facing apartment at the Sierra Towers, which ironically *was* Beverly Hills adjacent. Hiring the decorator who had done her office, she leaned into a Santa Fe style, complete with Navajo tapestries, a four-poster bleached wood bed, and a howling coyote in the corner.

"Beautiful," her mother said as she took in the décor, the view, and then her daughter. She had hoped that Beanie's promotion or at least the diet pills would cut away the fat, but a discerning up and down on her ever-expanding daughter in her Pucci dress that amplified rather than camouflaged her girth, dashed all hope.

Beanie noted Miriam's nonverbal disappointment.

Fuck her, she thought, as she led Miriam and Dr. Spitz out to the terrace, pre-set with terra cotta dishes, and surrounded by large potted cacti and various reptiles strategically placed to give the illusion of a desert landscape.

Knowing that Dr. Spitz loved soul food, Beanie had ordered a spread from Georgia Ray's Kitchen including fried chicken, mashed potatoes, collard greens, corn on the cob, biscuits with gravy, and apple pie.

As Beanie helped herself to a spoonful of potatoes, she saw Miriam give Dr. Spitz *that* look. She knew *that* look. It was the look that said *She's out of control.* Beanie had seen *that* look her whole life, and while she told herself she didn't care, she did, of course.

Her mother's voice, her mother's approval, her mother's disappointment, they all swirled around in her head creating a noise she could only quiet with food. Add to that the fact that her parents had just spent the afternoon with one of the skinny twins who'd announced her engagement to the son of one of Dr. Spitz's rich facelifts, and she took a second helping.

Her mother watched disapprovingly from the other side of the table. It was a chess match. The more Miriam judged, the more Beanie ate, and the more Beanie ate, the more Miriam probed, which would, of course, only make her eat more.

"Whatever happened to Moses?" Miriam asked, nibbling one kernel of corn at a time.

"He led his people to the promised land," Beanie said. Dr. Spitz laughed.

Miriam didn't. Instead, she watched Beanie pour a healthy dollop of gravy over a second helping of potatoes.

"I'm serious," Miriam said.

Beanie, mouth full, told her that he now ran the literary department in New York and the last she'd heard he was living in Greenwich Village and dating an actress or an actor. "He's tricky that way," she said flippantly, trying to show how little it bothered her, which of course had the opposite effect.

It suddenly occurred to Miriam that perhaps Moses had broken her daughter's heart. Perhaps he had left due to her weight gain, or worse, she was filling herself up *because* he'd left. Miriam softened. The thought of Beanie having to substitute food for love was crushing, yet the idea that she had withheld love and might have been a contributing factor eluded her entirely. She wanted to comfort her daughter, to lead by example, to share clothing, secrets, and lives. She yearned for the kind of relationship where they could talk to each other, not shoot barbs across a table filled with carbohydrates, but she was just so frustrated that Beanie had let herself go again that she could not hide her disappointment. It absolutely galled her that she had a fat daughter, and while Beanie wasn't obese, it was a hop, skip, and a side of fries before she'd be shopping at Lane Bryant, the store where fat women went for polyester stretch pants and flowery blouses with big bows to distract from big personalities.

How could Miss Rockaway have a daughter who shopped at Lane Bryant? It just didn't make sense to her.

Dr. Spitz, bless him, tried to change the subject, but Miriam, on a roll, went in for the kill. "Someone told me they saw your father a few weeks ago," she said casually, though there was nothing casual about it. "Apparently," she whispered, "he's gotten very big." She mouthed the word "big" silently, like you would "cancer."

Even the cactus pricks shivered.

"How big?" Dr. Spitz asked, ignorant as to Miriam's true motive, which was, Beanie guessed, to frighten her into starvation.

Miriam shook her head and told him she didn't know but that people were shocked. "And have you seen the wife?" she said to Dr. Spitz, raising her eyebrows to imply more than words. It was a mean-girl tactic that Beanie had seen her do her whole life:

"Did you see that muumuu Fritzi wore?"

"Did you hear what happened with the Carlisles?"

"Did you notice Stephanie's bruises?"

She'd ask open-ended questions, then raise her eyebrows and let you fill in the rest. But Beanie knew all about Janice Fleishman, her father's new wife.

She was fat, too.

Suddenly feeling protective of her sweet father, his new wife, and their fat lives, Beanie told her mother that she saw them both a few weeks earlier and that they seemed really happy. Miriam might have considered Janice Fleishman to be some kind of sideshow freak, but she was quite an accomplished party planner-slash-caterer in Pasadena.

"Her business is on fire," Beanie told them. "In fact, I've recommended Good Eats for the company Christmas party," she said, explaining that that was the name of Janice's catering business.

Miriam's eyes opened wide. *"Good? Eats?"* she asked, punctuating each word so the irony could not possibly be lost.

But Beanie, refusing to take the bait, smiled, nodded, and explained that Janice's business was so hot that if you didn't know someone inside, you'd have to book a year in advance. Then she shoveled macaroni in her mouth to drive her point home.

Later, alone on the terrace, she thought of her mother and Dr. Spitz, her father and Janice Fleishman, Ella and Scott, Barry and Moze, and even Mercedes and Harvey Khan. They'd all found their way to some semblance of happiness without her. Moze was floating somewhere between men and women, fame and infamy, and Barry was dating Morgan Fairchild, she'd heard. But Beanie couldn't be sure if that wasn't just another rumor he'd started. Either way, they were all moving forward, and she was stalled, less because she didn't have a partner and more because she didn't have an identity. And she was tired of complaining about it.

She took a deep breath and looked around, taking stock of her life, her home, and her gut. She *was* fat. Again. *Fuck. Fuck,* she thought, angry at Miriam for pointing it out, angry at herself for gaining the weight, angry at the Light Agency for not recognizing her brilliance except by association, and angry at Moze and Ella and Barry for all finding their way without her.

Miriam was right. In a business where you needed to be sharp and precise, where you needed an edge, being fat made you round and soft and sloppy. She thought for a minute about doing coke or diet pills as a sort of jumpstart to take the weight off quickly, but she hated not sleeping. *I'll join the Jane Fonda class downstairs,* she decided as she lit another cigarette, and took a second helping of pie à la mode.

Working the tumblers in her head, Beanie tried to figure out a way to be seen. If she could sign a client without Ella's help—be number one for a change—then maybe the agency, the industry, even her mother might value Beanie enough that she wouldn't need to Zamboni Ella out of her narrative when talking about her daughter's success.

But how do I get to them? was the question rattling around in her brain.

Suddenly she remembered something Sheila Day had told her months earlier when Sheila was trying to sign Sean Connery. "Honeeeey," she'd said, "sign the spouse. And if they're not married, sign the person they're fucking, or want to fuck."

It was a lesson that played out in real time for Beanie, who, at Sheila's insistence, became her emissary with Micheline Connery at a dinner she and Ella were giving for Kevin Costner and his *Untouchable* costars.

Sheila, who had naturally not been invited, told Beanie to send her regrets to Micheline regardless, and to try to get a number where she was staying. Sheila and Micheline had met in Cannes the year before and had struck up a friendship. Each time they socialized, Sheila was careful only to mention Sean in passing, concentrating instead on his wife, her photography, philanthropies, and their mutual friends. While she wanted Sean, she targeted Micheline.

"They're staying privately," Sheila said. "But let her know I'd love to throw a dinner for her."

While Beanie was doubtful, Sheila was certain. And as it turned out, Sheila was right. Micheline gave Beanie the number and Sheila threw Micheline a "girls'" dinner. Sean was not in attendance. With Beanie's help, Sheila courted and signed the wife of the man she wanted to represent. Four months later, she signed the man.

It was all about getting close to the people who were close to the people.

Beanie had been looking at it all wrong.

The answer, dear Brutus, she thought to herself as she thumbed through *People* magazine, *is not in the stars.*

It's in the people behind them.

BACKGROUND PEOPLE

If you want to know what Queen Elizabeth was saying to
her best friend, ask the woman holding her train.

—ONE WHO HELD IT

1989–1991

The first time Beanie had heard about background people was eight years earlier, in 1981. Locked in a windowless office in Central Files, she'd come out for a stretch and met an older man, perhaps in his mid-seventies, sitting in Ollie's outer office.

"They killed Marilyn, you know," the man had said conspiratorially.

"I'm sorry, what?" Beanie replied, not sure if he was speaking to her or himself.

"Marilyn," he'd said, annoyed that she wasn't following, and then continued, telling her that he knew Marilyn, he knew all the players, he knew the score. He'd seen it all. "Including the corpse," he'd added, explaining that this was hours before anyone had called the cops.

Beanie didn't know what to think as he rambled on about the young starlet who had been worshiped by many but misunderstood by more. He said he genuinely liked her, and Marilyn liked him, confiding that when she couldn't get Bobby or Jack or Peter on the phone, she'd call "Greenie"—that was her nickname for him, he'd explained, and they'd talk until she fell asleep. He nudged Beanie. "How 'bout that?" he snickered. "Marilyn Monroe called me to put her to sleep." He shook his head and told her the whole thing was a travesty, everyone had done everything they could, but once she'd threatened to go to Jackie, well . . . The implication hung heavy. He seemed sad and small, and assuming she was

Ollie's secretary, handed her his card and asked that she let Ollie know he'd come by.

"Who's Billy Greenjeans?" Beanie asked later after Ollie had come back from lunch. She handed him the card with his name, phone number, and an illustrated caricature. "He seemed like a lonely old man."

Burns smiled and told her that there was a time when a business card from Greenjeans would open any door, and not just at Light. "Billy Greenjeans was in the background of many lives," he told Beanie, explaining that he had been a big manager handling talent.

"Are managers different from agents?" she asked.

"Managers usually hire the agents," he told her, explaining that they were the people closest to the client. "And no one was closer to his clients than Billy Greenjeans," he said. "He represented big names like Red Skelton and Joey Bishop."

Beanie nodded, clueless as to who either was.

"And a lot of the guys in the Rat Pack," he continued, explaining that Greenjeans connected Hollywood to Washington, and vice versa. "So, Billy Greenjeans became the guy you went to in order to get to the guys you wanted."

Ollie brought a thick encyclopedic reference book over and opened it to the index where he traced his finger down the tiny print until he found Billy Greenjeans's name.

"There," he said, "and there, and there, and there . . . ," pointing out at least ten mentions of the small man with the big stories. Burns flipped from one page to the next where Beanie saw photographs of Frank Sinatra, Peter Lawford, Sammy Davis, Jr, and Angie Dickinson during random moments at fancy parties and intimate dinners.

But it wasn't the stars she was looking at. It was the man on the periphery of the stars.

Background people, Ollie had called them. "The ones you never notice, but they notice you. Look, see," he said, pointing out a particular photograph, "he's looking straight at the camera."

She held the book closely and saw what Ollie meant. There, in the deep background of every photograph, was a younger version of the man she'd met. Sometimes he was looking at the camera, challenging the photographer, but more often he was looking off to the side, surveying the action.

"He was the real deal," he told her. "Inside the circle, protecting their secrets."

Suddenly Beanie stopped and looked at Ollie. "He said they killed Marilyn," she told him.

Ollie shrugged. "He would know."

Beanie was dumbfounded. "It's the people on the periphery of the famous who become the authors of their legacies," he told her, then put the book and "Greenie" back on the shelf.

Either by Ollie Burns's parables in the outer offices of Personnel, or Sheila Day's strategy sessions about signing the spouse, the universe had been conspiring to give Beanie a direction. She needed to look at the people behind the people.

"Managers," she said aloud.

The way through the wave wasn't distancing herself from Ella, it was supplementing her, she realized. Beanie needed to establish a relationship with a manager so she could show how smart she was, how loyal she would be, and perhaps build a future where she could be number one. But in order to interest a manager, she needed a client of her own, someone they might want to represent. After all, she couldn't expect that a manager would seek her out.

It was a catch-22—until destiny caught it and intervened.

Adrienne Seabergh, who had once upon a time helped Beanie meet Nicolas Cage, was earning a reputation as one of the rising stars of the '80s. Often described as "Michelle Pfeiffer with a side of Madonna," Adrienne was beautiful, quirky, and spectacularly talented. While not a member of the Brat Pack, she was almost as hot, having done supporting and featured roles in *Desperately Seeking Susan, Footloose,* and *St. Elmo's Fire.*

Every agent in town was after her, but she'd been loyal to the man who'd represented her since she was eleven. Her loyalty, however, did not extend to the agency where he worked, so when he retired, her thoughts went to a young woman she'd met a few years earlier.

Less than two weeks after Beanie had devised her plan to court a manager, providence, dressed as a free spirit in cut-off Daisy Dukes, cowboy boots, and a button-down white shirt, showed up at the Sylvan Light offices, asking for Beanie Rosen.

You could feel the excitement as Adrienne strolled down the halls like a beautiful thoroughbred, uninhibited, unassuming, asking for directions to the shabby-chic office where Beanie sat, reading a script and eating an egg salad sandwich from Salami 'N' Cheese.

It was lunchtime, so Hawkeye had been out when reception had called, and Adrienne, who was on the cover of the magazines being delivered by the mailroom, told the receptionist she'd just make her own way.

Secretaries stealing some personal time came out of their bosses' offices to gawk, say hello, and walk with her. They weren't so bold as to ask for autographs but were thrilled nonetheless to know that Adrienne Seabergh was in the hallway.

"Beanie, someone's here for you," Randall Fink's secretary said, knocking on the door, then pushing it gently open.

Beanie looked up, and there was Adrienne Seabergh, all arms and legs and teeth and hair.

"I'm looking for an agent," she said to a stupefied Beanie, who hadn't seen her since she'd brought Beanie to Nick Cage's apartment. "Think you can help me?"

Beanie was flabbergasted. Light was thrilled. And all the other agencies were blindsided as a week later Beanie Rosen from the Sylvan Light Agency announced the signing of red-hot Adrienne Seabergh.

"I'm not the shit anymore," she told Ella.

"Damn straight," Ella said, proud and quite relieved.

"I'm going to do this on my own," she said, "without backup." Beanie was afraid if she got a number two, they would perhaps take credit or take over. She was flying solo, quite certain she could handle Adrienne and all her other responsibilities.

But as it turned out, she had her hands full.

Adrienne Seabergh was a wild child, testing the limits of her fame, living on the edge of life for the fuck of it. She needed less an agent and more an air traffic controller, navigating the speedbumps, helping her fly.

"Get her a job," Sheila advised in the weekly motion picture meeting, as Beanie announced that Adrienne was passing on yet another script.

"I just want something as great as her talent," Beanie said as Sheila made a giant jerk-off gesture.

"Honeeeey," she said, "her kooze is her talent, and even that, I hear, isn't anything to write home about." The agents, howling, loved when Sheila made derogatory comments and gestures.

Beanie, proprietary, didn't, and she continued to cull through scripts, looking for material with enough weight to show her client's talent.

A few weeks later Sheila called Beanie into her office. "You passed on a movie starring Dice?" she asked.

"It's crap," Beanie told her. "It's beneath Adrienne."

"Listen, Ingmar Bergman," Sheila said. "She's not exactly Sarah Bernhardt."

But that's where they disagreed. Beanie deeply believed not only in Adrienne's talent, but in her unselfconscious ability to peel away layers, her fearlessness to expose the truth underneath.

Sheila dismissed Beanie's idol worship and worried that Beanie was alienating studio heads and filmmakers, warning that if she wasn't careful, Adrienne would get cold, and Beanie would get blackballed.

"No one will hire your clients," she warned her, "out of spite."

But Beanie knew that nothing would burn Adrienne out quicker than a box office flop, so she continued her amorphous search for something that was both commercial and compelling.

And then, abracadabra, she found it.

Kaleidoscope, a film to be directed by Jonathan Demme, had a brilliant script about a paranoid schizophrenic who spends half the film in her delusion as a wealthy socialite and the other half in a mental institution. Described as *One Flew Over the Cuckoo's Nest* meets *The Three Faces of Eve*, *Kaleidoscope* was the project Beanie had been waiting for. Though it was not a big payday, she urged Adrienne to take the role, which resulted in a tour de force performance, garnering her an Oscar nomination and a number-one film at the box office.

It changed the course of both Adrienne's and Beanie's careers.

Suddenly, at twenty-eight years old, Adrienne was untouchable. The free-spirited artist who had never sought fame had it in abundance. There were new publicists and new attorneys and new friends and new apartments. Fearless, feckless, and curious, she was out of control, giving wild parties, spending recklessly, and beginning to get a reputation for being unreliable.

It was time for Beanie to consider her next move.

"Adrienne Seabergh needs a manager," she told Sheila, who thought it was a terrific idea. She felt that Beanie was spending far too much time with Adrienne and needed to leverage Adrienne's heat to sign other stars, preferably this time *with* Sheila.

Beanie, flattered, said, "We can be gold together."

"Fuck gold," Sheila said. "We can be platinum." Then she got to the business of helping Beanie choose a manager, suggesting Sylvan Light loyalists like Ray Katz, Sandy Gallin, or Larry Thompson.

But Beanie wasn't looking for managers who had been loyal to Sylvan Light. She wanted a manager who would be loyal to her. She needed to build her own army with someone so good that they would make Beanie better.

"Who are you thinking of?" Sheila asked.

"Stevie Lanzetti," Beanie told her.

Assuming she was kidding, Sheila rolled her eyes. "C'mon," she said. "I don't have all day."

But Beanie told her she wasn't kidding, explaining that she had thought about it a great deal and believed that Stevie Lanzetti, who represented everyone from Kevin Kline to Matt Dillon to Matthew Broderick to Jamie Lee Curtis to Emilio Estevez, would be a perfect fit. "They'd like each other," Beanie told her, explaining that Adrienne was about to move east, and Stevie was New York based.

Sheila looked at Beanie like she was nuts. "Are you out of your fucking mind?" Sheila screamed. "She's probably sucking Stieglitz off right now."

Beanie, remaining calm, told her she knew how close Stevie and Stieglitz were, but she reasoned that if Stevie got Adrienne through Beanie, Stevie would protect Beanie against Stieglitz. Ever since *Kaleidoscope,* the Alliance Group had been all over Adrienne anyhow, calling her weekly, sending gifts. And while Adrienne wasn't tempted, at a certain point she might be. Beanie reasoned that putting Adrienne with Stevie Lanzetti was a smart, proactively defensive move, saying that she'd have someone on the inside, telling Stieglitz to just stop it.

"Oh, yes," Sheila said sarcastically, "tell him to just stop it. That'll do the trick."

Sheila wasn't sure if Beanie was deliberately trying to sabotage herself or the agency or just being provocative. *Is she kidding?* she wondered, but then Beanie told her that she'd heard Matt Dillon and Matthew Broderick recently switched agents within Alliance, which was always a signal that a client was unhappy.

"And your point is?" Sheila asked.

"My point is, once Stevie gets to know me and likes me, presuming she does and she will, maybe she'll bring the Matts to me."

Sheila countered. "What if she doesn't? What if Adrienne gets unhappy and Stevie brings her to Alliance?"

Beanie shrugged. That could happen. But it was a chance she was willing to take, because if she was right, she would be the only person that Stevie trusted outside of Alliance. And that could be huge. In time.

It was a gutsy move and Beanie needed Sheila's endorsement. "Will you back me?" she asked.

Sheila considered. It was moronic, for sure, but Sheila needed Beanie's loyalty more than the office needed Adrienne Seabergh. Either way, it was a win-win for Sheila Day, and since she was collecting wins while waiting on the board seat, Sheila agreed. "Okay," she said. "It's the worst idea in the world, but I'll back you."

"Great," Beanie said, thanking her, and immediately headed for her office where she had Hawkeye put in a call to Stevie Lanzetti.

Stevie, whose real name was Stefanie, was a hands-on, brutally honest, tough-as-nails manager who didn't make small talk and didn't suffer fools. She read every script and manuscript, claiming that just reading a synopsis was for idiots and didn't encourage gossip, games, or bullshit. With her short black hair, and all-black ensemble, Lanzetti was a bit of a New York–based enigma. In her early forties, she was a creature of habit, driving her own car around New York City, eating at the same diner every day, ordering the same food, and wearing versions of the same clothing, no matter the season or occasion. Originally from the North Shore of Long Island, she detested travel, and other than monthly trips to Los Angeles on the MGM Grand Air, where the same car and driver would wait and take her to the same room at the Chateau Marmont, she rarely broke from her routine.

So, this request for a meeting with a Sylvan Light agent was out of the norm, if not her comfort zone.

Even using Adrienne's name as a calling card, it had taken Beanie three weeks to get the meeting.

"How can I help you?" Stevie asked suspiciously over coffee at the Chateau Marmont.

Beanie took a deep breath and shot her straight.

"I like your loyalty," she said. "Even if it is to the Alliance Group. I respect the fact that it's unfaltering."

Stevie looked at her. *What the fuck,* she thought, still not sure what Beanie's angle was. "I'm not interested in your clients," Beanie said. "I mean unless they're leaving. I'm interested in you," she told her, explaining that she was looking to strike up a relationship with someone whose loyalty was beyond reproach.

Stevie lit a cigarette and smiled. *This chick has balls,* she thought. She had to give her that. "What do the boys on the first floor think about you reaching out to me?" Stevie asked, eyes narrowed, weighing the truth in Beanie's candor.

"They think I'm nuts," she said. "But I told them that Alliance was already going after Adrienne, and I needed a linebacker who was great with material, who shot straight, and whose integrity wasn't limited to one company."

Stevie lit a cigarette. "What makes you think it's not?"

"Instinct," Beanie said. She was banking on the belief that if she brought a client to Stevie, Stevie would back her even against Stieglitz and Conroy. Beanie knew that she and Stevie were similar in many ways. Stevie had worked for Light in New York in the late '70s and, like Beanie, she wasn't recognized for her talent. "They judged you," Beanie said. "And my guess was, they were unkind."

"That's an understatement," Stevie told her. Unlike Beanie, Stevie left Light after a few years, began managing actors, and brought them all to Matthew Stieglitz and David Shipp at Alliance, vowing never to work with Sylvan Light again. She had found a way to survive in spite of them.

Over the course of their lunch, Stevie found that she not only liked Beanie, but admired her moxie and direct approach. That day at the Chateau Marmont, Beanie Rosen signed Stevie Lanzetti, and Stevie Lanzetti, a few weeks later, signed Adrienne Seabergh.

Over the next few years, these two background people guided Adrienne as she surpassed all the girls, the boys, and the benchmarks, inventing and reinventing what was possible for actresses, agents, and businesswomen who stood on each other's shoulders to reach new heights.

THE YOKO

When in doubt, follow the Yoko . . .

—A GINGER WHO DIDN'T

1990–1991

The story goes that sometime in the early '70s, after the Beatles had split, Yoko Ono asked John Lennon to leave. "I really needed some space," she said in an interview with David Sheff. "I thought it was a good idea that he go to LA and just leave me alone for a while." Lennon, also interviewed, told Sheff that at first he liked it. "Oh, you know, 'Bachelor Life! Whoopee, whoopee.' And then I woke up one day and I thought, 'What is this? What is this? I want to go home.'" But Yoko told him he wasn't ready to come home. Shortly thereafter he began an affair with their twenty-two-year-old assistant, Mae Pang. What people didn't realize until much later was that Yoko had arranged for the affair, assuring Mae Pang that she wouldn't mind and encouraging the intimacy. What seemed selfless and accommodating was actually quite pointed and strategic, as Yoko Ono effectively became confidante to both Mae and John, offering a shoulder, counsel, or just an ear. But eventually the thrill of someone new waned for the comfort of someone wise.

He never left home again.

The Gingers had referred to it as "the Yoko," and Mercedes Baxter had thought about it ever since Grace Khan died and Harvey Khan had suggested she move into the home on Stone Canyon. She had been wary, not only because Cheryl and Todd, Khan's adult children, barely hid their distaste for her, but Khan himself, who had admitted to sixty-nine but was actually seventy-four years old, had grown disgruntled. *Less short-tempered and more bored,* she thought. Living there was a conundrum. While she was not his wife, she was playing the part, and it was a thankless role without benefits. It was time for Mercedes to do the Yoko.

"What are you doing?" Khan asked one Sunday when he was getting ready for golf at Hillcrest and noticed that Mercedes was not. She always came along, read a book on the terrace, and waited. Dutifully. He liked knowing she was there. They'd have brunch afterward, sometimes with other members, then take a walk around the grounds, maybe play some bocce ball, or go to a museum. And then Sunday evenings they'd order in something decadent—spaghetti or pizza or lasagna—then watch a first-run movie in their screening room. Mercedes kept an eye on Khan's weight and his blood pressure, both on the rise, and only allowed him one free day a week where kitchen scales were confiscated, and calories weren't counted.

So, he was surprised, if not alarmed that she wasn't ready.

"What's wrong?" he asked. "Aren't you coming?" Then he saw her two Louis Vuitton suitcases and a small valise.

"No dear," she said calmly, "I'm not." Mercedes went on to explain that she needed space, and believed he did as well. "I'm going to take some time," she told him, saying that she was going to travel a bit, see some friends, family.

This utterly confused Khan. He thought that Mercedes was disassociated from her past and was surprised to learn otherwise.

Then she added a final blow that paralyzed him: "I hired that pretty blond floater who worked for Stu," she said. "Claire. She'll start tomorrow." Mercedes knew that Khan liked her, had heard his comments when he thought she wasn't listening, had watched his eyes follow her as she walked up and down the hall.

Khan was stunned. Guilty. Apologetic.

But there was nothing to apologize about, she assured him. This just made her decision that much easier. "Get to know her," she said.

And then she walked out.

. . .

Mercedes Baxter married Harvey Khan fourteen months later in a simple civil ceremony in Northern California attended only by Stu Lonshien and his new girlfriend Jennifer Banks, whom Mercedes had met that morning—Lonshien, the week before. After a brief honeymoon, she resumed her duties as the legal right hand of Khan, and according to some, was steadying that hand. There had been rumors that Harvey had suffered a series of mini strokes.

In early 1991 he began extending his weekends. When asked about his absences, Mercedes explained that he was taking meetings in Palm Springs, or at Hillcrest, or in Malibu.

No one questioned her beyond that, as many of the decisions that were coming from his office aligned with those of the board of directors, and in a don't-ask-don't-tell universe, it was easier to let sleeping Khan lie. Privately, however, there were growing suspicions that Mercedes Baxter Khan was quietly running things behind the scenes, writing memos, signing Khan's name, and authorizing actions that she thought he'd approve of. There had even been the suggestion that his compromised condition had preceded the nuptials, with the bride literally and figuratively leading him down the garden path, so to speak, even if his words of acceptance at the altar were slurred.

But on the first-year anniversary of their marriage, all doubt was erased, and whispers silenced as the happy couple allowed Sheila Day to throw them an intimate celebration for seventy-five people at the Hotel Bel-Air. Heads of studios, heads of state, and a sprinkling of stars such as Clint Eastwood, Tom Selleck, and Barbara Walters distracted from the fact that there was no family from either side in attendance.

There was no question to anyone present that evening: King Khan had his queen, and that queen had taken charge.

WHAT'S NEXT?

The greatness of our lives is not so much in what we
leave behind, but in what we send forward.
—SOMEONE WHO MIGHT HAVE HEARD STEVE
JOBS SAY THAT TO SOMEONE ELSE

1992

"Right this way, Miss Rosen," said the hostess at the Polo Lounge as she led Beanie through the main dining room toward *her* table on the outside terrace.

There wasn't a person she didn't see, or who didn't see her. In just a few years, Beanie had transformed into a version of whom she'd always wanted to be: a power agent with her own stars, her own table, and her own secretary. The girl who used to wear red jumpers and clogs was now in custom-made Donna Karan power suits, with statement gold jewelry and a man's Rolex—which communicated strength, she guessed, or perhaps equality, if only around her wrist. Beanie Rosen entered into the '90s with power, class, clients, style, and a hunger for more. She no longer looked up to Jamie Garland and Sheila Day: she looked over to them.

Emancipated from the chains of those who'd tried to stop her, Beanie Rosen, confident and self-assured, navigated the room, greeting stars and directors, making small talk and big deals.

Jamie Garland, who was lunching with Don Simpson, one of the producers of *Top Gun,* had promised him that Beanie would stop by. Jamie had already given Beanie the heads-up that Simpson had a script for Adrienne Seabergh that he wanted Beanie to reconsider. He knew that Adrienne trusted Beanie's judgment, and he hadn't been able to get Beanie on the phone.

Strange how the tables had turned. A few years earlier, Beanie had tried to get a meeting with Don, and even with Jamie's help she could only meet his head of development. Now Simpson needed Jamie to get to Beanie.

Hollywood is funny that way, she thought. *Ignore people at your own peril, and then when you need them, find mutual friends to smooth over the insults caused by your arrogance.*

Jamie watched as Kevin Costner joined Beanie. They stopped at Sherry Lansing's table to chat with her and Michael Douglas. Sherry, the new chairman of Paramount, was old friends with Douglas and new friends with Beanie. The two women warmly embraced while Douglas stood, greeting Beanie first, then shaking Costner's hand, pulling him in, whispering something private the way Johnny Carson always did on *The Tonight Show,* implying to anyone present, and everyone was, that there was intimacy, that they were connected.

And they were, in a way, since Beanie represented them both.

Originally, Beanie hadn't even been a number two on Douglas's team, but she had ingratiated herself to Gil Amati, his agent, and then to Douglas, recommending material she was reading for Westman but that she thought might be better suited for him.

Douglas was impressed, not just by her taste, but by the breadth of her capacity to absorb available material. Beanie read four newspapers a day and several magazines, scouring them for articles that could be optioned, reviewing unpublished manuscripts, screenplays, and projects that were still in the nascent idea stage. That's how she'd found a lurid tale about murder, sex, and manipulation that she knew only Douglas could do: *Basic Instinct.* Written by Joe Eszterhas, it would be, she believed, the kind of film you'd discuss around the watercooler Monday mornings; the kind you'd see once, then go back again because you just had to; the kind that would keep Douglas on top of the top tier of the top stars.

Gil Amati told him to pass. Beanie Rosen told him to take it. He took her as well.

While Costner and Douglas carried on their conversation, Beanie made her way to Jamie's table where Army Archerd, the big columnist for *Variety,* was holding court.

"What's Costner got coming up?" he asked Beanie, looking for a tip, a scoop, or if it merited, a headline.

Beanie, always guarding her words and her clients, simply replied, "Lunch," and then turned her attention to Simpson, assuring him that she was going to look at the script again for Adrienne.

While Simpson explained everything he would do in the rewrite, you could feel a distraction coming from somewhere behind them; a murmur that became a stir that became a noise so palpable it stopped Simpson mid-pitch.

Ella Gaddy had arrived with Scott Westman, and the room—already top-heavy with Douglas, Costner, and a few other luminaries—toppled over.

"It's a good day to be at the Beverly Hills Hotel," Jamie quipped, pointing out to Archerd that three-quarters of the stars present were Light clients. Add to that the fact that Scott Westman, who rarely frequented eateries such as the Polo Lounge, was there, it certainly was worthy of a mention.

But Archerd wanted more. "You cooking up a project maybe for them to do together?" he asked as Beanie smiled, excused herself, and walked over to Ella, who with Westman and Costner was already seated in the corner booth.

Being neither intimidated nor boastful, Jamie was impressed with how smoothly Beanie handled the columnist. She looked over at her protégé, so skilled and adroit, giving just enough to keep them curious but never revealing her hand. At that precise moment, as the two former secretaries huddled with the superstars, Jamie realized Beanie Rosen and Ella Gaddy were what's next. The baton she used to twirl as an adorable high school cheerleader had been passed without ceremony, but with a forward momentum that put her and Sheila Day in the rearview mirror.

Remnants of a past generation, Sheila and Jamie still played to the boys' club in order to play with them. Before this Anita Hill mess, Jamie liked to joke that she'd fucked her way to the middle, tolerating a pinch on the ass, or an off-color joke, all the while advancing without threatening, achieving without emasculating. Much like Sheila, who'd also fucked when she could and joked when she couldn't, the women not only survived but thrived because they never tried to be the men.

But that was the '60s, and this was the '90s, when you didn't dare joke about fucking or sucking or sexitarial favors. Because if you did, you'd be judged or perhaps ostracized by the Beanie Rosens or the Ella Gaddys or the newest breed of power women who set themselves apart from the generation that had come before. While Sheila and Jamie played to their femininity, Beanie and Ella and their acolytes played against it. And it wasn't just the Armani men's suits, or the Doc Martens, or the push for equal pay which of course they would never get; it was the realization that women in industry were no longer the exception, they were the rule, and the rules were changing. Fast.

For dinosaurs like Sheila and Jamie, the aperture was closing. If they didn't leave their mark soon, they would become relics or fossils, celebrated perhaps in memoriam. But if they could be insulated against irrelevance, they, like the men, might go the distance, working through their seventies and eighties, their images cast in bronze, reminding all that they, too, mattered.

And the only thing that would ensure their immortality was a board seat. For Sheila, at sixty-one, it was not only the next move, but it was also the only move; the last stand, the finish line, the glass ceiling for every woman in power who looked up and still saw a pair of men's loafers.

In the history of Sylvan Light there had only been seven seats on the board, so to think that there would now be an eighth, and that that extra seat would go to a woman, was preposterous. But it was also true: in six months' time, Sheila Day, per her contract, would be sitting shoulder to shoulder alongside them at the only table that mattered. And then once Sheila got in, maybe Jamie could follow, maybe others, and the power, the real power would finally shift. That board seat was a benchmark, and everyone from Sherry Lansing to Gloria Steinem to Beanie Rosen knew it.

If Sheila won, they won.

And Sheila Day was determined to win. She had worked hard to placate the boys on the first floor, while supporting all the female agents and file clerks and secretaries who'd looked up to her; presenting herself as their leader, their mentor, their role model, and their quarterback.

"If I can do it, you can," she'd say, all the while hiding her contempt for this younger group of aspirants with big hair, big attitudes, and big phones that weren't just in cars anymore but traveled with them, allowing anyone to reach them any time. The world had gone mobile, but not Sheila. She wasn't about to put a phone in her pocketbook and take it with her to restaurants, or the hairdresser's, or on vacation. She thought that was garish and desperate and uncouth. This younger group—the agents, the trainees, even the secretaries who suddenly insisted on being called assistants—were irritating and entitled, and as far as she was concerned, beneath her.

But she never told them how she felt. Because it didn't matter. All that mattered was the board seat. And in order to get that she needed the men, the women, all the key players who held her in place to stay put through the end of the year. It was a condition the board had made, an addendum to her contract. "Maintain the status quo," it read, and it was nebulous enough that she wasn't concerned. That is, until June of 1992, when suddenly, the alarm sounded.

"Moze Goff is in play," Jamie Garland said, coming into Sheila's office and closing the door.

"What the fuck?" Sheila screamed, balling up her fists in midair. She had been navigating speed bumps for years, but she didn't expect one so close to the finish line. All she needed was stability. There were just six months left before she got the board seat. "Six fucking months," she said, "and the cocksucker couldn't have waited?"

Jamie tried to calm her. "There's always rumors about him," she reminded her, which was true. There were always rumors about Moze Goff, who was flying with Geffen and Diller and private equity honchos. He was big time. Really big time, and Sheila had worked hard to befriend him, to help him, to promote him.

"Why the fuck is he doing this to me?" she asked, sucking the life out of her French cigarette. She really believed they were in good standing. "I fucking backed him in his fakakta idea about getting the office computerized," she reminded Jamie, who didn't need reminding. She'd heard Sheila complain endlessly about his request and his sense of entitlement.

Moze had come to her three months earlier, asking her to not only back him but help him convince the board to purchase one hundred and fifty computers for agents east and west. And even though the request was for half a million dollars, she rallied the board and urged them to listen.

"What's 'Next'?" asked Harvey Khan, studying a pamphlet that Moze had handed out for a prototype of the new computer system he'd wanted them to purchase.

"This is," said Moze dramatically, removing the cover off a large square machine with a three-dimensional "Next!" on the home screen.

Gathering around the conference table, the old men studied the new technology and listened as Moze waxed poetic about a superhighway of information, explaining that NeXT computers were the brainchild of Steve Jobs, who had recently been ousted from Apple and had started his own company.

"Sylvan Light will be the first company to try it," he said with pride. Moze and Jobs, both outsiders in a system they didn't respect, had bonded over their future vision of a world they were determined to create.

The board seemed dubious. The idea that each agent should be assigned a personal computer for electronic mail felt extravagant.

"It'll pay off in spades," Moze promised as they watched him type an email to Jobs in Silicon Valley and get a response seconds later.

"How about that?" Moze asked, turning to the board, expecting jubilation.

Instead, he was met with confusion.

"Why is this any better than a call?" Harvey Khan asked, uncomfortable that Sheila had put him in a position to turn the boy down. He liked Moze a great deal and recognized his value as a leading agent, but the idea that he expected them to shell out half a million dollars on one hundred and fifty machines that sent messages seemed frivolous. "There's only so much mail a person can take," Harvey Khan said, shaking his head in either disagreement or defiance of a future to which he refused to subscribe.

But Sheila, true to her word, argued with them over the next few weeks until she got what she considered a victory. "They're going to buy twenty-five computers as a test case," she told Moze, explaining that this was a huge win. "Honeeeey, give it a year, then you'll have computers coming out of your ass," she joked. She thought she had done a good thing. But, in truth, Moze flew back to New York and began questioning if he wanted to put his future in the hands of an archaic group of men who held on to the past as if they were holding on to their youth, and a woman who justified their pitiful offering as a win.

Moze understood that Sheila, wanting him to be grateful for the crumbs, didn't so much have a vision for the future, as she did a fear of it. She needed to keep the status quo, and he needed to disrupt it. So, while Sheila had thought she'd earned his loyalty, if not his respect, quietly he began to make other plans.

Three months later, suitors were lining up, and rumors were heating up. Some said Moze was down the line with Stieglitz, others said he was meeting with Sony chairman Norio Ohga to perhaps run Sony. Either way, there was enough smoke to motivate Sheila to fly to New York with a fire extinguisher; to reassure herself that Moze was stable, and to reassure Moze that come January 1993, she'd get him whatever he wanted, including all one hundred and fifty of his fucking computers.

Transparent about the board seat, but confident that he would understand that there was muscle to her promise, Sheila offered him complete autonomy if he stayed put.

He told her he respected her for her honesty and promised to think about it. Moze knew that he had her over a barrel. Sheila knew that Moze knew. And she hated him for it with every ounce of her being. But the finish line was within striking distance, and there was too much on it to lose a crucial player. She needed everyone to be happy. Until year's end . . .

THE EXIT PLAN

Let's get the fuck out of here.
—ELLA GADDY TO BEANIE ROSEN

1992

"We should look at office space," Barry Licht told Ella Gaddy, Beanie Rosen, and Howie Mishkin over dinner at Morton's. It was July of '92, two weeks after Sheila had flown to New York to meet with Moze and five months before she was supposed to be getting that board seat.

None of them knew about Sheila and her board seat nor did they particularly care, except Beanie. And Beanie was overwhelmed by the reality that they, herself included, were actually talking about leaving Sylvan Light and forming a management company. They'd been discussing it since January of that year when Barry and Howie had first approached Beanie and Ella.

Howie Mishkin, who had started in the mailroom just after Moze, was now a big television packaging agent, representing the creators and in some cases the stars of television shows including *Mad About You, Murphy Brown,* and *Home Improvement.* Because the Light Agency took a packaging fee from the networks, they could earn anywhere between fifty and one hundred thousand dollars per episode of any given show. So, Howie Mishkin brought in more commissions than Ella and Beanie combined. Barry also had hefty bookings now representing touring musicians such as Rod Stewart, Phil Collins, Elvis Costello, and most recently New Kids On The Block.

Slick, ambitious, and keeping to the straight and narrow—with an emphasis on straight—Barry Licht had grown restless at the Light Agency. This idea to leave had been gestating for a while and arose quite organically when Howie casually mentioned over lunch how much money the television packages that he'd put together were making for the agency.

"It's close to five million dollars," he'd said, which stopped Barry mid-chew.

Barry knew that packaging agents brought in a lot, but this was something else. Howie, who pulled in two hundred and fifty thousand dollars, plus car and bonus, had been happy with his salary as long as he didn't think about what he was leaving on the table. But Barry did think about it, and then started calculating how much Rod Stewart's last tour brought in—and New Kids On The Block. The office was making millions off the two agents, and the agents were settling for peanuts, a limited expense account, and a fancy car that Sylvan Light owned.

"It's bullshit," Barry said, and by January of '92 he'd invited Beanie and Ella into the conversation over drinks at his sleek new hacienda just off Kings Road in West Hollywood. It was a renovated Spanish bungalow he'd purchased for half a million dollars with three bedrooms, two bathrooms, a pool, and an outdoor spa with a view of where he wanted to go.

Beanie was in awe of his luxurious lifestyle.

"That's the problem," he said, beginning to sow the seeds of her discontent, "you shouldn't be." He laid out this idea of a management company, a cooperative, that would have a triad of categories: Personal Appearance, which he would run, Television, which Howie would run, and Motion Pictures, which Beanie and Ella would co-run.

"And," he added, "a production component." While agents were prohibited from producing, managers were not. To him, that was the kicker. He referenced Shapiro/West, the managers for Andy Kaufman and Jerry Seinfeld, who were making a fortune producing Seinfeld's hit series which was now in its third year. "You don't get rich being an agent," he told them, citing Geffen, Gallin, and Freddy DeMann, who represented Madonna.

Barry wanted to make a splash, a statement, enough noise to announce their presence with an authority that would attract other A-list stars in search of career management. But he needed Ella and Beanie for their smarts, their pedigree, and their stars. "If the four of us leave together, it would be seismic," he told them.

Ella, who'd been desperate to ditch the ten-percentery, totally got it. Her loyalty was to her clients—and to Beanie, of course. Besides, a less structured lifestyle suited her now. Her relationship with Westman was strictly professional, as he was rumored to be dating Uma Thurman, and she'd been quietly seeing a venture capitalist, Stirling Cowan, who owned several properties around the world, including a two-hundred-acre ranch outside of Lake Tahoe that Ella visited weekly. Thirty-two years her senior, Cowan would fly Ella up to Tahoe every Thursday in his private Cessna and back every Tuesday morning so she could attend the weekly motion picture meeting, which she began to resent. Loudly.

Finally, she just stopped attending.

Her disrespect and disregard for the rules was becoming too obvious; but Beanie, as her partner, would try to smooth things over, updating the agents on all client business.

Sheila, who feared Ella more than she detested her—and she detested her a great deal—said nothing about her absences, and the agents were forced to tolerate her rudeness.

But the truth was, Ella no longer gave a damn. For her, this idea of a new management company meant emancipation from a structure that had never truly suited her. She knew her clients would go with her, and she could work remotely if she wanted to, juggling calls, making deals, and going on set visits when necessary. She recognized the opportunity as a financial windfall, and Cowan, who was a millionaire a million times over, endorsed the move.

But Beanie was another story. Being an agent wasn't a stepping stone for her, it was an endgame. She didn't want to produce, she didn't want to manage, she wanted to be Sheila Day.

Of course, that annoyed Ella as her hatred for the senior agent had only grown over the years, and Beanie citing her as an example only inflamed it.

"I meant," Beanie said, quickly pivoting, "a legendary agent. That's what I want to be."

Barry knew how much Beanie had wanted to be an agent—after all, he was there at the beginning—but reasoned that no matter how good she was, they'd never recognize her. Not like she should be recognized. He was talking about the guys on the first floor, the ones who hadn't seen her value and still didn't. Not fully. "To them, you're just some girl who got lucky."

Over the next few months, Barry and Howie worked on Beanie, knowing that Ella, who was primary on Westman, would not leave without her. Beyond the fear of leaving, Beanie was concerned because she shared so many clients with Stevie Lanzetti, including Matt Dillon, Matthew Broderick, Kevin Kline, Kevin Bacon, and of course Adrienne Seabergh, who was the hottest young female star in the business. She couldn't pull any of them and wouldn't even try, lest someone suggest it.

They were stuck for a while until Barry had an idea. "Why don't we ask Stevie to join us?" he said. That way they could have an East Coast presence.

"Stevie would be brilliant," Ella agreed, urging Beanie to set a call and arrange a meeting the next week when Stevie was in town so they could all approach her.

Beanie was trepidatious, but she agreed, at least to set the meeting.

To her surprise, Stevie was intrigued. While she'd had offers before, this was different, primarily because of the television component. That, she knew, was where the money was. Besides, Barry had proposed an equitable split. "We'll all make equal salaries," he'd said, regardless of who represented whom.

Stevie left the meeting inclined to do it, but she called them the next day and said she felt like they needed another heavyweight in New York and suggested they go for Moze Goff. "I hear he's unhappy," she told them, oblivious to Beanie who was looking at Barry who was looking at the floor.

The Moze drama was water under a bridge so high neither Beanie nor Barry cared to look down. They never talked about him, or it, or what had happened afterward. Beanie knew that Barry's heart had been broken, too, that he had spun out, rebounded, and reset, burying his proclivities with a different version of Morgan Fairchild on his arm every month. He kept them rotating so no one ever got too serious, and no one ever guessed otherwise.

The closest she had gotten to talking about their shared past was when Beanie had once asked what ever happened to Marci Goldklank.

"She got married. Finally," he'd told her, toasting Beanie with a Diet Coke and a sigh of relief. He'd felt guilty, responsible, and emancipated from that life, but oddly chained in another of his own creation.

But she never asked him about Moze. It was too close. And now, here they both were, considering making Moze their equal partner.

"I mean, it would be huge," Beanie said. "Massive," Barry agreed. And it wasn't just Moze's clients, it was his swag, his know-how, his associations. He flew in a circle so high that studio heads had to look up. He was the whole package, and not just for a packaging agent. There were always rumors that the Alliance Group was taking a run at him or ICM or more recently Dell computers, which strangely made sense since he'd become consumed with New Age technology and had been frustrated with Sylvan Light and how slow they'd acted and reacted to the NeXT computer experiment. Maybe it was a good idea to approach him.

"I'll do it," said Beanie, nervous and excited to dip a toe into the Moze.

MOSES SUPPOSES ERRONEOUSLY

Betrayal is the only truth that sticks.

—ARTHUR MILLER

1992

On July 6, 1992, Beanie Rosen scheduled a lunch in New York with Moze Goff. Requesting some time to discuss a private matter, she'd sent him an electronic mail on the NeXT computer, figuring that was safer than phones or memos, and figuring he'd be impressed that she was using the electronic mail system that many agents still treated like a novelty.

Moze responded immediately, inviting her to his penthouse apartment on Gramercy Park. He was warm and welcoming and genuinely happy to see Beanie. Contrary to gossip, he wasn't dating Cher and hadn't a clue how that rumor ever got started. "I've never even met her," he said as he showed her around his two-bedroom apartment meticulously designed by Zajac & Callahan in a Mission style, heavy on woods and Warhols, light on personal effects.

Beanie, who wore a white Calvin Klein shirtdress short enough to show off her legs, but roomy enough without the belt to hide her middle, was impressed and charmed. They walked to his outside terrace, half a block long, with flowering plants and trees and fountains and grapevines creating his own little sanctuary. And then in the distance, peeking through the ficus, you could see the Chrysler Building.

"Who lives like this?" she said as his houseman brought them fresh lemonade. Beanie raised her eyebrows and mouthed, "Houseman?"

Moze laughed. He missed her sarcasm, her sense of humor, and the history they'd shared.

And while before her was a new and polished version of her old friend, Beanie realized that she'd missed him, too. They turned off their mobile phones, spoke of his parents and then hers, and spent the day laughing, reminiscing, and gossiping about the office. They both liked Sheila in spite of Sheila and worried that Harvey Khan seemed a bit off of late. She learned that Moze and Gil Amati had a timeshare together in the Hamptons, and that Jamie Garland might be having a little something on the side with Stu Lonshien. It didn't feel so much like old times as it did new times with an old friend.

He told her how good it was to see her, how much he'd missed her, how proud he was of her, and how grateful he was to her. Beanie wondered why she'd ever wasted time being mad. They were so much better as friends, and she began to see countless opportunities of things they could do together, especially if he joined them in the new company.

For the first time she was excited by the possibility of this management company as she launched into her pitch, stressing—obviously—confidentiality.

Moze seemed genuinely interested and told her that he believed that it would be massively successful. But he also said that he wasn't interested in management. He liked what he did, he told her, and while he didn't always like where he did it, he was, for the most part, content.

"I'm an agent," he said. And with a clarity that comes from absolute truth, she realized she was, too.

When she got back to LA, she told everyone that Moze was flattered by the offer and thought it would be huge, but he wanted to stay at the agency. And then she dropped the bomb and admitted that she wanted to stay as well.

While they were all disappointed, Ella was crushed, which surprised Beanie.

She knew that Ella had wanted her to go, but they had been on separate tracks for so many years that she just presumed Ella would be fine. The depth of Ella's despair touched Beanie, who encouraged Ella to go without her. She told her that they would still work together, that she was counting on representing all of Ella's clients so they'd be talking even more than they did now, only Beanie wouldn't be busting Ella's ass for not going to meetings.

"Excellent point," said Ella, smiling through tears. They'd worked and lived together for almost ten years, and just because they wouldn't be down the hall at an apartment or an office, it didn't mean that they wouldn't be as close. They'd still be connected.

Only differently.

That night Beanie and Ella went out, just the two of them, like old times, and spoke about their futures. It was almost as if the decision to separate had reconnected them with a renewed excitement for the unknown.

"It's like we're graduating, and one of us is staying in state and the other isn't," Beanie said.

Ella talked about her love for Stirling, about maybe even trying to have kids one day. She knew he was older, which was an understatement, but she believed he'd be a great father.

Beanie was surprised by her candor, as they barely broached the subject of children. It had been a non-starter for both of them. Ella had always been sensitive to any inquiries, past or future, and Beanie had never entertained the idea in any sort of real way, because she'd never had any sort of real boyfriend, except Moze.

"You and Moze should have a kid," Ella said. Beanie laughed, but Ella was serious, pointing out that it was untraditional enough that it might appeal to Moze.

"A child out of wedlock shuttled between coasts?" Beanie asked jokingly.

Ella shrugged. "Who else is he gonna knock up who understands him the way you do?"

Beanie looked at her and shook it off. “Maybe first we sign a client or two, then we work on a kid,” she told Ella, taking a shot of tequila.

“Here’s to you and Moze and all the little Mozes,” Ella said, raising her glass.

Beanie went to bed that night relieved, excited, and invigorated. She would still work with Ella as the agent to her clients, and now that she and Moze had reconnected, perhaps they would start working together more, forging a partnership, and she hoped, a renewed friendship.

That weekend, Beanie went into the office and sent Moze an email message saying how much fun she’d had with him in New York and inquired as to the recipe of his “houseman’s” lemonade. She closed asking when he was coming west next, angry at herself for not asking that question in person. It was fun, this electronic mail system, and she was hoping he was near his computer and would immediately answer.

But he didn’t.

Since she didn’t have a home computer, she went back to the office on Sunday to see if he had replied and was disappointed when he hadn’t. She thought about calling him, but that felt desperate and clingy, so instead she sent another electronic message saying that she’d heard George Lucas had left ICM and was thinking maybe they could go after him together. She had taken great pains in writing the email so that it was informative but casual, then waited around a few hours to see if he’d answer her.

When he didn’t, she figured he was probably in Amagansett at his summer share with Amati, without his computer or his mobile phone, and she would just see him at the motion picture meeting Monday morning, which they teleconferenced in from New York.

But Moze wasn’t at the motion picture meeting on Monday morning. Sheila, more annoyed than alarmed, took it as a sign of disrespect.

“Tell Moze,” Sheila said via teleconference to one of the junior agents in the New York office, “that motion picture meetings are not optional, and he should call me when he gets in.”

Moze never called.

Two hours later, in a memo to Harvey Khan, Sheila Day, and the board of directors, Moze Goff resigned from the Sylvan Light Agency.

Thanking them for the wonderful years of experience, he wrote that it was time to strike out on his own.

That was it.

A few short lines declaring his independence.

Moze wasn't going to be a manager; he was going to be an agent.

For himself.

It was a devastating blow to the agency as every client went with him and others called to see if they could. Professionally, it was a knife in Sheila's back. She had laid the stakes on the table; she had begged him to wait. And he had agreed, or at least she thought he had. Certainly he'd understood what was on the line for her. But he didn't care. Sheila was shaken. She left for the day without addressing the resignation, the troops, or any press inquiries.

She was devastated.

But not nearly as devastated as Beanie Rosen, who had opened her heart, shared her dreams, and confided *her* plans. "He not only withheld his plans from me," she told Ella, who'd come into her office as soon as she'd heard, "he didn't include me in them. He didn't ask if I wanted to go," she said sadly, still trying to wrap her head around it.

"Would you have gone?" Ella asked.

Beanie shrugged. That was beside the point. He didn't want her to. And that killed her. "Here I was telling him that we could work together and build something together, and all that time, he knew he was leaving, and he never said a word." Tears were falling down Beanie's face as the sting of his betrayal cut her into tiny pieces. "And it wasn't just me who he betrayed," she told Ella, explaining that he knew that Sheila Day was supposed to get the board seat at the end of the year, and that she needed all the agents to stay put to ensure she'd get it. "Now with him gone, she might not get it," Beanie said. Oblivious to the fact that Ella hadn't known about Sheila's board seat, Beanie had unknowingly given her the kill shot. And Ella took it.

One week to the day later, Ella Gaddy, Howie Mishkin, Barry Licht, and Stevie Lanzetti announced the formation of King's Road Partners, taking the agency, the industry, and most especially Beanie Rosen by complete surprise. They weren't supposed to leave until the end of the year.

If Moze's departure had wounded Sylvan Light, this was devastating.

The board held an emergency meeting as agents scrambled inside the agency to save clients and outside the agency to sign them. Between the clients the agency had lost a week earlier due to Moze's defection, and the ones they were poised to lose because of the latest exits, Sylvan Light was spiraling. The press was ruthless, alleging that agents were jumping ship due to poor leadership. All eyes were on Sheila Day, who was blindsided and speechless.

She wasn't the only one.

Beanie, stunned, asked Barry why they changed their plans.

Barry shrugged and told her, "Ella said if we don't leave now, she's out."

Thanks to Beanie Rosen, Ella Gaddy made sure that Sheila Day did not get her seat at the table that Christmas.

ET TU, BRUTE? . . .

The saddest thing about betrayal is that it
never comes from your enemies.
—BEANIE ROSEN, WHO HEARD IT FROM A FRIEND

1993–1994

"Listen, we've been friends for a long time, so I hope you don't mind me stopping by," Mercedes Khan said, standing at the door to Beanie's office.

Beanie, rarely at a loss for words, just sat staring at the petite woman poised in her doorway.

"May I come in?" she asked, presuming both a friendship and an intimacy that belied their relationship.

Beanie was speechless and simply nodded as the wife of the president of the Sylvan Light Agency, dressed head to toe in a black-and-pink-tweed Chanel suit, walked into her office and closed the door for privacy.

At forty-three, Mercedes, still youthful and fit at one hundred and two pounds, had the same short hairstyle, perhaps a shade darker than it used to be, with flawless skin and dewy makeup, and while she was ten years Beanie's senior, she looked like she was her contemporary. Manicured, polished, and stiff, Queen Khan assumed a mannered and authoritative stance. After all, she was the wife of the agency president, legally finding her way to the title she had zeroed in on a decade earlier like an assassin with a single bullet. And though she was asking permission to enter, Beanie had the funny feeling that she was the guest in Mercedes's office.

Mercedes sat gingerly on the chintz chair, balancing a thick P&C envelope on her lap. "I don't want to keep you," she said, "but I have something very important that I'd like to discuss."

Beanie, half expecting a drum roll, smiled, and waited.

"It would mean a great deal to Mr. Khan," she said, "and to me, Beanie," she added, without a hint of irony, "if you would sign a three-year contract with the Light Agency." She reminded Beanie that only the most important agents were given contracts, and Beanie was someone that Mr. Khan personally took pride in.

"You're homegrown," she said, as if either she or Khan had anything to do with watering her. She held out the thick envelope. "There's a mutual option for three additional years," she told her, explaining that the total compensation was more than seven million dollars, and that was just in base salary.

Beanie understood that Mercedes wasn't going to leave until she at least had an indication that Beanie would consider the highly unusual request. Much like the Morris office, historically Sylvan Light only gave contracts to key players, which signaled to Beanie that, in their eyes at least and at last, she mattered. While she already knew it, of course—by her client list, by the way people treated her around town, by the deference shown from parking attendants to studio executives—it meant something to her that they knew it, too.

They were finally acknowledging her worth. They couldn't afford to lose her.

By attrition, by resilience, and by sheer determination, Beanie Rosen had risen to become one of the most important and most powerful agents not only at Sylvan Light, but in the industry, representing superstars like Scott Westman, Kevin Costner, Dennis Quaid, Meg Ryan, Michael Douglas, Kevin Kline, Kathleen Turner, Adrienne Seabergh, and Matt Dillon, to name a few. The only people more powerful were Matthew Stieglitz and David Shipp, both at Alliance. But Beanie Rosen was on their tail.

It had happened, quite literally, overnight. Once Moze left, and then on his heels Ella, Howie, and Barry, it had put the office and the industry on notice, and a spotlight on Beanie.

"What would Beanie do?" people asked. There were rumors she would join Ella at King's Road, or perhaps join Moze at the newly formed Goff

Partners, or even align with another agency, like Morris, or Alliance, or ICM.

"You can't leave," Sheila had told her, coming into her office seconds after Ella, Howie, and Barry had left. After Moze had exited a week earlier, Sheila had been penalized, marginalized, and ostracized, and with the latest departures, she was now fighting for her life instead of the board seat. This would not be her legacy. She would not allow it.

Ella, in wanting to wound Sheila Day, had not only obliterated her target, but had also blindsided Beanie.

"Why did you do it?" Beanie asked, still reeling from Moze's betrayal a week earlier. She had called Ella over to her apartment to confront her. "You used information I told you about Sheila to hurt her."

"No," Ella said, "I used it to kill her."

They were sitting on her balcony a few hours after Ella and Howie and Barry had informed the agency that they were leaving. Silently sharing a cigarette, the two partners considered all that had happened, all that would happen.

Beanie hadn't had time to prepare herself or the clients.

"I've spoken to all of them," Ella told her, referring to the clients Beanie would now singularly represent. "It's all good," she said, adding that they should call them together tomorrow.

Beanie nodded, trying to get her head around the reality that Ella was no longer down the hall. She was out of sorts.

"It's not just about us, is it?" Ella asked.

Beanie shook her head. "I feel bad that I never called Moze after he left," she confessed. "He tried to reach out to me—I mean, after he resigned, he called me, sent me a few emails. But I deleted them," she said, deeply regretting that she hadn't even given him the chance to explain. After all, he had a right to leave, and maybe there was a reason he hadn't confided in her. "Maybe he didn't want to put me in a bad position," she told Ella. "We had just reconnected, and it was good. We could still be friends," she said, "and who knows, maybe we'll work together again."

Ella looked at her. "You think you can still be friends working at competing agencies?"

Beanie shrugged. "Maybe. Sure. Why not? I mean, it's not like I'm going after his clients," she reasoned. "Or he'd go after mine." And that's when Beanie noticed a strange kind of look on Ella's face.

"What?" she asked, confused and slightly annoyed.

Ella took a deep breath then slowly let it out, explaining that her phone had literally been ringing off the hook as soon as the news had become public. Everyone was hoping to get meetings with her clients.

Beanie nodded. "Okay," she said. After all, that made sense.

She had known that Ella would bring a few clients to other places just to spread the wealth. But she also knew Ella would protect her with Westman, Costner, Quaid, Turner, and a few others. "So, your point is?" she asked, watching Ella pour herself a glass of Pinot from a bottle she had brought outside.

"Moze was one of them," Ella said.

Beanie took a shallow breath. "Maybe he wasn't calling about the stars," she said, hanging on to a semblance of hope.

But Ella shook her head. "No," she said softly. "He called me about Scott Westman."

Beanie steadied herself and turned away.

Ella frowned. "I don't want to hurt you, Bean, but I also can't let you make a fool of yourself."

Beanie nodded, taking it in. Ella didn't want to hurt Beanie's feelings, but she needed her to know who this guy was. "And electronic mails aside, he is *not* your friend," she told her.

"Okay," was all Beanie could muster as she sat down next to the howling coyote.

"Not okay," Ella said, walking over and putting her arm around her friend.

Beanie turned her face away, trying to hide the tears stinging the corners of her eyes. "I would never do that to him," she whispered.

Ella, comforting her, said, "Of course you wouldn't, which is why you're you."

Beanie shook it off, standing, gathering her wits. "He must have thought I was a big fat idiot," she said, tears streaming freely down her face. "Sitting out on his ridiculous terrace with his ridiculous houseman, spilling my secrets while he kept his own."

"He's just ambitious," Ella told her.

"He's just stupid," Beanie corrected her. "He doesn't know how good I am," she said with a vengeance and resolve that made Ella sit straighter. "But I'll show him. I'll show everyone."

Ella sighed. She hadn't meant to work Beanie up. She just wanted to warn her. "For what it's worth," she said, softening, "he was very clear that he didn't want to take anyone from you. He just said that if Westman was ever unhappy . . ."

"Spare me," Beanie said, putting the cigarette out on the standing ashtray shaped like a cactus. "It's a passive-aggressive way of saying if Beanie blinks, I'm in the wings. But I'm not blinking. And his fucking wings are clipped." Then she turned to Ella, and with a renewed enthusiasm that took her by surprise, said, "Let's call the clients."

"Slow down," Ella told her, "I just need your word on something."

"What?" Beanie asked, anxious to get her show on the road.

"Sheila Day never gets near them."

Beanie sighed and nodded. *God, this is getting old,* she thought. Ella's hatred was profound and had not diminished despite the fact that she'd severely crippled Sheila with her early departure. But this wasn't a time to argue.

"I swear," she promised, reiterating that she would never commingle anyone that Ella worked with, with Sheila. Ever.

Ella smiled, hugged her, and they began calling clients, securing the representation of superstars.

And with that, Beanie Rosen became a powerhouse beyond not just her wildest dreams, but beyond the reach of any woman who'd ever come before her.

Including Sheila Day.

Which was why, six months later, Mercedes Khan was sitting across from her, offering on the board's behalf, on her husband's behalf, on behalf of their long-standing "friendship," a three-year contract, with an option for three additional years, worth an excess of seven million dollars. The Sylvan Light Agency was banking on Beanie Rosen to take them into the millennium.

And for some reason they thought their best shot to get it done was Mercedes Khan.

"Let's have lunch sometime," Mercedes said, inviting Beanie to come up to Stone Canyon, referencing the mansion she now called home.

Beanie smiled and nodded and told her how lovely that sounded, knowing she'd never take her up on the invitation. That was the house that Grace Khan had built, the one where she'd raised her children who no longer served a purpose for Mercedes, the home where Harvey Khan now sat, perhaps in his garden, wondering what the fuck had happened to his life.

In June 1993, eight months after Moze and Ella and the others had left, Beanie signed the contract Mercedes had hand-delivered, and the board, relieved, rewarded her with a five-hundred-thousand-dollar signing bonus, and the title of Head of the Motion Picture Talent Department.

"It's our way of saying thank you," Stu Lonshien told her since Harvey Khan was rarely in and only communicated by memos delivered by his wife.

They had essentially put Beanie Rosen in control of the future of the company, at least in terms of who she hired, and she'd felt empowered and emboldened to bring more women into the mailroom, as well as more people of color.

While she still answered to Sheila, at least on paper, Sheila nevertheless supported her on every request, including Beanie's desire to promote Hawkeye to agent, seconding Beanie on many of her most important clients who had come to love and respect Hawkeye almost as much as they did Beanie.

If Ella and Beanie had been a good team, Hawkeye and Beanie were a better one. Though Gil Amati had wanted to second Beanie on some of the bigger stars, Hawkeye was their choice, and she became the second on Westman, Costner, Adrienne Seabergh, and Michael Douglas—who no longer worked with Gil at all. And when Hawkeye heard that Moze Goff was going after *Disclosure,* Michael Crichton's new book about reverse sexual harassment in the workplace, with his client Harrison Ford in mind to star, she brought the book to Douglas—and with Beanie's help, took it off the market.

"Let's start finding material we can send to Ford," said Hawkeye, who was, Beanie thought, better than she had ever been.

Beanie Rosen was now a very wealthy woman flying in a stratosphere that her mother could only dream of. Still zaftig, she had her clothes personally designed by Norma Kamali to amplify and camouflage. Beanie dressed impeccably, always matching her shoes to her bag, and rotating chunky jewelry. Her hair, which she wore shoulder length and straight, much like Sheila's, was blown out three times a week, and cut once a month at home.

She had moved out of the Sierra Towers, paying back Dr. Spitz for the loan he'd given her a few years earlier, and into a four-thousand-square-foot Frank Lloyd Wright home off Nichols Canyon. It had a pool she never swam in, views she rarely noticed, and a houseman she barely spoke to . . . but who always served fresh lemonade.

MAJOR MINOR

I don't know half of you half as well as I should like; and I like less than half of you half as well as you deserve.

—J. R. R. TOLKIEN, *THE FELLOWSHIP OF THE RING*

1994–1995

Matt Stieglitz was leaving Alliance. That was the rumor. No one knew where or when, but what was clear, or at least crystallizing, was that he was done agenting. And what of David Shipp? There was talk he might leave as well. If they both left, many believed that Beanie Rosen at the Sylvan Light Agency would be the top agent in the business.

But no one wanted to believe it more than Beanie Rosen. While she dismissed the rumors as petty gossip, she also fueled them, letting it be known, indirectly of course, that with her list of filmmakers and superstars, no one had bigger reach. And if someone had the balls or ignorance to suggest Moze Goff as the heir apparent, they were dismissed with a disdain that informed exile.

In truth, Beanie's reputation had grown so large that other agents now vied to put her name next to theirs if only to make themselves or their clients seem more important. That was how rapidly the sands had shifted for her. Her client list was only dwarfed by her reach. And her reach was epic. Suddenly it was *her* name opening doors in entertainment, in politics, and in education, as institutes of higher learning sought Beanie Rosen to lend her name to their boards, or to give commencement speeches inspiring others. The world recognized her as an accomplished woman who had broken through, who would support other women in their climb.

When she talked about it, and she didn't often, as the backward glance was still too fresh, she'd recall that a mere ten years earlier she'd been in servitude to a misogynist, pouring her heart into his career, inhaling his drugs and his lies, believing that he would rescue her, until she woke the fuck up and rescued herself.

Now journalists were calling her, asking her to weigh in on whatever industry topic was up for debate. They recognized her not as an agent who siphoned off 10 percent of other people's income, but as an architect of careers strategizing for others how to break through, how to make their dreams come true. Her story became urban legend: from the Central File clerk to the superstar who represented superstars.

"The sky wasn't the limit," she was quoted as saying, "just a resting place."

Even her mother was proud.

Miriam Spitz, who used to brag that she was the wife of a Beverly Hills plastic surgeon, was now the mother of Beanie Rosen, the most successful agent in Hollywood. She no longer criticized or poked or questioned who or if she was dating, and even began complaining about the skinny twins, how they were leeches with their hands constantly out. They weren't like Beanie, who gave her mother Chanel purses for Chanukah and flew her on the Concorde.

Professionally, Beanie kept her circle tight, working closely with Stevie Lanzetti—and of course Ella Gaddy, who, in the spring of '94, at the age of thirty-seven, had a baby girl, whom she named Olive.

Shortly after Olive was born, Ella, whose reputation for being fickle was well earned, decided that King's Road would have one less partner, and left to form her own boutique management company with offices in Los Angeles and Lake Tahoe.

Barry, Howie, and Stevie, who'd relied on her clients to attract others, were shocked and furious, but it made sense to Beanie. Ella was always her own boss and had it not been for Garry Sampson and perhaps Beanie, she'd have left Sylvan Light and the structure of a company long ago. It was only a matter of time until she found her way to running her own shop, answering to no one. She flew to LA once a month, bringing Olive who, like Ella, was lanky and long with strawberry curls and a face full of freckles, and would stay with Beanie in her Nichols Canyon home.

Ella was happy and Beanie was happy, and their mutual clients were happy, most specifically Scott Westman, who in September 1994, opened his film *The Adventures of Major Minor,* which he wrote, directed, and produced to rave reviews and massive box office success, solidifying the fact that he was a triple threat—perhaps bigger than Eastwood.

Westman had poured five years of his life into *Major Minor,* writing and rewriting, terrified to do it, terrified not to. He assembled a cast of some of the biggest stars, including Tom Cruise, Michelle Pfeiffer, Jack Nicholson, Al Pacino, and Adrienne Seabergh. It was for him, an opus of sorts: a story about faith and destiny, questioning if the grass was really greener on the other side of life, or just a different shade. *It's a Wonderful Life* meets *Heaven Can Wait, The Adventures of Major Minor* was a resounding success, and not just for Westman, but for the two ex-secretaries who had pushed and sweated and argued and finagled a way to getting this very expensive fantasy film financed and produced. And they had done it together as partners and friends and equals. It was a stunning triumph, putting a cherry atop not just Westman's career, but Beanie's and Ella's as well.

Beanie, riding the wave of his triumph, had more power and more money than she'd ever dreamed, and all that was left on her to-do list that year was to make sure the agency didn't fire Sheila Day before giving her the board seat they were supposed to have given her two years earlier. After Moze had left, quickly followed by Ella, Howie, and Barry, the board had reconsidered the accelerated seat and informed Sheila's attorneys that they wouldn't even revisit a discussion until 1995, as per her original agreement.

Sheila, almost sixty-four, was out of bargaining chips. All that was left was leveraging the heat of others, specifically Beanie Rosen, who had enough clout with the boys on the first floor to give her that leg up and in. For Beanie, Jamie, Hawkeye, and any woman who'd dreamed of a seat at the only table that mattered, Sheila had to get in, and they had to make sure she did.

So, after the Westman premiere in September 1994, Beanie flew to

New York and had a sit-down with Stu Lonshien and Nat Rosenthal, two of the most lucid and powerful board members, to make sure Sheila was still on track.

Lonshien and Rosenthal assured Beanie that they understood how important Sheila was not only to her but to the agency, and promised that they were keeping an open mind. Still, they suggested it wouldn't hurt if Sheila could sign a star, implying, not so subtly, that she hadn't in quite a while.

"I'll ask Cruise for lunch," Sheila said, upon hearing their veiled threat. She'd said it so casually, as if ordering a sandwich from Salami 'N' Cheese, that Beanie presumed she was kidding. It was a Tuesday afternoon, and Beanie, who had just flown back from New York, was sitting in Sheila's office with Gil Amati, Jamie Garland, and Hawkeye.

Amati laughed. Sheila didn't.

"Why shouldn't he want to have lunch with me? I'm a good get, and I pick up the check," she said, pausing for comedic effect, then adding, "Sometimes."

No one expected Cruise to take Sheila's call, not on the first try, so the other faces in her office reflected stunned admiration as her male assistant's voice announced over the intercom, "Tom Cruise on one."

Tom Cruise, arguably one of the most talented and powerful actors in the world, was laughing and charmed within seconds.

It's as if he was waiting for her call, Beanie thought in awe as she witnessed the ease with which Sheila steered the conversation, demonstrating her wit, skill, and innate talent to woo talent.

Sheila and Cruise had met a few times in passing and had spent a few days together when she was visiting her ex-client Sydney Pollack on the set of *The Firm.* She knew she could make him laugh. She knew he liked her and was properly respectful and deferential for all she had done. And most importantly, she knew that he considered her one of the greats who had known the greats, and Sheila played into it, recalling anecdotes about Hackman and Brando and McQueen and how Cruise was both similar yet different, carving out his own legend for future artists to emulate.

Then she'd find her way to her signature move, praising the wife, praising him for choosing the wife, and the ultimate closer, praising them both for the work they had done together. There could be no better affirmation of a couple than cementing their artistry alongside the greats like Olivier and Leigh, Hepburn and Tracy, Newman and Woodward.

"Honeeeey, sign the spouse," Beanie could hear Sheila saying on a loop as she listened to Sheila heap praise on *Far and Away,* a film Cruise and Kidman had done a few years earlier, reminding Beanie that compliments were a currency that could pay in dividends if you knew how to give them. There was an art to bestowing praise, and Sheila, sincere without being effusive, wickedly funny, brilliantly erudite, was Picasso.

Deeply humbled by talent, Sheila found the balance between bullshit and hyperbole. By the end of the call, she had secured a dinner at Cruise's home followed by a private screening of his newest film *Interview with the Vampire.*

Perhaps all Sheila needed, Beanie thought, in awe of what she'd just witnessed, *was someone to show her a glimpse of who she could be by reminding her who she was.* Sheila still had it. And that was important to Beanie. She did not want to see the giant fall.

Over the next few months Sheila Day came alive, sending Cruise books, articles, ideas, anything to keep the conversation going without looking obvious, or worse, desperate. But given the fact that he hadn't been looking for an agent, she was keenly aware of the dance, never pushing so hard that she'd repel him.

"I'm close," she said to Beanie that Christmas after the Cruises sent her eight gorgeous Baccarat crystal goblets. "I can feel it." All she needed was an organic opportunity to let Cruise see her in action. Four weeks later, the opportunity presented itself.

In early January 1995, *The Adventures of Major Minor* was nominated for nine Academy Awards, including three for Scott Westman: best director, best writer, and best actor. He was a landslide favorite to win, and Ella and Beanie decided to throw a party in his honor.

Ella, who was supposed to fly in and co-host, was having difficulty with her second pregnancy and was advised by her doctor to stay put. Since she'd be flying to California six weeks later for the Oscars, her doctor advised she not risk two trips so close together.

Beanie was more than capable of doing it alone, as it was to be a relatively small dinner for seventy-five at her Nichols Canyon home. She had planned on reviewing the guest list with Ella, but Ella was preoccupied with Olive and bedrest, and just told Beanie to review with Scott so his friends, most of whom were teamsters, were included.

"And then," Ella said, "invite whoever the hell you want. It's our party, too, Bean!"

A few days later, Beanie got a call from Sheila Day, who had emailed Tom Cruise a funny article and received a response immediately, asking if he would see her at Beanie's that Saturday.

Sheila, who hadn't even known about the party, quickly vamped, telling him she was looking forward to it.

"Why would you say that?" Beanie asked, annoyed.

"Why wouldn't I?" replied Sheila.

Beanie took a deep breath and reminded Sheila, though it made her deeply uncomfortable, that her deal with Ella was that Sheila never got involved with their mutual clients.

"Honeeeey," she said, "did the cunt say I couldn't occupy the same airspace?"

Beanie didn't respond.

"Apologies," Sheila corrected, "I meant to say, fucking cunt."

Beanie hung up.

Sheila called back, promising she wouldn't even look at Westman. She was begging now, saying that this could close Cruise.

Beanie argued that the board seat was all but guaranteed regardless of Cruise. She wouldn't let them back down. Neither would Jamie.

But this no longer was about a board seat for Sheila. This was about proving something to herself, to the agency, to the industry, to everyone who'd wanted to retire her, to shut her down simply because they could.

She wasn't ready to stop, not nearly. "I could sign him," Sheila whispered. "Please."

There was something desperate about this request. As if the granting of it was a life-or-death situation, and perhaps for Sheila Day, it was. Everything came down to this one evening with Cruise. "I promise," she whispered to Beanie, "Scott Westman won't even know I'm there."

Unfortunately, others did.

Twinkly lights dotted the lemon trees as just under one hundred people, stars, teamsters, and studio heads ate, passed hors d'oeuvres, and then feasted on a buffet of sole meunière, filet mignon, scalloped potatoes, asparagus with hollandaise, and a pasta station all beautifully prepared by Janice Rosen's Good Eats.

Beanie, who never tasted a morsel, had been taking diet pills for the past several months in order to fit into her Christian Dior gown for the Oscars, and was already back at her fighting weight of 141 pounds and had selected for the evening a royal-blue Calvin Klein sheath dress, with a slit up the side showing off her slender legs, and matching Manolo Blahniks to elongate them. She wore her thick hair in a long French braid to highlight her newly rediscovered cheekbones, along with her sparkly new four-carat diamond earrings that she had gifted herself from Tiffany's.

"You bought retail!" her mother had shrieked, citing Rabbi Schnitzer's brother-in-law who worked in the Diamond District and would have given Beanie a substantial discount.

But Beanie didn't care, telling her mother if she played her cards right, she'd get her something from Cartier for her next birthday. Not surprisingly, Miriam immediately complimented the jewelry.

Beanie Rosen felt thin, chic, and put together as guests mingled around the outdoor firepit or roamed the flowering manicured trails of her property which, since she'd bought the land next door, was now over two acres, with a tennis court, pool, and guest house that was being renovated.

She only saw Sheila once that evening, right when she had first arrived.

"Honeeeey," Sheila had said, taking in Beanie's home, the catering, the guest list, "I couldn't have done it better myself." Then she thought about it and redacted, telling her that that wasn't true, she would have had less people, better lighting, and done a sit-down, as buffets were "taaaaaaacky."

Beanie, unoffended, laughed, and it was then that she realized Sheila was just a different version of Miriam. Maybe that's why she was drawn to her. Beanie was constantly trying to gain approval from both women who held it back just enough to keep her trying.

True to her word, Sheila never went near Westman, spending all her time with Tom Cruise, holding court, escorting him, introducing him, charming him, and Beanie hoped, for Sheila's sake, signing him.

For much of the evening, Beanie was focused on Westman, making sure he had a great time, introducing him to a few industry heavyweights whom she'd invited, meeting many of the teamsters he'd invited, and just hanging out around the firepit in the white Adirondack chairs with Hermes blankets provided by her houseman.

Westman liked her, she knew that, but that night he seemed to like her more. He was laser focused on her in a way he had never been before, not letting her out of his sight.

"Where'd you go, Bean?" he asked after she'd left to say goodbye to the head of Paramount Studios.

"Just showing people the door," she told him.

"They can find it themselves," he said, putting his arm around her proprietarily and not removing it. He held her closely, naturally as they walked around greeting people like they were a couple, which Beanie rationalized made him feel more secure. Ella and he had more of a familiarity, so normally she'd have been the one walking with him, touching him. For quite a while the town had assumed that Ella and Westman were an item, and they were until they weren't. But they had an ease that informed a deep connection.

Beanie had no such ease. She was self-conscious when his hand would accidentally graze her breasts and her nipples would stiffen. She tried to adjust, but each time she did his fingers would find them again. It was dark enough, and no one could see, but she realized by the third or fourth time that it was no accident.

She was aroused, and he was arousing her, and they both knew it.

While industry heavyweights talked box office and ate pigs in a blanket, the biggest star in the world was toying with his agent, telling her how sexy she looked, and though she knew it was wrong and hoped he'd stop, her panties said otherwise.

People began clearing out around eleven, and by midnight everyone had gone except Scott who, by that time, was wantonly rubbing his hands up and down her sheath dress, pressing against her so she could feel his desire.

"You're drunk," she said.

"You're right," he answered, and there in the backyard under the lemon trees heavy with fruit, and in front of the steam coming off the pool, he kissed her full on, and she kissed him back.

"I always wanted to do that," he told her lustily, holding her chin. He looked at her, waiting for permission, as she teetered on the precipice of right or wrong, client or lover.

Her knees were weak, her nipples hard as she leaned into him, giving enough of a green light to give them both relief. Beanie arched her back as he slid off her sheath dress and got on his knees, kissing and nuzzling her crotch. He laid her back on the grass as he continued the foreplay with Beanie writhing, moaning, and lost in an ecstasy she hadn't enjoyed since Moze.

Dizzy from multiple orgasms, she reached for Westman to reciprocate, but he just smiled.

"Let's go for a swim," he said, kicking off his cowboy boots and jeans.

Beanie had only been in her pool twice, and both times were to cool off. Now was no exception. Their lovemaking was erotic and lustful, starting in the pool and finding its way to Beanie's room, her houseman later making sure all evidence was folded, pressed, and hung.

DANGEROUS CURVES

Those fucking Doritos.

—BEANIE ROSEN

1995

Westman left for his home in Malibu early the next morning.

Beanie offered to make him breakfast, or coffee even, but it was a good hour drive from Nichols Canyon to Point Dume, so he needed to go. He kissed her, thanked her, and just before he left, she reminded him to read the new Bill Goldman script she'd sent him last week.

"FUCK, why did I say that?" she said, kicking herself after he'd left. *Ugh,* she was such a dope. She knew she shouldn't have slept with him and hoped it wouldn't be awkward now, but she tried to put it out of her mind as she got ready for the Women in Power luncheon. Jamie Garland was being honored and Beanie was supposed to give a speech and present her award.

After choosing a white Dolce & Gabbana pantsuit, which was still a little snug around the middle, she hopped into her steely blue Jaguar XJS, debating whether she should tell Ella about her night with Scott. Though they were partners, she decided against it since Ella had never shared the intimacies between her and Westman. And besides, it was a silly little drunken one-off, a fun frolic between friends.

"Honeeeey, they're not our friends," Beanie could hear Sheila saying in her mind, but either way, Beanie decided, as she drove to the Beverly Wilshire Hotel to honor the woman upon whose shoulders she'd stood, she didn't need to burden Ella with her bad call.

Instead, Beanie left her a quick message saying how great the party was, and how everyone had asked for her, and to ring her later. Then she rehearsed her speech about women standing with each other and for each other and decided that she would present the award to Jamie on behalf of both Beanie and her longtime partner and best friend, Ella Gaddy.

The next day, Beanie rolled into her office just before 9:00 A.M. She had meant to get in earlier and deal with some East Coast business and read the trades, but the diet pills had really been messing with her sleep.

She checked in with Sheila Day who was still on a high from the Cruise of it all. He hadn't signed with her but wanted her opinion on a few scripts.

Beanie became consumed by the fact that she hadn't heard from Westman all day Sunday—not that she thought she would, but she needed to get back to Columbia about the Bill Goldman script and she was still antsy about the course of events. So, she called him and left a message, asking him again to read the script as soon as possible, and to please call her after he'd read.

She also left word again for Ella, whom she hadn't wanted to bother but still hadn't heard from since the party, and reminded her to urge Westman to read the Goldman script and also that it was Dennis Quaid's first day of production on his new film.

She went to the motion picture meeting, followed by lunch, followed by a signing meeting, followed by a quick set visit. All the while, she kept checking back with her new male assistant, the son of a friend of her father's, as to whether Westman had returned her call.

He had not.

That night before going to dinner she put another call in to Ella, wanting to know if she was all right. It was unusual that she hadn't returned so many calls. But again, all Beanie got was her answering machine.

It wasn't until late Tuesday afternoon that she really started to suspect that something was amiss. Gil Amati walking into her office and closing the door only confirmed her suspicions.

"Moze Goff," Amati said, quietly, solemnly, "was spotted in Paradise Cove having drinks with Ella Gaddy and Scott Westman."

Beanie, knowing that Ella was on bed rest, initially dismissed it as absurd. "Did you see them?" she asked.

"No," Gil told her, "my assistant did. And he wouldn't make that up."

"I wouldn't be so sure of that," she said, dismissing the news and trying to focus on the work at hand. But she was unnerved. It was an odd thing for Gil's assistant to make up, and only exacerbated by the fact that she hadn't heard from either one of them.

Finally, on Wednesday morning, she did. By registered mail she received a letter from Scott Westman terminating Sylvan Light as his representative. Both Ella Gaddy and Harvey Khan were copied. Beanie, stunned, canceled the rest of her day and began calling Scott and Ella, panicked.

Neither answered.

Not wanting to share the news with anyone, she went down to Khan's office where Mercedes sat outside, holding her copy of the letter.

"What's this about?" asked Mercedes. Beanie shook her head, saying she just didn't know. Frustrated tears came as Mercedes guided her into Harvey's executive offices. Harvey wasn't there, of course, and Mercedes, who was strangely consoling, led her to the couch.

"Can you do anything about this?" Mercedes asked, offering her a box of tissues.

Beanie shook her head, unable to speak, and Mercedes held her.

How odd, Beanie thought, *that it would be Mercedes Baxter offering me solace.*

Mercedes, sitting beside her, tried to find the words, but was at a loss. "Is there anything I can do?" she asked.

But Beanie just shook her head, unable to tell her what an idiot she'd been, so careless, thoughtless. Inwardly she cursed herself, hating herself, wondering how she'd let it happen.

She was still trying to piece it all together. Westman must have told Ella that they had slept together, and Ella must have been furious. But would she have been so furious to have fired Beanie and set up a meeting with Moze? That was treachery on a whole other level. None of it made sense.

Still, she wasn't about to work it out with Mercedes Khan. Beanie stood, thanking Mercedes, and telling her that the answer lay with Ella, and she needed to find her.

It wasn't until seven o'clock that night that she was finally able to get Ella Gaddy on the phone. She had called Ella's assistant, Ella's nanny, and even Stirling Cowan, begging him through tears to ask Ella to call her, telling him that she didn't understand what had happened, and she really needed a best friend to speak to, but that, too, was Ella.

Finally, her phone rang.

Ella, sounding cold and detached, asked her to stop harassing her staff and her boyfriend. "Scott Westman has left Sylvan Light," she said, confirming, of course, what Beanie already knew. "For the time being," she added, "he's the only one." It was a thinly veiled threat that he wouldn't be.

"Why?" Beanie asked, her heart in her throat. She both feared and needed an answer.

"I know what you did," Ella hissed, "and I cannot and will not *EVER* forgive it." Beanie, crying profusely, apologized over and over again, rambling on about the fact that it was nothing, it meant nothing, she shouldn't have done it, they were both drunk, she didn't think Ella would mind, he'd left the next morning.

"It was meaningless," she sobbed, almost hysterical as Ella tried to get a word in.

"What are you talking about?" Ella asked when Beanie finally stopped for breath.

Beanie stammered, confused, "Aren't you mad because I slept with him?"

"With whom?" Ella asked.

"Scotti," Beanie said, not understanding. There was a long silence.

"You fucked Scott Westman?" Ella asked, aghast, surprised, disgusted. "And he fucked *you*?" she said, doubling down on the insult.

But Beanie, rather than being offended, was trying to play catch-up. "Isn't that why he terminated me?" she asked. "Isn't that why you're mad?"

Ella, now reeling from the depths of her partner's betrayal, spit out her reason. "He terminated you because you invited Sheila Day to a party that *we* were throwing."

Oh fuck, Beanie thought, quickly explaining that Sheila hadn't been there for Westman, she had no interest in Westman and never spoke to him or saw him. "She was there to sign someone else," Beanie said.

And that's when Ella screamed that she didn't fucking care why Sheila was there. She didn't want Sheila to sign anyone. She didn't want Sheila to win.

"SHE TRIED TO BLACKMAIL ME!" Ella screamed. "DO YOU UNDERSTAND? I FUCKING HATE HER."

And Beanie stopped. She'd never heard Ella scream, she'd never heard about any blackmail, and had no idea what it was that Ella had in her past that Sheila would use in any way to barter.

"El, I'm sorry," Beanie said, "I didn't know. I didn't . . ."

But Ella interrupted her, saying, "I told Scott that you broke a promise to me. And if you'd do it to me, you'd do it to him."

But she hadn't known about the sex. "And that's the kicker," she said, adding, "You fucked me. Then you fucked him. Well, at least you went out with a bang."

Then she hung up on Beanie.

Beanie sat stunned, trying to gather her wits. Ella was hurt, she got it. She shouldn't have invited Sheila, okay, bad move, but upon learning that, Ella had actually picked up a phone and called her archenemy without even giving Beanie a chance to explain.

Beanie went from being hurt to being furious to becoming enraged.

Ella knew what it would mean to lose a client of that stature, but to take him to Moze after everything that had happened between Moze and Beanie was a kind of cruelty that took Beanie's breath away.

Initially, she wanted to call Ella back and confront her, but to what end? Ella wouldn't answer, and even if she did, what she had done out of spite was more horrible than anything Beanie would ever do to anyone. Yes, she'd invited Sheila without thinking, and yes, she had fucked Scott Westman, but while both acts were thoughtless, neither were spiteful. What Ella did was premeditated and hateful.

Beanie gathered herself and started to formulate a plan. She was *Beanie Rosen,* after all, one of the most powerful agents in Hollywood, and she'd be damned to be defined by Ella Gaddy's definition of broken promises or loyalty, not after the low blow she'd struck.

Beanie didn't give anyone a heads-up that she was leaving, she just hopped in her Jaguar and drove toward Sunset Boulevard, calling Scott on the way. She got his voicemail, and then it occurred to her when she hit the Pacific Coast Highway that Scott often stayed at his guest house on the property nearer the ocean. She looked at her Filofax as she drove, but she couldn't find the number, and since there was a light drizzle falling, she called her assistant and asked him to go into the Rolodex to see if there was a number for the Malibu guest house under the name Tito, which was code for Westman.

He found it and connected her.

Scott, whom she'd been trying to reach all day, answered on two rings.

Beanie, taken aback, hadn't expected to get him so quickly or at all, and hadn't prepared what she was going to say. So she just spoke from the heart, rambling a bit but explaining that what had happened between her and Ella was a misunderstanding between old friends. She hadn't intended to offend her by inviting Sheila Day, but Ella hadn't given her a chance to explain. She didn't bring up the whole Moze thing because she didn't want to give Moze any power, so instead she pivoted, explaining that she wasn't asking him to choose between her and Ella. She understood theirs was a long and valued relationship.

"But at least let me explain myself," she told him. She didn't really give him a chance to say no, telling him she'd be there in forty-five minutes.

She was there in twenty.

Scott listened to Beanie tell the story all over again, and then told her that he and Ella had been together an awful long time, and she had been pretty mad about the whole Sheila thing, putting it to him, "It's me or her." Scott shrugged, telling Beanie he didn't want to leave, but he figured if she and Ella weren't talking, he didn't think he should stay.

And that's when he told her he'd met with Moze. "He's a nice guy," he said. "And you know, an old friend."

The bile backed up in Beanie's throat, but she knew enough not to act threatened. "He's a good agent," she told him, "I mean, I don't think he's me, but if that's what you want . . ."

Scott thought about it a beat and then told her it wasn't what he wanted. He wanted what he had. He said that if she and Ella could work it out, he sure would like the team back.

"Me too," she told him. "I'd meet her halfway, heck, I'd meet her three-quarters of the way if she's willing."

He shook his head, saying again that Ella was pretty mad.

"Yeah," Beanie agreed, "and she's also pretty stubborn." Then she confessed that it might be doubly hard to put things back on track, because in her confusion as to why Ella was so angry, she'd accidentally revealed that she and Westman had fooled around.

He smiled and shook his head. "Oh boy."

"I know," said Beanie. "I'm sorry, I just couldn't figure out why else she'd be mad. I told her I was sorry," she said, "and I promised that it would never happen again."

He smirked, stood up, took her in his arms and said, "Let's not go crazy."

And for the first time that day, Beanie laughed.

A few minutes later Westman called Ella, told her he'd spoken to Beanie, and that he wanted the three of them to meet. Beanie overheard him saying that he didn't want to wreck something as good as they'd had. She couldn't hear the rest as he walked into the other room, but when he came back he was smiling and said, "Feel like going to Tahoe this weekend?"

Beanie, relieved, hugged him, thanked him, and promised to never bring Sheila Day near him again. Then she got back in her car and put her head on the steering wheel, letting out a breath she'd been holding all day.

Somehow she had averted disaster and by the grace of God put Humpty Dumpty back together again.

It was half past nine as she pulled out of Scott's rambling estate and onto the Pacific Coast Highway, which was now thick with low-hanging fog.

In all the craziness of the day, she'd forgotten to take her diet pills and was hungrier than she'd been in a while. She looked for a McDonald's or something on the side of the road, but everything was dark. Fuck, she was hungry. She tried to distract herself, thinking about Westman and what a good guy he was, and Ella and how upset she must have been to have made that call to Moze. Beanie knew she had to forgive Ella, but she also knew she'd never forget how far Ella had gone to hurt her.

Ella's fight was deeper than Beanie's, and only Sheila knew why. Beanie toyed with the idea of asking Sheila what Ella was hiding, if only to get more insight into this woman she'd known for over a decade but apparently didn't really know at all.

She spotted a Thrifty Drug Store on PCH at Topanga and had pulled in when she realized that she'd run out of her house without bringing her purse. How silly she was to be driving without a license, or money, or any identification beyond her Filofax.

I should always leave a credit card in my Filofax, she told herself, as she pulled back onto PCH, speeding so she could get home and have her houseman make her a grilled cheese.

"I fucking earned it," she thought to herself. And then it occurred to her that there was a bag of nacho-flavored Doritos in the glove box. She had bought it at the store, then hid it the other day when picking up Miriam from her mahjong club. Miriam Spitz would not understand nacho Doritos. But Beanie, thankful that she'd salvaged them, did.

She reached for the glovebox, which was all the way on the other side of the car, and pulled out the Doritos just as her phone rang.

"Hello?" she said, trying to open the bag with one hand while navigating the phone, the turns, and the fog with the other.

It was Hawkeye calling to see if she'd heard the news.

"What news?" Beanie asked, hoping no one had said anything about the termination letter. She didn't need that kind of gossip, and besides, everything was under control.

"Matt Stieglitz has gone to Sony," she said, "and David Shipp is leaving to run Apple."

"WHAT?" Beanie screamed. "ARE YOU FUCKING KIDDING ME?"

Hawkeye, laughing with excitement, wasn't kidding. "Beanie," she told her, "you're on top. There's no one bigger."

Beanie didn't know what to say.

"Hello?" Hawkeye said. "Can you hear me?" But in that moment Beanie was stunned silent, almost reverential. "Hello?" Hawkeye said again.

"I'm here," Beanie told her, listening as Hawkeye explained that everyone was meeting up at Sheila's house—Gil, Jamie, everyone—and they'd asked Hawkeye to get Beanie. This was big news. They needed to be together. Beanie told Hawkeye to order food from Morton's, which was right around the corner from Hawkeye's place, and that she'd be there in twenty minutes to pick her up.

For two minutes Beanie Rosen drove with the knowledge and clear understanding that she had done it. She had scaled the mountain, dove through the wave, and made it to the top of the pyramid. Sure, there had been near misses and some fatalities, but she'd persevered. "I FUCKING MADE IT!" she screamed, pounding the steering wheel while biting down on one corner of the Doritos bag, trying to rip it open with her teeth, and pulling the opposite corner with the other hand, unfortunately leaving the steering wheel for a moment to chart its own course.

She never saw the cliff.

Beanie Rosen's last thought as the wheels spun in midair was, *Don't let my mother know I was eating Doritos . . .*

THE FINAL ZAMBONI

After the game, the pawn and the king go into the same box.

—ITALIAN PROVERB

Not if I can help it.

—MIRIAM SPITZ

1995

"They owe her," Miriam Spitz said, referring to the stars and the studio heads past and present who came one by one, in pairs, in packs, in Escalades and stretch limos to pay homage at the funeral of the woman many described as the most powerful female agent in Hollywood.

"Write 'the most powerful agent of all time,'" Miriam advised Army Archerd, who'd been invited, and Liz Smith, who'd flown in. And while it could be argued that there had been agents who perhaps were more powerful, no one was going to split hairs with Miriam Spitz, who was playing the mother-in-mourning role to the hilt. Whether or not it was true to life, it was true to Miriam, and once in print it would become the bedrock of her daughter's epitaph. Zambonied.

Moze Goff, who many were surprised had been invited, stood quietly in the back, nodding to Sheila Day with a small gesture Sheila chose to ignore.

"Eat a dick," Sheila said aloud to Jamie Garland, who turned to see the ire of Sheila's angst.

Dressed impeccably in Chanel suits with pearls and heels high enough to make sure they were seen, the two women scanned the room for others, keeping track, keeping score. Were she alive, they were confident that Beanie would've sat alongside them; past, present, future, an unstoppable trio of sheer will, each existing because the other had made room.

Jamie nudged Sheila as Ella Gaddy arrived, cutting a wide berth around both women.

"Taaacky," Sheila said loud enough for others to hear, referring to Ella's ruffled off-brand dress with black stockings and open-toed sandals. Anyone on the inside—and everyone was—knew that the two women so detested each other that Miriam Spitz had to personally call Ella Gaddy and assure her that she would not have Sheila Day speak on Beanie's behalf—which was a slap in Sheila's face. An insult. Everyone knew it. Sheila was a living legend who had, at least in her mind, promoted and supported Beanie Rosen, mentoring her, shepherding her, protecting her. "Without me, she'd be some pisher from Pacoima in trundle skirts with bow ties," she told her loyalists who advised her not to attend.

It was a conundrum. To snub Sheila Day so publicly without giving her a place of honor or honorable mention was a statement in and of itself, but Sheila wouldn't give Ella Gaddy the satisfaction of missing Beanie's funeral. Instead, she sat in the pews reserved for the superstars, wanting to ensure that proper respect was paid, and she didn't mean to the deceased.

Amongst all the people whose shoulders Beanie Rosen had stood upon, whose bodies she'd crawled over, whose careers she'd invented during her meteoric rise from file clerk to superstar at the Sylvan Light Agency, there was a rewriting of truth as Mercedes Baxter Khan, one of Beanie's "oldest and dearest friends," gave the eulogy.

If Hawkeye, who had been the first person to see Beanie when she came to the Light Agency looking for a job, and the last person to speak to her before she'd died, had been asked to speak, she would have said that Beanie Rosen had taken on the boys' club, beating them at their own game, and perhaps, in the end, becoming just like them. She wasn't looking to smash ceilings, glass or otherwise, unless they were blocking her way.

She. Just. Wanted. In.

And she got in, surpassing all who doubted, blocked, and tried to derail.

Hard to explain unless you were there: Sylvan Light in the 1980s, where people put their fingers in their mouths to see which way the wind was blowing.

Beanie Rosen knew how to blow.

EPILOGUE

Ella Gaddy had a baby boy that July and named him Bernie Rosen Cowan after her friend. She was lost without Beanie and tried to honor her memory by putting all her clients with Hawkeye, under the proviso that she never share them with Sheila Day. But without Beanie driving, she began to lose passion and focus, and other than Westman, let go of her clients, devoting herself to Olive and Bernie and life in Tahoe.

In the spring of 2000, Ella, forty-three, was contacted by an attorney on behalf of a twenty-one-year-old young man named Milo Williams who'd been searching for his birth mother. She flew to Chicago that December where the two finally met. He was tall, handsome, and had a passion inside him, much like his father, Ella said, telling him truthfully that Darnell, his father, had been a married physician who had never even known she was pregnant. She'd wanted Milo dearly, she explained, and knew he would be destined for greatness, but realized sadly that her own parents were not. She showed him pictures of Olive and Bernie, and he showed her pictures of his brothers and sisters and mother and father.

She had chosen well, and that made her whole.

The following year she left Stirling Cowan, Tahoe, and even Scott Westman, taking Olive and Bernie and moving back to Kentucky to help her brother Knox, who'd had a catastrophic fall and needed someone to take over the family business. The Senator, who'd had a stroke that left him partially paralyzed, was pleased that Ella had come back into the fold. Eve Lynn had died the year before, with tributes and obituaries about the death of the last debutante, and Alice Lee, now divorced, was living in England. So, it was left to Ella to uphold the Gaddy traditions of propriety and decorum that her mother had fought so hard to protect. Determined to leave her mark, she turned over the multimillion-dollar empire to their eldest grandchild, Milo Williams, who as a doctoral student at Northwestern University and president of the black student union, was now in charge of the Gaddy legacy.

Ella had found her way back home.

Mercedes Khan stayed at the Sylvan Light Agency as the right hand of Khan until he died in 2001. She never remarried nor had children, but she did reach out to her sister, who by then was widowed and living part time in New York. The phone call was cordial, and they made plans to get together, but didn't until 2011, at the age of sixty-one, when Mercedes visited Lucille, then seventy-five, who was suffering from early onset dementia. Mercedes introduced herself to the nurses as Lucille Goldstone's daughter, and she sat with her daily, reminiscing when Lucille was lucid, and keeping her company when she was not.

It was a mother-and-child reunion where both finally could be each other's patron saints.

Sheila Day never signed Tom Cruise and never got the board seat. Six months after Beanie's funeral, Sheila Day "voluntarily" retired, entertaining twinklies at her home and showing them clips of her *60 Minutes* interview, wiping away the stench of her second chapter as if it was nothing more than a footnote to an illustrious career.

When asked about Beanie Rosen, Sheila would say, "Honeeeey, we were just too fucking good for the cocksuckers," aligning herself with Beanie's rise and fall.

. . .

Hawkeye went on to become a super-agent, and then, later, the head of Columbia Studios. But before she left Sylvan Light, she convinced the board of directors to commission a bust of Beanie Rosen to be put in the lobby of the Sylvan Light Plaza, not too far from where they'd met when she was the receptionist and Beanie was a girl who just wanted in. Hawkeye was the first woman of color to ever be an agent at the company, and the first woman of color to run a film studio; and she credited her rise to the woman she'd worked for, with, and beside.

Beanie Rosen was the reason they named hurricanes after women. She stood on the shoulders of those who came before to reach higher than any woman had ever reached. The town mourned her in the way you do when someone dies too young, celebrating her in absentia with scholarships in her name and stories that were so much larger than the life she'd led.

They say when someone dies their life passes before their eyes in an instant. But that's not how it was for Beanie. For Beanie, it was more like a slow-motion ballet. Once she was airborne, she was angry—who wouldn't be? She didn't want to die. Not now. Not when she had everything to live for. She had saved the client, her relationship with Ella would repair, Stieglitz was gone, Shipp was gone, there were no more obstacles, the world was hers; but then, when she played the record out, looking at the Doritos floating around her head, she realized that maybe this was perfect timing.

She had reached the top, the pinnacle. So, what next? She had only to look to Sheila and Jamie and all the others who'd come before, who'd fought and struggled to leave their marks, and then disappeared, as if they never were. A quick slide to oblivion. Beanie didn't have a husband, or children, or a will, dammit. That would annoy her mother, who would dine out for the rest of her life on her daughter's greatness, claiming it as her own, Zamboni-ing out the Doritos, diet pills, and the just-in-case hiding places filled with junk food; making up boyfriends and adventures and a mother-daughter intimacy that never was.

And so, Beanie thought as her car sailed toward the rocks below, perhaps there was a kind of divine providence to going out on top. With Miriam Spitz guiding the narrative, Beanie would always be young, she would always be beautiful, and most importantly, she would always be thin.

The shining star who represented the shining stars, Beanie Rosen was thirty-five years old when she died, and while others would disappear into the ether, her impeccable timing for endings ensured that she never would. She would always be remembered as a force, a legend. Just the way she wanted.

And Beanie always got what she wanted.

Or died trying.

THE END (ISH)

ACKNOWLEDGMENTS

To Jennifer Lopez, my friend, my partner, my write or die, thank you for blowing your fairy dust into my dreams, for pushing me forward, and always reminding me that we are only limited by our own fears. Jen, you are the Thelma to my Louise, and I don't know what I'd do without your vision, your beauty, or your love. The wind beneath my shaky wings, thank you for helping me fly. In heels.

To Kevin Huvane, our friendship spans over forty years and you have been there every step of the way, no matter if we were agents together, or at separate companies, you stood for something bigger than competition. You lead with integrity and kindness and have been a partner, advisor, and mentor, always reminding me to hold my head high and stand in my truth. Mr. Huvane, you are a man without whom nothing seems worthwhile, and with whom anything seems possible. Our mothers are proud of us!

To Michelle Israel, for your friendship, for your patience, for your love, and for listening to this book aloud from the first page to the last, all the while acting like I was doing you the favor. Michelle, you made me believe that I could do anything. I am forever in your debt and you are forever in my heart.

To Benny Medina, who would not let me go a week without reading a chapter of this book to him and would nudge me once a month about deadlines. Benny, you magnificent dreamer, thank you for waving your magic wand over my world and making it so much more meaningful and beautiful. And thank you, partner and friend, for reminding me every day that the best is yet to come.

To Marcy Engelman, who urged me on, patiently listening to each chapter and even allowed me to FaceTime her so I could not only gauge her interest, but make sure she was paying attention! Marcy, you were there so many years ago on the old block in Pacoima that we called Arleta, and I love our life journey and wouldn't trade it for the world. Dear old friend, your enthusiasm was my engine, and your insightful notes were my compass.

To Jennifer Adams, my right arm; you rode in the car with me as I went to pitch a germ of an idea to the biggest publishers in New York City at the dawn of the pandemic. And you have stuck by my side ever since, holding me up from one film set to another as I formed and reformed the stories of these women climbing the stairs of their own ambitions. Assistant, friend, family, true north, I simply would be lost without you.

To Jennifer Enderlin: Jen, four years ago luck, disguised as my agent, led me into your office, where I rambled on about women with ambition in 1980s Hollywood who wanted a seat at a table where they were expected to serve. And while there was interest from others, it was never a contest. You understood and embraced each one of my flawed complicated characters with enthusiasm and love, and I knew from that meeting, you were my girl. Thank you for giving me a home to grow these brilliant, idiosyncratic, amazing girls into the women they needed to be and for sharing them proudly with the world. I am forever grateful.

To Elizabeth Beier, my trusted editor and now friend, who willed me to believe that my bunioned feet could scale this mountain in heels and loved every character, warts and all, celebrating their climb, their fall, and their journey. Elizabeth, you are a beautiful, kind, and gentle soul who took pity on a Hollywood producer and gave me time and room to find my way. Thank you for reminding me that brevity is the soul of wit, and for quelling my nerves about the steamy sex scenes, that you *insisted* I include.

To Brigitte Dale, the yin to Elizabeth's yang, you were stalwart and devoted in helping this fledgling writer find her way in the fast-paced world of publishing. Thank you for holding my hand, taking my calls, and answering my incessant questions. As I splashed around in the waters, you were my life preserver.

To Mollie Glick: Sweet Mollie, my first agent!!!! You held my hand and told me I could do this, I should do this, I will do this, and erased any doubt, and every fear. You're everything I want in an agent, and that says a lot!

To Via Romano, if ever there was an agent-to-be, it is you, sweet Via, who read every draft and gave *the best* notes. How lucky are the folks at CAA that they have you in the wings as the next generation.

To Amy Ferris, you brilliant lyrical author, who breathed life and hope and passion into the idea that I could actually write a book and were my shoulder and my muse, urging me on to finish. Amy, what an honor it is to call you my friend.

To Barbara Goldsmith, my sweet sister-in-law, who blocked out evenings to listen to whole sections, and then would call afterward with an insatiable need to know more. Barbara, your excitement was contagious and helped me climb (in flats) to finish this odyssey.

And last, but never least, my anchor . . . Daniel Thomas: my husband, friend, life partner. The calm to my storm. Thank you for indulging my stories, soothing my fears, holding me close, and being the safe harbor I can always run to. I love you dearly.

ABOUT THE AUTHOR

Ian Buiosi

Elaine Goldsmith-Thomas began her career at the William Morris Agency, and rose by the late 1980s to become the Senior Vice President of the WMA, and later the Senior Vice President of International Creative Management, guiding the careers of Julia Roberts, Jennifer Lopez, Nicolas Cage, Madonna, and many others. More recently, she has produced a broad, successful slate of films and television series that includes *Maid in Manhattan, Mona Lisa Smile, Hustlers, Marry Me, Emily in Paris, The Fosters,* and many others. She lives in New York City.